PRAISE FOR *THE VIBRANT YEARS*

"I would give this book five stars for the concept alone, but it's Sonali Dev's trademark character depth and beautiful writing that really make *The Vibrant Years* shine. A gorgeous story of evolving female relationships and how love, hilarity, and the bonds between three generations of women help them thrive in even the fiercest winds of change."

—Christina Lauren, *New York Times* bestselling author of *The Soulmate Equation*

"Oh, what a glorious tangle of love, career, the past, and family is *The Vibrant Years*! Sonali Dev writes beautiful prose and complex, delightful characters in this story of rediscovery and girl power for three generations of the Desai women. A delicious treat."

—Kristan Higgins, *New York Times* bestselling author

"A vivid and touching story of the relationships between three women who love each other and their quest to find each other's soul mates. Funny, fast paced, and insightful, *The Vibrant Years* gracefully explores questions of meaning and hope and regret and most of all the love between women. A beautiful book!"

—Barbara O'Neal, bestselling author of *This Place of Wonder*

"I loved this story of three generations of women navigating life, love, and the patriarchy. Sonali Dev's writing is lush and evocative, her characters vibrant with rage, humor, and wisdom."

—Virginia Kantra, *New York Times* bestselling author of *Meg & Jo* and *Beth & Amy*

The
VIBRANT
YEARS

A Novel

Sonali Dev

MINDY'S BOOK STUDIO

Published by Mindy's Book Studio, New York

www.apub.com

Amazon, the Amazon logo, and Mindy's Book Studio are trademarks of Amazon.com, Inc., or its affiliates.

ISBN-13: 9781662509261 (hardcover)
ISBN-13: 9781542036221 (paperback)
ISBN-13: 9781542036238 (digital)

Cover design by Kimberly Glyder
Cover image: © GUSAK OLENA / Shutterstock; © ganjalex / Shutterstock; © Aldo Pavan / Getty

Printed in the United States of America

First edition

This one's for grandmothers everywhere. The soft ones and the strong ones. But mainly for my two ajis, who were always both those things at once. Shantu and Kamla, thank you for never shying away from my questions, for never rolling me up in taboos, and for the gift of your stories. (Also, I still miss the taste of your food.)

A NOTE FROM MINDY KALING

What does it mean to live life on your own terms?

Sonali Dev's hilarious and heartwarming novel *The Vibrant Years* is the story of three generations of women in one family who are determined to find the answer to that question for themselves. They are at different stages in life, each dealing with their own issues, but they can lean on each other for advice, support, and, of course, laughter when nothing else works.

I was so charmed by the novel's rebel women. There's Bindu, everyone's favorite grandmother, who after years of going along with what was expected of her, finally reclaims her identity for herself. She's now the shiny new fish in her retirement community's dating pond. We meet Aly, who continues to chase her dreams, but when she realizes her employer will never give her a big break, she takes matters into her own hands. And there's young genius Cullie, who has created an app that helps millions of people suffering from anxiety, people like herself—and when the app's availability to help others is threatened, she won't let anyone get in her way, even if it means she'll have to step into the world of demoralizing dating apps. Luckily, she has a hot granny and a newly single mom to help her with the research . . .

The Vibrant Years is bursting with humor, banter, and cringeworthy first dates that kept me smiling as I read through the pages. But more than being just a fun read, it's also a timely tale about a group of underestimated and unrepresented women demanding respect and embracing their most authentic selves, who support and lift each other up through the most difficult times, which perfectly exemplifies the spirit of Mindy's Book Studio. I fell in love with this quirky family of women, and now I hope that you too enjoy the first Mindy's Book Studio release!

Poornima is the full moon.

Auspicious.

Romantic.

Illuminating.

Not rare, only rhythmic. Arriving every month with the dependability of breath. In, then out. Growing from a sliver to wholeness.

Hiding in the dark, then blazing to full, circular glory.

Only to disappear again, crescent by crescent.

But always whole behind the shadows.

They'd told him never to forget that he was the earth and she the moon.

That it was the only way. For both to know where they stood as they orbited the sun.

If she learned that she could be the earth too, and he let himself be the moon, they'd cause an eclipse. Plunge the universe into an endless night, burn it away.

Or, maybe,

They'd be blinded by darkness to relearn the light

They'd burn in the light to relearn the darkness

One nothing without the other

She sometimes the earth and sometimes the moon.

He sometimes the earth and sometimes the moon.

CHAPTER ONE

BINDU

The way a woman wears the color red tells you everything you need to know about how she sees herself. The first time I saw Bhanu, she was wearing a red bikini.
From the journal of Oscar Seth

It wasn't every day that someone left you a million dollars, without so much as a warning and no way to give it back, no matter how badly you wanted to. For years Bindu Desai had believed that life was a series of accidents waiting to happen, fragile beads strung together on threads of varying strengths. The only way to keep them from shattering was to stand utterly still and hold them as carefully as she possibly could. Then, twenty-six years ago, her husband had died, two days after Bindu's thirty-ninth birthday, and she swore to take them off and *Move! Dance!* She didn't care if the beads shattered. She was going to *live*.

But everyone in her neighborhood in Mumbai knew her. Mrs. Bindu Desai, wife of Dr. Rajendra Desai, mother of Ashish Desai, who was studying engineering somewhere in America.

Sure, her choice to keep wearing bright colors as a new widow was met with tolerant smiles, but when she'd worn her Western blouses and pants outside the house instead of her usual salwar kameez, the women in her building had started to avoid her. Especially if she dropped in on them after the husbands got home from work.

Turned out *Moving! Dancing!* wasn't quite so simple, because all her friends were still wearing their fragile beads.

Then her son announced that he was getting married to a woman he'd met at the University of Florida. They'd been in love for three years. Ashish had told Bindu about Alisha in confidence because his father would never be okay with his son marrying a Catholic girl. Even if she was Indian. Well, Indian American.

Alisha's parents were from Goa, but she had grown up in America. Being from Goa herself, Bindu felt like she'd won some special intraparental prize when Ashish had chosen a wife from her hometown. Too bad Rajendra would never know that she had won that marital contest.

He'd also never know that because he'd died and left Bindu alone, she'd been free to move to America and move in with Ashish and Alisha when they had Cullie while still in grad school and needed help raising her. Some accidents were actually beautiful.

Her daughter-in-law was one of Bindu's favorite people on earth. Sure, she was a bit—how could Bindu put this delicately—uptight? One of those people who always had to do the right thing. But Bindu didn't mind. She liked when people felt free to be who they were.

After Ashish and Alisha had gotten divorced two years ago, after twenty-three years of marriage, Bindu had chosen to go on living with her daughter-in-law. For one, Alisha had asked her to. For another, Bindu now moved and danced to her own tune. At least as best she could, which at sixty-five was not unworthy of pride.

That didn't mean, every once in a while, she wasn't livid enough at her daughter-in-law to want to drown her in the neighborhood pool. This morning they'd had one of those fights, triggered by something so insignificant that halfway through you forgot what started it.

Well, an empty chai cup started it. Bindu had left the blameless thing on the coffee table, preoccupied as she was with the unexpected million dollars. Why on earth would anyone leave such an obscene sum to a woman whose life he'd almost destroyed? What had he possibly hoped to gain, other than digging up old pain and secrets? Ever since the money had shown up, Bindu had felt like she'd been hit by a truck, one filled with every shameful mistake of her youth.

Alisha had snapped at Bindu, in her passive-aggressive way, about not using a coaster, probably preoccupied with some new stunt her bully of a boss had pulled.

"It's a table, Alisha! It doesn't have feelings. And it's ugly anyway," Bindu snapped back.

The coffee table was a gift from Alisha's mother. Which explained why it was ugly and why it needed so very much care. If Bindu had her way, she'd only ever buy furniture she could dance on, with heels!

Nonetheless, she shouldn't have said it, and from that moment on things had snowballed out of control. Hurtful words were tossed about, fragile beads shattering one by one, until Bindu declared that she was going to the open house at the retirement community that Debbie Romano had been pestering Bindu to accompany her to.

Debbie lived a few houses down from the house Bindu shared with Alisha in Naples, Florida. For years Debbie had been Bindu's walking buddy. They walked five miles daily, each committed to never missing a day.

Over the past year, Debbie, who was ten years older than Bindu, had turned repetitive in her conversation. Bindu responded by learning how to block out the parts she'd heard before. When you spent hours walking with someone, it might seem easy to confuse company with friendship, but Bindu didn't have that problem. Defining relationships and responding to them with exactly what they needed was one of her greatest skills.

"Maybe it's time for me to move out," Bindu had said in the final throes of their nonsensical fight.

Alisha had made one of her laugh-groan-scoff sounds.

If not for that stupid sound, Bindu wouldn't have said yes to Debbie, and Bindu wouldn't be standing here in a red summer dress she'd bought online, with nowhere to wear it to.

Elegant brass letters on a gray stone wall proclaimed that they were at the clubhouse. SHADY PALMS—LUXURY LIVING FOR YOUR VIBRANT YEARS.

If you were going to put a bunch of old—sorry, she was supposed to say "older" now, even though that made no sense—people in one place, why would you call that place something as fake sunny as *Shady Palms*? Palms should never be anyone's choice when seeking shade, especially if other options were available.

But they were here, so Bindu held her head high and walked through the arched entrance as regally as she could. Not easy with Debbie hiding behind her. If the outside of the clubhouse was impressive—all manicured landscaping and giant fountains—the inside was a veritable ode to showy elegance: a mullioned glass ceiling, mosaic marble floors, and an absurd profusion of indoor (still not shady) palms.

Bindu sent up a prayer of gratitude for her dress with its cute cold shoulders and gently flaring sleeves. As forms of self-soothing therapy went, Bindu had always believed that clothes, jewelry, and the perfect shade of lipstick were underrated. To say nothing of all the things a good hair day could fix in your soul. Thank heavens she'd touched up her hair color just yesterday.

These people did not look like they touched up their own grays with drugstore color. They looked like they'd been airdropped here, in chartered planes, straight from Beverly Hills. Bindu dragged Debbie to the circle of women gathered under the impressive crystal chandelier. Every one of them had blown-out hair, super-moisturized faces, and gold chains so delicate they were barely visible against the freckled crepe paper skin of their necks.

Eyes in all shades of blue and green and gold flickered Bindu's way, then flickered away without so much as a hint of acknowledgment. She might as well have been invisible.

Then their eyes landed on Debbie's blonde head, ducking behind Bindu. Smiles warmed every face. They introduced themselves to

Debbie with enough enthusiasm that the contrast in their reactions landed on Bindu like a slap.

Maybe she was imagining it.

"Hello," she said, trying to sound breezy, but her own accent sounded loud in her ears.

No one responded. The circle dragged Debbie in and closed up as Bindu stood outside it, taking in the wall of backs. The chill of the air-conditioning hit her exposed shoulders even as her skin turned clammy and hot. It was like menopause returning in a tidal wave. Had she used too much kohl to line her eyes? Was her lipstick too red? The sense of feeling all wrong tangled up her limbs. A girl from a lifetime ago, a girl Bindu had buried with a forgotten past, trembled back to life inside her. And her resurgence felt exactly like rage swallowed too long.

Escaping the turned backs, Bindu pushed past the oversize lead glass doors, slamming them hard enough that she heard some gasps behind her. Outside, the blast of heat and sound enveloped her but gave her no relief. A pool dropped into another pool by way of a waterfall and led up to a bar where swimsuited and sunglassed people laughed and chatted as though they had not a care in the world.

The phrase *vibrant years* had amused Bindu when she'd read it on the brochure, but looking at these deeply confident faces, it felt like the joke was on her. The sunshine was blinding, much like the rush of feelings she'd just experienced at the sudden reappearance of the girl she'd been. Unwanted. Unaccepted. Always on the outside.

She knew exactly why she was suddenly reacting with such ferocity to everything. It was the stupid money.

"Don't let them get to you," a kind voice said behind her.

She turned slowly, hand shading her eyes from the sun, not trusting the way the soft, deep tones settled the churn inside her. Her gaze landed on a pink golf shirt. She tipped her head back to look up his absurdly tall body and found hazel eyes, much like her own, studying her. Lines radiated from their edges like cobwebs pressed into skin. Lines that would never be considered this beautiful on her face.

Bindu hadn't thought of a man as beautiful in a very long time. But there was no other word for the gentleness with which he watched her. Not the sympathetic kind that grew more and more abundant in the way people treated you as you aged, but one that seemed rooted in humanity, in humor. As though he *knew* he could get her to see what he found so amusing about the situation that had just churned up the worst parts of her. A gentleness of equals.

"They're easily threatened." His voice was low, confident that people would focus to hear him no matter how softly he spoke.

"Threatened?" She let all the smoky huskiness of her own voice play out in the word, twist it with nonchalance.

It made his smile grow. He tilted his chin with the exact same impact as raising a finger and tracing her from head to toe.

It was the strangest compliment. But deadly, because it hit her where she never let men's compliments hit her. She'd spent a lifetime fielding men's gazes, their admiration, their lust. In recent years most younger men had stopped having that reaction to her, but men around her age still rarely gazed upon her as anything more than an object they'd like to possess.

The way he looked at her carried the weight of all those things. It *saw* how she must be looked at rather than mirrored it. Which made it different. But the part that caught her like the slow hook of a deep-sea fisherman was the clear displeasure in his gaze at how those women had made her feel.

"Are you new?" He seemed like a man who'd never once felt like an outsider.

In a flash she imagined his life in Hollywood-inspired vignettes: a high school athlete who got straight As. A father who called him "buddy" and shared life lessons as he tossed him a ball. A mother who baked pie and handed out supportive advice over it. A Mercedes-Benz and golf and a wife who kept a house that belonged in *Architectural Digest* and invited friends over for wine and dessert under a gazebo overlooking their lush garden.

Her gaze dropped to his hand, searching for a ring. But it was tucked into his pocket.

"I'm here with a friend," she answered.

"That's too bad. You should move here." For the first time his voice slipped from its confident pedestal. Just the slightest bit.

She threw a glance over his shoulder at the women still fawning over Debbie. "How can I resist?"

Another smile warmed his eyes. She'd been wrong about the color. They weren't hazel, like hers. They were green, like pond moss that made you slip off rocks.

"I think someone like you is exactly what they need." His tone was the warm water that cushioned your fall when you slipped.

Bindu didn't like it when people assumed they knew her. But since she'd just pictured his entire life without knowing him, she waited for him to explain.

"You're trouble."

The words body-slammed her, as if she'd run full tilt into a wall, one she'd built around long-ago memories. Glass beads crashed everywhere. It had been forty-seven years since she'd heard those words, since she'd almost let them ruin her life.

"Exactly the kind of trouble this world needs," he went on. "They need someone who'll pull them out of their bubble. Wake them up, you know?"

She felt off balance. "Setting the world straight is not my job."

Words her mother had said to her too many times. *The world is what it is. Fixing it is not your job.*

The resurrected girl inside her flipped her hair and flounced off like the heroine from an old Bollywood film. Bindu was about to follow her when a group of men approached him. Every one of them wore well-cut golf shirts in sunny pastels and khakis so sharply ironed they had edges. Their eyes strayed to Bindu as they greeted him.

One of them offered her a glass of wine. The pale-gold liquid sparkled in the sunlight. "Lee, who's your friend?"

Over the man's shoulder Bindu felt rather than saw the women who'd closed ranks on her start to stir with awareness, their attention turning in her direction, one by one.

His green eyes smirked. A challenge?

You're trouble. Yes, those words still held the power to move her to recklessness.

It had been a lifetime since she'd picked messages from a man's eyes, since she'd felt like this person.

Taking the glass of wine, she shook the hand one of the men held out. "Bindu." All on their own, her lids lowered and lifted slowly. Her shoulders straightened, making her immensely grateful for the drape and cinch of her dress, for the huskiness of her voice. Things about herself she'd let rust from lack of use. "This seems like a nice place to live."

The circle of men closed around her, laughter and questions and offerings of more wine, and cheese, and all the elaborate analysis of why a certain cheese paired with a certain wine. These were men who'd had time to explore the things they deemed fine. Men comfortable with success, but not so much that they were unconcerned with broadcasting it.

All of that set him apart from them. *Lee.*

When she looked back, he was gone, but the women had left the shade of the clubhouse and made their way out into the blazing sun. Bindu Desai was no longer invisible. And just like that, she knew exactly what she was going to do with the money.

CHAPTER TWO

CULLIE

Sometimes I wonder what would have happened if I hadn't caught Bhanu snooping around the hotel that day, looking for trouble.
From the journal of Oscar Seth

Six months later . . .

In for four, out for six. Cullie Desai counted her breaths as she made her way up in the elevator of the building she'd worked at for the past five years. For the first couple years after she'd moved to San Francisco, she'd had to do this almost every time she made the fifty-three-floor elevator ride up to the NewReal Networks offices.

Being a twenty-year-old genius college dropout in the big bad world of tech sounded far more glamorous than it had been. Although Cullie would never admit that to anyone. She needed them to believe she had this. She needed them to believe Shloka's future was bright. From the age of sixteen, when Cullie had first envisioned the app to help herself deal with her anxiety, a problem she didn't feel she could share with anyone, she'd done nothing but work on Shloka.

In for four, out for six.

She rubbed the short hair at the back of her cropped bob. The friction helped her breathe. Over the past year, she'd really gotten hold of things with the help of a good therapist and a prescription it had taken her far too long to admit she needed, in conjunction with her own app. She'd gained some control over the constant sense of dissolving into the air around her, from this thing that felt terribly close to fear but wasn't. Because fear gave you something tangible to avoid.

Her phone buzzed, and she looked down at it. You here yet? It was Steve, of course, and she was, of course, late.

She couldn't decipher the tone of the text, but that stubborn (and stupid) awareness sparkled across her skin. She tugged at the snug neck of the black crew she'd tucked into black jeans. *He went back to his wife, for heaven's sake, Cullie!* She tried to use her mother's voice to yell at herself, to snap herself out of this. Whatever this was. Because she hadn't slept with Steve for six months now.

He was waiting for her outside the elevator.

"You're late."

Focus on the fact that he sounds prickly. It's his dick voice. The one you hate.

The one she loved.

Because she was the prickliest of people, and his prickliness had made her feel like she was home when she'd first met him. When she'd beaten him, one of the judges, in the final round of that hackathon, and he'd reached out to her to see what she was working on.

This isn't your usual CS Geek code. It's . . . it's . . . beautiful. I've never seen anything like it.

Those words had landed like a caress on touch-starved skin.

"I texted Linda to let her know I was running late." Yes, she'd communicated with his assistant. Just the way he'd asked her to. It had been months since they'd spoken directly.

It's for the best, he'd said.

Best for whom? she'd wanted to ask. But smart people didn't ask questions they knew the answers to.

He grunted.

She tried not to let the sound hit her in the solar plexus and followed him to his office.

"How are you?" He shut the door behind her and left his arm there, caging her.

Not caging, exactly, because it was just one arm, but he felt too close.

Eyes the color of the Pacific met her from behind wireless glasses, and she needed to take those breaths again. *In for four, out for six.* How had she let a man who looked this harmless destroy her?

His face was open, bare of his usual defenses. Naked. The sudden shift sent alarm spiking through her nerves.

"Why would you ask me that? Is it Shloka? Did the board make a decision?"

Hurt flared in his eyes, all those grays and blues sparkling with it. "It's always Shloka with you, isn't it? Do you even care about anything else?"

How dare he! He knew Shloka was everything to her. She'd been working on it for what felt like her entire life.

"Are you really asking me that?" She'd given him her app. She'd let him take it to the VCs, trusted him to take it to market. They'd made a lot of money for a lot of people.

And then he'd gone back to his wife. A year after their divorce had been finalized. The happiest year of Cullie's life. His hand went to her cheek. So gentle she sank into it, her existence distilling to that one touch.

"I wish I hadn't met you when you were so young."

For the first two years after she'd dropped out of the computer science program at the University of Illinois at Urbana-Champaign and joined him to take Shloka to market, she'd been in awe of him. Or rather in awe of how in awe of her he was. His respect for her work, his faith in her: it had been like a drug that blasted her into herself.

Then it had started. The air brightened with awareness around them, saturated with need when their bodies were close. But he hadn't touched her. Not when they worked together sixteen hours a day. Not when they spent a week in Vegas at the Apps Supercon and she'd literally had to scream into her pillow at night, knowing he was in the next room.

He hadn't touched her at all until Shloka went to market, until after his wife had signed those divorce papers. It was why a little piece of her would always love him.

But what kind of asshole thing to say was that?

"Strange how you didn't think my age was a problem when we were screwing."

He yanked his hand away, as though she'd spat in his face. To her mortification, her body followed it.

"Do you really think I didn't?"

"We were together for a year. You had plenty of time to stop *the problem* if you'd really been worried about me."

Guilt and hurt flared again. The oceanic-blue darkening and brightening like the play of light on waves.

She knew it hadn't been just sex. They'd planned and strategized and created something fantastic. Suddenly, her skin prickled for an entirely different reason. Shloka was her life.

Slipping past him, she put distance between them. "Tell me what the board has decided. Are they funding the new features?"

His hand went to the nape of his neck and squeezed. Sympathy flooded his eyes. "I ordered you something to drink." He turned to his desk.

An iced matcha bubble tea sat on his desk, next to his coffee. Black with a packet and a half of Splenda.

"Wow. Bubble tea, a mention of my age. You're really leaning into the *little girl* narrative. How bad is it?"

Picking up the bubble tea, he held it out to her. "Extra boba."

"Now you're scaring me."

His eyes did that hurt thing again, but this time tinged with humor. "I would never manipulate you with boba."

Oh, he totally would. But she wasn't going to fall into their old banter. She was not going to let his manipulation work any more than it already had. She fixed him with her most cynical glare.

"This is business, Cal. It's not personal."

"Tell me what the board said or I'm marching into CJ's office right now." She headed for the door.

"Don't be this way. This isn't who you are."

Anger rose inside her, feeling too much like panic. *It isn't panic. This is anger. Name it. Anger and disappointment and hurt. Don't try to control it.*

She faced him, eye to eye. He was leaning back into his desk, making sure she knew he had this. His "I'm the rock to your waves" pose.

"They're not funding new releases of the app anymore, are they? Why? It's growing. There's eight million subscribers now. Why would they do that? What aren't you telling me?"

He took a deep breath, and his lean shoulders straightened. "They're going to start charging a subscription for it."

The icy bubble tea burned her hand. She slammed it down on the desk. "They can't do that." Eight million people took solace in Shloka, depended on it. In some cases, they were able to survive because of it. Cullie was one of those people too. "They pay for the Neuroband. They shouldn't have to pay a subscription too. That was part of the deal. The board promised me there would be no subscription fee. Ever."

"It's already done. The decision has been made. The company has to make money. If they don't charge a subscription, they'll have to sell it, Cullie." He made her name sound like Callie, and she hated that.

"It's *Cullie*!" she snapped. "Cuh-lee. How many times do you have to sleep with someone to say their name right?" It meant "flower bud," and it suddenly struck Cullie that every time he mispronounced it, the image of someone crushing petals formed in her head.

"Sorry."

She shoved back the heavy bangs that fell across her forehead. "Sorry for what? For stealing my app? You can't sell it. It's not yours to sell." But it was. She had given away enough equity that with the board's support, he could do whatever the heck he wanted.

She was never trusting another soul again. Ever.

Lies were the laziest form of evil, and Cullie refused to be an easy target. Not any longer.

"You know that's not my decision."

Of course it was. Everything between them had been his decision.

She marched to the door, and he followed her.

"This is business. Don't mix it with what we had."

Without another word she let herself out of his office and stormed to the CEO's office. NewReal was the umbrella company with a suite of apps for everything from meditation and anxiety support, like Shloka, to apps that helped you navigate emotional eating and count your way out of insomnia into sleep. A self-help conglomerate.

"Cullie." He pronounced her name exactly right this time, exaggerating the *uh* as though he were suddenly Indian or like he was mocking her. "Wait. Let's talk about this. Let's not make a scene."

Desai women do not make scenes. It was the one thing her mom and her grandmother would say together right now. In one voice.

"Yes, let's not." It would be a scene only if his betraying ass kept following her.

She knocked on CJ's door and opened it without waiting for an answer.

CJ was hanging upside down on her back-stretching machine. Cullie had never actually seen BDSM equipment, but this contraption had *dungeon of pain* written all over it.

"*Curlie,*" CJ enunciated in her British way, still upside down. "Give me a moment. The sciatica's been a whore lately."

Cullie kept her face utterly serious as CJ pressed a button and the machine rotated her the right side up.

"My best friend's a healer," Cullie said. "I can have him send you energy. My grandmother swears by his healing light." Bless Bharat for his woo-woo ways.

CJ unstrapped herself with impressive deftness. "Really? Why did I not know this?"

Because my asshole ex always got in the middle of every conversation we ever tried to have outside of Shloka.

"Send me a picture. His healing circle likes to have a photograph; it helps them channel energy."

CJ, who was the tallest woman Cullie had met in real life—nearly a foot taller than Cullie's own very average five-foot-four frame—walked right up to Cullie's face in her bare feet.

It took Cullie a moment to realize that the woman was holding her face in a smile. Oh. She wanted Cullie to take a picture.

Okay. Holding up her phone, Cullie snapped a picture. "Got it. You can't put a paid subscription on Shloka," she said.

CJ's eyes went to Steve, who had followed Cullie into CJ's office. "I thought you said she was on board with this."

"You bastard!" Cullie spun toward him.

He ignored her. As though she were too young for this conversation.

"I said she will be on board when she understands the benefits of the deal." He spoke directly to CJ.

"You let him speak for me without checking with me first?" Cullie threw the question at the author who'd written last year's bestseller about women in technology creating a safe space for one another. *Balancing the Ladder* had been hanging out on the *New York Times* bestseller list ever since its release without missing a week.

CJ blinked at Cullie, making it clear that no one had ever taken that tone with her.

"It's fourteen million dollars in profit. Plus, every app has a life cycle. This one is past its downloading prime and is no longer selling enough Neurobands for us to stay profitable. Why wouldn't we put a subscription fee on it? If we sell the app to another company, the first thing they'll do is slap one on." At least her tone was curious, fair. Not patronizing.

"We can't sell it. I can't have someone turn it into a hack meditation app like all the other ones out there." They had labeled it a meditation app, but Shloka was really a tool that helped you come back to yourself. It monitored your vitals during episodes that made you feel out of control and helped you work through and calm your emotions. It worked with the Neuroband Cullie had designed, a bracelet that measured heart rate and breath so the app could match them with ancient chants. Shloka realigned you.

Millions of people needed it to get through the day. Anxiety was at epidemic levels in the world right now.

"I know," CJ said. "That's why a subscription is our only answer. The projections are bad. It's going to be worth your while. Trust me."

"I already have more money than I know what to do with. I won't compromise something that helps people."

CJ let out the deepest sigh. "Just twenty-five," she said, almost to herself. "I'd like to meet your mother someday." She scratched her cropped hair—almost the exact same style as Cullie's—and studied Cullie as though she were a wonder. Well, she was, but the CEO had never looked at her this way. "My children blow through money like it's dust in a sandstorm. And they haven't made any of it themselves." Just as easily, her frustrated-mom face swapped back to her CEO face. "I need this subscription fee to meet my numbers, or it's my job on the line. We had a bad year."

"So did our competitors," Cullie countered, ignoring the sound Steve made somewhere behind her.

"Fair enough. But I can't save everyone else's job if I don't save mine."

"You said it was past its download prime in the life cycle. A subscription fee will make that worse. It will make customers drop Shloka en masse." Which meant people who needed it wouldn't be able to keep using it. "What if I gave you another app. A new one that starts a life cycle. One that uses the Neuroband so we get fresh sales on that hardware. But only if you keep Shloka funded and free."

Cullie had no idea where that had come from, but one elegantly tweezed brow rose as CJ met her eyes. "You have something you've been working on?" Her gaze swept to Steve, who'd been breathing heavily but wordlessly. CJ and the board had been begging Cullie for something new for two years.

Throwing Steve under the bus, wiping that patronizing smirk off his face: it would be delicious. But she couldn't do it. "I haven't told him about it. It's a passion project. No one knows about it." Not even Cullie herself, because she'd just pulled that out of thin air. Well, she'd simply have to come up with something.

"Can I talk to you alone?" Steve said behind her.

Cullie was about to tell him to take a hike when she realized he wasn't talking to her. He was talking to CJ. A fresh wave of betrayal rose like water in her lungs, so swift and brutal the Neuroband on her wrist vibrated for her to calm down. To hell with that. She was angry enough to blow out Shloka's algorithm.

She stepped between him and CJ. "Actually, CJ, I have some things I'd like to discuss with you privately first." If she sounded like a child, so be it. She might as well play to the audience.

CJ looked from Cullie to Steve and weighed their value in this situation against each other. Then she turned to Steve. "Why don't you wait in your office, and I'll let you know when Cullie and I are done."

CHAPTER THREE

ALY

She had no idea I knew that the bikini she was wearing was stolen. But not too many women wore red bikinis in Goa in 1974. And no woman I ever met wore it quite like that. As though the scraps of cloth were a lover and she knew exactly how lucky the bastard was.
From the journal of Oscar Seth

Aly adjusted her gray silk jacket over her trousers. She'd remembered to leave the jacket on a hanger, but she could hardly take her pants off at the office.

Aly hated—*loathed*—wrinkles. They were a simple thing to control about your appearance. Aly had no patience for the kind of person who shuffled through life with crumpled clothing as though they couldn't even bring themselves to care about their own appearance.

Joyce Komar, Aly's boss and the head producer at Southwest Florida News, never had a wrinkle on her clothing. Aly's own mother, the always perfectly put-together Karen Menezes, most certainly never did either. And here Aly was wearing wrinkled pants on a day as important as today.

Thanks to Meryl Streep, Aly's career dreams were about to come true. No more spot reporting on diversity stories. Finally, Aly was going to anchor her own segment, do a full interview.

Ms. Streep was scheduled to spend the winter on Marco Island as part of her research for her next film, which according to Aly's top secret insider intel was set in a retirement community there. Aly's best friend's son's boyfriend worked for Ms. Streep's talent agency, and he'd been able to get Aly in touch with her people. And Aly had snagged an exclusive interview for SFLN.

What on earth had possessed her to experiment with a new brand of trousers? There was a reason why Aly stuck with tried and tested things. The trousers were covered in those ugly horizontal wrinkles that ran across your crotch when you dared to sit down. It was the twenty-first century. Why did companies still make clothing that punished you for the act of sitting?

Aly checked her wristwatch. She had twenty-seven minutes before the editorial meeting that was going to change the trajectory of her career. She could feel it in her bones. Grabbing her purse, she ran out of her office. Wrinkled pants were not going to keep this from her.

It took her three minutes to drive to the Ann Taylor store, then another five minutes to run in and grab a pair of slim-fit black pants in a size six, twenty-nine-inch inseam. It had taken her years to zero in on the perfect combination of an interval workout routine and a diet so she could wear these pants and look like someone who fit the role of a news anchor. It took another five minutes to pay, then another five to drive back—because this was Naples, and she got stuck behind a driver who had nowhere to be.

Switching the pants out took two minutes. After that she touched up her lipstick, sprayed the flyaways from her chignon with her travel-size antifrizz mist, and gathered her iPad for notes. She was still the first person in the conference room.

Joyce followed half a minute later and smiled when she saw Aly. Her "There you are, on time as always" smile. As always, Aly wasn't sure if it was admiration or annoyance—another trait her boss shared with her mother.

"Our ratings are down two and a half points," Joyce said five minutes later to the seven people sitting soldier straight around the conference table she commanded like the captain of industry she was. Her perfectly styled blonde hair, polished blush nails, the humongous cluster of diamonds on her ring finger: it all announced, rather loudly, exactly how much she "had it all."

"Honestly"—she threw a loathing look around the table—"our content has been so boring these days, even I don't want to watch us."

They were a news channel; entertaining content should not be their job. But not one person at the table pointed that out. Aly sure as hell didn't.

"If we keep going this way, we're going to lose more sponsors, and you all know what that means." Joyce's I-smoked-in-my-youth voice was thick with insinuation.

Of course they all knew what that meant. Over the past five years, the size of their team had shrunk down to half. But Aly was still here, and that wasn't an accident. She was going to get that segment. She knew it.

Every time her ex-husband had laughed at her "pathetic optimism," the fact that she'd dodged the layoffs had kept her from internalizing the many, many ways in which he had tried to get her to drop her dream. She still couldn't understand why a man so kind and loyal, even smitten, had such disregard for this particular ambition. Enough to let it tear them apart.

Not that it mattered anymore. What mattered was this meeting today and what she did with it.

"Ideas for the Thanksgiving special?" Joyce said, a gauntlet tossed across the glass-topped mahogany of the conference table.

Aly would wait. She'd let Jessica or Bob go first—she could tell from their faces that they had nothing. If she went first, they'd just move to the next person, and then someone would repeat her idea, and somehow magically it would become theirs.

Not this time.

"The Chihuly exhibit," Bob said when no one else spoke. He let his words sit for a bit as though he'd just declared that Van Gogh had returned to life and agreed to doing an interview.

Aly tried not to roll her eyes. They'd already covered the Chihuly exhibit. Another one of her ideas that had ended up being covered by Slimy Bob, as her daughter, Cullie, had christened him.

"Since that piece was such a hit"—Bob added another practiced pause, lest anyone miss his anchor's timing—"I figured we could leverage it. Double down, you know. My niece is visiting from England. I'll take her with me, and we'll do a child's perspective. Have you heard a child speak with a British accent?" He said the words *British accent* in a British accent, and Aly had to suppress her gag reflex.

Joyce's smile was part indulgence, part skepticism. "You got a picture?"

Of course Bob had a picture, and he whipped it up on his phone in record time.

Oh, excuse her, it wasn't a picture, it was a flippin' video.

"Muh-mee, ah we go-eeng to the aht meusee-um?" a truly gorgeous child with the biggest blue eyes said in the most—and it hurt Aly to admit this—adorable accent.

Ovaries contracted around the table, Aly's included. It would have been a terrible idea, except for the fact that their viewership was going to lap this up like Anglophilia-flavored ice cream.

"It's a good idea. Maybe we'll use it for Labor Day. We still need something solid. Our Thanksgiving show is our flagship. Black Friday advertising is what keeps the lights on around here."

"What about that ex-con who's been painting boats?" Jessica said.

Joyce ignored her and turned to Aly. "You got anything that's not cute family members or rage art?"

This was exactly what Aly needed. Joyce coming to her.

Aly cleared her throat. "You're right, by Thanksgiving our snowbirds are here, and our viewership goes up forty percent. So we need this to get them to tune in for the rest of the winter."

Joyce was trying not to narrow her eyes at Aly to get her to cut the setup. Which meant she knew Aly had something good.

Damn it. Her face always gave her away. The last thing she needed was to lessen the impact by raising the expectations too much. *Just keep going*, she told herself. *Play it cool.*

"Meryl Streep," she said and left the name to dance there in the silence, on that shiny tabletop.

Every one of the seven people sat up.

That's how it's done, Bobby Cakes. She volleyed the immensely satis-fying mental grenade in Bob's direction before turning her focus back to her boss, who had her gaze trained on Aly as though she were a bull's-eye at an archery contest.

"Meryl's spending the winter here. Research for her next film about a retired chef with Alzheimer's. I was thinking an interview and a walk-through of the food trucks. A little 'How are you enjoying our lovely town?' conversation as we deep dive into her roles."

"Meryl," Joyce breathed, the word a benediction.

Aly wasn't even a little bit surprised. Meryl was who Joyce wanted to be when she grew up. Arguably, Meryl was who every woman who took her work seriously wanted to be. She was the pinnacle of her art. Let other journalists report on what destroyed the world every day. Art unraveled it and put it back together and shone a light on its darkest corners. All Aly had ever wanted was to bring art and artists to her viewers.

"Is that the evil boss from *Devil Wears Prada*?" Bob said, grinning.

The grin slid right off his face when five women and one gen-der-fluid person spun on him as though he had called into question their very right to exist.

"Sorry. A bad joke." The man cleared his throat and arranged his face in the most remorseful of masks.

Too late, buddy, Aly thought with far too much glee.

Joyce continued to glower, just in case the Only Man in the Room further misunderstood the Power of Meryl.

"Tell me you've watched *Out of Africa, Kramer vs. Kramer, Sophie's Choice*?"

The mask that was Bob's face did nothing to hide the pure terror. It was delicious. Aly knew it made her a terrible person, but: It. Was. Delicious.

"By next week's meeting, I need you to have watched at least ten of her films."

Bob allowed himself to breathe again. "Done. I'll watch fifteen. I mean, she's the most decorated actress of our time. It will be my pleasure."

Slimy bastard.

"How did you find out she's in town?" Joyce turned her attention back to Aly, voice trembling with excitement.

Aly accessed her inner Margaret Thatcher (as played by Ms. Streep, of course) and kept her gaze steady. "Insider tip. No one else knows yet. We're the only station with the information. Guaranteed."

Joyce opened her mouth.

"I'm not revealing my sources. The deal's off if I do." God, she hoped her plan was going to work. There was still many a slip between the cup and Aly's ravenous lips, but this time she was going to be brave. This time she wasn't going to settle. This time no one was taking this from her.

"Great. Set it up. You can be part of the production team. Jessica, make sure you've done your research. I want the interview to be flawless."

"Wait!" Yes, Aly raised her voice. Raised it all the way up. Maybe? She couldn't be sure because her ears were ringing. "You're giving the interview to Jessica?"

Joyce had the gall to look confused. "Well, Jess is the anchor of the show. Who else would do the interview?"

Me! Did the word come out?

"Me!" Aly said again. Or maybe for the first time. Then a second. "Me! You've been telling me you're waiting for the right interview to let me get my segment. What can be better than this?"

Joyce looked around the room. Color crept up her neck. Okay, great. Maybe Aly had gone too far. Maybe she should have done this privately with Joyce. But she'd wanted Jess and Bob to witness her victory. She was such an idiot.

"You've done an amazing job here, Aly," Joyce said, her tone exactly as coldly controlled as Karen Menezes's when she lost her temper.

What was that supposed to even mean? It sounded like something one said just before they fired you.

Aly had a verbal commitment on the interview, but it wasn't scheduled. Now that Joyce knew, she could easily reach Meryl's team and set it up on her own.

Had Aly made a mistake? Should she have made Joyce commit to giving her the segment before revealing the information?

Maybe she should have done that MBA, the way her mother had wanted her to. Working as a broadcast journalist who got to do anything of importance seemed to need more strategy than journalistic curiosity or investigative talent. Maybe she should have stayed in that technical-writer job the way Ashish had wanted her to. At least she'd still have a marriage.

Aly's heart was beating so fast, she barely noticed Joyce nod to the others. They shuffled out of the room with enough reluctance to prove exactly how thrilling it was to witness Aly's humiliation.

"Aly," Joyce said, voice oddly gentle. Dear Lord, she was trying to sound motherly. It made Aly want to bring up the salad she'd had for lunch. "That was unexpected. Is everything okay at home?"

"What?" Aly asked, open mouthed. *Don't say* what *like a street urchin; say* pardon *like the well-brought-up girl you are*, her mother's voice rang in her head.

"It hasn't been that long since the divorce."

At the cost of repeating herself: *What?* "Pardon?" she said.

"Aly, I know how hard it can be to find your feet after a divorce. It's only been two years since yours."

Please, God, she could not play the Sisterhood of the Commiserating Divorcées game with Joyce. From the office grapevine, Aly knew that Joyce had been divorced years ago from some sort of genius who'd also been a genius at philandering. All of it was irrelevant because five years ago she'd remarried, and her second husband seemed like the world's nicest man. Maybe marrying in your fifties was the answer. Unlike Aly, who'd been twenty-two and so, so stupid.

"This has nothing to do with my divorce."

"Is it your daughter?"

"Cullie is just fine. This has to do with the fact that you've been promising me a segment for almost ten years now."

Ten years! What had she even been thinking? How had she let someone string her along for so long? It was like Ashish all over again. She'd been too naive to see through him. Through what was important to him. Ashish—that's what had been important to Ashish. So long as he came first, so long as everything was about him, he'd been wonderful.

"You think I haven't tried to get you your segment?" Joyce gave the most long-suffering look. "Do you have any idea how many times I've proposed it to the board? I take this up to them at least once every few months."

That hurt.

"You know I give you stories. Make sure you're on air at least a few times a month. But you know how news is right now. Budgets keep getting slashed and slashed. We cannot do anything to displease our sponsors."

"Why would me anchoring arts and entertainment displease our sponsors?" Words were flying out of Aly today like they never had before, and Joyce studied her as though she had no idea who had invaded Aly's body.

For a long, stunned moment, Joyce didn't respond. Aly could hear her diversity-training seminar run through her head.

"You're a smart girl, Aly."

Aly wasn't a girl at all; she was a forty-seven-year-old woman. Which meant she at least had enough sense to not respond by correcting her boss about that.

Joyce went on, doubling down on the nonanswers. "This is southwest Florida."

Aly waited. She needed Joyce to say the words. *Say it.*

"Our audience is . . ." Getting up from her chair, Joyce moved to the chair next to Aly and cleared her throat with so much discomfort it sounded painful. "Our audience can relate to Jessica."

There it was. The storm inside Aly had gathered for too long without a tangible thing to break on, until now.

"I was born in West Palm Beach," she said, voice flat. "I went to the University of Florida. Jessica is from Wyoming."

Joyce cleared her throat again. Louder this time. Aly could see her patience slipping. "I didn't want to share this with the team yet, but I know you can keep it to yourself." Joyce's commiserating smile looked like it took all her effort to conjure up. "I just found out that we have another round of layoffs coming."

That couldn't be true, could it? Their ratings weren't terrible, and their sponsorships were up.

"Unless," Joyce added, "Tropical Juices renews their sponsorship." Before Aly could respond, Joyce put a hand on her shoulder. "I don't know why they're thinking about dropping us, but I cannot afford to make any sudden moves right now. Their sponsorship is up for renewal, and if they don't renew, we *all* lose our jobs. And you know there's no segment to be had for a woman your age on any other station."

Wow.

"But maybe if you let me leverage this story, it will push them to renew." She leaned closer. "Seriously, good job with this lead. I'm confident it can save our behinds. I mean, it's Meryl!" The first genuine smile brightened her eyes. "Let's use it to get Tropical in the bag. Then, as soon as they've signed, we'll announce the new arts and entertainment segment, with you as the anchor. Every Friday, a weekend-recommendations piece like you've been asking for. *Weekend Plans with Aly Menezes Desai.*"

Aly swallowed. *Weekend Plans with Aly Menezes Desai.*

"Has quite a ring to it, ha?"

It did. It had the best ring to it, and Aly wanted to nod and hand over the story. A fair exchange. But she didn't move.

"Take some time to think about it," Joyce said carefully. "Let me run a few things by the powers that be, and you get started on the story. Sound good?"

Aly nodded. Time to figure things out was always a good thing.

CHAPTER FOUR

BINDU

The actor's craft demands walking through the flames of your fear. It's getting naked so the world might see itself in you. It's violating your own boundaries. When Bhanu looked at me, I saw everything. And I wanted to be the camera.
From the journal of Oscar Seth

Bindu had never imagined that winning a game of pickleball could be so satisfying. Not that she was delusional enough to take credit for the victory. Jane, her doubles partner, had been a gym teacher for forty years. Any doubles team with Jane on it was unbeatable.

"The skort is lovely on you!" Bindu said as they left the courts. Jane and Connie, the two friends Bindu had made at Shady Palms, had dressed mostly in tracksuits when she met them, but they'd loved Bindu's style, so she had helped them love their own clothes too with a few marathon online shopping sessions.

"You're right. Winning while looking cute is so much more fun," Jane said, patting down her white athletic skort.

Bindu quite liked her new friends. Debbie Romano had chosen not to move into Shady Palms, and Bindu would never know why, because she hadn't spoken to Debbie since the open house.

"By the way, I got you something." Jane slipped a brown paper package out of her gym bag and handed it to Bindu.

Bindu had to laugh. "You didn't!" she said without having to open it.

Jane, Connie, and Bindu met for dinner and wine every Wednesday, and Jane and Connie had spent their last gathering dissecting, in thorough detail, the pros and cons of various lubes. It was a subject Bindu had no experience with, which the two women found hilarious. Bindu hadn't shared with them that a man hadn't been involved in her physical pleasures since her husband. There were plenty of ways to skin that particular horny cat on one's own. But everyone didn't need to know everything.

Her new friends, it would seem, had done quite a bit of indulging in the very eager pool of lustfulness that was Shady Palms.

"It might be time to put Richard out of his misery. The man has been following you around like a puppy dog the entire time you've been here."

"Maybe," Bindu said as they came to Jane's building and parted ways. But not before Jane wiggled her brows and declared that cute clothes weren't the only way for a woman to celebrate herself.

Bindu knew that. She also knew that she was listening to all the voices inside her—her mother, Rajendra, every person who'd ever looked at her and seen a slut unless she shrank herself into a tight little ball. But living life on her own terms meant she had to be intentional about it. She refused to let her choices be mere acts of rebellion. Freedom meant she'd do things for the right reasons, when she was good and ready for them. Because now she could.

Which didn't mean she didn't utterly revel in Richard's pursuit. After a long hot shower in her jewel-toned bathroom, she made herself a cup of chai in her quartz and glass kitchen and took it to her lanai. The roar of the ocean mixed with the melodic notes of old Bollywood ballads playing on the Bluetooth speaker Cullie had given her as sunshine poured life into her skin. She sank into her papasan chair and opened her email, anticipation making her heart race in the most exhilarating way.

As the sixty-five-year-old grandmother of a coding genius, Bindu was proud to admit how very much she loved technology. Who would have believed human beings could do this? Communicate across distance in real time, all the time? It was the kind of magic that had colored her grandmother's stories.

As a little girl, growing up in Goa, Bindu had wanted nothing more than to burrow into her grandmother's soft cotton sari and fall into her stories. She'd dreamed them into existence every night with herself as the hero, those worlds alive inside her in Technicolor like the movies her grandmother sneaked her into.

The princess trapped in a cave, plotting ways to escape as the prince fought seven-headed monsters and fanged serpents to rescue her.

The princess in disguise, strolling through bazaars, naively stealing food and being chased down for her crime, only to be rescued by a handsome rogue.

The princess throwing herself in front of the sword meant to pierce her warrior husband.

How naive it had been to believe herself the hero simply because she was part of the action. How she'd romanticized it all. She'd bought into her role as the one in trouble, the one making trouble, the one deserving of its consequences. Maybe she'd bought into it even more than everyone around her had. Because Bindu had never been able to control the even-more-ness inside her. Not once had it struck her as odd that every one of those stories had centered on men.

It's the way of the world. Another of her mother's aphorisms that made it possible to keep going no matter what you lost. A blessing. On the surface.

What would her grandmother have thought about email? A note composed in one corner of the world that miraculously and instantaneously appeared in any other corner of the world so long as you had a magic screen.

But like all magic, some witches would find a way to misuse this.

Seventeen emails from the HOA.

Really?

One would think drying bras on a clothesline in your own home was akin to streaking naked across a crowded bazaar in broad daylight. Or getting naked in front of a camera. But no, she wasn't going to think about that.

This was low even for them.

Then again. Undergarments dried just as well in your bathroom. But there was just such inexplicable joy in annoying pretentious people, Bindu couldn't help herself.

I don't want it to be the way of the world, Aie!

She'd been slapped across her face for saying that. The sting of her mother's palm across her cheek anytime Bindu "showed her true colors" had been just another way of the world.

The important thing was that Bindu had not turned into her mother. She was living her true colors now, and it didn't matter how long it had taken her to get here.

She skimmed her email. Richard (was there a more regal name?) was an author of some repute. Fine, the National Book Award was more than just *some* repute. The man sent the most beautiful emails. His words were caresses.

Those emails were the reason he had scored a third date. How many men described the bow of your lips as plump doves in flight? Your eyes as the harbingers of a storm?

Nope, nothing from Richard yet. To be fair, he'd written to her just half an hour ago, telling her that the eroticism of his anticipation for her company harkened his lost youth. That had sounded an awful lot like a euphemism for sex. Who used the word *eroticism* without expecting dinner to move their incipient connection from the ethereal to the tangible?

She shivered. Yup, she loved words. Possibly even more than she loved orgasms. The man was probably resting up for the night.

With a click that she told herself was more hopeful than desperate, she refreshed her inbox. It took a while to reload, as though it knew her impatience as she waited for it to scour cyberspace for love notes. Then: nothing.

Except, of course, the seventeen emails complaining about her red push-up bra. One of the best parts of moving to America was the beautiful undergarments.

"Rule about Unmentionables." Yes, that was the subject line. Stacked upon which were sixteen rows of "Re: Rule about Unmentionables" cc'd to twelve email addresses, each of them belonging to another pearl clutcher.

If they'd been cold at the open house, they had turned downright hostile after she'd moved to Shady Palms, this group of women who ruled the HOA.

Why oh why had she decided to take them on again?

Because if not now, then when?

The betrayal that flashed in Alisha's eyes whenever the topic of Bindu's moving out came up hurt. Bindu wished she could explain what had come over her that day at the open house. Even if she understood it herself, it would mean sharing things she could never explain. The things she'd done. The person she'd been before she was a wife and a mother and a grandmother. She'd worked too hard to put it all behind her, in the vault of the past, to survive.

Bindu had considered herself happy, living with her daughter-in-law in the house she had shared with Bindu's son. It wasn't as strange as it sounded. Bindu could hardly abandon the girl after her son had done it.

Ashish letting someone like Alisha go was something Bindu still couldn't wrap her head around. If anything, she'd worried about Alisha leaving her son, but never the other way around.

Maybe it was a curse. Desai marriages didn't last past twenty-two years. Bindu's mother-in-law had died twenty-two years into her own marriage. And when Rajendra had gone to bed one night and never woken up, they'd been married exactly those many years.

Cullie and Alisha saw her as the person she was today. They'd never had to see her as Rajendra's wife, atoning and atoning and atoning.

Where others might have dwelled only in regret and conformity, Bindu had chosen to find joy between the cracks in her life and her marriage. No one was going to take away the pride she felt in that.

After Alisha and Ashish got married, Alisha had been kind enough to invite Bindu to live with them. Not in a fake sympathy-for-the-poor-widowed-mother-in-law sort of way but in a families-stick-together sort of way. Because that was Alisha, with her inexhaustible need to do the right thing, the fair thing. Even when it wasn't the fun thing. Especially when it wasn't the fun thing. But Bindu would never have moved in if they hadn't needed help with raising Cullie.

For two years after the divorce, Bindu had watched with rage and regret as Alisha tried not to wilt from Ashish's abandonment, even as the poor girl struggled to understand the relief. Was there a mechanism on earth with more moving parts than a marriage? With the ratio between the good and the painful constantly shifting. Bindu's own marriage had been so many things, none of them visible on the outside.

Then the money had shown up, one million dollars after factoring in all the substantial taxation of two countries, a lightning bolt splitting the clear sky of their routine days.

Damn you, Oscar. You promised never to reach out.

If this wasn't reaching out, Bindu didn't know what was. So what if he'd waited to die before breaking his promise. Weren't you supposed to take your promises to your funeral pyre? She shoved away the grief she had no right to. His leaving her money felt like a flesh wound where the lightning had hit, ripping her open and charging the air with all the things she'd buried.

From the moment it had shown up, the money had been a live thing, gnawing and digging. A nebulous, untenable fear had gripped Bindu, a restlessness to do something and stop thinking about what Oscar's inheritance meant, what it might cost her.

The argument with Alisha had turned it all into the perfect storm. Every ancient and new repressed thing inside them had spurted up with unexpected force and torn through the care they'd taken with each other always. That moment too would have passed, like a million others before it, with the ease of a pressure cooker valve hissing its relief slowly. But then those women at the open house had shoved her back through the portal Oscar had opened with his money.

Bindu had leaped off the tightrope beneath her feet. It had felt like the promise of freedom. A promise that had destroyed her once. Back then she'd run away. This time there was nowhere to go.

You're stronger now.

That's what she'd told herself when she walked into the sales office six months ago and purchased the first home that had ever belonged to her and her alone.

She'd moved in almost immediately, but she'd never seen the man with the green eyes again. A part of her wished she'd had a chance to thank him, because whatever magic canyon she'd jumped over when she stepped into the poolside sunshine that day, it had let her into a life she might have missed if not for the challenge in those smiling eyes.

Well, she was too old to spend time thinking about green eyes when there were blue eyes that thought her precious enough to spin poetry for.

Yes, maybe she'd give Richard what he wanted. Fulfill the promise of *eroticism from his anticipation for her company.*

Over these six months she'd basked in a lot of male attention. Most of the men wanted only to flirt. Look good for the other men. Look desirable to the other women. Bindu didn't care. This was the most fun she'd had in years.

Actually, annoying the HOA was even more fun.

She refreshed the screen again, heady with the prospect of love notes. She let the anticipation soak through her, squeezed everything from this bright moment. Longing was a gift, rich with hope, tinged with the kind of pain that pleasured more than it hurt. What was gone was gone. All Bindu wanted was to revel in the simplicity of her life, the love of her family, the joy of doing as she pleased.

The screen gave her a slow dramatic refresh, then there it was. A new email. She smiled thinking about how over the top this love letter was bound to be.

Her eyes processed the words on her screen, and her heart missed a beat, then dropped in her chest as though she'd dived off a cliff just as the ocean beneath her disappeared, revealing only rock.

She thumped a fist into her chest, needing to dislodge her caught breath. Every flutter of excitement that had shimmered through her now burned like sparks. She stared at the words, willing them to be another hyperbolic love note from a decorated novelist.

Instead the words that sat there on her screen were ones she had dreaded for so long. Words that had been dancing like flames in her peripheral vision ever since the money arrived. Words that threw open every secret she'd ever buried, every fear she'd ever left behind.

It said simply: **Looking for Bhanu D.**

CHAPTER FIVE

CULLIE

For years before I met her, she'd been my muse. I'd dreamed of Poornima every night. The script possessed me like a fever. But I knew I would never make the film unless the Poornima from my dreams appeared before my camera.

From the journal of Oscar Seth

I have a hot date tonight." It wasn't quite the way one expected their conversation with their grandmother to start, but Cullie might suspect body swapping if her Binji didn't say something firmly ungrandmotherly at least once a day. "Get on video call so you can help me choose what to wear."

It was barely nine in the morning in California, and Cullie had been up working until four. But it was almost noon in Florida, where Binji was, so Cullie blinked the sleep from her eyes and dutifully switched the call to video. And was met by a close-up of her grandmother's ample cleavage.

"Binji, your girls are all I see." Cullie couldn't remember when she'd combined her grandmother's name, Bindu, and the Marathi word for grandma, *aji*, and come up with *Binji*, but it fit her grandmother perfectly.

Binji stepped away from the phone, which she always propped on the vanity in the bathroom of her fancy new condo when she needed fashion advice from Cullie. And by "needed" Cullie meant demanded, because the aim of the exercise was somewhat more complicated than it appeared. Her grandmother was a fashionista, and Cullie was . . . well, not. These sessions were meant to inspire Cullie to "live a little" and "find her inner diva."

To Cullie, that sounded like far more trouble than it was worth. At twenty-five Cullie sometimes felt like she had lived a little too much already. Done all the things people try to accomplish over their lifetime. And honestly, her inner diva just wanted to take a nap.

"Why are you still in bed?" Twirling around, Binji modeled the hot-pink wrap dress that hugged her unfairly spectacular body. "Don't the girls look great? It's this bra—it gives armor-grade support. These cutlets are like having fists shoved under the boob droop."

Cullie stretched against the high-density zoned-support mattress that was supposed to preserve the backs of deskbound workaholics. "That sounds painful. How is it fair that you look better in a fitted dress than your granddaughter? How come I didn't inherit all *that*."

Binji adjusted the ruched and wrapped fabric under her breasts, further magnifying the pillowy cleavage, which looked even better for the delicate lines that glazed her skin like brushstrokes on a canvas. "You *did* inherit my looks. You also inherited my son's insouciance, so you don't bother with the upkeep it takes to work them to your advantage. Do you know how much moisturizer has gone into this décolletage in the past two decades?" She twisted to give Cullie a view of her butt, which hadn't held up quite as well to gravity.

Sure, that might seem like a mean thought to have about your grandmother, but only to someone who couldn't see quite how stunning Binji was. No lies were necessary.

"Why don't they make bras for the bum? Cutlets are needed there too." Binji's brown-bordering-on-hazel eyes—which fortuitously Cullie *had* inherited *and* needed no upkeep—lit up. "How's that for a business idea?"

Cullie groaned. "Right. Brutts?"

"Yes! We should patent that."

Cullie rolled onto her side and propped the phone against the pillow next to her. "You sound like Ma." Because if her mother didn't turn every conversation into a lecture about "potential," she thought she'd waste away into the ether of bad parenting. "My one patent is causing me enough heartache right now."

As soon as the words slipped out, Cullie regretted them, because Binji's eyes started studying her as though Cullie were a diamond she was gauging for cut, clarity, and color.

"Don't compare me to your mother. I do not have a twig stuck up my lady parts."

"Ouch."

"A thorny twig too, lately. Tell me about this heartache business. Is Hot Steve causing you problems again?" Moving off camera, Binji started making sounds that indicated a dress change.

"No," Cullie mumbled. When an answer was too complicated, *no* was the perfect stand-in. *Hot Steve* was not the one causing Cullie problems. Cullie was. He was just using her problems against her.

"You should never sleep with someone you work for. It should be the first lesson women are taught in school." Binji came back into the frame, this time in a flowy white eyelet dress that was substantially lower on cleavage exposure. A little less New Binji.

Through most of Cullie's childhood, her grandmother had stuck to tunics and capris, with the odd caftan or midi dress thrown in, and saris and salwar kameez brought out only for special occasions. Always fashion forward and never anything like anyone else's grandmother, but this new superhot style choice was only six months old. Six months ago, Binji had mysteriously come into some money and bought herself a fancy condo where rich white people went after retirement to enjoy, and flash, their money.

It was yet another of the many ways in which their family had changed after Cullie's parents' midlife crisis divorce. But the ease with which Binji had made the transformation was both disconcerting and oddly natural.

"How would you know, Binji? You've never worked for anyone." *Must be nice*, Cullie wanted to add, but Binji would only remind her that the fact that Cullie had created an app millions of people used did not give her a free pass to be arrogant. Cullie wasn't in the mood to argue the point. Because, really, it kind of did.

A flash of annoyance passed over Binji's face. But then she smiled, her upbeat self again, and spun around, displaying a back exposed all the way down to her waist, with a deftly located band of lace across the back of her bra.

"Not only did I work in the home, but I was the best homemaker of anyone I know." Binji made a face. "Wait a minute. If you consider your grandfather my boss, then, well, I did sleep with him. A lot." She got that sharp, sexy look as she appraised herself over her delicate shoulder.

That look was all Binji: Old Binji *and* New Binji all rolled up in one. She always looked you full in the eyes, like she owned herself and she wanted you to know it. Maybe it was the contrast between her two grandmothers, but it was a look Cullie had learned to identify early in life.

"Seven days a week for most of our marriage," Binji finished with a wink.

"Oh my God, Binji! TMI!" Even as Cullie yelled it, she knew the redundancy of it. As "one of the most elegant coders of her generation" (thanks for that pressure, *Fortune* magazine), Cullie understood redundancy if she understood anything. TMI should have been Bindu Desai's middle name—her platform if she'd been a social media influencer. Binji thrived on Too Much Information.

"JEI, Curly-Wurly! Did you know that LOL really stands for *living out loud*?" She tucked her sleekly bobbed hair behind her ear. She had professional highlights now, replacing her usual drugstore boxed color

38

in dark medium brown. Another one of the changes since she'd moved into the schmancy new community.

"I'm pretty sure you're making that up. Just like you made up JEI. Just Enough Information hasn't caught on in popular culture for a reason."

"Popular culture is for sheep." Cullie mouthed it along with her grandmother as she made her favorite declaration. "Now, focus. Dress. Which one?"

"How old is this date?"

"Irrelevant."

"Relevant. Because: Do you want him to die of a boob-induced heart attack or a sexy back-induced one?"

The most adorable wrinkle folded between Binji's perfectly tweezed brows. She must have been late on her Botox shot. "It's urban legend that old people drop dead due to sexual stimulation. I did not raise you to be ageist."

"My apologies." Cullie forced herself out of bed and started riffling through her own closet—a veritable treasure trove of black shirts and black jeans. Binji was right, Cullie was too *insouciant* for daily clothing choices.

Not that how you dressed had much to do with finding someone to hook up with. Cullie might suck at relationships, but she'd never had trouble finding men to hook up with. A fact that would break her mother's heart and possibly even disappoint Binji.

"Cullie?" her grandmother said in her gentle voice.

Cullie didn't want to hear the next part. More than anything else, she hated being asked if she was okay. Who the hell was ever okay?

"I'd wear the white one and ease into the hot-pink one for a later date." She focused on her grandmother's film-star face and tried to gauge if this guy was special.

Binji scrunched up her nose, revealing how new she was at this "dating-shating thing," as she called it. Cullie had never seen her so much as mention a man other than her grandfather. Then the move to Shady Palms had happened, and suddenly Binji was the new hottie in town.

"One date at a time, my love. I gave twenty-two years of my life to one man. This time is for me."

Cullie couldn't imagine what it would take to put up with the same man for twenty-two years. The only person she'd ever slept with more than once was Steve, and look how that had turned out.

Her heart rate sped up when she thought about the fact that she had promised CJ a new app and she had absolutely no idea what she was going to give her.

And yet, oddly enough, Binji's words—words that told her to take a chance because mistakes weren't absolute, that one could reinvent oneself at any point in their life—those words made Cullie feel a little more confident that she would find a way to save Shloka. "The hot-pink one, then," she said.

"Good choice." Binji's smile was one of her signature extravaganzas of emotion, rolling together pride, affection, worry, and everything in between. "Why don't you give it a chance too?" Binji's voice dipped into softness, her kid-glove voice for her "sensitive" granddaughter.

"I don't think trying on clothes on a video call is my style."

"Funny." Binji leaned in, placing her elbows on the vanity, and fixed Cullie with a stare that meant she wasn't going to let Cullie deflect.

"I don't think dating-shating is my style." It was, in fact, the least productive thing Cullie could think of doing with her time.

"You know when I was your age—"

"I know, I know. When you were my age, you had a seven-year-old child." This entire pushing a living being out of the vagina was so vintage sci-fi; wasn't it time to fix it with technology? If Cullie wasn't so absorbed with Shloka, the idea might have been worth pursuing.

"That's not what I was going to say. I would never suggest that any woman marry at seventeen and become a mother at eighteen." This was true, and Cullie felt like a brat for falling back on her childhood pattern of melting down all over her grandmother at the first sign of uncomfortable feelings. Binji had always been there for her.

"That was, in fact, my point," Binji went on, as unaffected by Cullie's prickliness as ever. "When I was your age, only one thing was expected of women. That we find a man to take care of us. The path to our happiness was predetermined. Your path to happiness is so wide open, so limitless, that you don't even seem to know where to start looking for it."

"I don't need a man to be happy." Pursuing happiness by way of coupledom was absurd and too exhausting to contemplate.

"I know. God knows I've been happy these past twenty-six years without one." As soon as she said it, Binji seemed to realize that might have sounded disrespectful to the grandfather who'd died before Cullie's birth. She pressed a hand to her heart and mumbled a prayer. "May your grandfather's soul rest in peace."

That was Binji for you, the kind of contradiction in terms Cullie could never explain to anyone. "What I'm trying to tell you is that dating-shating is not about finding someone. It's about exploring what you want, about learning who you are. It's embarrassing how late in life I pieced this together. Until I moved to Shady Palms, I didn't even know how much living I'd missed out on because I bought into society's rules. You don't have those rules. So what is stopping you from living?"

"Just because we don't have the same rules as you did doesn't mean we don't have any or that preexisting notions have somehow disappeared."

Binji looked thoughtful. "That's a fair point. But at least you know that. So you can start undoing your own conditioning sooner. You don't have to wait until you're at an age when your breasts need prosthetic support."

Suddenly it was clear to Cullie why her grandmother had moved out of the house she'd shared with Cullie's mother after her parents' divorce. Binji was making up for a lifetime of FOMO.

"But isn't the purpose of undoing conditioning being able to do what we please? I already have everything I want."

Binji made a face. "You're twenty-five years old, Cullie! Your whole life is ahead of you." She didn't add that work wasn't everything, but Cullie heard it all the same.

"We don't all have to want the same thing, Binji!"

"Actually we do. We all want to be happy. And we all owe it to ourselves to try and find out what will make us happy. Even if focusing on what we can control is easier."

Cullie dragged herself to her kitchen and poked an annoyed finger into her blameless coffee machine, which was coded to give her the exact strength of brew she desired. "Again, what does any of that have to do with dating?"

The coffee machine let out a commiserating gurgle.

"What we find attractive about love interests says more about us than about them," Binji said in the wise grandmother voice she rarely accessed.

And it made Cullie stop in the act of reaching for a cup. She ran back to her room and picked up her iPad. Her heart was racing again. More importantly, her brain was racing. She wrote down Binji's words. "Go on," she said.

Binji winked. "I see going out with men as a journey of self-discovery. It's about finding us, not them. Think about that for a moment. And the next time you use Hot Steve as an excuse to write off all relationships, consider that you might really be writing yourself off."

Cullie wrote all of that down. Then deleted the last part about Steve. Yet again, her Binji might have found a way to save her.

CHAPTER SIX

ALY

When I first told her about Poornima, *I asked her if she knew what it was like to want something so badly it defined everything you were. She met my eyes the way only she ever did, slipping inside me through them, and answered, simply: "No, but I feel like I'm about to find out."*
From the journal of Oscar Seth

We need to find a way to get Cullie home." Aly's mother-in-law was one of those women who thought "I have a feeling about it" was reason enough to do anything. Without even asking, Aly knew that would be the answer if she asked Bindu why she thought Cullie should come home.

So instead, she said, "Aren't you the one who keeps telling me to get used to the fact that my daughter is an adult? If she needs to come home, she knows to come home."

They were grabbing lunch at Cullie's favorite Iranian place in downtown Naples. Under the bright Florida sun, a plate of khoresh bademjan sat on the wrought iron bistro table between them, almost all gone. The butter-fried eggplant layered on slow-cooked lamb was delicious when it went down, but now it sat heavily in Aly's belly, making her wish for the siestas of her childhood summers when she visited her grandparents in Goa.

"If only it were that simple. Cullie is your daughter and my grand-daughter. So, you know . . ." Bindu trailed off with all the drama of a film star. God knew she looked the part in her chiffon blouse over slim-fit linen pants. Those erstwhile Bollywood actors Aly's parents idolized had nothing on her mother-in-law.

"She's inherited that Desai pride," Bindu said in the perfectly husky voice that always made the broadcast journalist inside Aly envious. "And then there's the Menezes ego from your side."

"Why is it pride when it's your family but ego when it's mine?"

Bindu made a sound that was an eye roll turned into a scoff. It was all very sweet and dandy that her mother-in-law had chosen Aly over her son in the divorce, as she loved to declare, but recently Bindu Desai had changed so much that Aly was starting to think that this new avatar was best consumed in metered doses.

Nonetheless, Aly's Catholic guilt jabbed a brutal spike inside her. Bindu had never led Aly wrong when it came to her daughter. She had an uncanny sense for what Cullie was going through. Something that often eluded Aly.

"Fine. I'll call Cullie as soon as I'm done with my editorial meeting. I need to focus on the story I'm working on. I think this one's going to be it." A curl popped out of her chignon, and she pushed it back into place. Joyce was still "working on things," so Aly was pretty sure she hadn't been able to make contact with Meryl's people to poach the interview from her.

"You sound excited," Bindu said, tone careful.

Aly knew it was concern, but she needed rampant faith right now, not care. Aly's own parents thought she was a fool for harboring what they called her impossible dream. Well, she'd harbored it for ten years. And she'd lost her marriage over it—something her mother found downright sinful—so she was never giving it up.

Bindu and Cullie may have had their doubts about Southwest Florida News ever letting a forty-something Indian American woman be anything more than a correspondent for diversity stories, but they at least seemed to understand that Aly had the right to want what she wanted.

"I was able to book an interview with Meryl Streep." Ah, forget it, she let all the excitement racing through her show in her voice and bounced in her seat. She couldn't bring herself to add that she might not get to do the interview herself.

"Meryl!" Bindu said, her film-buff eyes lighting up like sparklers. "You're bringing them the mother lode. How can those idiots not know what they have in you!" The fierceness in her voice burned through some of the awkwardness they'd been tiptoeing around recently. It was this contrast between Bindu's unconditional support and the impenetrable skepticism Aly always got from her own mother that had made her spend the past twenty-five years hero-worshipping her mother-in-law.

Aly missed that. Missed the woman who'd been her rock for so long. The woman sitting across from her was still her *Ma*, but a chilly air curtain seemed to have fallen between them, even though they continued to behave as though nothing had changed.

Bindu slipped her credit card to the waiter, a tall blond surfer type. Aly could swear he blushed when Bindu smiled at him.

"Before I go, Ma . . . um . . ." Ugh, she hesitated.

Bindu slid her a sharp glance. Dammit, she knew exactly what was coming. Aly cleared her throat and soldiered on, because one had to do what one had to do. "Stacy from the HOA called. You've been ignoring their emails again."

"Did she now?" Bindu laughed her disinterested laugh and wiped a nonexistent spot off her big white patent leather bag. "I have a joke for you. It's a good one. I read it on Facebook: What do you call a coven of Karens?" She paused for the punch line. "An HOA."

Despite herself, Aly smiled. She found it particularly funny that her mother's name had suddenly taken on such pop-culture significance despite the fact she was an Indian Catholic woman from Goa. Still oddly fitting.

"No offense to our Karen, of course," Bindu added with a knowing smirk. "What did the coven complain about this time?"

The blushing waiter brought their bill back, and Bindu signed it with the flourish of a star signing an autograph.

"I know you enjoy annoying them, and I understand the sentiment, truly I do. But why would you hang bras to dry in your lanai? You know they have that right at the top of their bylaws." Aly felt like she was at Cullie's middle school, trying to explain to the principal that the other child had been calling Cullie offensive names for months before Cullie had hacked into her email and leaked the terrible things she'd been saying about people to the entire school.

"Don't you think it's a particularly stupid thing to have at the top of the bylaws? This is Florida. The lanai is the best place to dry your under-things. Also, Vanessa only complained because her husband bought me two margaritas and danced with me at last week's happy hour mixer. One would think she'd be relieved to have him off her hands for a bit. He looks like a mole rat. And he wants to be a naked mole rat, if you know what I mean." Bindu wiggled her brows.

"Ma! They've been married fifty years!" But God help her, she laughed.

"And isn't that punishment enough?" Bindu went on, studying her french manicure. "Fifty years! If the man wants to dance with a woman who can actually dance, why would you deny him that?"

"This is the twelfth complaint in the past six months." Aly tried not to sound exasperated.

"And every one of them is from one of the Grumpy Wives. The Sunny Widows love me."

"That's because you have them acting like you."

"What does that mean, Alisha?" Bindu pulled on her very trendy aviator sunglasses. Aly believed herself to be the kind of woman who was comfortable with having a mother-in-law who was hotter than she was and way more glamorous, but sometimes it was a lot. "Being a widow does not mean we're dead. It is not our fault that society encourages women to marry older men and then they go and kick the bucket years before we do, leaving us behind to count our toes."

Bindu had been widowed young, but she'd never been a Tragic Widow. Ashish's father had died before Aly married Ashish, but from everything Aly had heard—and from everything her ex-husband had internalized about marriage from his parents—Bindu's husband had obviously been a man who expected the world to revolve around him.

"You're the one who wanted to live in Shady Palms," Aly said, cracking open Pandora's box.

Bindu had moved in with Aly and Ashish during Aly's last trimester with Cullie, halfway through grad school. If not for Bindu, they would have had to change course on all their dreams.

People tended to have a range of reactions to Aly's living with her mother-in-law after her divorce, everything from horror to envy. But Aly had known no other life. All through Aly and Ashish's almost twenty-three-year-long marriage, twelve years in Fort Lauderdale and almost eleven years in Naples, Bindu had been part of their household.

After the divorce, Bindu had asked Aly what she wanted.

Please don't leave me, Aly had blurted out. Words she would never have said if the idea of more change hadn't made her feel like throwing up, words that would have killed Aly from mortification had she said them to a single other person on earth.

Bindu had stayed and made sure Aly's shock at Ashish's betrayal didn't suck her into the darkness that descended around her after the eerily quiet conversation with Ashish that ended their marriage. Then that stupid argument with Bindu had changed everything yet again, with just as much lack of drama.

Bindu had apologized. *This has nothing to do with our fight.* And promised to stay connected. *Nothing will change; I'm moving less than a mile away.*

Aly had finally sold the house that had turned into a bleak mausoleum to her marriage and moved into a smaller place, but she still didn't understand Bindu's decision.

If it was just the fact that the money had suddenly and mysteriously become available, then did that mean that Bindu had been waiting to move out all these years?

Asking meant risking what they had. And even if it wasn't what it had once been, it was still something Aly couldn't imagine life without.

"You could have continued to live at home with me," Aly said. "What's the point of trying so hard to get thrown out of Shady Palms now?"

If she'd meant to leave all along, Bindu could easily have joined Ashish in Mumbai, where he'd upped and moved to after he left Aly. Even more baffling was the fact that Bindu seemed to love that blasted community, even though she hated the coven that ran it. If anyone in the world had the ability to endear herself to people, it was Bindu. Why stop at these women whom she was obviously trying to emulate?

"You needed to move on with your life. A mother-in-law in the house couldn't possibly bode well for that." Bindu never added the prefix *ex* to their relationship.

She wasn't entirely wrong. Aly was starting to love the simplicity of her life. The ability to do whatever the heck she wanted whenever the heck she wanted was only a small part of it. Until Ashish left, Aly hadn't realized quite how much work marriage was. Actually, during her marriage she'd sometimes grasped it in flashes and fought to grapple with it, but she'd never considered that she had a choice.

Unlike her ex-husband. Obviously, it had always been a choice for Ashish. Because the moment things hadn't gone his way, he'd neatly exited the scene.

Bindu pursed her Gina Lollobrigida lips, stained an elegant yet risqué shade of ripe raspberries. "You're forty-seven, Alisha. Your life is just starting. The earlier you stop worrying about other people's opinions, the better."

Bindu was not usually the lecturing type. That job belonged to Karen Menezes, who could never let a teaching moment pass by without squeezing it for everything it was worth. Bindu had never been a conventional mother-in-law, but she'd only ever lived on the precarious line between living life her way and conforming, never pushing all the way into one side or the other. Until now. Now she was pushing against conformity with all the force of true regret.

Which meant she believed she had suddenly earned the right to dispense this particular life advice as though she'd always embodied it.

Not that this was a conversation for a quick lunch on a workday. "This isn't about me, Ma. I'm not asking you to be what the HOA wants you to be. But you insist you love living at Shady Palms. You love your Sunny Widows. So can you please stop annoying the Grumpy Wives for sport?"

With another scoff Bindu picked up the chocolate mints the waiter had left them, four instead of the usual two, and popped a couple in her mouth at once.

"I'm not your child, Alisha, so I owe you no explanations, but you know I don't sleep with married men. That doesn't mean I don't want to have fun." She held out one of the remaining chocolates to Aly, but Aly had already exhausted her calorie quota for today, so she waved the offering away.

"You know that I would never create any real trouble. But if you are going to be swayed by that coven and try to get in the way of me enjoying what's left of my youth, then I must ask you to stop." With a shrug Bindu popped the spurned chocolate into her mouth and closed her eyes as she soaked up the taste, making Aly's mouth water. Then, with a smug smile, she fed the last remaining piece into Aly's mouth and stood. "It's time you took a page out of my book. You're not going to look like this for too much longer. I know I make it look easy, but gravity is not forgiving, beta."

A smile broke across Aly's face. "You do make it look easy." Rising, she followed Bindu past a throng of tourists to her car. The happiness of the chocolate on her tongue warred with the failure to stick with her calorie count. This was such a perfect metaphor for how she felt about her mother-in-law that it made her laugh. "Also, I'm a bit terrified of what you think causing *real* trouble might mean."

Sonali Dev

Bindu threw her perfectly highlighted head back and gave a throaty laugh, making every man within a twenty-foot radius turn toward them. "You don't want to know. Shady Palms is filled with opportunity."

Her mother-in-law was right. She didn't want to know. What she did know when she got back to the station was that she was smiling for the first time that day, and she felt oddly filled with hope as she got ready to tell her boss that she'd thought about letting Jess do the interview and she'd decided against it.

CHAPTER SEVEN

BINDU

I knew she would be the death of me. I knew it the first time I met her. That she'd end me, burn down everything I believed about myself before I met her, before she showed me my soul and then took it.
From the journal of Oscar Seth

I bought you *penis*," Richard said when Bindu opened the door for him.

Her shock must've shown on her face, because he cleared his throat and held out a bouquet of the most beautiful flowers, each bloom a profusion of petals coalescing to form almost perfect globes.

Oh, he said peonies! Get your mind out of the gutter, Bindu!

"You okay, Bindu?"

She took the flowers from him. "Yes, of course. I love penis!" *Shit.* "I mean *peonies*." She enunciated the *o* hard this time and turned away quickly. Had anyone considered how unfortunately named these poor flowers were?

He was laughing when he followed her into her open kitchen. "I love a woman with a dirty mind."

All those shades of pink and magenta made a stunning contrast against the white quartz of her countertop. The sight made happiness glow inside her, and she used it to shove away her embarrassment.

"Let me find something to put your peonies in," she said, barely enunciating the *o* this time, face absolutely straight. "Wouldn't want any wilting."

He barked out a delighted laugh. "That's awfully kind of you. The propensity to wilt is the cruelest curse of these golden years."

She filled a vase and met his eyes as she arranged the plump blooms in an alternating pattern. "With peonies this large, a little wilting is of no consequence," she said, then burst into laughter.

"You're a gift, woman. Has anyone told you that?" His face was ruddy with his laughter, as though they'd been walking on the beach under the burning sun.

A memory from her youth in Goa—the salty breeze of the Arabian Sea whipping her face and snarling her hair—rose so starkly inside her she had to catch her breath.

"No," she said, the words leaving her before she could swallow them, "but I've been told I'm trouble."

"Oh, you're most definitely that too," he said, holding out his hand.

Holding hands was such a childish thing, or a little too American, and she wasn't sure she could do it. Rajendra had never held hands with her. Given how much sex they'd had, that realization made her suddenly and inexplicably sad.

She took his hand. It was tough and papery at the same time, like holding bunched-up newsprint. She imagined how many times his hands might have crushed up paper in frustration over words not doing his bidding, an image she'd seen in so many films.

But there was warmth under the leathery flesh. Life, even after more of it had been lived than was left to live.

He squeezed her hand and brought it to his lips and dropped a kiss on her knuckles. Oh yes, this man was definitely expecting more than just dinner tonight. The thought made her smile. A lifetime ago she'd loved this mix of power and nerves. Now it made feathery wings flutter in her belly.

"Let's get that dinner warmed up, shall we?" She'd cooked the meal yesterday. She was no longer young enough to cook all day, clean herself up, and have the energy to be charming at the end of it all. That had been her job for twenty-two years. She'd done it excellently and for long enough that it was well and truly out of her system.

Managing your energy and your assets was the key to aging right.

"Yes, please. Before my belly starts to growl," he said. "If I eat too late, I fall asleep right after. And I'm not planning on that." The suggestive smile on his deeply lined face made his shaking just a little bit worse.

Relax, tiger. "We can't have that, can we now?"

When she turned to the kitchen, he tried to follow. "How can I help?"

Ah, how she loved the 2020s. If Rajendra Desai hadn't died over two decades ago, the fact that men were now expected to help in the kitchen would certainly have killed him.

"Why don't you open the wine." She pointed to the minimalist wine rack on the kitchen island, one of Cullie's many housewarming gifts. "Pour us some, and regale me with stories of your National Book Award speech."

It was his favorite thing to talk about. Throwing her a look the most devout of worshippers saved up for goddesses, he got right to it.

If someone had told Bindu that she'd ever go on a date after she lost her husband, she would have called them delusional. When she was growing up, talking to a man she wasn't related to would have earned her a beating from her mother, so dating was an entirely foreign concept then. All she'd seen of love came from the movies her grandmother sneaked her into, the outwardly quiet yet inwardly volcanic form of love from Indian cinema of the sixties and seventies.

Then, at seventeen, she'd exposed herself to ruination. Rajendra had swooped in out of nowhere and married her and saved her from destroying her family's honor. Bindu had spent every single day of their marriage making it worth his while.

If gratitude were love, she'd loved him enough to last her a lifetime. It took an effort to shove away the sense of loss that had recently taken to rising inside her when she thought about her marriage, but she refused to disrupt the memories. Refused to think of them as anything but happy. What was the point of examining your past?

It was something Rajendra had said to her over and over as he unmolded and remolded her. *You are not that person anymore. Forgive yourself. What is the point of examining your past?*

Now, here she was, with a man named Richard eating her up with the bluest eyes as she moved around her kitchen in a hot-pink dress that showed enough cleavage that it would have caused her mother to disown her. Even now, all these decades later, making jokes about her mother disowning her felt, as the kids said, too soon. It made nausea churn in Bindu's belly, and she pushed it away, choosing instead to focus on how funny Aie's disapproval of her clothes had felt, years before it morphed into shame at having borne a daughter she'd only ever seen as a whore after one youthful mistake.

The pot of chicken curry on her professional-grade cooktop started to boil, and she gave it a stir, pushing away every thought of the past.

"You remind me of the first girl I ever loved," Richard said, handing her a glass of wine. The blue of his eyes was so much more fun to examine than the past.

It wasn't the most original of lines. He could do better, but she had to at least give him an A for delivery. His breath stuttered sincerely around the words. His gaze turned unfocused and dreamy in a way Bindu refused to think of as rheumy. He looked like Cary Grant, tall with coiffed hair and a lopsided smile, and she was holding on to that visual, thank you very much. A man who (usually) had a way with words and looked like Cary Grant did not come along often.

Oscar had been obsessed with Cary Grant. Not unusual for a filmmaker in India in the seventies. They were all obsessed with Hollywood back in the day.

Think Marilyn. That breathless sensuality. The way she meets the camera is pure eroticism. The pleasure she can make a man feel with just her gaze: most women can't make you feel that with their mouth on you.

Every woman on that set would have swooned in a horrified faint at his words. Rupa, the other actress on the film, would have run off and wept into her mother's sari in horror. But Bindu had laughed.

You're a dangerous girl, Oscar had said to her. *Trouble. You're trouble, Bhanu.*

Sometimes she thought he was the only man who'd ever really seen her.

Why couldn't she stop thinking these things? Why were these memories back? They were useless at best, dangerous at worst.

You're trouble. Exactly the kind of trouble this world needs.

Trouble.

This. This was why the memories were back. Because of that word and because of the email. Stop thinking about the email.

It was time to focus on the award-winning novelist in her kitchen, wielding words as foreplay.

"Her name was Melinda," Richard said, lips opening only on one side, much like Cary Grant. "And the first time I ever saw her, she was standing in a field of poppies in a yellow dress."

Okay, now he was just mixing up his memories with some greeting card photograph. She needed to feed him fast. As you aged, strange things happened when you didn't eat for long periods. Sugar levels, sodium levels, vitamin levels: you had to manage your body and mind like a machine, oiling and cleaning and running the various parts in turn lest they rust. Bindu's father had run a peanut oil mill. He had taught her to respect every part of a machine. Especially the tiniest components. They wore out without warning and were the easiest to ignore.

Most men she'd met didn't know how to do this. Especially the ones who'd been married. Especially the ones who'd been in long marriages where their wives had been their maintenance mechanics. Richard had been married five times.

Bindu found that astonishing and oddly freeing. The man clearly had no judgment whatsoever.

In the time that Bindu had lived at Shady Palms, she had learned a lifetime's worth about men. For instance, the older they got, the more they loved talking about their youth, even if they generously filled gaps with imagination. And for the married ones, the more they talked about themselves, the less their wives were interested.

Bindu had also learned more about herself than she'd ever bothered with before. Even though she had taken the tour of the model homes during the open house only to annoy Alisha, by the end of that tour something deeply buried had shaken loose inside her. The frayed rope of lies she'd been holding on to had suddenly snapped.

She'd needed to know what she had missed. What being by herself might tell her about herself.

A bead crashing to the floor. An echo of a forgotten word boomeranging back to her. *Trouble.*

Listening to Richard wax eloquent about his greeting card love made her want to throw her head back and laugh.

Until Richard's award-winning words, she hadn't let expectation be part of these dates. The entire point of moving here was to have fun. To have the kind of fun she'd seen shining on the faces of the residents that afternoon at the open house. The kind of fun she'd watched the film crew having years ago, always from the outside, her nose pressed up against the glass. Too young, too unpolished to be included.

The fun she'd suddenly become aware of having missed simply because of a few turned backs. How ironic that the coven had offered her this bounty. Not only had they woken her up to those memories, but they'd also offered themselves up as a symbol for all the things she'd never had a chance to fight before.

Until the open house, Bindu had thought there would be a relief to getting older. She'd finally be able to stop trying. Stop feeling different. Stop kicking herself for it. She'd been wrong. And she'd lost so much time because of it. You had to live life out, not wait it out.

Over the past six months she'd danced barefoot by a pool and kissed as she laughed and swum in a bikini and lain out in the sun with a cocktail and a book.

Every single male resident at Shady Palms had asked her out, and she'd gone out at least a few times a week. But she had rules.

She never went out with married men. She only ever went out for Indian food if they didn't generically call it "curry" or talk about heartburn when discussing it—or any gastric repercussions, for that matter. And if someone suggested she cook for him, she made him take her to the most expensive place she could come up with.

Being the most sought-after single lady at Shady Palms was not a trivial honor, and there really was no point squandering it.

"Beautiful Melinda might have been, but she did not have that rack." Richard winked at Bindu over the makhani chicken she plated on rice and carried to the bistro table by the windows overlooking the gulf. She loved the openness of her condo, all the spaces running into one another.

Usually she ordered in when friends came over. But she'd had a hankering for makhani chicken, and the Indian restaurants in the area tended to add a pound of sugar to the sauce. It was a curry, not pudding, for heaven's sake.

She could bear substandard food from other parts of the world, but for some reason paying for bad Indian food felt almost like a personal insult.

So she'd broken her own rule and cooked, but after what Richard had just said, she was starting to question the entire Richard situation. Another side effect of being in her sixties was that she found herself running out of patience in the blink of an eye. One moment, she was Bindu, here for all the absurdity in the world, with all the gentle understanding it needed. Then the next moment, she was done with anything that didn't make sense.

Sitting down at the bistro table, she crossed her legs at the ankles and fixed Richard with an unsmiling look. "You remember the color of her dress *and* the size of her rack. You hopeless romantic, you!"

He laughed and kissed her cheek before sitting down to her chicken, which 100 percent objectively smelled like heaven on a plate.

The imprint of his lips was dry on her cheek, and her annoyance melted a little bit. She handed him a glass of water. The only solution for dry lips was drinking a lot of water. The man was obviously dehydrated and in need of some fatty food.

She was right—she'd outdone herself. The chicken was delicious.

She waited smugly as he took a bite, but instead of effusive raving, he went a bit red in the face.

"Wow. This has cumin in it, doesn't it?" he said.

As quickly as she could, she dragged his plate away from him and handed him her own untouched glass of water. "Please tell me you're not allergic to cumin."

He stroked a finger across her cheek, the heat in his eyes making it clear that he was not dying. He was only a little red and breathing okay.

"Our generation does not have allergies," he said with the grandiose stupidity of many an old man. "My body just doesn't like cumin much. That's all."

"What on earth is that supposed to mean? Why did you say you wanted to eat Indian food if your body *doesn't like cumin*?" She wanted to smack him upside the head. But again, his sincerity was potent. The eagerness to please her made him look too young for his leathery skin. No wonder the man had convinced five women to marry him. "Cumin is the one spice that's literally in ninety-nine percent of all Indian food."

He shrugged, attempting to make his irresponsibility about his health endearing.

"How can you have lived eighty years and not have tasted Indian food?"

"I'm seventy actually." He sounded only slightly offended. And not even a little bit remorseful about never having eaten the most delicious of earth's cuisines.

"You write about the human condition. There is no human condition better than eating Indian food!"

He pulled the plate back, grinning at her as though she were the dish he wanted to devour. "Well, my human condition is about to expand, then, isn't it?" He poked a fork into the chicken and rice and took a bite with all the recklessness of a man who couldn't possibly have been celebrated across the world for his brain.

His face got redder.

"Don't be ridiculous, Richard." Taking the plate away, she made him another one with only rice and the koshimbir of tomatoes and cucumbers. "Let's not challenge the most basic human condition: being alive." She put the plate in front of him and tried not to kick him under the table when he looked relieved but too stubborn to admit it.

"This is delicious," he said as they ate.

She wanted to call him a liar, but his eyes were shining again, and she believed him. Even though she felt sorry for anyone who'd lived a life thinking rice with cucumbers and tomatoes was delicious, no matter how well she'd seasoned the salad.

After they'd gone back for seconds and put their plates away, they filled up their wineglasses and took them to the couch.

He dropped a kiss on her cheek and thanked her again for the food. The deep satisfaction on his face warmed her heart even as her head floated with the loveliest buzz from the wine.

Do it, Bindu. How long will you wait?

When he leaned toward her again, she met him halfway and let those no-longer-as-dry lips kiss hers. The sensation made the headiness she was feeling headier.

His hand went to her cheek, stroking as he deepened the kiss, slowly, tenderly. He was very good at this. Another reason for the five wives, she supposed. He did something with his lips, and she considered marrying him herself if he'd do it again.

Who are you, Bhanu? the deeply buried voice said inside her. *Who are you?*

Shoving the voice away, she scooted closer, and he pulled her into his lap.

Are you sure? she wanted to ask, but she'd never been at a loss for words because of a man's kiss, and she soaked up the feeling. He tasted of breath mints. He'd made the effort to slip one into his mouth. That made her feel somehow cared for instead of taken for granted. Plus, he was doing that thing with his lips again, and she didn't care about anything else.

Beneath her, his thighs didn't feel fragile. They felt solid and strong. The erection pressing into her butt most definitely didn't feel like it had seen seventy summers.

The mint clearly wasn't the only thing he'd slipped into his mouth. And yes, she was just as glad for that too, dammit!

He made a growling sound and took his kisses down her throat, even as his hands pushed her dress off her shoulders and found her breasts over the cutlet-stuffed bra. The man really did know what he was doing. Her nipples thanked him heartily for it by peaking against his caresses.

"I don't think I've ever made love to a more exquisite woman." Oh yes, he knew exactly what to do with those words.

Welcome back, Richard. Just keep it simple.

Pulling away, she skipped—yes, skipped—to the kitchen and pulled a tube of lube from a drawer. Thank you, Jane!

Richard grinned at the offering and pulled her onto his lap again. Yes, he most definitely knew what he was doing, and soon somehow she was straddling him, their hands in each other's hair. His was thick and lush. She pushed away the memory of Rajendra's scalp on her fingers under his thinning hair.

She kept her mind here, on the fire between her legs, the sparks tingling across her breasts, the warmth stroking her skin like feathers.

How he had her underwear pushed aside and found his way inside her with such deft speed she'd never know, but he was panting and shuddering, and she was right there with him. It had been so long. Good Lord, it had been too long.

With another heavy grunt he spasmed with almost youthful force, and she looked into his eyes. For one endless moment they filled with such intense pleasure, she forgot where they were. Then his eyes rolled up, and rolled up, the black pupils widening even as the blue irises disappeared into his lids. With another massive shudder his hands slipped off her, and his body slackened and went limp under her.

Things started to move in slow motion. He slid to one side, his back slipping against the couch, the fabric bunching under him as he slumped over. Then, with one last shudder, he went as still and heavy as a corpse.

CHAPTER EIGHT

CULLIE

At first I thought I was the flame to her moth. But the burning came when I lost her. I can only hope that the people who got to be in her life knew what they had.
From the journal of Oscar Seth

What do you mean, Binji killed someone?" Cullie was used to her mother and grandmother bickering since Binji had moved. But they would both basically throw themselves in front of bullets for each other.

Her mother never sounded so . . . what was the word she was looking for? So . . . bewildered, knocked off her feet. It was Mom's voice from when Cullie had dropped out of U of I's computer engineering program.

"I didn't say Binji killed someone," Mom said. "I said she might have caused someone's death."

"Oh, that's totally different, then." Sometimes having a journalist for a mother was the most annoying thing.

"Cullie, is this really the time for cheekiness?"

"Cheekiness? Now you sound like Granny Karen," Cullie said before she could think better of it.

"There's no need to hit below the belt," Aly said before *she* could think better of it apparently. Then she cleared her throat. "Let's focus on Bindu and not my mother, okay?"

Oh, you don't have to ask me twice, Cullie wanted to say. But Mom would feel the need to lecture her about respect and all the reasons behind why her mother's mother was such an inflexible, bitter grouch. Strange, because a constant state of bitterness pretty much defined Mom's relationship with Granny Karen. Fortunately, Mom's parents had packed up and moved back to India a few years ago, and it had stopped the day-to-day onslaught of Granny Karen's constant criticism and Mom's resulting blue mood.

"Tell me what happened. I'm pretty sure you wouldn't be sounding so calm if Binji had actually committed homicide. Wait, is Papa back in America?" The only person Cullie's grandmother was angry enough with to kill was her one and only child, Cullie's father.

Aly groaned. "Dear Lord, I don't know what I did to raise such a cynic. That's your father you're talking about."

"I know he's my father. And you're my mother. And Binji is my grandmother. That's why I know how badly Binji has wanted to kill Papa since the divorce."

"Cullie, can we please not make jokes right now. This is serious." She sounded serious enough. Then again, Aly Menezes Desai, anchor wannabe, always sounded serious, far more serious than Aly, Cullie's mom, who was probably the one Cullie had inherited her ill-timed humor from, not that she didn't work hard to hide it.

"You do sound like someone died," Cullie said, and her mother made a frustrated sound. "Fine, sorry. Tell me who died and why you're blaming the mother-in-law you secretly adore for it?"

As it turned out, Binji's "hot date" had just keeled over and died. "During sex. Or after sex," Mom explained in a tone that made it obvious she couldn't believe the words she was having to say.

"Was it during sex or after sex?"

"Cullie!"

"You're right. Both of those scenarios are equally horrifying. But it feels like an important distinction."

"I can't believe you're laughing," Mom said, her own voice shaking with that thing that masqueraded as mirth when unbelievably bizarre things happened, even tragic ones.

"It's really just my horror manifesting," Cullie said, even though there was an element of the absurd here that was pretty funny. Every person who knew Binji had made some version of a joke about her looks being killer. "Is Binji in trouble? Where is she? Are you with her?"

"I'm in her condo. We just got home from the hospital. The cops and EMT came, and we went with them when they took the body—"

Cullie gasped. "A b . . . body?"

"Cullie, honey, usually when someone dies, there's a body."

Things suddenly felt too real. "Okay, I'm leaving for the airport and getting on the next flight. Get Binji out of there, please." Binji loved that condo. This just wasn't fair. Well, even less fair to the man who'd died, obviously.

"She's refusing to go anywhere else. I tried to take her to my place, but she insisted on coming back here." Cullie tried to ask why, but Mom cut her off. "I'll explain everything later. The HOA is not going to make this easy. They're already trying to use this to drive her out, and . . . well, she's not going anywhere. I'm staying with her tonight." Her voice trembled, but she got it under control. "Are you sure you can get away? What about work?"

Shit, this was going to mess things up with what Cullie had promised CJ.

"Cullie?" her mother nudged. "You don't have to come. Ma seems fine. She hasn't said much."

"Binji hasn't said much?" Binji's constant state was saying too much. "Of course I'm coming. Will she talk to me now?"

"I think she's shaking her head." Mom sounded unsure.

"You can't tell if Binji is shaking her head or not?" When you didn't know if Binji was shaking her head, that was bad. Everything Binji did was dialed up. Her gestures and expressions weren't loud, exactly, because there was an elegance to them, but they were visible, in your face, in this inescapable way. Cullie had always thought of them as Bollywood mannerisms.

"She hasn't said much to me yet. She tried to talk to the cops, but they realized she was in shock because she kept opening her mouth, and nothing came out. The doctor gave her something to calm her down, and the cops said they'd be back tomorrow."

Before Mom had even disconnected the phone, Cullie had bought tickets to Fort Myers and was checked in. The flight left in two hours. She could be at the airport in half an hour if she hurried.

Crawling to the back of her closet, she retrieved her overnight bag and stuffed it with a few black tights, tanks, and tees.

Have Binji get on Shloka, Cullie texted her mother. Have her use the Tranquil++ track. That should help her relax.

Knowing that she'd created something that could do this, help someone in crisis, relaxed Cullie. The stress she'd been feeling about the deal she'd proposed to CJ had disappeared when Mom called. Now it was back full force and clamoring for attention. Needing to protect Shloka was a flood inside her. Binji in crisis only made the flood swell.

All through Cullie's life, Binji had been her shelter from every storm. Be it her first upper-lip wax to shut down the bullies at school, or the spontaneous meltdowns in her head that she'd never been able to share with her parents, or the time Steve had gone back to his wife and Binji had flown out to see her. Cullie hadn't been able to talk about it, but she'd put her head in Binji's lap while she stroked her hair and told her stories from old Bollywood films the way she'd done when Cullie was little.

Which wasn't to say Binji was not the one to blame for putting all sorts of ideas in Cullie's head that kept complicating her life. The idea for Shloka had come from Binji chanting with her to help her sleep when she was a child, a practice Cullie had then started to use to deal with her racing thoughts. And now, thanks to Binji, she'd told CJ she'd been working on a compatibility app.

A dating app? CJ had looked bored. *There are fifteen hundred of those on the market, at last count.*

What we find attractive about love interests says more about us than about them. Cullie had repeated Binji's words, desperate to keep Shloka free for the millions of people who needed it. Cullie would be the first to admit that she didn't know much; most things people got passionate about bored her into blanking out of conversations. But the fact that Shloka had to stay subscription-free, that she knew with the kind of certainty she could not explain. *What we call dating is really a journey of self-discovery. Or at least it only turns into something meaningful if it is also that.*

The words had sounded like hooey even as Cullie said them, but CJ's dark eyes had sharpened with focus beneath her lash extensions. And Cullie had known that her grandmother had saved her ass yet again. *I have a plan for an app that identifies matches based on self-discovery.* Not only did she not have a plan—she had no idea what that even meant—but CJ's favorite buzzword had veritably exploded around her head like fireworks. *It works with the Neuroband. So our Neuroband sales should skyrocket too.* Cullie had shot the last arrow right into the heart of her argument.

I'll talk to the board. We'll need to see a mock-up soon. That's all Cullie wanted. A chance to change the board's mind.

For the past twenty-four hours, she'd furiously played with dummy code. The walls of her room were plastered with paper covered in flow-charts and notes. There was not a chance in hell this was going to work with the approaches she was taking. With Shloka, she'd known exactly what to do. The design and code had been alive inside her, and getting it out had been like one of those firetruck hoses. Unstoppable.

With dating. Nothing.

Cullie groaned. Her grandmother was hot enough to cause people to die from orgasms, and here she was at the peak of her biological attractiveness, and men went back to their wives after test-driving her for a year. *Test-driving*, by the way, was what Granny Karen called dating. Actually, she called it "letting men test-drive you." Which was one of the many reasons why eight thousand miles away was just the way Cullie liked her.

You'll figure it out, the voice inside her said. Binji's voice.

Pulling the paper from her walls, she stuffed it into her backpack, then threw in her laptop, test hardware for the Neuroband, code notebooks, and her medication. Then she slung the overnight bag over her shoulder and took the elevator to the lobby.

Her car would be here in ten minutes. Just enough time to let the front desk know to forward her mail, because she planned on staying for as long as Binji needed her.

"Are you going somewhere?" The last voice she expected to hear pulled her out of her thoughts as she got out of the elevator.

Steve?

He pointed at the bag hanging from her shoulder.

She kept walking. "Nope." It served as both an answer and her general reaction to his being here. He hadn't been here since they'd broken up. "What makes you think it's okay for you to just show up here?"

"Why are you treating me like this?" How had she ever found his voice attractive? Now she wanted to reach down his gullet and yank out his voice box with her bare hands.

Wow, Cullie. Calm down.

The Neuroband on her wrist vibrated, and she took a deep breath.

"You mean why am I treating you like someone who tried to steal the most precious thing in my life?"

"Is that what this is about, or are you hurt about something else?" He had the gall to look knowing and sympathetic. The bracelet heated again, and she took another breath. *In for four, out for six.*

She blinked up at him, feeling a little bit like Mona, her Cabbage Patch doll from childhood, wide eyed and hapless. She'd stopped playing with Mona for a reason. Grounding herself in that visual kept her from shoving him across the tiny lobby of her building.

"Yes, Steve, the fact that you screwed me for a year and then went sniveling back to a wife who'd cheated on you and bankrupted you makes you the kind of prince I care about more than an app that can keep people from taking their own lives." Thanks to the bracelet on her wrist, her voice came out calm. It helped that suddenly she felt nothing for this man who'd once made her feel so much, it had been like an illness. "Oh, to have the confidence of a mediocre man."

He looked like he couldn't decide if he should be angry or hurt. "You're many things, Cal, but I could never imagine you being this bitter."

How could she not laugh at that? Because, wow. He didn't know her at all. Cynicism and bitterness were literally her most defining qualities, something she'd been accused of displaying in the cradle.

Her phone buzzed, and she looked at it. The car was two minutes away. There was no way in hell she was telling the front desk to forward her mail in front of Steve. He would know exactly zero about her life from now on.

"The other day, we started on the wrong foot. I'm sorry, I can't seem to think straight when you're near me." His eyes intensified. His breath turned shallow and labored. This sincere facade was what had stripped her bare.

Do not feel. Don't feel things for him, Cullie. What is wrong with you? A lot, but that didn't mean she'd let herself be an airsickness bag for his emotional vomits ever again.

"Don't blame me for your inability to think." She pointed at his face. "And your puppy dog eyes lost their power when you tried to destroy my app."

He opened his mouth to deny it, but before he could, she walked away. Getting people to pay for Shloka was sacrilege, no matter what capitalism said about it.

He followed her. "What did you say to CJ? She took me off the Shloka team. I was the only one there protecting your interests, Cal."

"You were right before. You have lost your ability to think. So let me simplify it for you," she said with all the meanness she'd ever been accused of. "Your version of protection involves stripping me down first and then giving me your coat. Leave me alone, and find someone else's work to steal, because you're never getting near Shloka again. Or me. And for the last time, it's *Cul*."

"Okay, I know paranoia is part of"—he rotated a hand around his head—"all the shit you have going on, but this is not about Shloka, is it? Someone told you, didn't they? Did Roxy call you? She called you, didn't she, and told you about the divorce?"

Cullie's brain was still stuck on the fact that he'd just insulted not only her but every human being who'd ever struggled with any kind of illness, mental or otherwise. Fortunately, her brain worked faster than his ever would.

She pressed a hand to her head, the Bollywood pose for regret. "Did she tell you she told me?" Cullie had never spoken to his ex-not-ex-had-she-ever-been-an-ex? wife.

Just like that, it was clear in his face.

What. An. Idiot. She'd. Been.

"Did you never file for divorce in the first place, or did you file for it and then change your mind?"

He stood there, mouth open, trying to figure out if she'd just figured it out or if his wife had called her. Finally he settled on a face that said the answer to her question wasn't relevant. But it was the most relevant damned thing.

"It's the first, isn't it? You told me you were divorced when you hadn't even filed for one."

"I meant to. I contacted a lawyer. But you know how it was between us at the beginning. It was impossible to wait. You didn't want to wait any more than I did."

All the lies he'd told her splashed like acid inside her head. One corrosive drop after another. "If that's true, if you really believed I was too into you to wait for you to leave your wife, why did you lie about the divorce?"

His gaze dropped to the floor, the first sign of shame.

But he didn't know what shame was. Shame was being taken for a fool when you prided yourself on being the smartest person you knew. Shame was trusting a liar when you prided yourself on trusting no one.

"The point is, it was never about Shloka," he said, smug again.

"Oh, it was always about Shloka." The time he'd waited was the time it had taken them to take Shloka to market. He'd made sure she'd trusted him completely and handed him the app before he made his move. "Start looking for another job. Because I plan to make NewReal billions, and you won't see a cent of it." With that she walked away.

CHAPTER NINE

ALY

I'd spent so much time agonizing over how to ask her to do Poornima. *But all I had to do was narrate the script and she was as lost in it as I was, the two of us equally helpless in our passion.*
From the journal of Oscar Seth

Sunshine flooded into Bindu's kitchen, making the quartz counter-tops shimmer as Aly poured the lemongrass and ginger chai into three cups. It was past noon, but both Cullie and Bindu were still asleep in Bindu's bedroom. More accurately, Cullie was passed out and Bindu was pretending to sleep.

Aly was supposed to have taken the couch, but she hadn't been able to. So she'd put a comforter on the living room rug and slept there. She'd expected to be plagued by dreams of dead bodies. Instead she'd dreamed of Joyce and her mother fighting over her while Bindu laughed.

The sleep aid the doctor had given Bindu had turned her limp and restless at the same time. By the time it had finally knocked her out, it was well past midnight. Just a few hours after that, Cullie had arrived on the red eye and fallen asleep next to her drugged-out grandmother.

Aly had taken the day off today—even though it was the most awful timing, and Joyce had made sure Aly knew that—but she'd gotten a few hours of work in before she'd heard Bindu getting up to use the bathroom and then promptly returning to bed. As un-Bindu an act as anyone could imagine. When Bindu had responded to Aly's "Morning, Ma!" with pretending to be asleep, Aly had turned to Bindu's own fix for all things: chai.

The invigorating smell of it filled the condo, and Aly hoped it would be enough to infuse life back into her usually overenergetic mother-in-law.

Unlike Aly's own kitchen, Bindu's bordered on messy. Bindu described it as "artfully disarrayed." Not to be confused with Aly's artless perfection. To her credit Bindu never said that last part, but she did laugh when Aly added it as a joke.

That morning Aly had cleaned up out of habit. Then she'd felt bad, because Bindu had always made the effort to keep their kitchen—when they'd shared one—as perfect as Aly liked it. So Aly moved some things back to their disorderly places. The sugar pot on the island, the spice grinder on the counter, the kitchen towel not perfectly aligned on the oven handle.

Truth was, she'd never seen Bindu like this. Bindu tended to smile at the height of the flu; she made jokes at funerals. The blankness in her eyes since the previous night—a Bindu knocked off her game—had scared Aly. The ways in which Bindu was different from Aly had always been a comfort to her. Bindu worked harder than anyone to color outside the lines as much as she could. The irony made Aly smile. Her mother-in-law was super wound up about never appearing wound up.

All through their marriage Ashish had thought it "adorable" how tightly wound Aly was. Maybe that's why she had married him. Her need to be good, to be *correct*: it was who she was. And when a man like Ashish Desai had loved her for it, she'd had not one single complaint.

Aly used her discretion, and common sense, to define what was right, instead of her mother's way, which involved letting community and religion dictate it.

Karen put her role as a devout Goan Catholic mother above everything else. Heavy on the discipline, light on the fun. She did nothing without the permission of her priest, talked incessantly about Goa and how everything there was perfect, and believed with all her heart that the only way for life to end up okay was to thank God for it, preemptively and constantly. An oversize blanket to cover all her bases and keep any of her blessings from slipping away. For Aly it had always caused a perpetual sense of holding her breath.

Now she let it out, long and cleansing.

As Aly poured heated milk through a strainer into the teacups—because Cullie would gag if even a bit of milk skin escaped into the chai—it struck her out of nowhere that Bindu's new home was scattered with pictures, framed prints sitting on tables and shelves and hanging from walls in artistic clusters. Most of them were of Cullie. A few of Aly. There were even some of Bindu in her youth. Pictures one might mistake for Gina Lollobrigida. Seriously, the women could be twins.

The bouffant hair, the winged eyeliner, the lush, darkly painted mouth, the regal high cheekbones. The chiffon sari with its psychedelic geometric print was where the similarities diverged.

How had Aly never noticed that there were no pictures of Ashish in the condo? Putting the milk pot down, she started opening drawers. Encountering everything from absurdly large stashes of nail files and lip balms to . . . oh . . . lube.

She noticed that the tube of lube was open, as though someone had hurriedly thrown it into the drawer. Aly snapped it shut and wiped up the little that had leaked out and forced herself not to have any feelings about that. Not a single one. She continued snooping through the drawers. Well, it wasn't snooping. Bindu had said repeatedly that her home was Aly's home.

And there it was, tucked way at the back of the bottom drawer, under a stack of notepads. Two metallic picture frames with Ashish's smiling face. One was Aly and Ashish's engagement picture. When they'd been at their happiest, knocked sideways by the serendipity of finding each other, sitting under a tree with their arms and legs intertwined.

The second was of Ashish as a baby in faded sepia tones, toothless and abundantly joyful, with the thick head of hair. Her ex-husband's crowning glory was something he'd been blessed with in the womb.

How Aly had yearned to have hair like that. Silky, bountifully thick, with just enough of a wave to make it look like he had used product on it even though he just used body wash. Too lazy to even open the bottle of shampoo sitting right there in their shower. Or just too complacent in the blessing that was his hair.

He'd taken it for granted, just as he'd taken all his other physical attributes for granted. The lean body, the flat belly, the unfairly white teeth, the glowing skin. Never carried them like the advantage they were.

When Aly had first met Ashish in her freshman biology class at the University of Florida, he'd been fresh off the boat and entirely unaware of it. She had noticed, with a shock of awareness, almost immediately after first meeting him, that something about him had felt inexplicably familiar to her. Before she knew it, being in his presence had become wrapped up in this sense of having found something she'd been searching for. A bright light amid the dreariness outside her. A leak in the pressure inside her.

His grungy rock-concert T-shirts; his overgrown hair and careless stubble; the nerdy glasses: she'd never met anyone so comfortable in their skin. More significantly, she'd never met anyone so oblivious of her own frizzy curls, her rounded body, or the undulating scars on her cheeks from teenage cystic acne.

Four years into their relationship, they'd been sitting under an oak tree on campus, his head in her lap, her back against the craggy trunk, her fingers playing in his hair, when he'd told her she was his deep shade in the beating sun that was life, singing it to her in his golden voice.

One look at you
and a thought brushed my mind
Life is the desert sun
and you the deep shade of woods

An ageless Urdu ghazal, a ballad from a Bollywood film they both loved about a young couple who wanted to live life counter to the world's expectations.

It was the moment that had cemented who Aly was in her own mind, made her fall into herself. She'd loved being *that*: soothing shade in the brutal sun. An Oasis.

It was the moment she'd realized that Ash didn't just not see her physical flaws, but his mind processed them as beautiful. Back then, before she knew that his most ruthless criticisms would cut at something much more deeply buried than physical beauty, he'd lit her up. Exactly the way the rays of sunshine had found their way through the thick oak canopy above them that day.

Ashish had turned his head in her lap and looked up at her, his hazel eyes soft and burning at the same time, slightly unfocused because he had taken off his glasses. "You know what? We should marry each other. Nothing else is ever going to feel this right."

That was Ashish. That proposal. Him in a nutshell. An edge of insult threaded through with the purest emotion. It wasn't until much later that Aly figured out how he used those two things to balance himself out. The dismissive cynicism that kept him from getting too invested in anything that might take away his control, and the purity of unfiltered, uncomplicated feelings. He constantly juggled those two things in order to survive without ever having to face any uncomfortable parts of himself.

When Aly had met his mother, she'd known exactly where the happy, loving parts of him had come from. But it was also where his belief that no woman could be enough had come from. He barely ever mentioned his father, but the dynamic of his parents' marriage had taught him that a woman's job was to constantly prove her worth.

The kicker was that Bindu didn't even know how much she constantly worked at proving herself. She thought she was so different from Aly. But Aly just didn't know how to hide it.

After grad school, Aly hadn't been able to pursue a job in TV because the hours and the intern's pay hadn't fit with their goals. She'd put her dream on hold until the time was right. But as soon as her dream had taken form and become attached to her individual goals, it had stuck in Ashish's eyes like a dislodged lash he couldn't extract. Aly's parents' reaction had been much the same as Ashish's, but Bindu had found a vicarious joy in Aly's getting the reporter job at SFLN. At her *living on her own terms.*

It was her mother-in-law's favorite phrase. Whatever that even meant.

Well, in this moment it meant that a man had died "following the act of coitus," as the doctor had declared when informing them of the death.

Bindu had blinked up at the doctor, who looked far too young to be declaring deaths, as he walked away, and then turned to Aly. "This isn't the first time I've found a man dead, you know. I was the one who found Rajendra. I didn't need a resident to tell me what I already knew."

Saying the words had turned Bindu's skin paper pale, leaving behind a constellation of freckles across her cheeks. Since then, Bindu had barely said a single word.

Aly stuffed Ashish's pictures back in the drawer and ignored the inexplicable anger that burned inside her. The reason those stupid pictures were in that drawer was that Bindu thought they would hurt Aly's feelings if they were on a wall. Aly hated when Bindu coddled her.

Why do you need to be coddled so much? Ashish had always said to her. *You women want to play the feminism card, call it equality, but all you want is to be coddled.*

Slamming the drawer shut with more force than she usually allowed herself, she set the cups of tea on a tray and took it to the bedroom, where the barest amount of light filtered through the blinds.

No, she would not let her ex-husband's voice tell her that letting Bindu stay in bed so long was coddling her. A man had died in her arms. Well, not in her *arms*, exactly.

Embarrassment heated Aly's face at the inappropriate urge to laugh. Cullie and Bindu were rubbing off on her.

Except *that* Bindu was nowhere to be found this morning. Her irreverent—"extra," as Cullie called her—mother-in-law seemed utterly snuffed out as she pretended to be asleep while Aly stood there, studying her over a steaming tea tray.

"Morning, Ma," Aly said. "Chai's ready!"

Bindu sniffled and kept her eyes closed. She hadn't cried, but her perfect button nose was bright red with holding in tears.

"I used a lot of lemongrass and ginger. I bet you won't be able to complain about there not being enough," Aly said, placing the tray on the nightstand.

When Bindu continued to pretend to be asleep, Aly put a hand on her shoulder. "Ma, it's noon. If you don't get some chai in your system, you're going to get a headache."

"Too late for that." Finally a response.

"Do you want acetaminophen?"

Bindu pushed off the pillow she was hugging and sat up. Her eyes were puffy, and her hair was pressed up on one side. The batik kaftan nightie she was wearing seemed oddly droopy around her. As though she had shrunk overnight.

Her phone buzzed next to her, and she stiffened, a tremble going through her at the sound.

"Is it the coven again?" Aly picked up Bindu's phone.

The fact that Bindu just sat there and didn't grab the phone away said a million words.

"Those bitches," Cullie said from under the block-printed Jaipur quilt. "That phone has been buzzing nonstop."

Bindu patted Cullie's burrowed head and finally took the tea from Aly.

"What is wrong with them?" Cullie popped up with the sheets still on her head.

The messages on Bindu's phone were nasty. Ugly.

"Maybe you should kill them, too," Aly said, more angrily than she'd intended.

Cullie sat up. The quilt slid off. "Mom!" She threw Bindu a gauging look Aly didn't understand.

Bindu pushed Cullie's thick bangs off her forehead, the heavy silken strands exactly like her father's. Then she turned hurt eyes on Aly. "Did you just accuse me of killing someone?"

"What? No!"

"You said *too*," Bindu and Cullie said together, with matching accusatory tones.

Aly pinched the bridge of her nose. "I'm sorry," she said, kicking herself for her callousness because Bindu looked numb, shaken. "That came out wrong."

"Do you really think I killed him?" Bindu said, then pressed her hand to her face.

Cullie threw her arms around her grandmother and a look of rage at Aly. "Binji, come on. Mom was making a tasteless joke about killing the coven."

Really, Cullie?

Aly put a hand on Bindu's shoulder. "I was. Of course I don't think you killed him. No one thinks that."

"Well, these witches do." Bindu pointed to her phone.

Cullie took the phone and held it up to her grandmother's face, and the screen unlocked to a picture of Cullie holding the *Forbes* magazine declaring her one of the most influential thirty people under thirty.

"Give that back." But there was no force in Bindu's voice.

"What is wrong with these women?"

"What are they saying?" Aly reached for the phone, but Cullie moved it out of the way and furiously swiped her thumb across the screen.

"An eviction notice? Who is their lawyer? Daffy Duck? Did he even go to law school?" She made a buzzing sound as she speed-read through the emails. "A PR nightmare? It's only a PR nightmare if they leak it to the media and lie about how it happened. This is a senior living facility. People drop dead all the time." She threw a quick look at Bindu. "Sorry, Binji. I don't mean you. You're a baby here."

Bindu waved away her words. "How do they even know the . . . the circumstances under which he died? Could the police have told them?"

"No," Aly said. "Your conversation with the cops is confidential. There is nothing incriminating about what happened. The coven is just making assumptions and trying to turn this into something it's not." Juvenile complaints about bras might be funny. But Bindu had watched a man die, and going after her now was downright cruel.

"They want us to get angry," Bindu said, calm again. "The only way to get back at them is to not react to their pettiness." Something about the coven turned Bindu into a block of ice, immovable but bloodless. Well, this wasn't the time for that.

"Pettiness?" Aly put down her cup, because anger was making her hands shake. "This is not pettiness. This is bullying, and this is not the time to ignore bullies. This is a time to hit back."

Bindu put her chai down next to Aly's. "Really, Alisha? You won't tell them to take a hike about some bras hanging in my lanai, but now, when it's something I'd rather not talk about, you want to fight?"

"You're the one who's always telling me to fight. Bras aren't worth fighting for. Not letting someone threaten your right to live somewhere is worth fighting for."

"The fact that Richard and I were having relations is not anyone's business."

Cullie looked up from her phone. "Who's Leslie?"

"Why? She's the HOA secretary. I've never met her, but she keeps trying to be the good witch. She usually calms the rest of them down when they get their chaddis in a knot." She turned accusatory eyes on Aly. "She was the one who got them to back off about the bras when Aly thought I was the one who should back off."

"Stop bickering with Mom for a minute. It looks like this Leslie might be our best bet. But she wants you to meet with the HOA."

"I'm not doing that."

"Like hell you're not." Aly stood, heart beating fast, and pressed a hand to her hip. "If you don't shut these women up, they will drive you out of a home you love. Enough is enough." She held her hand out to Bindu.

Bindu didn't take it. "And yet you let that manipulative boss of yours bully you every single day."

That wasn't the point right now, was it?

"Mom is not wrong. Let's at least see what this Leslie has to say," Cullie, who always, always sided with her grandmother, said.

Bindu took Aly's hand and stood.

Cullie continued to study the emails on Bindu's phone. "Don't worry, Binji, let's go see what these jerks want, and if they mess with you, I'll hack into their bank accounts and bankrupt them."

Aly was about to respond when both grandmother and granddaughter held up hands in an identical gesture. "It's a joke," they said together, as though they'd invented the concept of humor.

Cullie stopped short in her study of Bindu's phone and looked up at her grandmother, eyebrows drawn together quizzically. "Binji, who's Bhanu D.? And why do you have twenty unopened emails about where to find her?"

CHAPTER TEN

BINDU

"Why does lying get a bad reputation?" she asked me once when I worried about all the lies she was telling her family to shoot Poornima. *"Isn't film-making lying? It's spinning tales. Digging into a lie so hard that it helps you get to the truth."* It was easy to forget that she was seventeen.
From the journal of Oscar Seth

Her acting days, short as they were, had served Bindu well her whole life. When the camera turned on, it was as simple as letting the words you were saying, the person you were being, become the truth. Slipping into an alternate moment, letting it take this one over. Sometimes it taught you something new about yourself, and sometimes it saved the person you needed to be.

When Bindu had taken her phone back from Cullie and calmly told her that Bhanu was a friend who used to be an actress, Alisha and Cullie had believed her without even the shadow of a doubt. Obviously, Bindu still had it.

That pesky person had been sending her five emails every day. It made her so angry, she almost yearned for the coven's emails.

How idiotic of her to let Cullie go through her phone. But what had happened with Richard had erased everything else. And it had been so long since she'd had to hide something.

It didn't hurt that Alisha and Cullie were currently throwing Bindu a pity party. All that mattered was that they hadn't deepened the interrogation. She'd take it. This was one thing Bindu was never discussing with anyone. Not ever. It was her business. Hers alone. The shame of those memories flushed across her body like a fever.

It had been decades since she'd thought about Bhanu. Every memory of all that nonsense was long gone. None of it took up any space inside her. Not even a little bit. Not the scandal, not the death threats from her own mother, not the blazing joy of facing the camera, of being pierced by it all the way to her soul, of being seen. Nothing.

The lady doth protest too much, Oscar's long-ago voice said in her ear. The velvet note of knowing so vivid, it was as though he was standing behind her. Too close. His body straining toward her even as he held it back.

A man of rare integrity. That's what Oscar's obituary had said. She let the involuntary pang of grief wash through her. She knew she had no right to grieve him, but the grief found its way inside her regardless. If she forced it away, it would only fight harder to take up residence. So she let it lie and covered it up until it was ready to leave.

Letting her mind feel this old wasn't something she usually allowed herself, but exhaustion overwhelmed her. Memories crawled inside her like spiders climbing over each other.

Shouldn't older memories disappear as new ones were added? Why was the mind so elastic?

She needed to get dressed. Alisha and Cullie were right; it was time to get this Leslie person to shut down this nonsense with the coven. Reaching to the back of her closet, Bindu picked out a kurti. Modest enough for a day in court when you were on trial. Whatever it took to get Leslie on her side she'd do. Including shrinking herself back inside her kurtis. But she'd let them throw her out of her home over her dead body. And it would have to be *her* body, not Richard's.

What the hell!

It took all her strength not to scream the words. How could this be? All these years she'd waited to have sex, and *this* is what happened?

Whore.

Whores spread diseases that kill people and then die of them, her mother's angry voice whispered in her ear. No! She was not old enough for ghosts to start talking to her. *Enough.*

"I am not a whore, Aie." She spoke the words. They were a whisper, but she had to speak them. They echoed off the jeweled tile of her bathroom.

Whatever you are, as long as it stays in our bedroom, there's no shame, Rajendra whispered in her ear.

Bindu yanked off the kurti she'd pulled on and reached for one of her wrap dresses.

Leslie was going to have to be on her side exactly the way she was.

"Everything okay, Ma?" Alisha asked from outside the bathroom door, and her kind voice—a voice that had recently taken to annoying Bindu for being too compliant—calmed her today.

"Not yet." Bindu pushed the door open and let herself out. "But it will be once we let the bullies know they can't push us around." With that she left her beautiful condo and took the elevator down to the glass-and-marble lobby, flanked on both sides by her girls. They made their way to the HOA office, marching in like the warrior goddesses they were.

Mary, the receptionist at the HOA office, was possibly the prettiest girl Bindu had ever seen. Definitely the sweetest. She sparkled like a sequined button on the starched lapel of the HOA. Reaching over, she took both of Bindu's hands in hers. "I'm so sorry, Mrs. Desai. You okay?"

Obviously, the coven had hired her as the sugar coating around their bitter pills.

Bindu squeezed her hands. "Thank you, Mary. It was horrible. But I'm okay."

"He was one of my favorite residents. Always brought me the best books after he was done reading them." Her voice trembled.

Accepting condolences for Richard's death felt wrong. They'd been on three dates. Bindu didn't even know if he had a family. Should she send a card? Flowers?

"I know how much he loved his books. That means you were special to him," Bindu said, surprising herself when her voice trembled too.

Mary rushed around the desk and gave her a hug. And burst into tears.

Within seconds the shoulder of Bindu's dress was soaked. Bindu patted her, taken aback by the turn of events. "There, there. It's going to be okay." She had no idea Mary had been so close to Richard. Unless the poor girl got this attached to all the residents. In which case, this job was not a good fit for her.

With another squeeze, Mary pulled away. "I'm so sorry. It's just that I've worked here for five years, and every day Richard brought me coffee, and we chatted for hours. I used to write little stories, and he'd read them and tell me to spend more time on my writing." She smiled the saddest smile. "But not everyone can feed themselves with their passion, can they? He hated when I said that."

Bindu plucked a tissue from the pink quilted box on Mary's desk and dabbed her cheeks.

This only made her eyes fill again. They were the same beautiful blue as Richard's.

"He had a very hard time talking to people. I'd only ever seen him happy these past few months," Mary said, giving Bindu a worshipful look. "After he met you. He was like a little boy when you agreed to go out with him. He made me help him buy a shirt online. A blue one. He said you loved his eyes."

Bindu felt tears welling up and pushed them back. "I did." Her voice cracked some more, and she felt completely ridiculous. "He had the bluest eyes I'd ever seen." She'd told him that so many times.

This time Cullie handed Mary and Bindu tissues, and someone cleared their throat behind them.

Mary started and turned toward the sound. "I'm so sorry, Leslie. I didn't mean to burst into tears."

Bindu spun around to see who this Leslie was that Mary felt the need to apologize to for her grief. But the silken voice hit her before her eyes found him.

"That's perfectly understandable. Please don't apologize." It was the green-eyed man from the open house. "Hello, Mrs. Desai."

"That's not Leslie!" The words flew out of Bindu before she could stop them, and he smiled, exposing the pearly whites that had made her think about the perfection of his life.

He offered her a hand. "Leslie Bennet. My friends call me Lee."

She let his hand hang there. "You've been on the HOA board this entire time?" When those women had been hounding her about one thing or another.

Apparently she'd read the kindness in his eyes, in his voice, wrong.

"I guess someone like me wasn't exactly who they needed," she said, and his eyes smiled some more. *Trouble*, indeed. He'd just wanted to be entertained.

"It is. But even I didn't quite estimate how much you enjoy being trouble."

"Watch yourself," Cullie said, getting between Bindu and him.

He offered Cullie the hand Bindu had rejected. "I'm sorry, I didn't mean to be rude. You must be the genius granddaughter."

"Excuse me?" Bindu said. How could he possibly know anything about Cullie? She'd never seen him after he'd called her trouble and incited her to move here.

"I'm sorry. Richard liked to talk about you." That was all the explanation he gave before leading them to the gilded and wainscoted meeting room and shutting the door behind them.

"Is no one else joining us?" Alisha asked, holding his gaze.

Her daughter-in-law in her tiger-mom avatar was a terrifying thing, her beautiful curls pulled back in a bun, one brow raised, those large jet-black eyes ruthless with judgment. Bindu had watched her slay the elementary school vice principal when he'd misunderstood her soft voice as weakness and tried to tell her that Cullie had behavioral issues when what she'd been doing was standing up to being bullied.

"I made sure it was just me." He slid a pointed look at Bindu. "It wasn't easy."

"Why are you acting like you're doing me a favor?" The gall of him! "I didn't ask for the cov—the HOA to not be here. I'm not afraid of them. I've done nothing wrong. Unless you're suggesting that I have?"

"My grandmother is the one who's been through trauma here, and your vicious little group should be sending her flowers to sympathize. Not flooding her inbox with threats." Cullie was the hardest person in the world to charm, and Bindu had never been more grateful for that fact.

"I know. I'm sorry," he said, still pouring on the charm and gloriously wasting it on Bindu's favorite person on earth.

"So we're here for an apology, not an eviction attempt, like your band of bullies suggested in their emails?" This from Alisha.

"It's a little bit more complicated than that," he said, gaze slipping between the three women. He was obviously used to speaking to a roomful of people and making them feel like he was entirely focused on each one individually. "Would you like some coffee or tea?" He pointed at the chairs around the meeting table, inviting them to sit down, but Bindu would give him even more of a height advantage than he already had when hell froze over.

Cullie picked up a bottle of water from the sideboard and pointed it at him. "What we'd like is for you to get to the damn point." She pulled out the chair and plopped into it with some force.

"Well then, let's get to it." *Leslie* pointed to the chairs again, and when Alisha and Bindu didn't sit, he sat down. If Cullie's rudeness bothered him, he didn't show it. "Richard was a heart patient."

"I know." The doctor who'd declared him dead had told Bindu that Richard had a pacemaker. "I mean I know now. I didn't before."

He met her gaze, every hint of amusement gone from his eyes. "His family wants to sue."

"Excuse me? Sue whom?" Alisha asked.

Bindu sagged into the sideboard. What in God's name was happening?

"Is it a crime to not know a friend's health history?" Cullie said.

"Richard had a family?" Bindu said. He'd had five ex-wives, for heaven's sake. Of course he did. He couldn't possibly have been as alone as he'd seemed.

Alisha went to Bindu and took her hand. Cullie stood and did the same.

"Yes, and he also had a substantial amount of money." Leslie's gaze took in the three of them standing there, hands linked, registering something that made the green of his eyes deepen.

"I guess what they say about writers being starving artists isn't true." Bindu threw a look around the ornately appointed conference room with jazz music piping softly through artfully concealed speakers. "Then again, he lived here. Obviously he wasn't a pauper."

"I'd be careful what I say," Leslie said. For words that harsh, his voice was kind.

"Are you a lawyer?" Trust Alisha to ask the right questions.

He nodded, perfectly pomaded silver hair barely moving. "I'm the person Richard entrusted with executing his will."

"Why would we care about his will?" Bindu said, starting to lose patience with this drama. The headache that had been nudging at her ever since she'd stupidly let them give her something to knock her out yesterday pushed forward. She kicked herself for waiting until noon for chai.

The weighed-down, and weighing, look in his eyes only pushed the headache closer. He took a long, meaningful pause. "Richard left everything to you."

"What?" all three of them said together.

Bindu yanked her hands out of Alisha's and Cullie's and pushed off the sideboard. "How?" She started pacing. "Why?"

No one answered. No one said a word. Alisha, even Cullie, stood there slack jawed. But Fancy-Pants Lawyer didn't have the luxury of sitting there, studying her as though she were on a witness stand. To hell with that.

She pointed at his face. "You've made a mistake. That's not possible. I barely knew him."

He had the gall to raise a brow at her.

"Cut the judgment and say what you're thinking. I need answers," she said.

His eyes softened. "It doesn't matter what I'm thinking. Rich obviously thought he knew you well enough to leave his life's earnings to you. And also all future royalties from his books."

What the hell, Richard!

"That makes no sense!" Yes, she raised her voice.

He stood and approached her as though he meant to comfort her, but she stepped away, and he stopped. "His family agrees with you. He has five children from his five marriages. I'm pretty sure they're all going to come together to fight his will."

"How much is it?" Cullie asked.

This time Bindu did cut her off. "I don't care. I don't want to know. I don't want it."

His eyes narrowed. She didn't care. He could take his assessing eyes somewhere else.

"It doesn't work like that. My job is to make sure Richard's wishes are carried out. And . . ." He swallowed. "And to make sure there was nothing suspicious in the fact that he changed his will so close to his death. Obviously, the circumstances of his death don't help."

Bindu sat down. She didn't care if his height gave him power. More accurately, her legs didn't care, because they gave out.

"The circumstances of his death?" Alisha said, ears picking up the important parts, Ganesha bless her. "That sounds an awful lot like an accusation. Isn't there a conflict of interest here? You seem to be coming at this from a place of bias, given the harassment your HOA has been inflicting on Bindu for months now."

The flash of surprise on his face was almost comical. He couldn't believe that someone had dared accuse him of anything nefarious. Never mind the accusations he'd been generously tossing Bindu's way. "The HOA board is concerned about the negative press from the death of a resident as famous as Richard under these circumstances. I'm working with them to allay their fears."

Bindu pressed a hand to her heart, and yes, she gasped. "The poor things. First the bras in my lanai and now a friend's death in my home. *Their* fears are certainly what need to be allayed here." She turned to Cullie. "Does Amazon deliver smelling salts?"

Cullie gave him a glare for the ages, and he looked down at his shiny shoes.

"It doesn't sound like executing Richard's wishes is all you're interested in," Alisha said, yet again slicing through the noise to what mattered. "How well do you know the family?"

"It's admirable how much your daughter and granddaughter support you," he said, looking directly at Bindu. If he meant to use their connection and win them over with flattery, he didn't know who he was dealing with. "It says good things about you."

Cullie stepped into his space, eyes fiery with anger. "Don't act like you're Binji's friend to manipulate her when you don't know the first thing about her. She can see right through the likes of you. We all can."

Bindu squeezed her granddaughter's hand and tapped her own wrist to remind Cullie of her Shloka bracelet—their code for "calm down."

"Answer the question," Alisha said, also turning up her glare. "Are you representing Richard's family?"

Leslie pinched the bridge of his nose as though the conversation had completely slipped out of his control. Good. "Of course I'm not representing the family. Rich was a friend. I'm not representing anyone but him."

"And what, you think your friend couldn't possibly think enough of me to . . . to . . ." Never mind, Bindu couldn't finish that, because it was beyond ridiculous that Richard had left her anything at all. Let alone all his wealth. This was Oscar all over again.

A thought flew in from nowhere. Could the emails about Bhanu be coming from Oscar's family? Had Oscar done something stupid on his way out too? What was it with these men wanting to lay claim even as they moved on to their next life?

"Never mind," she said. "You're right. The money belongs to his family. Not to me. And I don't care if you believe me or not. But I had no hand in his . . . his . . ." Dear heavens, a man had died while having sex with her.

The room spun a little, and she dropped back in her chair.

Alisha and Cullie were on her in a second, faces tight with worry, forcing a bottle of water at her until she drank.

When Leslie tried to ask if he could get her something, Cullie pushed him back and got up in his face again. "You can't accuse someone of murdering your friend with her vagina and then act all worried when she faints from the shock of it."

Oh, Cullie! Despite herself, Bindu's shoulders started to shake. With laughter, Ganesha forgive her. "Cullie, beta, please! I did not faint."

Seeing Bindu let a laugh escape, Cullie cracked a smile, and Alisha let a small one nudge at her lips too, even as she shook her head disapprovingly.

Leslie studied them with some confusion. Bindu didn't care. This is how they dealt with tragedy, and she didn't need him or anyone else to understand.

Alisha turned on him. "You can take your preposterous accusations and your friend's money and do whatever you want with it. Just leave us alone. We want nothing to do with it. And since you're a lawyer, let me put this on your radar too. If your HOA doesn't stop harassing Ma, we're going to be the ones doing the suing, and it will not be pretty. So if the bad publicity is what's making them act like middle school bullies, then you'd better tell them that they don't know what bad publicity looks like until a discrimination suit hits them."

Curls had flown loose from her prim bun. Her dark eyes had gone large and livid enough to shoot sparks. Alisha was blazing, and Bindu wanted to high-five her, but the room spun a little bit again, and she had to squeeze her eyes shut. She hated how helpless she felt when she opened her eyes and Alisha was handing her more water.

Pushing it away, she took Cullie's hand and pulled herself to standing. There was a reason she never took sleep aids. Her body reacted terribly to them. She'd been too thrown off her game yesterday to remember not to take one.

Leslie looked genuinely concerned now, even a little shaken. Well, good. Until the stupid drug was out of her system, Bindu was going to ham it up for him. The nerve of him! To walk in here pretending to protect Richard's interests to support his little coven.

"I'm sorry. I should have been more sensitive. I do know that Rich had a high opinion of you," he said as though making that concession hurt his lawyer brain. "We can discuss this later. You should get some rest."

"There's nothing to discuss," Bindu said, following Cullie out of the room. "I've said all I need to say."

He opened his mouth to respond but then took in the daggers Alisha and Cullie threw at him and closed it again. His nod was courteous, but the look in his eyes made what she already knew clear. They weren't done with this. Not by a long shot.

CHAPTER ELEVEN

CULLIE

My greatest fear was that she'd end up with someone who'd break her. Not because she was fragile. But because without meaning to, I taught her that breaking yourself is the only way to love.
From the journal of Oscar Seth

Chinese takeout had been the only option to cheer Binji up after Richard's funeral. Cullie's cooking skills might have been rudimentary at best, but no one could accuse her of being anything but spectacular at ordering things online. If *grubhubbing* were a verb, it would be Cullie's signature verb.

She'd outdone herself, ordering all Binji's favorite dishes: Szechuan shrimp (that Binji insisted on calling prawns) and Szechuan chicken and Szechuan fried rice and pretty much every dish on Lotus Garden's menu that started with the word *Szechuan*. Because Binji associated it with spice. *Real spice.*

"See, this is real spice," Binji said, red nose sniffling from the heaped spoonfuls of the hot sauce she had slathered on the already spicy food. "Not the American version of spice. Which, frankly, is embarrassing to taste buds everywhere."

Cullie rolled her eyes, but Binji didn't look restless and sad for the first time in the week Cullie had been home. Getting to go to Richard's visitation seemed to have helped. Richard's friend Mary had made all the arrangements for his funeral, which seemed odd considering he had a family that was eager enough to sue for his money. Mary had been kind enough to invite Binji to say her goodbyes privately, before the coven and others arrived.

Cullie and her mother had stood with Binji as she chanted a prayer over the casket, then tucked a tube of lip balm under Richard's hands, hugged Mary, and left.

They'd driven home in silence, then changed out of the white clothes Binji had asked them to wear out of respect for the dead and showered before the food arrived.

The spice had accomplished the rest, because Binji looked like herself again, in possession of herself and the universe. A combination of the goddesses Laxmi, Saraswati, and Parvati in the Amar Chitra Katha comic books Dad had read to Cullie every night in his most dramatic voice. On days like today she missed him so much, it was like a physical ache. Or maybe she just missed the simplicity of her childhood.

"Ma, that stuff can burn a hole in your intestines," Mom said, popping a spoonful of white rice into her mouth.

"I'm sixty-five, and I've been eating food five times spicier than this from the day I was born." Cullie couldn't believe she was thinking this, but she was so relieved to have Binji's extraness back. It had been terrifying to have it gone. "So my intestines are either like a sieve by now or they've become thick skinned, like me," she declared fiercely, before delicately—because she was Binji—sliding a massive oily red *prawn* into her mouth.

Mom patted Binji's shoulder and took a bite of her own shrimp. Even without the extra-extra-hot sauce, Mom's nose was Rudolph red. But she looked happy too. American Chinese takeout—as Binji called it—was Desai catnip.

"You're resilient, Ma. That doesn't make you thick skinned," Mom said gently. "You've handled all this admirably."

Binji's chopsticks paused on their way to her mouth. She gave Mom a half-tolerant, half-grateful smile. "Honestly, I have no idea how to handle it. I wish I'd had a chance to become friends with Richard." She bit into another shrimp and chewed carefully. "All I know about him is that he loved words." The saddest smile lit her eyes. "Even when he talked, it was like he was writing his own dialogue. And taking immense pleasure in it. Like he was never separate from his art."

"That's actually lovely, Ma," Mom said. They were so much better at this, knowing what to say to each other in the wake of death. All Cullie seemed able to do was make inappropriate jokes about her grandmother having couch coitus just to make her grandmother laugh.

Binji put her chopsticks down, that sadness in her eyes turning to purpose. "You and Cullie have that too. You know that, right?" Suddenly Binji's eyes were burning with something Cullie had never seen there before. Her gaze moved from Cullie to Mom. "Love for what you do. Work that feels as essential as breathing, that lets you dig into yourself, makes you feel alive. Hold on to it. Everyone doesn't have that."

"I'm sorry, Binji," Cullie said before she could stop herself. Sometimes she forgot that Binji had spent her life taking care of other people, and it made Cullie livid.

If Cullie had punched her grandmother, she would have looked less hurt. But the blast of pain was gone in a flash. If there was anything that could keep her grandmother down for long, Cullie was yet to discover it. Binji was like the endless earth, and calamities and adversity mere bolts of lightning swallowed up into its grounding soil.

Mom patted Binji's hand. She, on the other hand, was thrown so hard by things, she never got back up. Case in point: the divorce. Good thing Cullie had already been an adult when her parents decided to give up on their marriage out of the blue, because if Cullie hadn't been, she would have found it impossible to navigate never saying Dad's name in Mom's presence.

"Did you ever have something like that?" Cullie asked. "Something that made you feel alive?"

Binji opened her mouth, then shut it. "You," she said finally. "Taking care of you."

Instead of making Cullie feel better, that made her feel worse. But before she could say more, Binji threw her another fierce look. "How is your new app coming along?"

It was Cullie's turn to shove a humongous clump of noodles into her mouth. For the past few days Cullie had continued to struggle with a mock-up. One corner of Binji's bedroom floor was carpeted with sheets of paper containing Cullie's dud ideas.

Emails from CJ filled her inbox, along with a few from Steve.

How had she ever thought of him as Hot Steve? Now the only thing hot was the anger that gripped her every time she thought about him. How stupid did you have to be to let a married man lie to you about being divorced? It was the oldest con in the book, and Cullie would never, ever let herself forget how easily she'd fallen for it.

The incentive of rubbing Steve's lying face in the success of a new app was a powerful force. But how did one code something they didn't understand? Coding wasn't just typing out a string of numbers and letters and symbols; it was solving a problem, creating from nothing what you wanted to bring into existence.

As someone who sucked at everything in the general vicinity of romantic relationships, there wasn't a less qualified person in the world to do this. Falling in love, being in a functional relationship: all those things she'd sold to CJ were basically Greek to her. Scratch that. For the price of off-the-shelf language-learning software, she could learn some Greek by the week's end. What's more, she found the idea of learning a foreign language mildly exciting. With dating . . . nothing, and consequently no idea where to even start with this program.

"Cullie?" Binji said, studying Cullie as though she knew exactly what had just passed through her brain. "Why are you frowning at those poor prawns like that? Don't take your smooth forehead for granted, beta."

When Cullie didn't smile or respond, Binji and Mom exchanged the Look.

"What's going on with Shloka?" Mom asked the question for both of them.

When Cullie looked surprised, they exchanged another look.

"The child is hilarious, no? Who does she think raised her?" Binji asked Mom, pointing her chopsticks at Cullie's face.

"You only get that look on your face when something is happening with Shloka." Mom circled her chopsticks around Cullie's face too.

Suddenly they were two artists working on one painting, with chopsticks for paintbrushes.

"I thought the app was growing," Binji said, washing a mouthful of shrimp down with the last bit of wine in her glass. "What's wrong?"

"You have enough of your own stuff to worry about right now," Cullie said. "More wine?"

"What stuff of my own do I have to worry about?" asked the woman who'd just had a friend die on her couch. "If I'm being perfectly honest, I'm tired of thinking about what happened. We can't change the past, but we can fix what's wrong now. Stop deflecting."

Fine.

So Cullie told them. Not about Steve's betrayal. Because she wasn't ready to watch Mom's heart break in her eyes. But she told them how the board was breaking their promise and planning to slap a subscription fee on Shloka. Destroying the thing that so many people relied on. She told them how she'd panicked and thrown Binji's words at CJ in the form of an idea for a dating app.

For the first time today, Binji beamed. "You're welcome!"

"I'm not hearing the problem," Mom said. "Having something new to work on is great." She opened her mouth to say more, but then another look passed between her and Binji, and she didn't.

It wasn't like Cullie didn't know what Mom wanted to say. It had been a few years since Shloka went to market. There was a team of developers working on it now, not just Cullie.

At least neither of them tried to explain to her why a subscription wasn't such a bad thing. They got why it would be devastating, and knowing this eased the mountain Cullie had been feeling buried under.

"I've been trying to come up with a plan to send CJ. She keeps telling me to send her what I have."

Naturally CJ didn't doubt Cullie's ability to execute whatever idea she came up with. Problem was, there was no idea. And Steve had to know this. He knew exactly how much relationship stuff was not Cullie's thing. How long before he convinced CJ that Cullie was lying?

In his last email, he'd accused Cullie of being vicious. *I needed a woman who felt more for me than physical attraction. A woman who could access other feelings.*

The asshole.

"So send her what you have," Mom said with all the cluelessness of a mother who'd never had to deal with her child struggling with homework or bad grades.

"I've got nothing, Mom!" Cullie snapped. "I pulled this out of thin air because of Binji. I have no idea where to even start."

"You came up with the design for Shloka when you were sixteen. This is so much more tangible." Mom looked baffled.

It wasn't tangible to Cullie. Not even a little bit. Sometimes her mother really didn't get her. The mountain burying her piled right back up.

Thankfully, Binji was right there with her. Their three-way dynamic. Binji translating between them. "The reason Shloka came so easily to Cullie was that she understood the problem she was trying to solve," Binji explained.

Mom looked like she always looked when the topic of Cullie's mental health came up. At once disbelieving and completely convinced that she understood it better than anyone else, simply by virtue of having birthed Cullie.

It was a conversation neither one of them wanted, or knew how to get into.

Cullie understood only too well how her mother processed the fact that Cullie "had issues." Cullie's first memories of the waves of noise came with her mother responding by telling her to remember that she was perfect. But that just meant that the *imperfection* of a mental illness didn't fit in with that. Over the years Mom had found a way to tidy it all up by creating the narrative that Cullie was her brilliant child whose brain had parts that worked in overdrive, therefore making other parts of her brain not work as well.

Cullie had once overheard Mom explaining it to Radha Maushi, Mom's best friend. She'd said it was like being a runner. You could either be a sprinter or a marathoner. And the more brilliant you were at one, the more challenging it made the other. It was a matter of focus. In Mom's view, Cullie's brain's focus was taken up with code and numbers, so "processing other aspects of life" got neglected.

For many years, Cullie had believed it was a choice too. And no matter that her therapist had set her straight; she sometimes still liked thinking of it as a choice. Because that meant that when she decided to focus on it, she'd know how to make it go away.

"Binji's right. I was the problem I was trying to solve," Cullie said, tone ironic.

"Maybe that's the case with this *problem* too," Mom said, trying not to be intrusive.

"When was the last time you went on a date, beta?" Binji never had a problem being intrusive.

Binji grinned with more than a little self-satisfaction. As the veritable truckload of roses sitting on the table proved, she was suddenly something of an expert on the matter of dating-shating now, because new suitors were already circling.

A grunt escaped Cullie before she could rein it in.

"Exactly!" Binji mimicked her grunt, managing to turn the sound entirely nonsensical. "You have never dated. You have never looked for a person to be with."

She was aware. She hadn't gone looking for Steve. He had fallen into her lap. As had all the boys she'd slept with in high school and college. Cullie had lost her virginity at sixteen. Mostly because she'd never been great at holding back her curiosity. She'd had to know what the big deal about sex was.

As someone who had a hard time understanding what everyone around her was chasing—freedom, achievement, pleasure—sex had felt like the shortest path to figuring at least some piece of it out. It was amazing how easy it was to fool around in high school if you didn't care about things like popularity or gossip. Her reputation for being able to hack lives away with a flick of her hand meant no one dared share anything about her online.

"You've never had to *search*," Binji clarified as though Cullie might have missed her meaning.

"I don't want to search now!" In fact, could she undo having found Steve, please.

"You're twenty-five years old." This from Mom, as though Cullie wasn't aware of her own age. "How can you not want to search? It's a natural part of being human. Unless you've suppressed that part of yourself so hard that you don't even know you've done it." Mom applying her worldview to psychoanalyzing Cullie was Cullie's least favorite thing, so she ignored it.

Binji's face softened but her eyes sharpened. That fierceness was back. "Every girl should meet a man who makes her feel exactly right. At least once in her life."

What did that even mean? Steve had made her feel good. But what was feeling *right*? Parts of Cullie never felt right. Other parts of her always did.

"Or at least that's the dream," Mom said. "That's why this app has potential. Because everyone feels the need to search for the one who makes them feel that way." She looked so determined to show no feelings, Cullie's heart twisted for her. But then she went on, and the sympathy evaporated. "Aren't you curious? Lonely for companionship?"

"Talk about the pot calling the kettle black," Cullie said, ruthlessly pulling out one of Granny Karen's many favorite old-world idioms. "You're forty-seven, Mom! Aren't you afraid it will be too late? Aren't *you* lonely for *companionship*?"

Mom picked up the leftovers and started slapping lids on them. "Who said I'm not?"

Great, now Cullie felt an inch tall. Dad had been an idiot to walk away like that. Even if her app could just help Mom find someone, that would be enough.

"I'm definitely lonely for companionship," Binji said, "or are we not using that as a euphemism?"

Mom and Cullie both stared at her.

"It's been a week since a man died in your arms!" Mom burst out. Work pressure must have been getting to her, because she only said things like that when something was blowing up elsewhere. But at least the sadness was gone from her eyes.

"Technically he died between her legs." Well, if they were letting truths fly.

"Cullie!" Mom smacked Cullie's shoulder.

"How long have you been holding that one in, beta?" Binji said, letting a smile escape. But then she stood and stared down at the two of them. Purpose shone ominously in her eyes. Something inside her seemed to have changed during this conversation. "All jokes aside. We're sitting here discussing being lonely for companionship as though it's something we have no control over, as though it's something we don't understand."

"Because we don't," Cullie said.

"Well . . ." Binji looked like she was about to yell, *Eureka!* "Then there's only one thing to do about it, isn't there?" She paused, creating one of those pregnant silences that was so filled with the thought-grenade she was about to expel into the air that all Cullie could do was clench for impact.

CHAPTER TWELVE

ALY

Bhanu didn't lie to Rajendra Desai about Poornima. *She told him the truth. I've spent all these years wondering what it cost her.*
From the journal of Oscar Seth

Aly had seen that look in Bindu's eyes before, and it did not bode well. Cullie leaned into Bindu's pause, and Aly felt her own excitement rise. They exchanged looks, three sets of eyes lobbing the potential of an idea, brimming with anticipation over its possibility to be great. Or terrible.

And boom! Just like that Aly knew exactly what was forming in Bindu's head.

"You're going to make me say it, aren't you?" Bindu picked up her wineglass before realizing it was empty.

"We're hoping you won't," Aly mumbled, even as excitement fizzed like misguided bubbles inside her. She filled Bindu's glass with the last few sips left in the bottle.

"You can't do this without firsthand research." Bindu fixed Cullie with one of those looks that came so easily to her: gentle firmness.

"I do need to do the research," Cullie admitted grudgingly, with the same expression she'd worn when Aly had taken her to the dentist as a child. "What I know about dating apps, or even dating for that matter, could fit on a Post-it Note."

Aly typed in the words *dating app* on her phone and started scrolling. "Did you know there are over a thousand dating apps out there?"

Bindu looked lost for the first time in this conversation. Her mouth opened, then closed without sound.

"I know, Mom. And ten of those have tens of millions of people on them." Aly should have known that Cullie would have all the data at her fingertips. Ashish had brought home a T-shirt for their daughter from a conference once that said "DATA DIVA." The words were long faded, but she still wore it.

"Tens of millions of people who obviously aren't getting what they want from it." Aly skimmed the statistics in what seemed like one of a thousand think pieces on dating apps. "Your chances of finding a meaningful relationship on a dating app are about twelve percent."

"That's terrible." Bindu downed her wine and looked around for reinforcements. "Why so low?"

"Is it terrible?" Cullie said. "It sounds high to me."

"Either way, the point is to raise it, right?" Aly said, still poring over her phone, because this was a whole entire world she knew nothing of. "And to do that, we have to know what's out there and how it works."

For a few seconds the silence in the room swirled with possibility again.

"You need test cases," Bindu declared finally, so much flourish in her voice, one would think she had written all the code and handed Cullie a finished app.

In high school, Cullie had paid people to test Shloka by writing their essays and doing their calculus homework. Then it had started helping people, and the word had spread, and everyone had wanted to help her test it. Aly remembered the pride and terror of seeing Cullie become that obsessed.

Suddenly her daughter, who'd needed to be mainlined discrete calculus problems to keep her from bursting with restlessness, had lost herself in gathering data and tweaking her design. There could be no bio app without someone to test the prototype. The entire thing was based on the idea that the human physiology reacted to thoughts and feelings. Ashish had worked with Cullie to build the bracelet prototype in a friend's workshop.

Through it all, Cullie had known exactly what to do.

Cullie pushed her hands through her bangs, her worry tell. "We're jumping a few steps here. We don't even know what we're testing."

"So let's figure it out one step at a time," Aly said, starting to pace. "Those apps are right there. How hard would it be to learn how they function and then analyze why they do or don't work?"

"Then it's just a matter of fixing the parts that don't work." Bindu stood and joined Aly in her pacing.

They were in full entrepreneur mode now. The Desai women, ready to solve the world's problems.

"What if dating apps aren't our competition? What if we come up with something that makes dating apps better, more effective?" Bindu threw out. Her mother-in-law was truly a wonder.

Cullie bounced in her seat. Her grandmother had obviously landed on the heart of the problem in one elegant swoop.

"Binji! That's brilliant. We need something that sits on top of existing dating apps and makes them work better for each individual. Since who we find attractive has more to do with us than them."

Bindu grinned, totally settling into the Goddess of Love avatar she'd taken on since moving here.

"A way to personalize these generalized apps." A sparkle of excitement crackled inside Aly.

"Exactly!" Cullie looked fierce. It had been too long since Aly had seen her daughter this way. Not bored and disillusioned by the world but like she actually gave more than a surface-level damn. Not quite her Cullie from high school, on fire with what she wanted to do, but with sparks of her lighting up the edges.

"So, test subjects," Cullie said. "I need someone to actually use the apps so I can mine them for user flow and user experience data. A place to start figuring out what I'm even trying to figure out." She jumped up from her perch at the dining table and started pacing too. All three of them were pacing now, crisscrossing each other. "Someone I can trust to be honest, and someone who can start helping me right now."

The pregnant silence returned as they stopped, facing each other. They had circled back to Bindu's idea.

Suddenly, a nervous knot tightened in Aly's belly. It had been too long. The idea of dealing with a man's opinion made her nauseated. She hadn't been a fan of Ashish's opinions about her work, but she'd never had to perform for him the way she'd always had to around men before she met him.

Thinking about how much she missed that was stupid. Not to mention useless, because she had no interest in paying what it cost to have it again.

She went to the wine rack on the kitchen counter and studied their choices.

"Usually the best place to start anything is right where you are. I can't think of a better place to start than here." Bindu patted Aly's shoulder, then took the wine bottle Aly had picked out and started searching for an opener.

"Here where?" Aly said, suddenly certain that she wasn't interested in being part of this. Her reflex to clean up kicked in, and she started gathering the takeout containers.

"Right here with you, Alisha. You're the perfect test case. Stop hiding in my refrigerator," Bindu said.

"A perfect test case would be someone who's interested in finding someone." Aly had thought she'd found her soul mate once. She'd been wrong. "I already found someone, remember? And realized I don't like it that much." The refrigerator air was cool on her face as she put away the food. "No offense to you." She popped her head out and looked at

Bindu, then went back inside and adjusted the fried rice before popping her head out and throwing Cullie a look. "Or you."

"No offense taken," both of them said together.

"Just because one relationship didn't work out doesn't mean you stop living," Bindu added, and a memory of Ashish's face when Bindu had told him she was staying with Aly flashed in Aly's head.

True to form, he'd swept his hurt under nonchalance. *Since everyone in this family has decided to do only what benefits them, I don't care what you do, Ma.*

"I'm living just fine, thank you very much. And I need to get home and finish up some work, or my living will be taken away." Aly manufactured a smile.

Cullie rolled her eyes at Aly's feeble wordplay and took the bottle from Bindu. "Binji's right. Stop using *making a living* as an excuse to not *live*. You're doing this, and that's that."

Aly opened and closed some drawers. Where was the damned wine opener? "Doing what exactly?"

"Test-driving dating apps for me so I figure out a way to . . . you know . . . save my living."

Bindu clapped her hands and plopped into a dining chair. "Alisha's going to date. Brava!"

"No, Alisha and you both are going to date. This is all your fault for putting ideas in my head. You're the one going on about putting yourself out there. So let's step outside the Shady Palms pool. There's no way you're getting out of this."

"Getting out of it? I was afraid you might want to leave me out of it." Bindu winked delightedly at Aly.

"Perfect," Cullie said. "Let's get profiles set up for both of you on Twinge. That's the app with the biggest market share. Then we'll try other apps." She reached for their phones, and they both pulled them away.

"Not so fast. You're the number one dating demographic," Aly said. She hadn't been skimming those articles for nothing.

"You're doing this too," Bindu said.

"I'm too close to this. And stop trying to use this to get me to date." Cullie crinkled her nose.

"Well, Shloka was such a success because you created it for yourself. So the 'being too close to it' argument is meaningless," Bindu said. "And you're right. I'll use whatever I can to get you to date. Both of you. It's a shame that you live in a time when you can do this and you're too afraid. It's time for you to figure out that there are hotter Steves out there. Also *better* Steves." She threw Aly a glance. "And finding your soul mate is a gift, but losing one is not an excuse to stop living. Like everything in life, soul mates serve their time, and once they do, it's time to move on. Our souls are not so limited that they can only have one mate."

Bindu had to be the world's strangest mother-in-law.

"Cullie and you can start, and we'll find more people to join in as we figure out what we're looking for. I simply don't have the time for it. Maybe after I get the segment," Aly said.

"The segment you plan to get after giving your Meryl interview away to Relatable Jess?" Bindu said.

"You gave the Meryl story away?" Cullie raised her voice, and damn it, Aly did not need both of them on her case. "What the hell, Mom! Bharat's boyfriend pulled all sorts of favors to get you that information."

"I didn't give it away."

"You haven't yet. But you're going to," Bindu said with all the ominous confidence of a soothsayer.

"I may not have a choice. It's the cost of being in the news business. You have to give the sponsors what they want. Only then can you get what you want."

Bindu stared up at the ceiling and threw a "What do I do with this girl?" plea at the recessed lights. "They're telling you the sponsors want all their stories to come from someone who is not a brown woman. How can you believe that they're magically going to change their mind about that after you give them the story that's the best chance you have to prove them wrong?"

"This is bullshit, Mom! You have to hold on to what the sponsors want and leverage it to get what you want. That's business." Cullie looked like she wanted to shake Aly. "Business is all leverage. Which is why you and Binji have to help me do this. So I can build an app that can be so profitable, they won't touch Shloka. We need to put an end to having our chains yanked because we happen to love what we do."

Love so sharp squeezed inside Aly that she teared up. She cupped Cullie's cheek. "I'm so proud of you. I don't even know where you got so much wisdom from."

Bindu cleared her throat. "I know where she gets it from."

How could Aly not smile? "I can't get on Twinge. I can't go out with strange men. I was terrible at it when I was young, and the idea gives me hives now." She ripped the foil off the wine bottle with more viciousness than she'd intended. "I'll come up with another way to help you. Just not this. Where is that damned corkscrew?" She yanked every drawer open again.

The look Cullie threw her was equal parts disappointment, frustration, and stubborn disregard for anyone else's wishes. When Cullie got that look, there was no derailing her. Just as Aly was trying to figure out how to make a getaway before she did something she regretted, the doorbell rang.

"If that's Leslie, throw him out." Bindu jogged across the room and hid behind the fridge as though this were a sitcom. Leslie had been pushing for another meeting with almost Cullie-level single-mindedness.

"Gladly." Cullie marched to the door, hungry for a fight, and pulled it open as though tossing Weaselly Leslie to the curb would fix their problems.

"Surprise!"

"Dad!"

The crash of the wine bottle hitting the floor sounded across the condo. The gasp that escaped Aly was louder than the crash.

The smell of wine flooded the air even as red splattered like blood across Aly's white trousers.

Her ex-husband beamed at their daughter, picked up the suitcase sitting next to him, and let himself in.

~

Karen Menezes was not for the faint of heart. But today, Aly really did not have the strength to deal with her mother. After Aly had mortifyingly dropped the bottle of wine, the only way to make sure everyone knew exactly how unaffected she was by Ashish's unexpected arrival was to let Cullie set up a profile for her on Twinge. As Ashish watched. Because to hell with her fear—she was doing this. Finally, she'd made her exit with all the dignity she could muster and a smile so breezy she deserved an Oscar for it.

The phone rang again. After the day she'd had, Aly should have been able to ignore her mother's call without guilt.

Usually, the time when Aly got off work and drove home coincided with the time her mother went for her morning walk in Goa. Aly called her mother dutifully every second day. If Aly missed a day, Mummy simply gave her the silent treatment the next day.

She never called Aly herself. This was her third call in five minutes. Aly answered the phone.

"You never told me that your husband was planning to visit you," her mother opened without a greeting. "You never tell your mother anything." Naturally, Mummy had to be in her element today.

Aly bumped her forehead on the steering wheel.

Ashish had been on American soil for a matter of hours, and already every bit of peace from Aly's life was gone.

"Never mind all that," Mummy continued with the patience of a passive-aggressive saint. "I'm so glad you're finally seeing sense."

Their calls always lasted under fifteen minutes, during which Karen found a way to tell Aly that she was praying for Aly to see sense and get back with her husband.

Ashish had obviously filled Aly's parents in on his plans.

"I didn't know he was coming. Unlike you. So how was I supposed to tell you?"

"What's wrong with the fact that he checks up on us and keeps us posted about things? It's not every day that you find a son-in-law like that. I light a candle and say a novena for the blessing every Wednesday."

"He's not your son-in-law anymore, Mummy," Aly said without heat because no matter how many times she repeated the words, they fell on obstinately unreceptive ears.

"In the eyes of God, he will always be."

Aly imagined her mother crossing herself and resisted banging her head on the steering wheel again.

"I feel like God's a little less rigid than that." The words were out before she could rein them in.

Her mother paused, unused to getting what she deemed back talk from her grown daughter. Usually, when they arrived inevitably at this point in their conversation, Aly changed the subject. With four of her mother's siblings living in the same apartment building after retirement, it was easy to deflect the conversation to what was happening in one of the aunties' or uncles' lives. "He is a merciful God, but you cannot treat His understanding frivolously," her mother said finally.

"I did not leave my husband, Mummy. He left me. Did you want me to chain him to my bedpost?"

Her mother gasped.

Aly almost gasped too, with the force of letting out the words that had been trapped inside her for so long. A fierceness beat in her heart. She felt like she'd thrown herself from a high-rise without hitting concrete, and the force of it almost lifted her off her seat.

"Don't be crude, child. Worse, don't use your crudeness to hide from the truth." Her mother yanked her back to reality. "You refused to

move to India with him. So technically you are the one who left him."
For someone who barely altered her tone no matter how brutally she
wielded it, Mummy stressed the words *you* and *him* with the force of
a bad actor.

After being in India for five years, Mummy was losing her American
deadpanness. Americans tended to believe themselves loud. But they
mistook their confidence and entitlement for actual largeness of mannerisms. You had to watch a Bollywood film once or attend one Indian
party to know how wrong they were.

Aly could have told her mother that Ashish had known she would
never move to India, which amounted to him choosing to leave her.
She could also get into how he'd used returning to India as the final
battle for power in their marriage, and she'd failed the test. But Karen
was not the kind of person who allowed her opinions to be changeable.
It would count as a moral failing.

"In either case, he's only here for a short while. He'll be back in
India soon, I'm sure. So please don't expect anything to change."

"I don't expect, I pray. His will be done." With that Mummy went
on her merry way, the crash of the waves on Varca Beach the last sound
Aly heard before the phone went silent.

"I love you too, Mummy," Aly whispered—fine, hissed—at the
phone before tossing it onto the passenger seat.

The phone was about as moved by Aly's declaration as her mother
was by Aly's feelings.

CHAPTER THIRTEEN

BINDU

Poornima turned out to be everything I'd ever dreamed it would be. But it destroyed something more beautiful than anything I could ever have dreamed of.
From the journal of Oscar Seth

I have an appointment, so you'll have to eat by yourself," Bindu said to her son as she poured water into the flour and started kneading the dough for rotis.

She couldn't get herself to say the words *I have a date* to him.

What made it worse was that this wasn't even one of her living-her-life dates. It was one of Cullie's research dates from Twinge.

It had been a couple of days since Alisha had smashed a bottle of wine to celebrate Ashish's return (and they called Bindu dramatic) and then allowed Cullie to create a dating profile for her (with a big fake smile plastered across her face). Ashish had pretended not to watch, his lips pursed in that way he'd always pursed them when he didn't get his way, ever since he was a boy.

Well, good for Alisha for squeezing every passive-aggressive drop of mileage out of the situation.

Bindu wasn't going to complain, because talking about the app had been a good way to avoid a conversation about Richard's death. Turns out Cullie had told Ashish about it. Which is why he was here. Bindu wanted to be angry at Cullie, but how could she not have told her father? Ashish might have failed at being a husband, but he'd always been a good father. After the divorce, Cullie was the one person he'd constantly been in touch with.

That didn't mean Bindu was going to fill Ashish in on the details. Neither about Richard nor about having coffee with a man they'd found on Twinge who made music videos in Bollywood and Hollywood. Like every other remotely successful person, he was now retired in Florida. It was a surprisingly good match, so maybe this app-shap business wasn't as random as it sounded.

"You don't have to make me rotis, Ma," Ashish said in the voice that all his life had meant the exact opposite of the words he was saying.

She knew she had spoiled him. But wasn't that the job of mothers?

Throughout his marriage, Bindu had watched as he helped Alisha around the house. Her mother's heart had been so proud of every diaper changed, every dish rinsed, every plant watered. In retrospect, she was ashamed of her pride. Alisha had done all those things too, ten times over. And all she'd heard was people praising Ashish for what a good husband he was.

Dusting the flour off her hands before she started kneading the dough in earnest, Bindu gave the pot of fish curry a gentle stir before covering it and leaving it to simmer.

Her mind strayed to Alisha. Bindu was hungry for an update on how her date had gone the previous night. Before Ashish had shown up, Bindu had sensed the tiniest spark of excitement in Alisha about this dating thing. That poor woman really needed something nice to happen to her.

Bindu threw a look at her son. He'd made his declaration about her not needing to make rotis for him and then gone back to his phone. She tried not to let the prickle of annoyance grow. He was her only child, and of course she was happy to see him. It had been two years since he'd abandoned his family. So it had been two years since she'd seen him. They talked every few weeks, but it was the longest in her life that she'd gone without seeing him.

Contrary to popular belief, Bindu *had* tried to stop him. Karen Menezes had called her incessantly after he left, telling Bindu to be a good mother and appeal to her son to forgive Alisha for whatever she'd done.

Karen was exactly the kind of woman Bindu had spent her life avoiding. One of those women who believed themselves too genteel, too pious, too virtuous (yuck, that word), too everything for lesser mortals. She had sided squarely with her son-in-law in the divorce, making it even more impossible for Bindu to not side with Alisha.

Bindu had tried to get her son to see that all marriages had their ups and downs. Staying when the going got tough was the only secret there was to a long marriage. What she'd really wanted to do was scream at him that he was a lucky bastard to have Alisha and Cullie, and he was being an idiot. But somehow, with Ashish she couldn't stop being the compliant Bindu she'd been with Rajendra. The mother who'd had to be sensitive enough for both parents. The mother who was always compensating.

I deserve to be happy too, Ma, he'd said. *Why does only Aly get to chase her dream? What about my dreams?*

Maybe past generations were wise to decree that the dreams of two people could never both be important in a marriage. They were opposing forces, and opposing forces always tore things in half.

You were lucky to never want anything more than a family and a home, he had said to Bindu as he filed for divorce. *And look at how well you did it.*

It had been one of those moments that had hammered Bindu like nails in a coffin, slamming into focus all the things she'd allowed to die. All the things she'd had to hide from him. *For him.* As always, she'd buried the hurt where she couldn't feel it.

The day Alisha signed the divorce papers, Bindu had sat next to her daughter-in-law filled with an indescribable rage and told her that she wasn't going back to India with her son.

Please don't leave me, Alisha had said with the exact kind of vulnerable hope with which Cullie used to ask if she could sleep in Bindu's bed when she had nightmares. *Just until all of this makes sense.*

For as long as you need, Bindu had answered.

Bindu checked on the fish curry one last time. Realization wafted through her like the nuanced but unmistakable aroma that signaled that the coconut in the curry was perfectly cooked. For someone who worked so hard not to appear disruptive, Alisha never backed away from the things that were important to her. Her ability to identify what she wanted to dig in her heels about was uncompromising.

Why had it taken Bindu so long to see this?

Bindu, on the other hand, for all her gregariousness, had spent her life focused on the small, unimportant things to compensate for never being able to ask for anything truly important.

The lid dropped from her hand and clanged on the pot. She leaned on the countertop, strength draining from her in a rush.

Ashish finally looked up.

"You've been kneading that dough like it's responsible for everything wrong in the world," Ashish said, his boyish smile displaying the one crooked tooth that Bindu had loved so much when he was a boy. "Do you need help with it?"

Bindu had the urge to laugh. It might have been the first time in her life that her son had asked if she needed help.

She was about to kick herself for being so happy with the fact that he had offered when he put down his phone and washed his hands. Then he pulled the plate of half-kneaded dough away from Bindu.

A rush of love washed over her, and she didn't even know why.

"What time is your appointment? Don't you need to get dressed for it?" he asked as Bindu gawked at the deftness with which he started kneading the dough.

"I've lived by myself for two years, Ma. I had to learn how to make my own rotis."

Actually that was not true. In India you could easily hire someone to make rotis for you.

"People change," he added without a hint of smugness.

Do they? she wanted to ask, but then she saw herself in the mirrored surface of her refrigerator, and the question fizzled on her tongue.

"What else did you learn?" she asked instead, tidying up the mess from cooking.

He met her eyes with something suspiciously like regret. It was eerie how much like her he looked. "That Aly was right. Following your dreams isn't easy, but it is the one thing you owe yourself." Was that look he was giving her accusatory? She'd never stopped him from following his dreams. Had she?

"Working on the concert circuit was amazing." His golden-hazel eyes lit up, and somehow they were so much more beautiful on him, so beloved. But the passion in them was new.

Why are you back? She couldn't ask that without having to get into the Richard situation.

For all her joy in seeing him, alarm bells sounded in Bindu's head.

He was tanned and longhaired again, with the unkempt stubble from his college days that had bothered her so much then. Something about seeing him like this made the years in between feel like they simply hadn't happened. The clean-cut years when he'd worked behind a desk for two decades, hair neatly trimmed, jaw neatly shaved, tie neatly knotted.

The years when he'd turned into Rajendra.

It had been a relief.

It had been a horror.

She'd buried the memories so deep that the fact that they were stirring made her want to throw up. What if Ashish found out?

Why had she taken Oscar's money? Why hadn't she just given it away or hidden it like everything else to do with Oscar?

Excusing herself, she went off to change. Her marriage had taught her not to keep people waiting. As a military doctor, Rajendra had had no patience with unpunctual people.

"Looking pretty, Ma," Ashish said when she came out dressed in her purple Lucknow tunic over white linen capris.

Not only was the dough kneaded, but he picked a perfectly round roti off the tawa pan and placed it on the flame. It swelled to a sphere, and the smell of flame-charred wheat filled the kitchen.

The memory of the sweet boy he'd been rose so pure and huge in her heart, she pressed a hand to her chest. The way his eyes had shone when he told her he loved her clothes and how pretty she looked. He used to pick flowers for her from the bougainvillea that spilled over their fence.

But Rajendra hadn't liked the idea of a boy who picked flowers and noticed the colors of his mother's saris. By the time Ashish was ten, he'd turned his focus to running around the lane, playing cricket and football with the neighborhood boys and making just enough trouble that his father could tell his friends stories of Ashish's shenanigans. But never so much trouble that Rajendra couldn't brag about his son's grades and his ranking at school.

Ashish had seemed to enjoy his sports and his studies well enough. When he'd shown no interest in medicine, unlike his father, and chose engineering instead, Rajendra had seemed perfectly fine with it. The one thing Ashish had made sure he never let slip around his father was his love of music.

Bindu had asked him once if he was interested in taking singing lessons. It had resulted in one of those teen meltdowns about how she didn't understand him at all and how she wanted to ruin something he loved as a hobby by turning it into yet another thing they could brag to their friends about.

Now all these years later, he'd decided to run off and become a sound engineer on a concert tour, becoming the exact kind of person Rajendra would have been ashamed of. Then again, Rajendra might have been even more ashamed of the fact that his son had not been able to bend his wife to his will.

What good did second-guessing the dead do? It wasn't like it could give you any meaningful answers.

What is the point of examining your past?

"Does this appointment have anything to do with Cullie's new app idea?" Ashish asked, carefully smearing a generous spoonful of ghee over the roti he'd just taken off the flame.

Bindu weighed her answer even as the smell of ghee melting on a hot roti distracted her. She could use Cullie's app as an excuse for her social life. But she couldn't get herself to be that disingenuous. So she simply said, "Yes."

"You never could say no. Not to Cullie or to Aly." He gave her a look that wasn't accusatory, but kind. "Or to me." He sprinkled a thick layer of sugar on the ghee-soaked roti, rolled it up, and handed it to her.

A sugar-and-ghee roti roll was one of Bindu's favorite treats. A simple indulgence she'd often rewarded herself with when she made rotis for Rajendra and Ashish every day. He remembered.

She let the flavors cartwheel across her taste buds, and tried not to ruin the moment by crying. "Why would I not help Cullie when I can? Why would I not help any of you?" It had been her job. Taking care of her family. It was the career she had chosen.

You wanted to work, and now you have a job. That's what her aie had said to her on her wedding day. *Taking care of your family is your job. Why should it be any different from working in a film or in an office? It's what your mother and your grandmother and her mother before her did.*

She'd done that job well. Better than her mother ever had. She'd put every bit of her heart into it. And nothing would ever dilute her pride in that.

Ashish grinned at the shameless joy with which she chewed. He seemed to be seeing her for the first time. "Was the man who died part of gathering data for Cullie's app?"

Her surprise must've shown, because he raised both hands to show . . . what? That he was not digging for information? That he was not judging her?

She savored the last piece of sugar roti, determined to not miss even a bit of the deliciousness or to not tiptoe around at least this truth. The new life she'd built for herself was something she loved. Richard's death was an accident.

"Richard and I were friends before Cullie needed help with the app."

He looked almost surprised that she'd responded, but also relieved, because it gave him permission to go on. "Why would he leave you his money? And why would you think about not taking it?"

A layer of sweat beaded along her hairline. They were talking about Richard's money right now. Not Oscar's. She would never let Ashish find out anything about Oscar's. Ever.

Did he know the circumstances under which Richard had died? Bindu hoped Cullie had at least had the sense to not divulge those details to her father.

"I have no idea why he left me the money. But I do know that I did nothing to deserve it. So I won't take it." It's what she had told Weaselly Leslie when he'd called again that morning. The man was like a recurring rash. He wouldn't go away.

Of all the people on earth, why did *he* have to be Richard's lawyer.

Trouble.

Her stomach did another churn. The echo of that word from long before Leslie had uttered it made her head spin. She should've known she'd be punished for taking Oscar's money.

No! She needed to stop taking on the mantle of blame for other people's actions.

Oscar should never have broken his promise.

There was too much neither of them should have done.

Unlike Richard, Oscar had not left her everything he owned. It was a neat little sum, but it didn't even scratch the surface of the wealth he'd accumulated. Just his home in Bandra had been sold for several million dollars. Bindu knew this only because she had always been a Bollywood news junkie. It had nothing to do with the fact that her brain zeroed in on any scrap of information she'd ever been able to gather about him.

This also meant that she knew that Oscar had real estate all over the world, including London and New York, and he had left his children as rich as Kubera, the god of wealth. A thought arced like an electric current through her brain as she remembered that one of his grandsons was named Rishi.

Ashish watched her as she looked down at her phone. She had three missed calls and voice messages from a number listed as "Possibly Rishi Seth" from that morning. How had he even found her number?

"Ma, this is Richard Langley we're talking about, right? The guy who wrote *Death of a Whore*. He was a famous playboy back in the eighties, nineties, and heck, even the decades after that. What were you doing hanging out with him anyway?"

"*Death of a Whore?*" That was the name of one of Richard's books? She had the uncontrollable urge to laugh.

Before she could say more, her phone rang. "Possibly Rishi Seth" flashed on the screen.

Bindu squeezed the quartz of her breakfast bar until her fingers hurt. *Get ahold of yourself.*

"Listen, beta. I need to leave. Thanks for the sugar roti." It was time to shut this Rishi person down.

Oscar's lawyer had assured her that the inheritance was completely private, untraceable to her. Another lie. She no longer had the luxury of burying her head in the sand and hoping the problem would go away. If they wanted the money back, she'd have to sell the condo.

She loved her new home. She'd finally found herself here. But she loved nothing more than her family. Letting the door close behind her, she answered the call with the curtest hello she could manage.

The response was a surprised intake of breath, then complete silence.

"Hello?" she repeated angrily, ready to disconnect.

"Don't hang up, please." The voice shoved her into the past. Time and space spun around her so fast, she reached out and caught her balance on the wall. "Thank you for answering! I'm sorry, I wasn't expecting you to. You caught me by surprise."

It was Oscar's voice. Clear as day all these years later. A voice that strung together so many notes, it was like an entire harmony. Unchanged.

Goose bumps danced across Bindu's skin, dotting her from head to toe like pin stabs. The sugar roti pushed up her throat.

Silence stretched again, and she made her way to the stairwell used mostly for emergencies and let the heavy fire door close behind her.

"My name is Rishi Seth. I'm Oscar Seth's grandson." He let that hang in the air, as though he knew exactly what that name meant to her.

Bindu sank down on a step, the stagnant stairwell air heavy in her lungs.

In a moment she'd fake not having any idea who Oscar was. But first she needed to catch her breath.

"I just need a few minutes of your time. I promise it won't take long."

She cleared her throat. "Do you mean the old Indian actor-director?" Her voice was steady enough, but she was grateful to be sitting down.

He'd obviously not been expecting her to lie, because there was another long pause.

"Yes, my grandfather made twenty-seven films. He is widely acknowledged as one of India's best filmmakers." Was that amusement in his voice?

"Congratulations?" Oscar would have been proud of how well she'd emoted that. *Inflection is what sets the great actors apart.* She sounded utterly at a loss for why he might be calling her. "But what does that have to do with me?"

The boy cleared his throat. "It appears my grandfather had some unfinished business. I believe you might know something about it."

Bindu stood, heart hammering, then sank back down because her legs gave out. This wasn't about the money? It had to be. If it were about anything else, she didn't know what she'd do.

"Listen, I have no idea what you're talking about, and I'm late for something. You have the wrong person."

"Mrs. Desai, I promise I mean you no harm. I'm also a film-maker. I was very close to my grandfather." His voice trembled, and Bindu thought of Cullie. "Thing is, I miss him terribly. If you knew him, you know that he was the best human being you could ever meet."

Oscar's smile blazed to life in her head. If there were kinder, more vulnerable eyes on earth, Bindu had never in her sixty-five years encountered them.

She dabbed her eyes on her sleeves.

"Just five minutes of your time. Please," he said in Oscar's voice.

"Fine. What is it you want?" The words slipped out before she could stop herself.

"Actually, I can't talk about it on the phone. Can we meet, please? I have something to give you."

A secret is a cosmic impossibility. Nothing stays eternally hidden. A line from *Poornima* whispered in her ear.

Bindu sprang up. Suddenly her panic was so strong it made the slamming of her heart hurt.

This mess could not be anywhere near her family. Cullie, Alisha, Ashish: they couldn't know what she'd done. Ashish, her beautiful, confident child. His face at every age flashed in her head.

How dare Oscar put her in a position where this boy could destroy the life she'd built?

"Listen." She sounded strong now. Tears well and truly gone, swallowed up by rage and regret. "I don't care who you are, but I want you to leave me alone. You said your grandfather was a good man. Then respect his memory, and for his sake, if no one else's, don't contact me again."

Before he could answer, she disconnected and let herself back into the safety of the hallway. As she waited for the elevator, she put herself back together in the mirror.

"Damn you, Oscar," she said to her own reflection, fully aware of how dramatic she was being. "How could you let this happen?"

CHAPTER FOURTEEN

CULLIE

The woman who cleaned the room that we used to view the day's rushes found some stills from Poornima *that the AD left lying around when he went to grab chai. The woman was Bhanu's cousin. What she turned out to be was the inevitable blade that unravels every deception.*
From the journal of Oscar Seth

It was hard for someone like Cullie to fill out a profile on a dating app. She had no interests. Unless you counted coding, but that was more like listing "living" or "breathing" as an interest. Finally, unable to bear how much it annoyed her to see all the various things people were supposed to feel passionate about, she picked animals.

She liked animals well enough. They were certainly easier to deal with than humans. Her family had had a dog when Cullie was growing up. Duke had passed away when Cullie was fifteen. He'd been her best friend her whole life—something Radha Maushi's son, Bharat, would take umbrage to. Because he was the kind of person who'd use the word *umbrage* in casual conversation, but also because he shared Duke's title as Cullie's best friend.

Mom and Dad had both been too heartbroken to think about another dog after that. They all were. Well, Binji had thought Cullie *needed* another dog. But Binji never pushed Mom and Dad about anything. It probably had something to do with her awful parents, who'd turned her into the kind of parent and grandparent who "let her children live their own lives."

Plus, Binji worked hard to never be pushy about what Cullie needed in terms of her mental health (a term Cullie had started to use in the context of herself only after therapy). Unlike Cullie's parents, Binji listened. Which was why Cullie had been able to tell her that she didn't want another dog. She couldn't replace Duke.

Cullie still missed him. Mom and Dad had adopted him from a drive to find homes for dogs orphaned in Haiti that Mom had been doing a story on for the campus newspaper she worked at as a grad student. The traumatized poodle had turned into their fat and happy baby.

The good news was that never getting another dog saved them all from a custody battle over a dog. Not that Mom and Dad would have battled over anything, so eager were they to prove their own maturity. An "amicable" divorce was supposed to be easy on children. But Cullie wouldn't describe her parents' strangely bloodless tearing apart of their family as easy. Her therapist had pointed out that a silent disease with invisible symptoms could be just as painful as a visible one. Cullie was glad she'd found Dr. Amita Tandon.

Cullie was also glad, and shocked, that Mom was helping her with the app research. Which meant that Cullie had to pull on her big-girl panties and give it an honest shot too.

Choosing animals as her passion had resulted in hundreds of matches. An alarming number of them men who seemed to spend an unhealthy amount of time inside a gym. This was not an affliction Cullie shared. She was completely at peace with her squishy tummy and her early-onset arm flaps.

Enter: narrowing her search to people who abhorred exercise. And bingo! She had nine matches. Extra bonus, the Neuroband registered true elation when she'd claimed herself as unhealthy.

Gaurav Amin and Cullie had texted a few times before deciding to meet at the food truck pavilion in Naples. Just as she got there, an Indian guy who seemed to be searching the crowd made eye contact. He was kinda hot, in a skinny, nerdy way (Mahatma Gandhi glasses, hello!) and surprisingly similar to his picture.

Making his way to her, he pulled her into a hug. A bit much, but instead of her usual kick of discomfort when people made unsolicited physical contact, it felt friendly. Unthreatening. As though he'd known her for years.

"Cullie?" he asked, after he'd hugged her, which was a bit backward.

"Who's Cullie?" she said, startling him before he burst into a big belly laugh. He had a dad laugh, the laugh of an older person, self-claiming and unabashed.

"Hot *and* funny?" He did an elbow pump.

Unfamiliar flutters sparkled in Cullie's belly. Could one fall in love at first sight? She felt lighter than she had in a long time.

Her Neuroband was in its perfect zone. Heartbeat, blood pressure, adrenaline, dopamine, all of it nicely buzzing along in harmony.

Good thing Binji had forced her to put on lipstick, because she even felt hot.

Let's highlight that gorgeous mouth, her grandmother had said.

You're only saying that because I have your mouth, Cullie had whined, but she'd let Binji hand her one of those glossy lip stains that stayed put until you scrubbed it off with industrial cleaner. Binji was a vocal fan of specialized cosmetics for aging faces. Cullie agreed: her grandmother's cosmetics were the best things ever.

Now, thanks to Binji, Gaurav's gaze did a quick and adorably discreet dip to Cullie's mouth. The bubbly feeling in her belly did another happy skip.

"So *Cullie* is an Indian name, right?" he asked.

She wasn't thrilled it was his first question, but he looked so earnest, she decided she was going to stop judging him and follow Bharat's advice from their phone call this morning and "let this date happen."

"Yup. But my parents decided to spell it using American phonetics. I believe the Indian spelling is K-A-L-I. Which would turn into *Kaali* on our American tongues."

She was babbling, possibly for the first time in her life, but he grinned, so she couldn't bring herself to care. "That would make you the goddess of war instead of an unblossomed flower bud."

"Yup, completely different vibe."

"You look like a Cullie," he said, a sincere smile crinkling his eyes.

She smiled back. "Honestly, everyone who knows me thinks I'm more Kaali than Cullie. You speak Hindi?" He'd known the meaning of her name without her having to tell him.

"Yes, my parents refuse to speak to me in any other language. It used to annoy me when I was younger. But it means I can speak the language my family speaks *and* my parents can't keep secrets from me by speaking in Hindi. So win-win."

"You should teach me. I speak very little Marathi, but I understand it. My parents and grandmother use Hindi for secrets. My childhood was filled with, 'Is ladki ka kya karna hai?'" She knew her accent was terrible, but it made him laugh that adorable laugh again. "But I do know the words to all the Hindi songs because my family is obsessed with those. And I only know what those mean because my grandmother loves translating the lyrics." Binji could spend hours explaining every nuance of the romantic ballads.

He started humming a song, and to both their delights she recognized it. "Dekha tujhe to ye samjha jaana . . . ," he sang, his accent sounding like Dad's and Binji's.

"Hota hai prem mastaana," she joined in, sounding terribly off key.

They laughed, their laughter threading together seamlessly, unlike their singing voices.

"I love that song," she admitted.

"Really? It's terribly cheesy," he said with a scoff. But the smile that followed was so warm and inexplicably familiar, she ignored the scoff.

Stay in the moment, her therapist's voice said in her head.

They did a tour of the food trucks, studying the chalkboard menus as they chatted easily. Turned out he, like her, had grown up in Florida. In West Palm Beach, not far from where Mom had grown up. He'd recently moved to the Fort Myers area for work.

They picked up their food: vegetarian tacos for him and sweet potato fries for her, because she just couldn't order meat around someone who was vegetarian. Certainly not around a vegetarian veterinarian.

They settled into a bench, where an older couple scooted over to make a place for them. They had three dogs with them, all of whom headed straight for Gaurav the moment he sat down.

The frail old man tried to pull them away, politely scolding the pups. But Gaurav lowered himself to the dogs' eye level and patted their heads and said it was okay. This somehow led to three tiny dogs pressed into him as he ate.

The fries were good. She asked him if he'd like some, and he complied, eating one and then offering a few to the dogs. Then letting them lick the heck out of his hands. Which he then used to eat his tacos.

When he offered Cullie a bite, she feigned disinterest. Dog-slobber tacos were on her no-no list, but she was determined not to judge him, since both Bharat and Dr. Tandon seemed to be perched on her shoulders, whispering in her ear not to do it. The conversation meandered lazily, touching on people they knew in common from West Palm Beach, friends of her grandparents.

"So, your profile said you loved animals. I thought you'd enjoy a trip to my sanctuary."

"Sanctuary? I thought you were a veterinarian." She watched as he fed pieces of shredded cabbage to one of the mouth-breathing pugs.

The couple got up to leave. The dogs did not like that. They started whining, and the owners had to drag them away. Gaurav bid them farewell with at least an equal amount of regret.

"I'm a veterinary therapist," he said, shoving his dog-slobber-covered fingers into his food. "But my life mission is to rescue and foster traumatized animals. The ones no one wants to adopt. I've built a sanctuary for them." He reached out and patted her hand with those very hands, and she reminded herself that she'd meant to wash her hands anyway.

There, she could too live in the moment! She even tried to focus on the fact that the touch of his hand felt nice, the slobber notwithstanding. Her family would be proud of her.

"I think you're going to love it," he said as they got out of their cars after a short drive and approached a blue-vinyl bungalow on a shady street.

Gaurav jogged up to his front door and threw it open with the excitement of someone sharing the entrance to a treasure-filled cave.

The first thing that hit Cullie was the smell. Like a punch to the nose, knocking the breath out of her. She was trying to stay in the moment and everything, but the place smelled like a full-body immersion in animal slobber, tinged with alarmingly acrid poop. So escaping the moment seemed much more sensible.

Not that there was any escape from . . . well . . . from any of it. The *sanctuary* was basically his house. It might have been cozy if it didn't look like a tornado had hit it. A tornado that had hit a pet store first and then carried all its contents and dumped them in here. Oh, and the tornado had also churned up a sewer. And a septic tank.

He ran his hand through his nerdy hair, which suddenly didn't look as cute when she considered how many times he had touched it with hands he'd determinedly refused to wash when she'd stopped to wash her own before leaving the food truck pavilion.

He took her hand—God, could he please not do that—and dragged her into the backyard. She reminded herself not to touch her face, something she tended to do when she was nervous.

Okay, so she'd been wrong. In there wasn't the sanctuary. This fenced yard with bald patches on brown grass was the sanctuary. Some twenty dogs ran at him at once. Also a pony. Unless that was a very large donkey. She couldn't be sure.

There was a wild gleefulness to the animals as they jumped all over him. A glee he mirrored as he let each one lick him across his face. Suddenly Cullie was certain this was *not* a moment she wanted to stay in. The deathly smell was multiplied a hundredfold out here. The sensory onslaught of what was happening was so consuming that she didn't notice something slithering by her feet until that something thumped against her leg. She jumped.

A flipping iguana!

Correction: a yard full of flipping iguanas.

There was a picnic bench behind her, and she jumped onto it, all the way on top of the table, the touch of the iguana still crawling across her skin.

If Gaurav Amin noticed that his date was doing a terrified, violated dance on a tabletop, he hid it well. With utmost calm, he tried to hand her what looked like wilted cabbage. She could no longer identify vegetables because the smell was killing her brain cells.

"Here, feed them. It will help you get over your fear," he said condescendingly.

She was quite happy with her fear, thank you very much. What she needed was a new set of olfactory nerves. Correction: he needed that more than anyone else in the world.

"They're harmless," he said, condescension turning to annoyance.

She was feeling quite harmed. "They look like they want to eat me."

"Iguanas are vegetarian." Yup, definitely annoyance. "And there are no recorded cases of domesticated iguanas eating live humans."

Where was the sweetheart who'd sung a Bollywood song with her?

She shoved his cabbage back at him, and he started tearing it up and giving it to the iguanas, fortuitously drawing them away from her.

"What is that smell?" she asked, unable to contain herself any longer.

"I've been gone all day, so I haven't done my pickup," he said with the kind of meanness people reserved for empathyless jerks.

"Pickup?" Yes, she squeaked.

Now he looked at her like she was stupid. No one had ever—*ever!*—looked at Cullie like she was anything but intimidatingly brilliant. "Yes, healthy dogs poop. There's no stigma in it. Want to help me scoop?"

That would be a no. She reared back, trying not to fall off the picnic bench and refusing to think about scooping ice cream. She loved ice cream, and she would not allow this experience to ruin that for her.

Too late. She was never eating ice cream again. If she got out of here alive.

"I thought you said you loved animals." That whine was certainly not attractive, and her Neuroband was backing up the realization that her initial reaction to this guy had been a complete and utter lie. She was never again, ever, staying in the moment.

"I do. But when was the last time you bathed these poor creatures? Also, is having so many animals in a backyard this size legal?" She heard Mom in her voice, and it was oddly comforting.

"Overbathing dogs can give them eczema." He picked up what looked like an old two-gallon ice cream tub (seriously, she was never eating ice cream again) and a hand shovel. "Do you know why your nose is all scrunched up right now?"

She had no doubt he was going to tell her.

"A lack of love."

He whistled, and all the animals seemed to flow in a wave to one side of the yard. Squatting down in the part of the yard they'd cleared out of, he started poking at whatever was left of the grass. "Do you know what love is, Cullie?"

She should have run for her life, but it was like being hypnotized, this compulsion to see what he was going to do next. *We're on a date! And you're scooping poop!* she wanted to scream, but screaming meant breathing, and that meant inhaling.

"Love is accepting the ugliest parts of those you love."

She couldn't argue with that. Also, generally, she couldn't argue, because that too involved breathing.

He scooped up an alarmingly large lump and brought it to his nose.

"Oh my God!" Cullie jumped off the bench. Iguanas or no iguanas.

"Love is knowing your pets so well you can identify their excrement by smell alone!"

"I'm pretty sure that's not what love is. But please don't do that."

He held up another vile lump, and nausea washed over Cullie like a tidal wave. "This is Maisey's. It has a faint smell of corn. Maisey likes—"

That was it. She was running. She heard barking break out behind her, but she hadn't taken a breath in too long, and her head was going to explode.

She ran through the house and into the front yard. By the time she was in her car, survival had kicked in. Tires screeching, she fled.

Until she pulled into the parking lot of Binji's building, she'd had not one single thought but *Run, Cullie, run!*

Breathe, she told herself. *It's safe. You're safe. There's no smell here. You can breathe.* But the moment she sucked in a breath, the smell was everywhere again, filling her nose, her brain. She needed a shower desperately. Jumping out of the car, she broke into a run.

And ran headlong into someone who appeared out of nowhere. Someone who most certainly did not share her loathing for the gym.

It was like bouncing off pure muscle. She landed on her butt on the hot blacktop, the impact jolting through her. He, of course, had caught his balance, as gym rats everywhere were wont to do.

He leaned over and gave her a hand. "Oh shit. I'm so sorry, I didn't see you." He had an accent that sounded a little like her father's.

She let him pull her to her feet, but there was something on her shoe, and she slipped—much like someone in this stupid rom-com she was suddenly stuck inside. True to the theme, he grabbed her elbows and steadied her.

Before she could pull away, the fresh scent of him hit her, the impact even harder than when she'd bounced off him with her entire body. It was like sunshine on a rainy day, like water in a desert, like all the bad similes in every love song ever. She almost pressed her nose into him and sucked up the smell, desperate for relief.

It took her a moment to realize he was doing the same. Well, he was sniffing in her general direction. The difference was that he wasn't having a set-me-free-with-your-scent moment. He was having a what-the-hell-is-that-stench moment.

"What on earth is that smell?" he asked, scrunching his nose.

She pulled away, because in their olfactory exchange she'd forgotten that he was still holding her.

Crap, she'd probably stepped in something while running across the yard to make her escape.

"It smells like diarrhea from eating rotten fish."

That did it. All the nausea that had been roiling inside Cullie rose up her throat. Running to the closest flower bed, she bent over and brought up her guts. Then went on bringing them up until she felt like someone had scraped her insides with steel wool.

The nice-smelling guy with the soothing accent was still there when she was done. Great, he'd witnessed the entire thing. She couldn't be sure, but she thought he'd actually stroked her back as she retched. Now he magically retrieved a bottle of water from his backpack.

Tapping the cap to show her it was a fresh bottle, he twisted it open and offered it to her.

She drank. Her throat was raw from the force of her throwing up.

"Maybe we should wash that off." He pointed at her shoe, and another wave of nausea squeezed her stomach.

"Yes, please." Pressing her sleeve into her nose, she poured water on her shoe and imagined Gaurav Amin smelling it to decipher which dog it belonged to.

When she looked up he was smiling, because she was laughing.

"Want to share the joke?"

"You don't want to know," she said, then added, "Thank you. And sorry. I learned quite a lesson today."

He gave her a curious look. "A hangover doesn't go well with the smell of poop?"

It was barely eight in the evening. How did he figure that math? "I wish it were a hangover."

"Words I've never heard anyone say." He smiled, and an aggressive dimple sank into one cheek. It stunned her so much, she didn't smile back.

This seemed to hit him hard. Something rippled through him then, turning him suddenly serious. "I'm sorry. I'm . . ." His eyes dipped to her collarbone, searching for something. "If you're sick, that was really insensitive of me."

"I'm not sick."

He looked shaken, so she reached out and touched his hand. "Everything okay?"

"Yes, yes." His smile was back, the wave of pain gone from his eyes. He shook his head as though reprimanding himself. "You're the one who just emptied her guts. I should be asking you that question."

"I'm not sick, and I haven't been drinking. But you wouldn't believe the day I've had."

"There must be something in the water," he said, mouth twisting in an oddly familiar way. Had she met him before? "I'm not having a whole lot of luck with my day either."

"Did you go on a date with someone who made you smell dog poop?"

The laugh that spurted from him was so sudden, it sprayed her. "I'm so sorry," he said, embarrassment suffusing his expressive face, and rushed to extract wet wipes from his backpack.

She had the odd urge to hug him. "That's okay. You won't believe the things I've encountered today." A little spittle was nothing. But seeing him pulling out wet wipes restored her faith in humanity. And hygiene.

"Did you say your date made you smell dog poop?" His large, thickly lashed eyes widened with shock.

She put the wipes to good use, scrubbing her hands so hard they turned pink. "Yup, he can identify his dogs by the smell of their poop." She started laughing, and he joined in.

Their laughter vibrated together, tapering off into awkwardness when they remembered they were strangers.

"You win." He swallowed and pointed at the flower bed she'd thrown up in. "It all makes sense now. Where did you meet this specimen?"

"Long story, but I found him on Twinge."

"Maybe use a different dating app next time?"

"Really weird that you say that. Which one do you use?"

The awkwardness was back in the way he studied her. How were they talking about dating apps like old friends?

"I've never used one." He sounded offended. Oh my God, he was vain. "Never needed one." Yup, vain as hell.

For the first time, she noticed that he wasn't just hot—he was dramatically beautiful. If you liked square-jawed model types who liked gyms. She herself was someone who went for skinny nerd types. And no, one bad experience was not going to make her rethink her type.

They stood there like that for a beat. The overheated blacktop smell of the parking lot mixing with the smell of the oleander blooming around them. The smell of home. Being able to register that smell was more relief than she could contain, and she sighed. It made him smile. Something he seemed to do often and widely. Possibly because he believed those dimples were making women everywhere swoon.

Now that she had noticed it, it jumped out at her. How full of himself he was. It was in how he carried himself, with loose-limbed confidence. As though he were someone.

"Why has *your* day been awful?" she asked.

The smile slid off his face. The proud shoulders slumped infinitesimally. "I came here on important business," he said as though he'd been waiting to say those words to someone, to let them out. "But I think I'm going to have to go home—to Mumbai—without a resolution." He looked so upset that Cullie was gripped by an unfamiliar urge to comfort him. Pat his shoulder, do something.

This was the second time she'd had the totally out-of-character urge. Maybe it was all those years of seeing her parents help people who'd just arrived from India. Taking them shopping, showing them around, trying to ease something they recognized and related to at a visceral level, the transition from outsider to local.

"Maybe I can help you," she said, then realized they didn't know each other's names. "Cullie Desai." She offered him her hand.

His eyes widened as he looked down at it, but then he grabbed it with both of his own. "That's a pretty name. You have no idea what your offer to help means. Thank you. I'm . . ." Looking up to meet her eyes, he seemed to lose his train of thought. Cullie felt a blush warm her cheeks under his gaze. "I'm Rohan. Rohan Shah." And then he smiled as though he'd been waiting his whole life to meet a girl who made him forget his name.

CHAPTER FIFTEEN

ALY

Bhanu once asked me, "Why are we supposed to be ashamed of our own nakedness? Doesn't that turn the vessel we live in, our most precious possession, into an ugly secret?"
From the journal of Oscar Seth

Radha and Aly had been friends since sixth grade. They'd become friends when Rick Johansson—possibly the most handsome human being Aly had ever encountered in her earthly life—had tossed Aly's cilantro-coconut chutney into her hair and told her that she *and* her food smelled "like ass." It had been a bafflingly unintelligent insult, but it had stung.

The upside was that when the time had come to write her college essays, Aly had mined gold with that experience: a child of immigrant parents learning what being othered in her own country felt like and the journey she'd traveled from that feeling of helplessness to being the winner of the John F. Kennedy prize for promising American teens as a high school junior.

The other upside—the far more valuable one—was that it had given Aly her best friend. Radha Kambli had used the incident to start an anti-hate club at Washington Junior High.

Washington's Activist Teen Coalition for Hate Interception and Tolerance. WATCH-IT for short. It had become known as the Watch-It-Rick-Johansson Club in school, because no one could ever remember what Radha's acronyms stood for except her. It was certainly the last time someone had poured an ethnic food into the hair of the person of that ethnicity in the cafeteria (food fights for other reasons continued undeterred).

To no one's surprise, Radha had gone to Harvard and was now a human rights lawyer in Miami and still the best thing that had ever happened to Aly.

"It does make sense that Cullie told Ash that a man died in his mother's home," Radha said, turning around to face Aly as they crossed the bridge that led over the shrubbery from the downtown Naples parking lot to the beach. "You'd want someone to tell you if a man died in Karen Auntie's . . . well, never mind. That's absurd."

"Is it horrible to laugh?" Aly asked, laughing. The blast of salty ocean air made a heady combination with the lightness she felt in Radha's presence. "You're the only person on earth who can make me laugh right now. And thanks for making me think about Mummy and sex at the same time, as though my marriage hadn't completely turned me off it for life already."

"Liar. That was the one thing that wasn't broken in your marriage." They stopped to slip off their sandals and leave them by their rock and then set off on their walk. Radha had several clients in the Naples area, and whenever she was in town, walking along the ocean the way they had done growing up in West Palm Beach was a given.

Aly savored the feel of cool sand between her toes and tried not to drift off into the past. "If you call getting stuck in a cycle of having horrible arguments, then falling into long silences, and then having makeup sex not being broken." Because that's where their marriage had ended up in its final years.

"Sounds fabulous, actually," Radha said. "Not just fabulous, it's genius! Taking the boredom out of marital sex by only having makeup sex."

"Should we slap an acronym on it and start a club?" Aly said, still laughing.

"Hold on, I got it. MOAN—Marital Orgasm-Apology Network. I like the sound of that."

The man running past them turned around and gave them a thumbs-up.

Aly was laughing so hard, she was in tears. "I hope you don't mean for it to be a secret society. It might be hard to keep it quiet."

"Good one!" Radha said delightedly. "MOAN, the sound of a happy marriage."

When their laughter died down, Aly found herself frowning again. "The last thing I need right now is to deal with Ashish. I thought I was done with that. Isn't divorce supposed to be the end of having to deal with your spouse?"

"Not if you're roomies with his mother. To say nothing of coparenting. Coparenting takes divorce into the death-and-taxes category. There's no escaping it." That was Radha-the-lawyer speaking.

Radha-the-wife was as content with Pran as anyone married for twenty-five years could be. Which is to say, she believed he was the best thing that had happened to her, 40 percent of the time. She had married Pran in the most unexpectedly traditional arranged setup. After being dumped by her college boyfriend over email, she'd taken "things into her own hands" and told her parents to show her "what they could come up with."

They'd done well. Not only was Pran one of the most solid people Aly knew, but he was also the most irreverently funny. Ashish and he were as close as Radha and she, and the loss of their four-way dynamic was one of the saddest casualties resulting from the divorce. Aly had lost the community of families Ashish and she had been part of after the divorce, but losing Pran and Radha's couplehood friendship was the part that stung most.

"I still think Cullie shouldn't have told Ashish. Is it weird that I feel betrayed?" A wave skimmed close to Aly's feet, and she let it lick the tips of her toes without breaking stride.

"Honesty or coddling?" Radha matched her stride easily and threw Aly a sideways glance through the barely salt-and-pepper strands she refused to color, unlike Aly, who'd been obsessed with not letting her gray roots show since the ripe old age of thirty.

"Coddle me, please," Aly said, knowing full well that Radha was incapable of not speaking her mind.

"I don't believe for a moment that Ashish came down to check on Bindu. That does not sound like him at all. Although this is the first time a dead body has been involved in your ma-in-law's shenanigans, so even I'm out of my depth here."

Radha loved Bindu—even more than people usually did—so Aly laughed. The memory of dropping a wine bottle from shock was so mortifying, it made her cheeks burn. If Radha knew she'd done that, she'd smack her upside the head for giving Ashish's ego even more oxygen.

But Radha was right. There had to be more to her ex showing up than taking care of his mother. Ashish and Bindu's relationship didn't work like that. Bindu showed up. Ashish expected her to always be there to make everything okay. Until Aly and Ashish's divorce, Bindu had never reneged on that understanding.

The converse of that was not part of the equation. Her mother-in-law was almost pathologically independent. She'd never needed any taking care of.

"Ashish knows you're here for whatever Bindu needs. You do realize it's weird how you and Bindu are together. Pran's mom is a whiny witch, and she gets worse with age."

"Maybe guys are only nice to us when we don't get along with their families, and when we do get along with their families, they take us for granted."

"Who the hell knows," Radha said. "Men want us to believe they're uncomplicated. It's such a lie. They're like knots under wax. How do you ever unravel a hidden snarl?"

"Ashish doesn't even pretend to not be complicated. He loves being complicated."

For the first ten years of their marriage, Aly had worked herself to the bone, worked a job that sucked her soul dry, taken care of the home front, the cooking and cleaning, raising Cullie, building a healthy social life, though Bindu had helped. Aly had made it possible for Ashish to travel for work and establish himself as a respected professional, so his hard work had been financially rewarded. Without her, he wouldn't have been able to do any of that.

It wasn't until he'd built a career where he made enough money to cover both their paychecks that she'd taken the SFLN job. The opportunity to be on TV, chasing a story, bringing things to light for the audience: it made her feel alive. It gave her the kind of joy she couldn't explain.

And yet she'd had to explain it over and over again, to everyone.

For the first couple of years, she'd even held down both jobs. Ashish hadn't been happy, but so long as nothing changed in his life, he'd been patronizingly supportive. Then she'd decided that if she didn't put more time into it, didn't give all of herself to it, she wasn't going to be able to get where she wanted. Another two years of staying on an intern's salary but doing a reporter's work, and she'd been able to move into reporting full time.

That was when Ashish's gloves had come off.

Aly had started to get regular pieces where she got to be on air. It was only a few times a month, but friends started to introduce her as "our local celebrity" at parties. People started to introduce him as her husband. He'd laughed, exploding with good humor. He'd played at being a great sport, made jokes about how he planned to retire once they finally realized her talent and made her an anchor. He'd always had a ruthless tongue on him. She'd even found his irreverence funny. But then he had started to draw blood.

For years he'd done laundry, because he was only home over the weekends and that was the least he could do, because he knew how much she hated doing laundry. It was an act of love that had meant more than all the flowers in the world he could have bought her. As soon as she made reporter, he stopped helping around the house. Not completely: just enough that she felt it. He started praising the success of his friends' wives.

When their friends took a trip to Europe, he'd say things like, *His wife is a director at Google. Naturally they can afford it.*

If someone moved into a bigger house, bought a nice car, he'd say, *Must be nice to have the comfort of two real incomes.*

At first Aly let the hurt flare into anger. Every spark he threw her way burst her into flames of temper. Then she started to grasp how badly their marriage was stretching under the strain of how differently they saw their situations. She tried to explain her side to him. Tried to show him how important this was. How the potential of it was huge. If she made anchor, she'd make up for all the income she'd lost.

For tracts of time he seemed to understand. Then she'd show up on TV, and he'd fall back into the precision cuts of his words.

I had a meeting, but I caught your piece in passing. It was blink and miss, but you did great.

Didn't Bob get his anchor job at twenty-five?

The phrase "you're misinterpreting everything I say" became easy currency in every argument. He used it to justify all the blood he drew.

Bindu's support, Cullie's struggles: it all piled up against her on the scales that became their marriage. Then Cullie dropped out of U of I, and Ashish stopped trying to be subtle, if he'd even tried before.

Naturally, your daughter thinks it's okay to be flighty and to chase after things on a whim.

Aly had never chased a damn thing on a whim in her life. That was the moment when she realized that the man she'd fallen in love with because she believed he saw her—really saw her all the way to her soul—no longer did.

"So you have no idea why Ashish is here," Radha said, pulling Aly back to the present.

"I don't really care," Aly said. "I have bigger issues to deal with right now. Joyce is hounding me to give her the Meryl contact. Thankfully, Meryl's people are doing a great job keeping things under wraps. Your son is my favorite person on earth for getting Sam to make the introduction for me. I owe Bharat."

"Well, I'm leaving all my wealth to him, to say nothing of my C-section keloid scar, so he'd better help my best friend. The fact that he'd help you even if I told him not to is beside the point." Radha pushed her hands into her shorts pockets. She always got restless when she perceived an injustice. Probably why so many of her cases were pro bono and the thing about leaving her son wealth was a stretch.

"I can't believe that Joyce is playing hardball with this," Radha snapped. "It's absolute horseshit. I have to agree with Cullie and Bindu. If she's making you hand this over to Jessica, she's never planning to give you your segment. There is such a discrimination lawsuit here—"

"No." Aly needed this job. "I love this job." She'd been miserable at the tech company. SFLN had given her a chance just when she'd thought she'd have to give up on her dream. "It takes time to change things. I want to do this on the basis of my work, not using legal action."

Those were possibly Radha's least favorite words. She believed there was no better way than legal recourse to change anything that was worth changing. The fact that Aly was stretched to the limit must have been obvious on her face because Radha didn't point out—as Aly knew she badly wanted to—that Aly had only gotten her job as a diversity hire. Which was a result of discrimination laws.

"Aly, sweetheart, it's true that we all know why they gave you that job. But you've kept that job for ten years for a reason!"

They had reached the pier, and it was time to turn around before the crowded part of the beach invaded their peaceful walk. She couldn't be late today. She had a date.

When Aly didn't respond, Radha took a breath and switched topics. "How have the dates been going?" Radha's face went from worried to gleeful in a fraction of a second. These days, getting Aly to hook up with someone was her second-favorite pastime, after pressing her to "sue the bigotry out of her employer."

"The first guy was obviously only interested in finishing coffee and then making out in the restroom," Aly said.

"I still can't believe he straight-out asked you that."

"I'm a pretty fit forty-seven-year-old. But seriously. I'm not having sex anywhere but on a bed."

"So you considered having sex with this guy?"

"Yikes. No! I'm just saying. Even if he hadn't made slurping noises while drinking his coffee, or had a pornstache, or hadn't only looked at my breasts when we talked . . ."

"Or suggested sex on your first date."

"In a bathroom stall! Even then. He was a no. But I met a guy on Tuesday who seemed like there were no terrible red flags."

Radha rubbed her hands together in glee. "Yay, no *terrible* red flags! Sounds like kismet!"

They laughed and then Radha got serious again. "So, this might come to something, then? Even though you're only doing it to show your ex that you've moved on. Well, whatever it takes."

"This isn't about Ashish. It's about Cullie. How can I tell my child I don't want to help her?" Even so, Aly couldn't believe she'd let Cullie create an account for her on Twinge.

Aly groaned, because having Ashish watch had actually been mortifyingly satisfying.

"Aly, I love you with my whole heart. But seriously, you need to get out more, and you need to get the hell over that loser you married."

"I thought you liked Ashish."

"Everyone likes Ashish. Being likable is a genetic predisposition with the Desais. They are annoyingly likable. But, sister mine, he's treated you like shit, and it's all sorts of pathetic that you're still hung up on him."

Aly picked up her pace, the tips of her ears warming with anger. "How can you say that? I am not hung up on him. In fact, I'm so over him that by extension I'm pretty sure I'm over men. All of them. That's how much I'm over him." She crossed her arms, because they tended to start flailing when she got this angry.

Radha stared at Aly in that way one stared at a window after they'd scrubbed it clean enough that birds were cracking their skulls flying into it. "You just heard yourself, right?"

"I hate you."

"You love me. If you're looking for a date you've already written off, why don't you go out with that syrupy doctor your mom's been hounding you about. Word on the street is that he wanted to be a priest when he was young. It might be kinda hot in a Fleabag sort of way."

Aly made a horrified sound, and Radha laughed. Tungsten. Who named their child that?

Ashish had called him Filament. Aly hated that she'd found that funny. But the man looked alarmingly like the human version of a filament inside a light bulb, wiry and strangely triangular. She hated that she laughed now. "First, that's just creepy on too many levels. He's like a cousin, given that Mummy and his mom have been friends since before we were born."

"That's not how cousins work. I mean, if Bharat and Cullie fell in love, that wouldn't be weird at all."

"Given that your son is gay, it would be."

"You know what I mean. What's the second point?"

Aly looked confused.

Radha made her signature impatient face. "You said *first*. That means you were going to say more before I interrupted you."

"Yes. You're ignoring the fact that Mummy wanted to set me up with Tungsten before I married Ashish. Now she'd never set me up with anyone because Ashish and I are still married in the eyes of Our Lord and therefore in her own eyes. Until death do us part, remember?"

Aly tried not to feel the rush of relief she now felt about her parents' having moved back to Goa after retirement. When they'd first moved, she'd been angry. Why would you move to a new country, have children there, then abandon them? Aly knew they'd left after she was a grown adult, and really, she might have prayed for Mummy to move to the moon a few times, but there was still something self-centered about it. Mummy called it "taking care of themselves," because God helped those who helped themselves and all that. Which was fair. It still rattled something inside Aly. Maybe if her parents had not moved back, Ashish would never have gotten it into his head to move back either.

The sky was starting to turn pink with the setting sun, and Aly reminded herself of the lightness of these past two years. After the initial shock of Ashish leaving had faded, the relief hit her. Not being in a state of struggle all the time was nice. Now that Ashish was back, that inexplicable struggle was the first thing that had returned.

It wasn't something Aly could explain, not even to Radha, but somewhere along the winding road of marriage, Ashish had become synonymous with needing to prove and claim her identity. To continuously ask herself why she was okay with things she would never let her friends put up with.

"Trust me, I don't need you or my parents to comb through your network of eligible men. All I'm doing here is testing an app for Cullie," Aly said as they found their sandals again.

Radha nodded, accepting that without question. "Drink?" They often made their way to Hobnobs for a drink and some truffle chips after their walks.

"I wish," Aly said forlornly. "But no time before the date."

"Well, don't sound so excited," Radha deadpanned. "If you're going to show Ashish up, at least show him up with some enthusiasm."

CHAPTER SIXTEEN

BINDU

The way she smelled was incomparable. When I told her that, she brought
me the parijat flowers she wore in her hair. I wrote that into the script.
Just like Bhanu, Poornima would be indistinguishable from the ethereal
scent of parijat. And the audience would smell her across the screen.
From the journal of Oscar Seth

It had been years since Bindu had experienced trouble falling asleep.
As a young girl, she'd burned with too much wildness—wild yearn-
ings, wild imaginings, wild hope—to sleep. And when she did, her
dreams were so vibrant they'd felt like flames consuming her, a fever.
Adventure and romance had played on the screens of her closed lids like
Technicolor projections.

Then those impostors had been beaten out of her by the battering
ram of consequences (as her mother had so neatly summed up her
disastrous youth). She'd made a fortuitous escape from having to walk
the streets selling her body (as her mother had so ominously predicted)
and landed instead in the safety of matrimony (which her mother had
so graciously taken credit for).

All through her marriage Bindu had worked hard to force her nights
into dreamlessness. The practice had served her well, bringing her peace

where restlessness could have corroded her mind. In widowhood it had helped her keep her mind where she was instead of letting it get lost in the past or wander off into the future.

Now her restless dreams were back, with a vengeance over forty years in the making. Ever since she'd heard the ghost of Oscar's voice on the phone, ever since his grandson's obvious affection for him had filled her heart with unreasonable warmth, even as the boy threatened to destroy everything she'd built, all of it was back. Subterranean lava that had been nudging for fissures too long.

What she'd felt for Oscar Seth had been volcanic. Untempered, destructive. What she'd felt for herself when the camera turned on had fanned her very being into an inferno. Oscar had used that, then abandoned her. Left her burning in those flames.

Bindu had not pulled herself out and rebuilt herself to let someone shove her into it again.

Nothing would touch the life she'd built. It wasn't a lie. Her family wasn't a lie. She watched as her granddaughter pushed a piece of chocolate painted with twenty-four-karat gold into her mouth.

Between Cullie and Bindu, they'd made their way through half the too-large, too-ornate box of assortments. Alisha, on the other hand, had allowed herself only one.

"So, you and I went on dates from hell, and Binji met a man who sent her flowers that look like they were harvested in paradise by celestial beings." Cullie made a pleasured sound even as she glowered affectionately at Bindu. "And chocolate that was definitely crafted by celestial beings, probably from the organs of magical creatures."

She was not wrong. Bindu had never tasted anything quite so delicious. Cullie reached across the table to pluck the card from the flowers that took up more than half the dining table. It was even more elaborate than the flower arrangements in the clubhouse run by the coven.

Alisha tried not to smile as Cullie mimed a gag reflex and skimmed the words on the card. Love so strong it was almost painful tightened around Bindu's heart for these two. The world would never see them like this, entirely comfortable in their skin. This was a world they had created, the three of them, because of who they were. This belonged to her, to this version of Bindu.

Since the Richard tragedy, the tension between Bindu and Alisha had receded to the background. Bindu could only hope that it would disappear entirely from there.

It had been weeks since Jane and Connie had been able to make their weekly wine o'clocks or pickleball. It wasn't just their fault. Bindu had canceled first, the day after Richard's death. Truth be told, with Cullie and Ashish here and everything she had going on, she'd been more than a little preoccupied. The fact that neither of her Sunny Widows had reached out much had barely registered.

Now, if only Weaselly Leslie would stop hounding her about Richard's will, they could just leave the entire incident behind. Bindu had stopped taking his calls or answering his texts after he'd refused to let her sign away the inheritance. At least Rishi Seth had left her alone since the phone call.

Then there was Cullie's app. It had given the three of them a joint purpose. Alisha had come over after work, and it was just the three of them for the first time since Ashish's return.

He had left town to meet with some concert organizers in Miami. When Alisha arrived and saw that he wasn't here, her relief had been loud enough that she might as well have smashed another bottle on the floor.

Cullie was still rolling her eyes at the card. "How I pity these flowers. For I expect them to survive not a day in the shadow of your beauty," she read out loud.

Alisha laughed.

"Does he work for Hallmark?" Cullie asked.

"If Hallmark existed in the seventeenth century," Alisha said. "For who starts sentences with prepositions but the most pretentious."

"Is it bad?" Bindu asked, trying to suppress the prickle of irritation.

She was not going to think about the parijat flowers from her garden or how she'd picked them for Oscar. It had been too many years since she'd smelled the intoxicating scent or thought about how he had looked at the fragile garland of the orange-stemmed white blooms as she held it out to him.

Leaning over, Bindu smelled the expanse of roses packed together to create an ombré effect, from a deep red to a pure white in an almost perfect fade. "It seemed sweet enough to me. Albeit a bit grandiose."

"Grandiose is one way to put it," Alisha said.

"Cheesy is another," Cullie added.

They were in fine form today.

Bindu ached to join in their laughter, but she couldn't seem to find her way there. "Maybe you two need to be a bit more generous." She tried not to snap.

"Sorry," Cullie said, looking anything but apologetic. "I didn't realize the difference between a date who sends you two hundred roses and one who exposes you to biohazardous conditions was a matter of generosity."

"I'm not asking you to be generous to Noseless Veterinarian." In fact, if Bindu got her hands on the man, she was going to knee him in the gonads. "I can't believe you went to his house with him," Bindu said. Usually, she worried that Cullie trusted no one, but knowing whom to protect yourself from and whom to trust: that was the vital thing. A thing Bindu had learned a little too early in life. Or maybe too late.

Alisha and Cullie exchanged a look that said Bindu couldn't possibly understand their plight. Why, because of some chocolates and roses?

"It's easy for you to judge, Binji," Cullie said. "You've never done anything stupid in your life."

Bindu knew Cullie meant it as a compliment, but her words fell on Bindu like the slice of a knife. She turned to Alisha but found no understanding there either.

"This comes easy to you, Ma. Making friends, men, dating. It's a good thing. We wish we could be like you."

"Dating? Until six months ago, I'd never been on a date in my life!" They knew this.

"And yet look at the flowers littering this place," Cullie said. "You don't know what it's like to be stuck in a humiliating situation, to not know how to get out of it."

Bindu swallowed back the laugh that threatened to burst from her. If she didn't swallow it back, she was going to cackle like someone who'd lost their hold on reality.

"Remember the man who packed up my leftovers, including my half-eaten bread, and took it home? After he'd made me pay for dinner," Alisha went on. "And the one who spent the entire time filling me in over coffee on all the foods that gave him gas. I get scavengers and flatulents, and you get extravagant gifters and Hallmark poets."

Bindu looked from one teasing face to the other. Her girls, who were her whole life, the two people in the world who knew her best, knew nothing about her.

Cullie doubled over with laughter, and Alisha smacked her on the back.

"I still can't believe you waited until he shoved poop in your nose to run!" Alisha said.

They shuddered in unison through what they thought was humiliation. What would they think if they knew what real humiliation looked like?

Bindu manufactured a smile, but it took everything she had.

Alisha and Cullie studied her as though they'd suddenly noticed that she wasn't with them. *Why isn't this cracking you up?* their curious gazes asked.

"Listen," Bindu said. "It's been two bad dates and a few underwhelming exchanges over the phone. We're doing this for Cullie's app, remember?" Her eyes slid from Alisha to Cullie.

One of the reasons Bindu had suggested helping was that both Alisha and Cullie needed to get out more. To live more. She didn't want them to reach sixty-five and have this sense of having let life pass them by.

"We can't stop until Cullie has what she needs. And if we find love along the way, that's just a bonus."

Alisha's eyes went round with horror. Bindu might as well have suggested mud wrestling, which honestly wouldn't be a bad thing for Alisha to try. "I am most certainly not looking for love," Alisha said as though her dearest wish was to undo the time she *had* been in love. "Before we go on, I need both of you to be very clear on that. I'm only doing this to help Cullie get something to NewReal."

"Breathe, Mom. It won't kill you to believe in a little magic." Those were the most uncharacteristic words that had ever come out of her granddaughter. Had she just used the word *magic*?

Cullie noticed the shock on Bindu's face. "It's not like we're asking you to skydive out of a plane," she added, throwing in a little more of her usual prickliness. Did she think Bindu was that easy to fool?

Alisha studied the roses as though something about them had turned suddenly disturbing. "Honestly, it feels like you are."

"It's dating, Alisha!" Bindu snapped, mood cartwheeling again. "How can you compare it to jumping out of a plane? It's just being able to go out and enjoy someone's company and maybe find someone who makes you feel seen. And you have limitless choice." She spun around, such annoyance burning in her that Alisha stepped back from the ferocity of it.

Before Alisha could respond, Bindu held up her phone. "On here, in your hand, you can scroll through your choices, filter . . . *filter* by things that make you happy. And you can do it without having to hide it from anyone. And you're acting as though all of this is a curse."

"I never said it was a curse," Alisha said gently, obviously seeing right through to the storm that had suddenly sprung to full, violent force inside Bindu. "But if it's a choice, then I should be able to choose not wanting it."

Bindu blinked and dropped onto the couch, winded by the outburst.

"Ma, you okay?" Filling a glass with water, Alisha came to her. "You don't have to do this so soon after what happened with Richard."

Bindu blinked again, and some of that trancelike anger inside her cleared. "Richard? You think this is about Richard? This isn't about Richard. This is about the fact that someone like Richard can exist."

Cullie spurted a laugh. "Except Richard doesn't exi—"

"Cullie!" both Alisha and Bindu snapped.

"Stop it! Both of you." Bindu glared at Cullie. "At your age, if I so much as looked sideways at a man I wasn't married to, they called me a prostitute." Then she turned to Alisha. "And at your age, I was widowed and expected to spend the rest of my life in the demure memory of my husband. Do you not understand what you have? What we as women have?"

Cullie looked like Bindu had slapped her. "Binji, are you crying?" She looked at Alisha so helplessly, and Alisha looked so lost in response, that Bindu was struck by the fact that they had never seen her truly upset.

No one ever had. How was that even possible? Her feelings had once been so huge, she'd had to work to breathe around them. Not just how she'd felt about Oscar and *Poornima* but about everything. How free her grandmother's stories had made her feel, how stifling her mother's rules had felt. The joy as she'd run into the ocean. The humiliation when Rupa, one of the actresses in *Poornima*, accused her of stealing her earrings when Bindu wouldn't show the security guards the parijat garland she'd hidden in her bag for Oscar because she'd known they'd laugh at her if they found it.

It had all been huge. Her laughter, her tears, even her whispers. Everything loud inside her. Powerful. And now she couldn't recognize her own raised voice.

Ashish, Alisha, and Cullie had always teased her about having a flourish for the dramatic, but they'd only witnessed the tip after her iceberg had been swallowed up by the ocean. She'd been method acting a role as herself for forty-eight years.

Eyes bright with worry, Alisha squatted in front of Bindu and tried to take her hand. But Bindu sprang up and slapped away tears that surprised her more than anything else.

There was a reason she'd put herself away. Big feelings hurt.

"Of course I'm not crying. I just wish you could understand how it used to be." They would never know. Never get it. "This moment, the thing we're trying to do together, my mother would have disowned me for this. She would have held me down and pushed poison into my mouth with her own hands. We have each other. We have these opportunities, and you two won't stop being too scared to be vulnerable."

For a full minute no one said anything.

Hypocrite, a voice whispered inside her. She cleared her throat. This portal into her past would take her nowhere but right back into the pain. Not just for her but for those she loved. It was not the same as what Alisha and Cullie were doing. "Cullie, what do you need to get this app business done?"

"Why don't we go over what we learned and what we could have done differently," Alisha said, trying to relay a silent message to Cullie to let it go.

Listen to your mother. Bindu sent her own silent message Cullie's way. Letting it go, the way Alisha was so easily able to, was the only way to survive this world.

CHAPTER SEVENTEEN

CULLIE

At its heart Poornima *is the story of what life demands of us and a woman who dares to use it to claim what she wants.*
From the journal of Oscar Seth

Mom and Binji were making chai to dissipate the tension after Binji's outburst. The smell of lemongrass and ginger mixed with their bantering over the right quantities of those ingredients and wafted into Binji's bedroom. Cullie tried to let it calm her but failed. She stared at the mess of paper and Post-it Notes pinned all over the walls of the nook in Binji's bedroom that Cullie had taken over. None of it made even a little bit of sense.

Her work was supposed to be her solace, her distraction technique when her brain started to vibrate with uncontrollable thoughts.

A massive wave washed over her, and she sat down on the bed and starfished her arms, giving up resistance and letting the anxious feeling pass through her. *In for four, out for six.* She slipped on her headphones and let the chants from Shloka ebb and flow with her breaths. Finally, when her Neuroband registered her body's coming back into balance, she picked up her laptop.

"Are you sure a dating app is what you want to do next?" Mom asked, entering the room as though it were filled with land mines.

Binji followed her, still looking a little off balance. Her reaction earlier had been the weirdest thing. For the first time in her life, Cullie felt like maybe she didn't know her grandmother as well as she thought she did.

"Neither of us is particularly interested in dating," Mom said, handing Cullie her chai (and her agenda) and sitting down cross-legged on the rug.

Cullie shrugged, wishing everyone would stop saying that to her. A message from Rohan popped up on her screen, and a smile quirked her lips before she could suppress it.

Maybe dating wasn't rocket science. "I didn't think I was. But you were right. There has to be better than Steve out there."

"Definitely," both Mom and Binji said together, which made them smile too, making the tension in the room melt away.

Binji sat down on the bed next to Cullie. "You seem to be enjoying this more than you thought, right? Despite Noseless Veterinarian."

Cullie shrugged again, barely hearing her grandmother, who cleared her throat in response to being ignored.

"Sorry." Cullie shut down the text window and looked up. "Just helping a friend with where to find lingerie for his sisters."

Binji and Mom gaped at her and sidled closer to get a peek at her screen.

"So, lessons learned. Let's do this," she said, refusing to meet their probing gazes. "You're right, Binji. Noseless Vet might have scarred me for life, but it was just one date. You're not hating it, either, right?"

Binji nodded, a faraway look softening her eyes. "I do enjoy the flowers and the chocolates. But what I like most is the sense of freedom to choose."

"I thought you chose Ajoba," Cullie said.

The bitterest laugh spurted out of Binji. She slapped a hand across her mouth, horrified that she'd laughed. "I did. But back then we used the word *choice* rather more broadly. Never mind all that. My point is that this online dating cannot all be an empty promise," she said fiercely.

"Our first experiences prove otherwise," Mom said, obviously still convinced that they might be barking up the wrong tree with the app.

Cullie and Binji cut her identical looks that said: *Coward.*

"Fine. Do we at least know what we're trying to prove?" Mom said, making an "I'm going to be brave now" face.

"Aren't we trying to find a way to make online dating more effective?" Binji said.

"And less painful?" Mom said, getting into it.

"More effective, less painful. Check and check." Cullie scrunched up her nose: the memory of the foul smell was back.

Following close behind it was the way Rohan had smiled when she'd smelled him. She started tapping at her keyboard in earnest. "I did a little hacking into Twinge's code to find out why we were matched with these particular men from the millions of people on there." This was her zone, the space where she felt fully in possession of herself.

"That's a good place to start. If, from the endless volume of options, these were the options we got matched with," Mom said, "then something is wrong."

"Since it's all data driven, either they're gathering the wrong data or we're giving them the wrong data," Cullie said, her brain and her fingers on the keyboard moving as one.

When they had signed on, Twinge asked a bunch of generic questions that seemingly spoke to nothing in particular and then parsed keywords from the answers as criteria for the matches.

Cullie had said "love animals and hate exercise" to narrow her options.

"To be fair the poop-smelling vet satisfied those qualities," Mom said.

Binji had put in "love wine and world cinema" and done okay. So, then, were the results random?

"I'm not saying there was anything wrong with the man," Binji said. "Especially when compared with what happened with you two. He obviously has good taste in flowers." Her tone suggested there was a *but* coming.

"Or a personal assistant who does," Cullie pointed out.

"True." Binji scratched at a nonexistent spot on the sleeve of her caftan. That uncharacteristic restlessness was back. "But at dinner he ordered my meal for me, without even asking if he could. And he was excited that I'd never had a job."

How had Cullie never considered that not having worked outside the home was something that bothered Binji? She'd never gone to college, and she'd often said that the women of her time, especially military officers' wives, hardly ever had jobs. Had it always made her this . . . this *unhappy*?

Binji met the question in Cullie's eyes with deliberate blankness. The most un-Binji look ever. She wasn't going to go there. "He basically spent our entire time together talking about himself. But that's probably because I am very good at acting interested."

Cullie's fingers continued to fly across her keyboard. "Between the three of us, a few horror dates and one good one would have been acceptable. But if our rate is one hundred percent duds, then that's terrible." She was back to square one.

Who was she kidding? She'd never left square one.

"Even if we could find a way to prevent the truly terrible ones, that would be something," Mom said.

Binji looked at Mom as though she'd hit on something major. "That's an important distinction. What defines *truly* terrible?"

"Smelling animal poop and conversations about gas seem pretty terrible," Mom said.

"Again, this becomes about who we are. What makes us cringe varies from person to person. Even being asked to have sex in the restroom. I'm sure there are women who are seeking men out for that same reason.

My point is, that's not how you—*you*, Alisha Menezes Desai—define excitement. But someone else does."

Cullie gave her grandmother a smile that she hoped said *I worship your brilliance.* "What we find attractive about people says more about us than about them! You called going out with someone a journey of self-discovery. About finding us, not them."

Binji looked sad again. "That's how it should be, don't you think?"

Absolutely. Cullie hadn't understood what Binji had meant before, but suddenly it made perfect sense. Her brain was racing at full speed now. "The questions apps like Twinge ask are supposed to tell people things about one another, so they can judge if they find those things attractive. But a thing is attractive to you because it appeals to something inside you that's part of who you are."

Cullie tapped with some flourish and pulled up some information. "Let's take Noseless Vet. One of my answers on Twinge's profile was, 'I'd rather spend time with animals than humans sometimes.' Which was a stupid thing to do, in hindsight, but it made him pick me. One of the things he said on his profile was, 'Obsession with your work is the purest form of self-love,' which probably made me pick him."

"And under less gross circumstances, passion for work is something you two might have had in common," Binji said.

Cullie shuddered, but she wasn't wrong.

"How can you know that unless you've met? What kind of data could have prevented that date from happening?" Therefore saving her from lifelong nightmares. Cullie bounced in her seat. "That's the million-dollar coding question."

"When my friends set up their children for arranged marriages, it was based on a deep knowledge of their children," Binji said. "Just like if Bharat were to set you up with someone. So your code would need to have the kind of deep knowledge a parent or close friend would have to sort through choices."

Cullie's fingers flew across the keyboard. "So what I need is to write something that layers over the code of existing dating apps. An add-on functionality that mimics a parent's or friend's knowledge and parses the matches based on that."

"But even better because instead of someone else's knowledge of us—however deep—we're relying on our own knowledge of ourselves," Mom said.

"A question that identified how much you loathe putting yourself in dangerous situations would have eliminated the guy who wanted to take you cliff jumping," Binji said.

"But not without knowing what I identify as dangerous situations," Cullie said. That time she'd run as soon as he said the words *cliff jumping*.

"So, 'Would you call skydiving exciting or dangerous?'—questions like that?" Cullie adjusted the flowchart. It was a mess, but now it was a mess she might be able to work with.

"Also how much. Like would you rather poke your eyes out than ride a motorcycle, or are there certain circumstances under which you'd do it," Mom said, her expression jubilant. This did feel like they were getting somewhere.

"So, answers on a sliding scale," Cullie said.

"The way those Myers-Briggs and other personality tests do it," Mom added.

Cullie stopped typing, put her keyboard down, leaned over, and threw her arms around her. "Mom! That's genius. We need a personality test that focuses on relationships." Cullie's brain was spinning. "Then I build an overlay app that sits on top of existing dating apps to search the information they collect and have it tie into the personality test. It's not going to be that straightforward. But—"

"It's a place to start. A relationship personality test that looks inward," Mom said. "Relationship ID Personality! RIP for short."

Cullie laughed. She loved Radha Maushi and Mom's acronym obsession. "Identifying the questions to pin down your Relationship ID Personality, your RIP, that's the challenge."

Suddenly Binji frowned. "There's something else we haven't considered. Will people tell the truth about who they are? Do they even know? I'd never thought about how much I hated not being able to make choices until recently. Maybe not even until we had that conversation today."

For a few moments they were all silent.

Was it possible to be honest about yourself? Also, didn't you change with time? Cullie had always thought she'd found one kind of man sexy. Now she couldn't understand why her heart gave little skips every time Rohan's messages flashed on her screen.

The cursor blinked at her; she was lost again. "Binji, what would you have chosen had you been able to choose?"

That unfamiliar restlessness that had been burning at the edges of Binji's eyes flared. "No man has ever asked me what I want. Men have always tried to solve my problems for me—solve me." Her eyes widened with surprise at having verbalized it. "It would be nice to meet a man who simply asks and doesn't make assumptions because of how I look."

Cullie's and Mom's brows flew up in unison. They stared at her, mouths agape.

"You can't ask me questions and then react like this when I'm honest."

Well, the question was: Why had she never been honest about these things before?

Maybe because they hadn't asked her before.

Mom recovered first. "So you want a man who appreciates a woman's brains and not just her looks."

"Well, I want them to appreciate my looks too, and it's not just my brain but who I am. The things I like to do, the way I feel about things, the way I treat people, what makes me laugh. So my looks, my brain, and who my particular combination of those things makes me."

"Okay, so then a man who . . ." Cullie trailed off.

Complete silence. There was no possible way to quantify any of that.

Again Mom broke the silence. "We're going to have to start with something a little more tangible to come up with this RIP thing."

"Let's break it down," Cullie said, and turned to Binji. "What are the things that you're happiest doing? What are the things you'd rather die than do?"

Binji nodded. "When am I happiest? Well, this, now, being with you two. Being able to tell you both how I feel but also knowing how you feel. Talking. Really talking. But also shooting the breeze and saying nothing of importance."

Cullie typed furiously as Binji talked. "What else? Hobbies? Why do you love your films so much?"

"Because I can lie on my couch and escape. Become other people, travel to other places, other times. But also lose myself in the art of it. Especially in old films. Films from simpler times, when less happened in a scene but it pushed harder. Where you had no escape from it. Where everything wasn't moving, and you could focus on the characters, fall into them—what they were thinking, what their eyes and bodies were trying to tell you." Her gaze went fuzzy; she was inside those films, lost. "I like to cook but not when someone asks me to," she went on. "I like to dress but not when there are expectations attached to how I should look."

Cullie had the urge to apologize: for not knowing these things, for all the countless times Binji had cooked for them.

"So, having your opinion valued. Being taken care of," Mom recapped.

Binji seemed to be unable to stop, as though a dam had broken. "A man who cooks for me and listens to what I have to say instead of writing sonnets to what he sees when he looks at me. Maybe?"

Cullie's fingers went wild typing. When Mom opened her mouth to say something, she made a grunting sound to stop her.

"I think I might have a list," Cullie said after a few minutes of running a search across the hidden data in the top three apps. "I used a sliding scale for some of the things you said. It's very, very nascent and minimal, but look at these matches now."

They studied the matches. Mostly men who wanted to take care of others but also seemed to value independence in others. The expected stereotypes: nurses, doctors, chefs. But also men in construction and technology.

Finally, Binji settled on a fifty-seven-year-old chef who proclaimed himself busy and looking for someone who valued her own time and liked being pampered as much as she liked to do the pampering. Also someone who valued the planet and was passionate about reversing the damage humans had done to it. Someone who wished for a simpler time.

Binji grinned, back in her element. "I think I might be in love with him just based on his profile."

CHAPTER EIGHTEEN

ALY

Every time they humiliated her, called her a thief, laughed at the way she pronounced a word, she raised that determined chin and gathered it up into the fire she had inside her. Then she used it when the cameras turned on to burn them all down.
From the journal of Oscar Seth

That was really good, Aly!" Praise from Joyce landed on Aly as it always did. Like droplets landing in the dry well that was Aly's need for approval.

Aly knew she was not lacking in love. Cullie, Bindu, Radha: that love was deep and solid. Then why she'd let herself turn Joyce into the echoes of her mother, she had no idea. Why did human beings need love from where they wanted it rather than from where they were getting it?

Aly thanked Joyce. She'd reported on a frog farm that a family was cultivating in their backyard. The family's dog had almost taken a chunk out of Aly's calf, but other than that it had been as mundane a story as a reporter could find. It was, in fact, the nth in a line of mundane stories Joyce had been assigning to her.

Punishment for putting her in a corner with Meryl? Who knew. But if this was the price for getting in that interviewer's chair, she'd pay it.

After Aly had tried to be okay with letting the interview go, Cullie and Bindu were so disappointed in her for even considering it that she was unable to do it. So she'd written a show plan so perfect, even Joyce had been unable to do her usual *This is nice, but Jess will get more eyes on your work.*

Not only were Aly's production notes impeccable as ever, but she'd taken extra care to make sure her interview questions were based on her deep understanding of Meryl's work—something neither Bob nor Jess could claim. Then she'd straight-out begged Joyce to let her do the interview. Joyce hadn't said yes. But she hadn't said no either. It helped that Joyce had not been able to make contact with Meryl's team for the interview.

The pride Aly felt at fighting for it bordered on sinful, but she wasn't Karen Menezes, so she reveled in it. The idea of letting someone else use her hard work yet again made her sick to her stomach.

This time she had Joyce by her Meryl-loving ta-tas. Joyce had been "working through things with the sponsors" for weeks while Aly waited patiently, because it was a concession she'd never before made.

"We can't mess up the Meryl interview," Joyce said as Aly followed her to her office after they'd watched some footage in the war room. "Our ratings have been dismal this past month."

The Chihuly piece had garnered almost no views. Which was surprising because Slimy Bob's niece was even more adorable on camera than they'd expected. That was the audience today. A snoring dog got millions of views, and news channels struggled. No one knew how to crack that code. Aly had worked on a piece last week on fifteen-year-old twins who had become Instagram influencers with two million followers by tasting tacos around the Miami area.

Jess had done the interview. The teenagers had been impressive, giving tips on how to become "voices that people connected to" with heart-tugging earnestness. But really, the only wisdom about something going viral that you could confidently dispense as a tip was that it was entirely random.

"A Meryl Streep interview should fix that," Aly said with a goodly amount of smugness. Even as blasts of quick and fickle obsession rolled through the mass consciousness in endless waves, real art still held. A parallel stream of the world's consciousness still worshipped talent.

"Good job on that too," Joyce said. "That should sustain us for a few months. But we still need programming that keeps bringing viewers in." Then she brightened. "The initial reaction to the ads we've run about a new entertainment segment has been encouraging. We have a new ad hinting at the Meryl interview. I want you to see it."

Aly's heart felt like it was going to explode in her chest. She looked over Joyce's shoulder at her computer, trying to contain the urge to bounce on her heels.

The first thing that flashed on the screen was a close-up shot of Richard Langley, staring at the camera with soulful sadness for the injustices in the world.

Mysterious Death of Florida's Favorite Literary Star Tainted by Scandal about Estate

It had been almost three weeks since Richard's death, and the media had done some nice obituaries and not covered it more than that. But this headline meant Richard's family was still hoping to make trouble about the will.

Joyce made a frustrated sound. "Don't you just want to kick all men in the balls sometimes?" The bitterness in her voice was deeper than usual. "Did you know I was married to this asshole?"

What? No, Aly most definitely did not know that.

"My first husband. I met him in grad school, when he taught a class at Columbia as an adjunct. He's John's father. As narcissistic as they come. He left all his wealth to his last hussy."

Shit! Shit! Shit!

Joyce's older son was named John Langley. Somewhere in the far reaches of Aly's mind, she'd known this. She made a strangled sound.

"Aly, you okay? Do you need to sit down?"

Aly shook her head.

"I wish I could get my hands on that woman. How can someone have such little self-respect?" Joyce said, filled with indignation. Before she'd married her current husband, they'd had an affair for two years while he was still married to someone else. "Seriously, Aly, are you okay? I'm sorry. Did Ashish cheat? Is this triggering you?" She looked around as though the lawsuit Aly might bring for being triggered in the workplace was hiding in a corner.

"Ashish never cheated," Aly said. There were a million ways to betray someone. Cheating was only one of them. All the same, Ashish had been unflinchingly faithful.

Joyce made a scoffing sound. "Well, fidelity is such an archaic construct. I don't care that Richard was a serial cheater. But you don't do that to your children. You don't steal their legacy from them. It's a good thing this woman is hiding. Because when this story comes out, she's going to regret stealing from a man Florida worships."

With a fierce click she closed out of the news piece and opened the promotional video.

Vignettes of Meryl Streep in her most iconic roles flashed across the screen. A voice-over Aly had recorded boasted about having their town graced by Meryl's glorious presence. Then Aly flashed on the screen—Aly Menezes Desai, anchor of the new segment *Weekend Plans with Aly Menezes Desai*.

"It's just a concept," Joyce said.

But Aly didn't care. It was everything.

~

For the rest of the day, Aly had to work hard not to think about Richard and Bindu. At least Leslie was protecting Bindu and keeping her anonymous.

The last thing Aly was in the mood for was a date. But she'd set it up, and she wasn't about to let Cullie down. At exactly six o'clock Cullie pulled up in front of the SFLN building to give Aly a ride. She'd been using Aly's car and working on her app at a coffee shop near Aly's office. There was something strange yet cute about having her daughter drive Aly to her date. A throwback to when she'd driven Cullie around.

One part of Aly wished Cullie had picked something else to use her coding skills for. The other part wanted to believe that finding someone to be with was as simple as finding your relationship personality on a sliding scale and then matching it with someone.

Of course Bindu's theory had merit. Who we fell in love with . . . that magic thing that tomes were written in praise of . . . it was basically about what we sought in the world, what we wanted out of life.

What was it about Ashish that had called to Aly? Why had meeting him felt like coming home? Was it because he had an ease with life she didn't have? What did that say about her? The thing that she did know with clarity was what had pulled their marriage apart at its seams, slowly, steadily, until it had torn. He'd been unable to support her work. But why? That was the piece she wished she could understand.

The date Cullie's algorithmic magic had chosen for her today was an artist, which was totally up Aly's street. As always they'd texted and talked on the phone first. He'd invited her to be part of one of his art shows. So here she was.

Aly had offered to take Cullie home first, but she said she had plans too and needed the car. She'd been cryptic about the plans, but of course Aly was happy to let her have the car.

When they got to the park, instead of dropping Aly off and leaving, Cullie parked.

"Why are you parking?"

Cullie pretended to search for something in her backpack.

"Cullie?"

"I have to pick someone up. Just call me when you need to be picked up, and I'll swing by to get you." Her phone rang, and she answered it with the hesitation of someone who did not want her mother to know who she was meeting.

Aly sighed. Cullie was twenty-five. She deserved her space. And Aly needed to focus on finding her date. She headed off with some confidence. She'd done this enough now that it didn't feel like she was heading to the gallows.

The last guy Aly had gone out with had been lovely. They had bantered over coffee. He had beautiful eyes, which he'd used quite effectively to bore into Aly's soul the entire time, making her think he was, you know, into her.

As it turned out, he wasn't, because he didn't respond to any of her messages after that. Apparently, this was perfectly acceptable now. Cullie told her there was even a term for it: *ghosting*.

Mom, you have no idea how lucky you are to be ghosted for the first time at your age. Most of us have been ghosted at least seven times by the age of seventeen.

That made no sense. When Cullie was little, she used to ask Aly about dinosaurs as though Aly had been alive to experience them first-hand. Suddenly Aly felt like Cullie might have had it right. She felt positively prehistoric.

Ever since meeting her ghoster, Aly had started to wonder if she'd been missing something. The little tremble of attraction in her belly had been . . . nice.

George Joseph, the artist, not only had two first names, but he also had two of Aly's favorite assets: a nice voice and a nice smile. Both great for the little tremble of attraction in her belly. Which instantly registered something on the Neuroband she was wearing.

He beamed at her as she found him at the amphitheater outside Bonita Beach. He even gave her a firm handshake and friendly hug. "I'm so excited to meet a fellow art lover," he said in his lovely voice.

He held out a brown paper shopping bag filled with clothes.

She threw a skeptical look at it. "I thought we were going to the art museum." She was wearing a super-cute lime-yellow halter blouse that showed off her cut shoulders and arms, which she worked hard on every day, thank you very much, with skinny jeans. Was something wrong with her outfit?

Was this a new phenomenon, like ghosting, where your date brought you alternate clothing choices?

"We *are* at the art museum," he said, voice laced with meaning.

Meaning that bounced right over Aly's head.

Suddenly some floodlights came on, and a squeak escaped Aly because a statue moved.

"I'm a human installation artist. Today, I thought you'd enjoy being my partner."

"Partner?"

"We have fifteen minutes before the opening of the exhibit."

"Exhibit?"

Yes, she turned into a monosyllabic echo when she was caught unawares, so shoot her.

"It's not a big deal," George said. "We just dress in bronze bodysuits that turn us into statues and then strike some poses. You'll be amazed at how much fun it is."

Before she could tell him she wasn't interested and make her escape, a familiar laugh sounded behind her. She avoided the urge to spin around, because it couldn't possibly be.

It was.

"Sounds like the perfect date," her ex-husband said, amusement so loud in his voice he might as well have been yelling.

"Why, hello. I'm George Joseph." George beamed at Ashish, and Aly finally turned.

She wanted to ask what he was doing there, but it would turn a bizarre situation into an embarrassing one. So she stood there silently, refusing to make this easy for him.

"I'm Ashish. Aly's—"

"Old friend," Aly said. "I wasn't expecting to run into him."

"Cullie said she was driving you here." Cullie. The little traitor. "I figured it would be easiest to meet her here."

Right.

George looked lost.

"So, these bronze clothes. What kind of statues do you play?" Ashish asked with a little too much sincerity.

George found himself again. "Adult statues. The exhibit is called *Love Poses*."

Sure enough, there was a huge banner with the words *Love Poses* scrawled across it right above them. A banner Ashish had no doubt already seen.

"Yeah, good luck getting Aly to do that," Ashish said, his most annoying grin in place.

You're just not the kind of woman they're ever going to put on the air.

Aly was going to disown her only child.

"Oh." George Joseph produced the most adorable pout. Darn it, he was so sweet. As opposed to the evil glint in her ex's eye. "I thought she might—"

"He has no idea what I will and will not do."

"So you'll do it?" both men said together in entirely different tones, one all excitement, the other all challenge.

Aly snatched the bag from George and stormed off to the public restrooms.

"Cullie is waiting for you in the car," she threw over her shoulder as she left, hoping he'd be gone by the time she returned.

He was. But George was right there. Hair and beard and all of him alarmingly bronze. And . . . well . . . he seemed to be stark naked. Well, fake stark naked. Seeing her expression, he grinned, flashing bronze-painted teeth behind bronze lips. The whites of his eyes were the only part of him that was not bronze.

But coming back to the nakedness . . . was that a prosthetic, um, organ hanging from him?

Aly shoved the bag filled with her clothes at his fake junk.

"This is an adults-only installation. Don't worry," he said, pointing to the seven other couples also dressed in metallic leotards. It wasn't until she saw the other statue couples that Aly looked down at herself. Yup. Her bronze leotard had embossed, and quilted, nipples.

She squealed in shock and then let her gaze drop lower, to the pretty lifelike wiry bronze fuzz between her legs. The restroom had no full-length mirror, and Aly had been in such a rage, she hadn't noticed.

She yanked the bag back and covered her own fake junk this time. "Are you out of your mind?" she said.

"Art is about normalizing the natural world."

What did that even mean?

"How can we love and accept each other if we can't even accept our own bodies?"

"But this isn't my body. It's quilting and . . . steel wool?"

"I thought you said you loved art," he said, a whine showing up in his voice. "Come on. Where's your sense of adventure?"

Before she could respond, or run for her life, a woman—painted entirely silver and also bedecked with fake genitals—brought him a jar of bronze paint. "So real," she declared, voice choked with emotion, studying Aly from head to toe.

"Truth," George said, and they slid into a joint trance of examination.

Aly threw a glance around the garden to make sure Ashish was gone. Because if he wasn't, she was going to have to run away to Antarctica and never show her face again.

"Your friend is gone," George said, beckoning her with the brush dipped in bronze paint. "I sensed a lot of negativity in him. You shouldn't let his energy bind you. If you let it keep you from reaching for this gift of experience, from living your life, doesn't his negativity win?"

Aly squeezed her eyes shut. And shoved her face at him. "Let's do it," she said as paint brushed down her nose, knowing full well that she was going to regret those words.

CHAPTER NINETEEN

BINDU

When I wrote Poornima, *I hadn't planned on playing that scene out on film. But then I hadn't planned on Bhanu turning into Poornima. With her whole soul. And there was no way to keep that final surrender, that ultimate claiming, from the audience.*
From the journal of Oscar Seth

The chef, with his pure-white ponytail and almost glacially blue eyes, slipped his hand into Bindu's. It was a good hand, warm and capable. They walked along Marco Island's main beach, the art deco high-rises lining the ocean dwarfing them. A salty gust of wind hit her, and she pushed her hand against her sun hat to hold it in place. Nostalgia for Goa slid down her skin like a monsoon shower.

"You're a vision," Ray the Chef said. Yes, he'd introduced himself that way: *I'm Ray, the chef.* Now Bindu could only ever think of him as Ray the Chef.

"I'm Bindu," she'd answered, followed by a pause that had nothing substantial to fill it. Bindu, the grandma, the mother, the widow? The actress who could've been the defining moment in the career of one of the world's most celebrated filmmakers, had the world been a different place? The latest addition to a community for your vibrant years?

If she had to choose one, she'd choose that last one, because she did feel vibrant. And honestly, that was the one thing still within her control: who she was now.

"You look like you were born to walk by an ocean." Ray the Chef was still talking. His voice was gravelly with sharp edges, like someone used to issuing commands in a kitchen. A distinctly male tone in her day. Now she smiled every time she thought about her Cullie having it too. This unapologetic authority.

"Funny you say that," she said, slipping her hand out of his to adjust her hat and retie the strings at her chin. "I was born a few feet from the ocean."

This seemed to delight him. Ice-chip eyes glittered in a way that made Bindu think of him tasting a new dish and then throwing a chef's kiss at it.

"In Goa, India," she added, loving the taste of her hometown's name on her tongue.

"Goa!" he said, also savoring the word. "It's been years since I visited. Some of the best food I've ever eaten."

She wasn't surprised. Almost every American she'd ever met who'd been to India had visited Goa. Agra, Jaipur, and Goa were the trifecta of India's tourist meccas.

"Vindaloo, now there's a dish a chef can become obsessed with," Ray the Chef said, pulling her out of her memories. Memories she wished she could shove back inside the vault. "And xacuti, and sorpotel. I love that the names have Portuguese roots."

"Goa was a Portuguese colony until 1961." Bindu had been born in Portuguese Goa. By the time she was five, Goa had become one of India's union territories. Not that it had changed much about the way Goan people lived. The grand families in their mansions nestled in coconut and cashew groves on cliffs overlooking the ocean. The working fishermen huddled tightly in their hutment communities on the sandy beaches. And families like hers, wedged into the middle, dotted the winding lanes that snaked through the lush green countryside.

Talking about her hometown with this stranger was oddly relaxing. It was also disconcerting how the universe threw things at you once you unlocked thoughts. Ever since Oscar's grandson had invoked his grandfather and shattered Bindu's hard-won armor, Goa had moved to the front of her mind, and now here was someone who'd, quite unexpectedly, been there.

They meandered along the sparkly sand, climbing rocks that broke up the beach like scabs on skin. The urge to hum as she walked pushed inside Bindu, but she smiled at how ridiculous it would seem to him to hear her break into an old Bollywood ballad. *Not a first-date thing*, she heard Alisha say in her sensible voice.

They talked easily, skimming topics until they landed on two things they both seemed to like talking about: food and nature. He, like many native Floridians who loved the planet, seemed seized with the worry of disappearing beaches. He'd traveled across the world in search of sustainable food resources. Apparently the earth's population was on the verge of an unsurmountable food shortage.

"Ready for lunch?" he said when they'd walked for a good hour and Bindu had internalized some of his panic about how close they were to destroying the planet.

His skin was ruddy with the sun (no ozone layer!), highlighting the lines on his face. When they'd talked on the phone before they met, he'd asked if she had a food preference or if she was okay with being surprised. Being surprised had sounded perfect. But how could the man talk about food when they were all going to starve to death soon?

How had she gone from nostalgic yearning and peace to apocalyptic panic in under an hour? Well, maybe because he'd walked her through some pretty vivid end-of-days scenarios. And those glacial blues were not for the faint of heart when they predicted doom.

Bindu was shivering when they entered the restaurant. The smell of soy and ginger caramelizing on cast iron hit her, and she felt instantly better.

The inside of the restaurant was overcooled, as restaurants in Florida tended to be, and tiny. Not surprising, because the ocean crashed beside them, and even this much space had to cost enough to feed Florida for a day.

There was one occupied table, and now that she was inside the restaurant, there was something earthy threaded into the caramelized-soy smell. Bindu couldn't tell if she liked it or not.

"I love that you care," Ray the Chef said, fixing her with his blue gaze. "Not many people are this affected by what humans have done. We're all walking around, shoving our feelings down because we believe we can't do anything about them. But what kind of life is that? Are we even human if we're this desensitized?"

At this point she wasn't sure if she wanted to be human. All the times she'd thrown food out because she'd rather toss it than consume the extra calories burned inside her like an accusation. Was she even deserving of forgiveness?

"Ray-man!" A skinny man rushed up to Ray, and the two men gave each other a complicated shoulder slap that turned into a half hug. They said something to each other in a language Bindu hadn't heard before. It sounded so foreign that she wondered if they'd made it up. Then again, all languages sounded made up when they were foreign to you.

Ray introduced the man as the chef-owner of the restaurant.

"Beautiful," the chef-owner said, taking Bindu's hand and trying to bring it to his lips before Bindu realized what he was doing and tugged it away gently. They barely knew each other, and this wasn't Regency England. Plus, the fear for Earth's impending doom was still trembling in Bindu's belly.

Ray's friend—she'd missed his name in the kerfuffle over the Regency hand kiss—led them to a dark corner inside the restaurant, which was decorated to feel like a tunnel burrowed into the earth.

Not the most appetizing choice, but they had bigger things to worry about.

"I'm not sure I can eat after our conversation," she said to Ray as his friend left with a promise to send out a meal that was going to change their lives.

Ray laughed with the kind of fondness she'd imagined on Rajendra's face at Cullie's birth. Only instead of being jointly responsible for the creation of a perfect grandchild, this was being jointly horrified at the future.

"You're going to love this place." With the tip of his finger, he touched her breastbone. "This pain you're experiencing, this discomfort, that's the love in your heart for humanity. In another half hour, you're going to feel so much more at ease, trust me. This restaurant isn't called Taking Earth Back for nothing."

She hadn't noticed the name of the restaurant. But she liked it. It made her think of vegetable patches in backyards and fish from nets dragged out of the sea mere feet from the markets where they were sold. How idyllic Goa had been, and all she'd wanted was to break free from it.

"It's a nice name," she said. "Is it seafood?" Even though a surprise cuisine had sounded exciting, she wasn't comfortable with people ordering for her. It reminded her of her childhood, when her aie put the leftover fish and vegetables on her plate after feeding her father.

For all the things Rajendra had controlled in their marriage, he'd gladly and gratefully eaten everything Bindu put on the table. It had been a lot of great food Bindu worked hard at, but he'd acknowledged and appreciated that, and that was something.

"Eating seafood is desecrating the oceans." Ray's eyes flashed with an unholy rage that changed the air between them somewhat.

Before she could respond, a waiter brought out huge white plates and placed them on the table. Each plate had what looked like the tiniest gray dumpling at the center, drizzled with perfect lines of a very green sauce.

Ray popped it in his mouth, and his eyelids dropped with appreciation.

"What is it?" Bindu asked, bringing the dumpling to her mouth and trying to be discreet about smelling it.

"It's a rice cake."

She popped it into her mouth. Hmm. It tasted like . . . well, like chewing on a mushy earthen pot.

"What kind of rice?" These days they ground all sorts of things up—or "riced" them—and called it rice.

"Do you want to take a guess?"

Clay? she wanted to say, but she was too busy trying to swallow, which wasn't quite as easy to do as it should have been.

Before he could answer, another big white plate showed up. This time the tiniest bowl sat at the center, filled with a bright-yellow soup dotted with what looked like sesame seeds.

Bindu's cell phone vibrated, and she looked at it. Weaselly Leslie. Again. The man was relentless. What would it take for him to see that she had no interest in speaking to him?

Ray picked up the yellow soup and downed it in one gulp. It had been hours since Bindu had eaten, and that was a long walk. That rice cake wasn't exactly making her want to take a chance on this soup. She picked it up and tried to sip it, but the consistency was gelatinous, and the entire cold glob slid into her mouth.

"Nobody poaches crickets quite as well as Amey," Ray said.

The words registered in Bindu's brain exactly as the soup passed down her throat. Her stomach somersaulted.

"Isn't it amazing? If people knew that insects could taste like this, so much of the bias would be gone."

The gloppy soup wobbled up her gullet.

"What's wrong?" Ray reached out and took her hand.

Her phone rang just as bile rushed into her mouth, trying to bring the soup with it. Swallowing it down was the hardest thing she'd done. She yanked her hand away and pointed at the plate. "What did I just eat?"

"Wasn't it great?" Ray said.

Actually, it had been awful. "What kind of restaurant is this?" She looked at the menu and realized belatedly that the letters were . . . oh dear Lord . . . worms.

"Amey is trying to reverse the stigma on eating insects. It's the future of food. The only way to solve the—"

The phone rang again. Bindu answered it with a desperate jab at her screen.

"Hello," she croaked. "Oh my God, where are you? No! This is the first time my phone rang. I swear I'm not ignoring you."

"Okay," Leslie's confused voice said at the other end.

The waiter brought out another giant white plate, and Bindu pushed her chair back, the scrape of the legs loud against the slate floor.

"Oh, you're here? Already? I didn't think we were meeting until much later," she said into the phone, voice on the verge of tears.

"Bindu?" Leslie said at the other end, sounding concerned. "What's going on? Are you okay?"

Ray gave the plates the waiter put down on their table a loving look. It looked like paella, but instead of shrimp there were curly-tailed bugs and chunks of something brown.

The bile Bindu had swallowed made another resurgence in her mouth. "Fine. Fine. I'm sorry. I should have paid attention. I'll meet you outside. Don't be angry."

"You can't leave," Ray said. "This is Amey's pièce de résistance."

"Just tell me where you are." On the phone Leslie's concern had turned to alarm. She heard him moving around. The need to throw up was so strong now, she grabbed her handbag. Moving helped.

Babbling on the phone helped. "Oh gosh, yes. I'm done here, don't worry. Seriously. I didn't realize I double-booked lunch. It's on Marco Island beach. I'm not that far."

Leslie was saying something, Ray was saying something. The chef had come out and was saying something, but all Bindu could think about was getting away from the room where she'd swallowed bugs and emptying her guts.

The next thing she knew she was crouched over the commode of the impossibly tiny restroom, bringing up her lunch. By the time she could stand again, there was nothing left inside her. If she let her brain think about it, insects crawled up her throat.

"You okay?" Ray was knocking on the restroom door.

When she went back out, he had the gall to look disapproving. She had the unholy urge to push past him and run. So she did. She made her way through the dark restaurant that now smelled like the moist dirt of worm hills. The thought made her stomach lurch again.

"Please," she threw over her shoulder because Ray was at her heels. "I have to go. My husband found out I'm on a date. Sorry."

The man stepped back. "What?"

She had no idea where that had come from, but she blessed the brief period she'd fancied herself an actress. "Yes, I know. I'm a horrible person. Sorry. But he's violent. The last guy I went out with didn't end up well."

"What?"

Letting that horrified note in his voice hang in the air, she fled.

As she left the restaurant, the heat and light of the Florida afternoon hit her like a body blow. She embraced it. Her legs moved, and she let them take her away as quickly as they could. Away from those tunneled earth walls, that smell, those crawly tails sticking out from between fat orange fragments.

An ugly belch escaped her. The sun burned her skin. Yanking her sandals off her feet, she ran full tilt at the ocean.

When she finally stopped, winded, and dropped down onto the sand, she realized that she had remembered to grab her bag, but she had left her hat behind. Her favorite hat. Just as she was contemplating ways to get it back without coming in contact with Ray or the restaurant—even just thinking about either made the crawling sensation in her throat worse—she heard someone call her name.

Ganesha, please, no!

She was proud of how limber she was, but it still took her a moment to stand up on the soft sand. Making a run for it wouldn't be easy. Nonetheless, she stumbled away from the sound of his voice, pretending to not have heard it. In the absence of runner's legs, she would use compromised hearing.

"Bindu, you forgot your hat!"

Ugh, that made her stop. But forget it, she couldn't turn. She'd have to sacrifice the hat. She broke into a jog.

He ran around her and stopped in front of her and held out her hat.

"You really shouldn't be here," she said. "My husband can be dangerous."

He was in the middle of executing an impressive eye roll when she looked over his shoulder as though she really had a husband with anger issues and he really was chasing them. Now that she'd committed to it, she found herself unable to back away from the farce she was barreling down.

"Listen, I know what you're doing," Ray said just as someone else called her name.

They both spun around, equally surprised as Leslie ran at them, face florid with rage.

Dear Ganesha.

She ran at him before he did something stupid. What the hell was he doing here, anyway?

"Oh gosh, honey," she shouted. "I told you I was okay." Then, pressing a hand against his chest as though she were holding him back, she turned to Ray, the word *run* in her eyes. "We're just friends. We were just having a friendly lunch. Don't hurt him, please."

Both men looked shocked as tears started to stream down her face, surprising her more than either one of them.

"Go, please, go. Before something bad happens." She turned pleading eyes—with award-worthy tears—at Ray. Why wouldn't the idiot take his cue and run?

Before Ray could react, Leslie lunged at him, again seeming to surprise himself even more than the rest of them. Finally, Ray broke into a run. Instead of stopping, Leslie continued to chase him, terrifying Ray so much that he dropped the hat with a squeal and flew.

Leslie stopped, bending over to catch his breath. Then, picking up the hat, he walked back to her.

She was on her knees in the sand, laughing so uncontrollably her stomach hurt. He sank down next to her. Like her, he was wearing white linen pants, which were now as stained with sand as hers.

He opened his mouth a few times but couldn't seem to make words. When finally she stopped laughing, she realized that he was laughing too and looking a little dazed. He had on one of his pastel golf shirts, lavender today. Being on his knees had dislodged his always-tidy shirt collar, exposing a freckled and tanned chest. That electric sensation in the pit of her stomach from the first time she'd met him arced low in her belly.

His gaze rested on hers. He was a man thrown off his game. "What was that?" he said just as she said, "What are you doing here?"

Another spark slashed through her.

Instead of answering, she stood and started walking toward the road. She'd have to call a rideshare. Alisha was at work, and Ashish had driven out with Bindu's car to Fort Lauderdale to see some friends.

Leslie fell into step next to her. "You sounded like you were in danger," he said, answering her question.

So what? she wanted to ask. But something about it felt like fishing or going places she had no interest in going with someone who'd made it clear how much he disliked her.

"I was," she said instead. "But I am fully capable of getting myself out of it."

"Ah," he said, spinning a finger at the spot they'd just left. "So that unhinged-husband thing was you getting out of it yourself?"

"If you hadn't shown up, you wouldn't have had to participate. I didn't ask you to come."

"You sounded terrified on the phone."

So her acting chops were alive and well, then.

The thought shouldn't have made so much joy burst inside her.

"I . . . I wasn't terrified. Just terrorized. By insects."

He raised both brows.

Ah, forget it. If she looked stupid, she looked stupid. What did she care what this uppity, judgmental man thought of her? She'd faced enough of that to handle it in her sleep. "The man took me to a place where they serve . . ." She cleared her throat. "Insects."

A laugh spurted from him. "That Taking Earth Back place? Shit. Don't you read the Shady Palms message boards? It's been on the blacklist for months."

Silence settled between them at the mention of the message boards.

"Why would I be on the message boards? It's not like I'm welcome there."

"Since when has that stopped you?"

Her step faltered.

"I'm sorry," he said, quickly, sincerely. "I didn't mean to say that."

"Then stop. Stop acting like you know me or we're friends. You don't even like me." And yet he'd rushed here when she was in trouble. She hated men like him. Men who believed themselves so honorable, their own wishes didn't count in the face of the good of others. "I'm not your charity case. Just leave me alone."

He was still holding her hat. She snatched it out of his hand and started walking again, opening her rideshare app as she went.

"Bindu." Why was he still following her?

"What?" She'd always prided herself on being the kind of person who never snapped at people, but to hell with that. She stepped into his space and flung the word at him with a fury she couldn't control.

He didn't so much as blink. "I never said I didn't like you." It was a whisper, his green eyes so defenseless, it was like she'd stripped him bare. "I don't think I've liked anyone this much in a long time."

181

Silence burned around them like the brutal sunshine singeing her skin. Their breath became the only sound as they stood there, not knowing what to do with the words he'd just said.

Well, snap out of it, Bindu.

"Is that why you called me trouble? Because you liked me so much? Without knowing the first thing about me."

"Is that why you're so angry with me? Because I called you that?" He searched her face, confident that there was more, as though he *saw* that there was more. Story of her life. Men who thought they saw her.

She stuck a finger in his face. "One, I'm not angry with you. I don't do anger. Two, how would you like someone you'd never met throwing that word at you?"

"You think I meant it as a bad thing? You're exactly the kind of trouble I've always wanted to be. The kind of trouble that changes things. Anything worth doing in the world only ever gets done because of the troublemakers. Especially the troublemakers who know exactly why they want things. Because it's right to want them. Not because it's easy."

Her stupid heartbeat sped up. "Well, you're wrong." She'd always chosen easy. "But thanks for turning me into your preconceived notions."

He blinked, then swallowed. "Haven't you done the same? Assumed who I am?"

It was her turn to blink and swallow. She'd written his entire life history the first time she'd met him.

Suddenly he looked young and lost. "Even if you have, it doesn't make it okay that I did too," he said slowly. "I'm sorry." He pushed his hand at her. "Can we start over? I would love to get to know you, if you'll give me a chance. I'm Lee Bennet. I was a county circuit judge for twenty years. Recently retired. Widowed for ten years. One daughter. She lives in Ann Arbor, Michigan. I'd love to be friends."

This level of cheesiness from him was so unexpected that she took his hand and shook it. And giggled. It had been years since she'd giggled.

"That's a line straight out of a Bollywood film. Where the hero asks the heroine to be friends with him."

His smile was nervous. "And? Does she comply?"

Ah, what the hell. She'd eaten bugs today; she could do anything. "She does." She gave his hand another shake. "I'm Bindu Desai, and yes, I'd like to be friends."

CHAPTER TWENTY

CULLIE

How she could bear to go through life with such vulnerability, I'll never know.
When I asked her how she was never afraid of anything, she said, "If I'd been afraid, I wouldn't know what it was like to love you. If ever I'm afraid, I'll remind myself that being fearless gave me you."
From the journal of Oscar Seth

Here! I fixed yours, but my life is still an unmitigated disaster," Cullie said as she handed Rohan's computer back to him, his earth-shattering crisis solved.

Tears of relief sprang into his eyes. He hadn't been exaggerating when he said the file she'd saved was his life's work. With a quick swipe of his face against his shoulder, he wiped away the evidence, and a raging and unfamiliar warmth squeezed at Cullie's heart.

She'd never met anyone as completely comfortable in his skin as Rohan. *Borderline cocky* might've been a more accurate description if not for the way he wore his emotions on his sleeve. When he'd called her, he'd barely been able to breathe from panic.

Over the past two weeks, he'd called her for all sorts of reasons. Advice on where to shop for groceries. Where to find cosmetics for his three older sisters, who kept sending him shopping lists from India. That was when he wasn't texting her. To be fair, she'd been texting him at least as much.

At first it was only to test if the little uptick in her heartbeat when she heard from him or saw him was real. It was, and she liked it. It had even made hitting a wall with the app bearable.

The matches had only been getting worse. After their last experiences, Mom and Binji were refusing to help anymore.

"I think I might have fallen in love with you just now," he said, staring at his screen.

Cullie couldn't be sure if he was talking to her or to the file she had saved, which he was looking at with some seriously smitten eyes.

Then he turned those smitten eyes on Cullie. She had to smile, because he had what she'd come to think of as Bollywood eyes, the brown of burnt amber transparent to every feeling. Over-the-top eyes.

She'd never been attracted to men like him.

He is so *your type*, she'd told Bharat that morning. And he was. All intense with purpose yet gentle, like the quietly dramatic sky over the ocean before sunrise. Those deep dimples swooshing into that square jaw—soft over rugged—multiplied the impact many times over.

"May I at least see what this invaluable file I saved is?"

He stiffened imperceptibly. "It's a digital print of the film I spent a lot of time restoring." It was his passion, film preservation and restoration. *Films are time capsules*, he'd said to her when he first told her about it, the love for his work burning in his Bollywood eyes. *The only way to go back to 1950 in any meaningful way is to watch a film from 1950*. "There are privacy issues. So I can't show you." Then he got all sincere in a way that had taken to burrowing under her skin. "But I want to."

"Fine," she grumbled, surprised at how much his integrity moved her.

They were in the sitting room, every surface piled with stacks of paper and notebooks. How much was it costing him to stay in a suite like this? He'd been here over two weeks. She'd joked about it when she first got here. Since he was still struggling to get his debut film made, it felt like a lot. He'd responded with a quick "Trust funds have their benefits."

"Now that you've saved my life," he said, eyes warm with his boyish grin, "I can't rest until I've solved whatever is making your life a disaster." With an aggressiveness she hadn't seen in him before, he saved the file she had rescued from the guts of his motherboard like the badass she was and turned to her.

"It's not just a disaster," she said. "It's an unmitigated disaster." Why had she thought she could create an app for a thing she understood so little? The last two dates she'd been on had been oddly silent and monstrously awkward, and she'd promptly laughed about them with Rohan afterward.

"Why do people say *unmitigated*? If they were mitigated, they wouldn't be disasters."

She slow-blinked. "That's deep." It was strange that they'd been friends for only two weeks. She felt like they'd known each other forever, and making friends was not one of Cullie's strengths.

"Maybe you're unable to code this app because you don't know what you hope to accomplish with it. Maybe it's just a matter of identifying your goal."

"Wow, I can't believe you just low-key mansplained my job to me?"

His smile turned only the slightest bit sheepish, because of course he had. "So if it's mansplaining when a man says something you already know, then when a woman does it, it's . . ."

"Help?" she filled in helpfully.

"Ah. And you're telling this to a man who has three older sisters. Very *helpful* older sisters, I might add." Something about his face tended to turn both younger and older when he mentioned his sisters.

"Well, aren't older siblings *supposed* to be wiser than you?"

"Wiser, huh? Thank you, only-childsplainer."

"Ha! Did I miss the part where people with siblings have had to put up with only children assuming they know everything better?"

"So women never assume they know better than men?"

"They aren't trained by society to assume it. Were you ever told there are things you won't understand simply because you're a man?"

They were both sitting up now, leaning into the sparkly tension that suffused the air like glitter.

"Like fashion, and cooking, and decorating?" He made a thoughtful face. All his mannerisms were so darned expressive, it was maddening.

Every man ever would make the same argument. Cullie was a bit disappointed that Rohan would do it too. She didn't bother to hold in her sigh, because they might as well both behave like they were in one of those Bollywood films Binji loved, hamming up every feeling that passed through them.

"Sure, if fashion, cooking, and decorating were things generations of men hadn't been allowed to do before you, and even now men weren't allowed an equal shot at. As far as I know, men do quite well at fashion and cooking and decorating and always have. My best friend is a chef in New York City, and I'm pretty certain no one has ever told him he couldn't be one because he's a man."

Bharat felt the pressure to add an Indian flair to everything he cooked, but he'd be the first to tell you that being a man had never gotten in the way of his being a chef.

"Fair," Rohan said, and she knew he meant it, because instead of teasing her, his Bollywood eyes were now telegraphing concern. They were a potent thing, his eyes.

For a few seconds she sat there lost in them, the sparkles electrifying the air between them. A lock of hair fell over her eye, and his hand twitched as though he wanted to push it back, but then he seemed to catch himself, and something in his eyes darkened. "So, is that what's going on with your app?"

Her hand went to her hair, slapping it out of her eyes. "Excuse me?" She used the tone she used to get people to back off, but it didn't seem to register.

"This unmitigated disaster," he went on calmly, as though the moment he'd destroyed had never happened. "Does it have to do with being told you can't code because you're a woman?"

She laughed. "No one who's seen my code has ever been dumb enough to say that."

Instead of backing away the way people usually did when she told the truth about her genius, he smiled, and the sudden tension between them sank into his dimples and disappeared. "Given that you are the best coder on the planet."

Fine, she'd told him that when they'd first talked about their jobs. His response had been that he wanted to be one of the better filmmakers on the planet someday.

"Still, the pressure to get it right has to be a lot," he pushed.

"The reason I need to get it right is because I can't create something that isn't the best. Or at least the best thing I can create. Which makes it . . ."

"The best," he finished with her.

Twin smiles bloomed on their faces again.

"Is that why you have only one?"

And boom! The smile slid right off her face again. She pushed herself off the chair. Was he for real?

"I have only one because I'm frickin' twenty-five years old. How many multimillion-user apps have you heard of other twenty-five-year-olds creating? I'm not a damned factory. But if I don't get this to work, my asshole ex is going to destroy what I built."

He leaned back in his chair lazily. "So you're not letting being told you can't code because you're a woman get in your way. You're letting your ex get inside your head."

"I'm not working eighteen hours a day to prove Steve wrong." Or was she? "And even if I am, it needs to be done. I do need to prove him wrong because he is wrong."

She sat back down, and he reached out and touched her hand. Warmth spread beneath her ribs, calming her and heating her up at once. This was just who he was, touchy-feely. It must have been all those sisters who obviously adored him enough to have cuddled the hell out of him as a child.

Or just biology. It had been too long since she'd been touched by a man, since she'd had sex. She'd gone out with more men in the past few weeks than she had in years, and for someone who enjoyed sex and didn't mix it up with unnecessary emotions, the fact that she'd wanted none of them was disconcerting.

Rohan smiled, in that way he had of smiling with his eyes, and need bloomed inside her. "But is this particular app the way to prove him wrong? It's obviously something you're not interested in."

The urge to punch him right after wanting to climb him like a tree, followed by the slippery desire to share every one of her thoughts with him, was incredibly disorienting.

"And now you're telling me how I feel about my work. That's worse than mansplaining."

"Actually you said those exact words to me yesterday." They'd gotten into the habit of sitting at the café outside his hotel and working almost every day the past week. She trying to make sense out of the nonsense that was dating apps, and he working on the documentary project he was more obsessed with than she'd ever seen anyone be with anything. Except herself with Shloka.

"Honestly, I wasn't really into it when I started, but now I feel like it cannot possibly be this hard if more than half the world's adult population is in relationships. As a woman of science, I'm feeling pretty darned compelled to crack the code."

Between Mom, Binji, and her, they had gone on twenty dates in three weeks. Every date had been some level of a disaster. And the ones that hadn't been downright ghastly had been meh.

"Well, I guess that's the next-best reason for creating a dating app, after wanting to help people find someone to be with." His over-the-top eyes met hers, and that sparkly warmth slipped lower into her belly.

"I'm not certain it qualifies as help. Given the misery relationships seem to cause."

"One crappy ex nullifies all happy relationships, then?"

"Do you know any happy relationships?"

"I think my parents were pretty happy."

"I thought mine were too. Well, happy in the Desai way."

"What does that mean?" The man could hold your gaze endlessly.

"I don't know how to explain it. We make ourselves miserable in our quest for happiness, so we're kind of obstinate about it. Does that make sense?"

"Not even a little bit. But it sounds wonderful."

"Before you start imagining happy family portraits, I did tell you my parents are divorced, right?" Before he could ask about the divorce, she added, "How long have your parents been married?"

"They were married for thirty-five years. My mother died three years ago. She was sick for five years before that."

Pain so harsh it almost edged into panic flooded his eyes, and Cullie had a sense that she'd seen him like this before. The memory of his eyes flashing with pain like this nudged at her, and she pushed at it, trying to unravel it.

"Cholangiocarcinoma, a.k.a. bile duct cancer. One of the worst cancer survival rates. But she sent it into remission for a year after two years of treatment before it raged back." He said all of that as though he were talking about someone other than his own mother.

She thought about Mom and what life might be like without her and felt sick to her stomach. Suddenly she remembered how he'd looked at her when he'd thought Cullie had thrown up because she was sick that first time they'd met.

His arms wrapped around himself. "I'm sorry. I shouldn't have brought that up."

She sidled up to him and laid an arm across his shoulder.

It made him laugh, a laugh that came from deep inside him and shook out through his shoulders, which were bulging with gym-rat-level muscles.

"Okay," she said, unsure if she should be offended. She must be totally off her game if hugging a guy when he was sad made him laugh.

When she pulled away, he looked at her with the saddest eyes. "I'm not laughing at you. My mum was obsessed with seeing me 'settled down' before she died. So much so that she once suggested I use the fact that my mother has cancer to get women. Her exact words were, 'There should be some advantage to this thing.'"

"That's the sweetest thing I've ever heard. She sounds lovely."

He wiped his eyes on his shoulder again. She couldn't tell if the tears were from laughter or grief or both. "She was amazing. Big—not her size, her presence. One of those unapologetic people who radiate something special because they love who they are so wholly. She always said loving yourself is a foundational requirement of knowing how to love anyone else and that most meanness in the world comes from self-loathing."

"She sounds a lot like my Binji. My grandmother. She's like that. Big. A lot. But also the kindest, softest person I know. She's hard to explain."

He paled. Maybe comparing his dead mother to another woman was insensitive.

Before Cullie could apologize, he cleared his throat. "I'd love to meet her sometime. Your grandmother." He said it with such tentativeness that she wanted to hug him again.

"Of course, you should come over for dinner. She would love you. She's also an amazing cook. Especially if you like Goan food."

"What kind of monster doesn't like Goan food?"

"See, you're the exact kind of cheesy that would totally get to her." He was definitely getting to Cullie.

"What about your grandfather?" he asked. "Did he die before you were born, or did you know him?"

"How did you know my grandfather is dead?"

He blinked. "I . . . um . . . I . . . you said you grew up with your grandmother around, but you've never mentioned your grandfather, so

I just assumed that she lived with you after you lost him. I didn't mean to suggest . . . it's really nice of you to invite me over." He sounded adorably nervous.

"I have to warn you that there might be some subtle—or unsubtle—attempts at matchmaking." Their eyes met, and his already flushed cheeks colored some more. "Ever since this app business started, my family seems to have decided that my singleness might be something they can solve." Needing to be solved was one of Cullie's least favorite things.

"What? They don't buy into your belief that relationships cause misery?" He pressed his hand to his chest.

She mirrored his hand-on-heart action. "I don't see you, Mr. Pushing Thirty, with a wife either." As she said them, the words gave her pause. He'd been a little jumpy today. The attraction between them seemed to have come to a boil, and he seemed to be holding himself back.

He couldn't possibly be married, could he?

The question must've shown on her face because his strong brows drew together. "Come on, Cullie." He sounded angry for the first time since she'd met him. "You think I'd hide being married?"

"Sorry." Suddenly she hated how all over the place her reactions to him were. "Of course I don't think that. But I haven't known you long enough to know what you would and would not do. What if you've also lied about being a filmmaker and are actually an actor?"

He looked stricken.

"I'm kidding! For someone I've just met, I totally trust you. I'm here. In your hotel room, feeling safe." They were standing a little too close, and maybe she was being an idiot, because maybe it was dangerous to feel so safe when she also felt more vulnerable than she ever had. She didn't do vulnerability, no matter how much Binji's words from the other day rang in her head. The last time she'd gone anywhere near it, with Steve, she'd paid dearly. "Well, mostly safe." It came out a whisper.

He finally did it: he pushed the hair that had flopped onto her forehead back. Something electric crackled beneath his fingers, surprising them both. His hand stilled, but instead of pulling away from the burn, he let the back of his fingers trace her cheek, light as feathers. The reverence in his touch made her tremble. She'd never been touched like this. Her body filled with the need to reach for it, to rise up on her toes, to give in to the curiosity, to see what the deal with that lush mouth was.

He withdrew his hand, fingers trembling from the effort, breath shallow.

The rest of his body was still close. "I was engaged once." He swallowed, gaze steady on hers. "She was one of the residents on Ma's oncology team." He smiled. "Ma did get her wish of seeing me settled. Actually, Ma's efforts at matchmaking were epic while she was in the hospital. She was convinced Leena would make me happy. As it turned out, Leena wasn't happy with how sad I was after Ma passed. So she left. Because she 'owed it to herself to be with someone who at least tried to be happy.' It took my feet out from under me. I've been gun shy since, I guess."

"What a piece of work," Cullie said, anger burning her throat. What was wrong with people?

The brown of his eyes turned almost black, her anger reflected in them as something else. Another moment vibrated between their bodies. Breath caught in her lungs as she waited for him to lean into her again. The potential kiss that had just suffused the air between them lingered like a heady scent.

The only time Cullie had ever held herself away from a man was with Steve, because he'd been married.

Rohan pulled away, again. This time backing up a few steps.

Maybe it was a good thing. To not do this. To think it through. Cullie had never thought a kiss through. She'd never been afraid of losing a friendship. This tenuous connection was already pushing into precious territory. She'd never been friends with someone she'd slept with.

"That's something we have in common," she said as lightly as she could. "We both have terrible judgment in relationships."

Dimples dipped into his cheeks, the barest smile, but the relief of taking the hurt from his eyes was a head rush.

"Also, see, I was right. Relationships do cause misery." God, he'd looked miserable a second ago.

He laughed at that. "Heaven help anyone who's trying to convince you that you're wrong, Cullie," he said, voice laced with too many things. "Also, see, you don't actually believe in the app. So I was right too. How will you design something you don't believe in?"

She dropped onto the couch.

He dropped down next to her.

"I guess that's what I'm trying to figure out. How to believe in it," she said. "How can *you* still believe after that?" How did one betray someone over their grief? "Isn't sticking around for the hard stuff the heart of it? Not one person I've been matched with has made me feel anything but terrified for the human race. Yesterday a guy told me his opinion matters more than mine because he's a billionaire."

She'd been matched with an entrepreneur, for obvious reasons. They'd gotten into a political debate about taxing businesses, and finally, when he couldn't come up with an argument to change her mind, he'd told her that he was a billionaire, so he knew what he was talking about better than her.

Rohan started laughing so hard he choked, and she had to thump his back. "Did you not tell him you were the legendary Cullie Desai, the creator of Shloka?"

"You mean the unimpressive Cullie Desai, who's hit the ripe old age of twenty-five with *only* one app to her name?"

He touched her cheek again, the pad of his thumb skimming her skin as though he couldn't help but do it. "That's not what I meant. If there's one word to describe you, it's impressive." There it was again, the sincerity that made her want to slide closer to him.

But he pulled away again, and she got up and went to the desk and grabbed one of the notebooks.

He was at her side in a moment, taking it from her before she could open it and pressing it to his chest so possessively that the feelings that had been swinging wildly inside twisted together.

She reached for it again, but he stayed her hand with his. "Cullie, don't." His body was touching hers. The smell of him that had flooded through her like relief the first time they met swept through her. "Please." The whisper landed on her hair, dislodging a lock.

"Why? What are you working on? Is it something salacious?"

He laughed. "You wish." His filterless eyes filled with restlessness. "It's the opposite of salacious." He turned away from her.

Something about the set of his shoulders sent alarm ringing through her. She walked around him.

"Rohan, are you crying?"

He sniffed. "It's my grandfather's journal." He squeezed his eyes shut, then opened them again, storms raging inside. "It's his account of a love affair from his youth. He gave it to me on the day of his death." A tear slid down his cheek, and she wiped it, then stepped close to him and wrapped her arms around him.

He didn't wrap his arms around her in return, but she felt the pain inside him, tried to soak it up.

"I'm guessing it wasn't with your grandmother." The muscled warmth of his chest was shockingly comforting. It might make her forget her prejudice against gym rats.

"No."

She waited for more, but he said nothing and just stood there as though he wanted to put his arms around her but couldn't. She took his hands and placed them around herself.

He pulled away. "God, Cullie, please. Please don't make this—"

It should have been humiliating. It should have sliced her ego in half, but something else was going on here, and it surprised her how clearly she knew that.

Is this what you mean, Binji, when you said to be vulnerable?

"You don't have to tell me. I understand your loyalty to your grandfather. I'm sorry I intruded. I would not break Binji's confidence for anything. I would kill to protect her."

Instead of easing him, her words seemed to make things worse. "It has to do with the documentary I'm working on. It's too important. I can't talk about it yet." He stepped close again. "It's not that I don't trust you. I do. We've only known each other a few weeks. But I . . . I've never felt this easy, this comfortable, with anyone, ever. Our . . . we . . . I just want you to know that, okay?"

"You sound like you're about to say goodbye. If you run away in the middle of the night, I will hunt you down. Unless, of course, you're married. In which case I hope your wife kicks your ass for doing this."

"Cullie, please." He sounded so helpless. "I won't go anywhere without telling you. That's the one thing I can promise you. I won't leave without saying goodbye. I can't go anywhere until I figure out how to . . . how to get this person to meet me."

"Why don't you just show up at her door. I'll bet she won't be able to resist your charm."

He didn't smile. Not a bit of his cockiness was anywhere in sight.

"Can I help? Maybe I could call this woman, appeal to her on your behalf?"

"You're already helping me more than I deserve. But can you . . ." Why was this torturing him so much? When he unabashedly asked her to help with all sorts of other things.

She waited.

"Can you . . . am I still invited to dinner? I'm really missing home."

"Of course." She started laughing. He was just so darned adorable, her heart might melt from it. "I can't wait for you to meet my family."

CHAPTER TWENTY-ONE

ALY

It was what Rajendra Desai would demand in return for paying me off to release Bhanu from the film that scared me. That's why I did what I did. Or maybe I was just jealous of him having what I couldn't.
From the journal of Oscar Seth

Aly needed her monthly Mediterranean dinner date with Bindu today. A tradition they'd started after the divorce, when Aly had done a piece on the best Mediterranean restaurants in the area. Cullie usually flew down for it. Which was a bit excessive, but being so successful so young had to have its advantages.

Just as Aly left work and was getting into the car, she saw a missed call from her mother. Aly had been avoiding her, because all Mummy wanted was to ask how Ashish was and where he was and why Aly wouldn't see sense.

Not calling her mother back when Aly was on her way to a dinner she was looking forward to would be the sensible thing to do. But she just couldn't do it.

"One of these days you'll call your mother because you want to talk to her and not because you have to." Mummy always had the best openers.

Usually Aly would lie and say what her mother wanted to hear, that she didn't call her only out of a sense of duty. Actually that wasn't a lie. She did want to call her mother. She wanted to tell her about Meryl and the fact that she might lose everything if Bindu's connection with Richard Langley came out. She wanted to laugh with her about her naked-statue date.

"Isn't calling the important part, Mummy?"

"Are you driving? You know I don't like you talking to me when you drive."

Aly held back her groan. "Things are really busy right now. If I didn't catch you on my drive, I'd miss you. How does it matter that I'm driving?"

Mummy drew a breath. "You don't understand. Ravina's daughter died while driving and talking on the phone. You always misunderstand what I say. Maybe if you tried to understand people, you'd see why Ashish has come back to you."

Aly let out that groan, but not without hitting the mute button. "I always use the speakerphone when I drive." She would never tell Mummy that her cousin's daughter had been under the influence of enough drugs and alcohol to qualify as an overdose when she'd died in that car crash. Ravina had suffered enough with losing a child. She didn't need the family's judgment and blame.

"As if Ravina's daughter didn't have a speakerphone," Mummy said in a huff and then got a call from one of her sisters and hung up on Aly.

Aly was about to execute the head-on-steering-wheel maneuver she needed to survive these calls when the phone rang again. Despite her best efforts, Aly's heart did a little jump of hope as she imagined Mummy calling her back to finish their conversation. Maybe even apologize for hanging up on her. Maybe even end the conversation with an *I love you*.

It was Cullie, which was a far better option. Aly tempered her voice before she said hello.

"Did you just talk to Granny Karen?" Cullie asked as soon as she heard Aly's voice.

Aly made a sound of affirmation, still unable to make words without more pathos than she wanted to saddle Cullie with.

"In that case, never mind," her child said gently.

"Never mind what?"

"Nothing." Her voice said it was certainly something. Aly had a suspicion she knew what it was.

"Cullie, just say it, beta. What do you need?"

"Mom, sorry. I didn't do this on purpose, I swear. But is it okay if Dad joins us for dinner?" She sounded so heartbreakingly tentative.

Aly hated when Cullie felt the need to tiptoe around her feelings. She'd sworn that her child would never have to do what she'd been stuck with her whole life. She tried to force herself to say that it was okay, that they were still a family and Aly could still be around Ashish. But she couldn't, not without the sense of betrayal that slashed through the center of her rib cage every time her mind went anywhere near her ex-husband.

She could not wait to rub *Weekend Plans with Aly* in his face. She hadn't told anyone yet. It felt too tenuous, too long awaited. Every superstitious belief about jinxing it congregated in her wary heart.

Ashish was back from his cryptic business travels, so their family gatherings were about to get awkward again. Why hadn't he gone back yet? Where was the "call of his homeland" now?

"I didn't tell him about it. He just remembered that we do Tagine Tuesdays and invited himself," Cullie said when Aly didn't respond. She sounded so unsure, so young. Her absurdly precocious daughter hadn't sounded young when she *was* young.

"Cullie, beta, you don't have to apologize for wanting to have dinner with your dad. Of course you want to spend time with him."

"Thanks, Mom. But Tagine Tuesdays are ours, you know?" Cullie's voice went flat again, and Aly knew there was more.

If Mummy hadn't just gouged out all the things Aly should have put away long ago, she wouldn't have hesitated. She would have put her breeziest voice to good use. They were both Cullie's parents. He was Bindu's son. They were a family.

"I know Tagine Tuesdays are ours. This doesn't change that. He's not going to be here long." Then, before she could stop herself, the question slipped out. "Is he?"

Silence stretched as her child tried to figure out how to not betray either parent.

"I'm sorry," Aly said quickly. "I should not have asked you that. I didn't mean to put you in the middle of this." But she needed Ashish to go back to India so they could go back to their lives. And she could stop doing stupid things to show him up. She almost groaned at the memory of the naked bodysuit.

"I am literally the actual middle of this," Cullie said, her voice more pissed off than hurt now.

"I really am sorry."

She made a classic impatient Cullie sound, back in all her glory. "Why are you sorry, Mom? I'm an adult. You have the right to live your life." Another frustrated groan, this time laced with a laugh. "I just sounded like Binji, didn't I? What I meant is it's not like I wanted you or Dad to stay in a marriage that made you miserable."

They'd never been miserable. That was the thing that kicked the hardest. There had just been miserable parts. That also meant that she needed to be a grown-up and let Cullie and Bindu have a family. It struck her that Ashish had made the effort to stay out of her space when she was with Cullie and Bindu.

"Thank you. And of course your dad can come. I'll be perfectly civil."

Cullie laughed. "Isn't that the default Aly Menezes Desai state?"

She meant it as a compliment, but it still stuck like a thorn in Aly's side.

Be nice.

Be nice.

Be nice.

Mummy's voice whispered in her ear.

"But thank you," Cullie said happily. "And since you are in such a generous mood, can you also give Dad a ride?" There it was, the thing Cullie had been trying to figure out how to slip in.

"You don't have to do it, but he's on your way. He can't get a ride-share because the drivers are protesting that new law and disrupting service. Binji and I are already here. But of course he can—"

"Cullie. I got it. I'll pick him up."

Cullie's relief was palpable. "Thanks, Mom. Just sent you his location. You're the best."

"I am, and don't you ever forget it." Then, with a fierceness that made her grip her steering wheel, she added, "I love you, Curly-Wurly."

"Love you too, Mom."

There, Mummy, His will be done only when you help Him do it.

Like the cresting and ebbing of waves, her mood went from upbeat to subterranean when Ashish let himself into the car that had been his dream car before he'd switched up his dream.

He was wearing khaki shorts and a white linen shirt. The jerk!

It was his 100 percent get-lucky clothing choice. That's what they'd called it. Because, well, something about Ashish in a linen shirt was unbearably sexy. And a white linen shirt? He was the beach and the surf of their Goan ancestors given human form. She suppressed the urge to scream into her fist.

For him, it had been her in a sari. Well, her in anything, but if she put on a sari, Ashish was going to take it off her. They'd been late for many a party. They'd even missed the first dance at her cousin's wedding because they'd stopped at the hotel to change between the church and the reception. They'd worn "Western formal," as Indians called it, to the wedding, and the reception dress code had been Indian wedding wear. She'd had to drape her sari twice. Because . . . Ashish.

One quick glance, and he knew exactly what his clothes had made her think about. He handed her a brown bag. "Got you something."

"Why?" she said, bewildered.

"They're Miller's cookies."

Aly's heart did a painful twist, and her grip crushed the paper bag, leaving her with zero dignity. "You shouldn't be buying me things. Let alone food. Don't buy me food, Ashish!"

His jaw tightened. His eyes softened. She hated that she could read his face this way, this stranger with her husband's mannerisms and memories. "I was in Gainesville. And Miller's was right there. How could I not grab you some?"

In college, Aly and Ashish had stayed up many a night studying and stuffing their faces with these oatmeal raisin cookies from a store tucked away at the edge of campus. Aly had consumed them by the truckload when she was pregnant, then craved them after they moved to Fort Lauderdale halfway through her pregnancy.

Ashish had made sure she had an unending supply. He'd had a client in Gainesville. He'd work twelve-hour days all week and fly back for the weekend on Friday evenings. He'd never come home without a box of cookies.

When they'd first met, he'd found it hilarious that oatmeal raisin was her favorite cookie.

Why is that funny? she'd asked.

Because it's so apt. If you were a cookie, of course you'd be oatmeal raisin.

Because it's delicious?

Because it's the most sensible cookie. I mean, it's practically a granola bar.

The answer should have upset her, but it had made her feel like he got her.

What would you be if you were a cookie? she'd asked him.

You tell me.

A macaron.

He'd grinned. *Because I'm beautiful and fancy?*

No, because you're frivolous and entirely nuts. She hadn't known then that, like a macaron, he wouldn't last. Macarons, too, tended to be gone too fast.

She'd been sick and oddly lonely through her pregnancy. Until she'd had to get off her feet in the last trimester and Bindu had taken a flight from Mumbai to take care of her. Aly's own mother had been busy with caring for her father one town over. Not because Daddy was sick but because he needed her to.

When Aly didn't open the bag, Ashish took it back and opened it. "You can eat one and give the rest to Ma and Cullie." He held one out and said in the tone that had gotten her to do all the things she would never have tried if not for him.

She snatched the cookie and took a bite, resisting the urge to put the entire thing in her mouth, then rage eat the whole box.

"You look good," he said. Throwing the words out quickly, as though he knew he shouldn't be saying them but couldn't help himself. That pretty much described everything he'd done toward the end of their marriage.

"Can we not do this today, Ashish?" Actually, could they just never do this. Ever.

"What happened?" he asked.

She stared at the road. She shouldn't have said the word *today*—that had to be what tipped him off.

You goaded me into the most humiliating experience of my life.

Your mother has inherited my boss's child's inheritance.

"I just spoke to Mummy." Why did she settle on that? When she should not have said anything at all. But being able to say the words without having to modulate her tone made her giddy with the oxygen that hit her lungs. One of the gifts of their marriage had been how well Ashish understood the snarled-up tangle that was her relationship with her mother.

"How are they?" His voice was odd. He was obviously trying to figure out if she knew that he talked to her parents.

"You tell me. You talk to them more than I do."

"You live with my mother." There was anger in his voice. His all-the-suppressed-things tone.

"Lived."

"It's just physical separation of spaces. It doesn't change anything." Was he talking about them? They were divorced. Or hadn't he noticed? Or did he mean Bindu? Or both?

It was obvious from his face that something was bothering him. She refused to fall into the pattern of being his fixer.

"Ma seems different. In that condo." He frown-smiled. "It's funny, right?"

"Is it?"

"Come on, Aly. I mean, it's *Ma*. Those dresses. The dates. I can barely recognize her."

"Actually, she seems more herself than I've ever seen her be before."

His smile turned incredulous, and Aly braced herself for something about her turning everything into "psychobabble about identity."

Instead he said, "It's strange how you two—now three—support each other at the cost of everyone else."

At the cost of everyone else? "She's living her life, enjoying opportunities she's never had before. Why is that a problem?"

He let out a bitter laugh. "Living her life? Or is she trying out someone else's life? What was wrong with her life with us?"

What he meant: Why was it not enough for Bindu to be his mother, his father's wife, his daughter's grandmother? Just the way he'd wanted Aly to be his wife, his mother's daughter-in-law, his daughter's mother first.

"Why does her life have to be only what fits yours? Why should you decide which life is hers to want? How long does she have to fit the role you've set? She's a whole person. Why does she have to put that away to make you feel loved?"

Instead of looking like she was attacking him and attacking back, he paused. Was he thinking about it? Ashish never thought about things she said. His only defense, ever, was offense.

His brows drew together, his lips pursed. Her words seemed to have hit something inside him. "Why do roles feel like bondage to you? Men have predefined roles too. Don't you think we struggle with them too?"

He'd always told her that she'd been able to quit her job and follow her passion because he held down his job, because he sacrificed his passion and did what needed to be done for their family.

If you decided to follow your passion, I would support you, she'd said.

But I won't because I care about what this family needs, he'd responded.

When he'd decided to move back to India, he'd thrown that back at her, extracting his pound of flesh. *You said you'd support me if I decided to follow my passion. Now I am. Let's go back home.*

But this was her home. *Our life is here, Ash. Why can't you work on concerts here?*

Because this isn't my music. My music is in India.

I just got made reporter. I've worked for ten years to get here. I know I'll get a segment soon. I know it.

You know that's not true. They'll never give that to you. It's too late. You're past forty. If they were going to give you a shot, it would have happened by now. Why can't it be my time now?

I can't.

And I can't put my dreams away anymore. I need you to give back.

That's how easily it had ended.

"I guess you're right. Maybe we all need to stop struggling with our roles and let them go," she said. Because if they didn't let go, the deadlock would suffocate them.

The concession seemed to roll through him like relief. He smiled again. "Is that what that statue date was about, then?"

She felt her face heat. "Wow, really, you're going to bring that up?" Mortification burned through her.

A laugh lit his eyes, but he didn't let it out. "Come on! You had . . ." He made wiggly fingers at his crotch.

"I will kill you if you say it." How had she let him goad her into wearing a naked bodysuit? With steel wool pubic hair sewn into it.

Aly hadn't been able to sleep for two days after that because she kept jolting awake from the memory of someone grabbing her butt when she was supposed to be frozen in a sensuously athletic pose.

Remove yourself from movement. Separate yourself from your body and watch from without. George Joseph—a man Aly hoped never to lay eyes on again—had whispered those words with the kind of pseudo-Zen self-importance that should have made her run as soon as she heard it.

The butt grope had done it. She had removed her body from the entire bizarre situation and fled the scene she'd been subjected to only because of Ashish. Damn him.

Oh God, what if it got out? George Joseph had assured her that pictures were not allowed at the exhibit, but maybe she'd been naive to trust him. What if Joyce found out? Joyce took nothing more seriously than the public image of her anchors.

For a moment Aly was so distracted by the fact that her stupid date might cost her the shot she finally had that it took her a moment to process that Ashish was watching her as though he could see every thought passing through her head.

He let one spurt of laughter out. "You always said I pushed you to do things you ended up enjoying."

She had not enjoyed Naked Art Guy.

He got serious again. "I was never trying to put you in bonds. I loved how fierce you were under all that Karen Menezes conditioning."

A blast of pleasure warmed her. Then terror turned her cold. This was precisely the problem. That he knew exactly what to say to get to her. "You liked when I was fierce except when it was for something I wanted, not something you thought I should want."

Again, he didn't get defensive. "Aly, listen. I did that. I know. I'm not making excuses, but it's all I ever saw. If you'd ever met my father, you'd understand." Unfamiliar sadness flashed in his eyes. "You're not the only one with conditioning. All I wanted was to not be like him, and I ended up . . ." He wiped a hand across his face as though it was that easy to wipe everything away. "Can we talk, please? Maybe after dinner. I have to tell you how these two years have been. I've . . . I've had the most amazing experiences. And I would never have found what I found if it weren't for you."

Wow. Was he really telling her how wonderful leaving her had been? And he *was* making excuses.

He paused, again, obviously seeing what she'd heard in his words. "If I hadn't seen you fight for what you want, I . . . I would never have been able to do it."

"Well, congratulations," she said as they parked. "Bindu and Cullie are waiting."

"Aly, I think you're misunderstanding what I'm trying to say."

"Of course I am. Don't I always? But you know what, we no longer have to understand each other. We just have to be civil so Cullie and Ma can still have a family. Can we do that, please?"

"That we will always be." He shoved his hands into his pockets and nodded. "But we're more than that. Can we talk, please? One dinner. I'll cook."

She waited for him to say something about how she owed him that much. But he didn't. And he was going to cook for her.

"I'm not going to help you or clean up or anything."

He gave a lopsided grin. "You can even complain about how badly I cleaned up. Please."

"Fine. Tomorrow." But she didn't add that it was a date. Because it wasn't.

~

After dinner Ashish went back to Shady Palms with Bindu, and Cullie came home with Aly. They'd had enough wine at dinner, so they made themselves hot chocolate in their favorite mugs and took them to the couch.

Aly had been determined to have a good time despite Ashish's presence, but when she'd ended up having a good time, it had been disconcerting. But it was still worth it, because Aly couldn't remember the last time Cullie had looked like this. Light. Happy. She was staring at her phone with the widest grin on her face. This had happened all through the evening. It had been happening a lot lately.

Even when Bindu and Aly had informed her that they were done with the dates and that they'd given her enough to go on, she'd thanked them and gotten to work with what she had, filled with purpose, not dread.

"So, are you going to tell me what that grin is about?" Aly asked.

Cullie looked up from her phone, and her grin did a weird thing where it both brightened and shook a little.

"You know that thing Binji was talking about when she said every woman deserves to meet someone who sees her the way she wants to be seen? Someone who makes her feel right?"

Aly sat up. For years Aly had trained herself to temper her reactions for Cullie so Cullie wouldn't feel overwhelmed. Ever since the day of Bindu's uncharacteristic outburst, Aly hadn't been able to stop thinking about vulnerability.

Case in point: her daughter was opening up to her.

Cullie had seemed really strong these past couple of years. So Aly went for it. "Is it one of the dates? Do you feel like you met someone?"

"That makes it sound weird, Mom!" Cullie frowned.

Aly kicked herself for getting carried away, but then Cullie smiled again, this time tentatively.

"It's not one of the dates."

Aly should have known. It was the app. With Cullie it was always her work.

"I met him in a parking lot when I was throwing up. I know that sounds terrible." But she was grinning in a most un-Cullie way, and it sounded anything but terrible. "It was right after Noseless Veterinarian." She grinned again. Then she cleared her throat. "Mom?"

Aly made an encouraging sound. Too afraid to say actual words.

"You and Dad. Things were . . . they were okay today, right?"

This had to do with Ashish?

"Why do we have to bring your father into this?" Aly said, and Cullie's grin disappeared.

"Sorry."

Great going with the vulnerability, Aly!

Aly didn't want Cullie to be sorry.

"No. I'm sorry." Aly reached out and squeezed Cullie's arm. "Seriously, I'm sorry. I shouldn't have said that. You can mention your dad around me. I mean that."

"Okay."

"Cullie, please. What were you going to ask about your dad?"

Cullie took a sip of her hot chocolate. "With Dad . . . you grew up here, and he grew up in India. Was that . . . sorry, I know you don't want to talk about Dad, but . . ." She trailed off.

Aly gave her arm another squeeze.

She thought about Ashish in that white linen shirt. All that they'd been. The effort he'd made today. Not once had he tried to step into the spotlight. He'd been content to listen as they discussed the app and what a disaster their research had been.

Bindu's Worm Eater had made an appearance. Bindu had played the horror to the hilt, with an expression that said, rather loudly, *Queens don't share what they suffer.* Well, she hadn't suffered pubic hair extensions on a bodysuit.

Yes, Naked Art Guy had made several appearances too and made up most of the evening's comedic entertainment.

"We weren't always broken," Aly said, before the invisible gag tightened around her words again. "When I met your father, what Ma said that day was exactly how it was. The way he saw me. That's exactly who I wanted to be." Her heart hurt as she said it, but it was also freeing. Crushing the block of ice that had encased her for so long.

"I'm sorry," Cullie said again.

"I don't want you to be sorry. I want you to know that our divorce has nothing to do with you."

"I'm twenty-five, Mom, you don't need to do the 'Mommy and Daddy will always love you' bit."

"That's not what I'm doing . . . just . . . well, I want you to be able to talk to me. To ask me things. I know you're uncomfortable talking to me about . . ." She made the effort not to use her hands, kept them in her lap. "Some of your struggles."

Cullie put the mug down on the coffee table and turned to Aly, eyes too hesitant. *Are we really talking about this?*

Yes. They should have talked about it a long time ago. How had they not?

"Did I make it hard for you to talk to me about it?"

"Of course not!" Cullie said a little too fast.

"Cullie, tell me. Let's fix this."

Cullie laughed. "Fix what, Mom? Me? This is the problem. You go straight into fixing-me mode."

Aly had the urge to press a hand to her mouth. "Oh God." She did do that.

Cullie looked miserable. "But I'm not broken. I have a condition. It's not your fault. It's not my fault either."

"I know, honey. I know you're not." When she'd tried to fix Cullie, she'd only made her feel broken. How had she not seen that? "I'm so sorry I made you feel that way."

"You didn't on purpose." Cullie's big hazel eyes, eyes that had made Aly want to weep from their defenseless innocence when Cullie was a baby, looked careful again.

"Say it, beta. You're not going to hurt me."

"It's just that for a long time I didn't know what was happening to me. And Dad and you worked so hard. And then you both became so sad and preoccupied, I just couldn't tell you. I'm sorry."

"Oh, Cullie, stop apologizing. I'm the one who's sorry. I am so very sorry." She'd spent so much time trying to be a good parent, and she'd missed the basics.

"But I'm really doing well now. Shloka helps, and I have a therapist who's helped me learn not to fight the feelings. And, Mom"—she paused—"I take medication."

"Honey, that's wonderful. You've taken care of yourself. I'm proud of you and so ashamed I wasn't there for you."

"You were there. You are. It was me too. I had to figure this out for myself. You know how stubborn I am."

"You, stubborn? No!"

Cullie laughed, but her eyes were thoughtful. "Can people really change, Mom? Because I feel different."

Aly wiped her eyes. "I guess they can. Because I feel different too."

"Who knew it was possible to improve on perfection?" A grin tugged at Cullie's lips again.

"So," Aly said. "This guy. He's from India?"

The grin spread across Cullie's face, running rampant across it and brightening her eyes, and she didn't even try to hide it. "I've just met him. So no one's doing anything weird like getting married, okay?"

"Okay."

Cullie barely seemed to hear her. "He's nothing like me, Mom. He doesn't even know how to retrieve a file from his motherboard."

"What? People like that exist?"

"Very funny. But it's not just that. We have no idea what the other person is talking about when it comes to work, but I know exactly how he feels about it. He makes films. Documentaries. And restores and preserves old celluloid film. But he's just so . . . I don't even know what to call it. Nice? Decent? But also . . ." She colored. Her Cullie was blushing. "You know, really hot."

Aly found her hand pressed to her mouth. She had never seen Cullie like this. Then she pulled her hand away so Cullie wouldn't think she was overreacting and shut down again, because seeing Cullie like this was the best thing that had happened to Aly in her entire life.

When she'd first met Ashish and told her mother about him, her mother had been terribly excited that he was from India, but then she'd been heartbroken that he wasn't Catholic and then doubly heartbroken when he'd refused to convert.

But Ashish had won them over. By becoming the son they'd never had. For her.

"Mom, will you stop trying so hard to manage your reactions, please? It's okay for you to be thrilled that he's from India."

"I'm not thrilled because he's from India. I'm thrilled because of how you're talking about him. Do we get to meet him?"

Yup, her cheeks were definitely flushed. "Is it okay if I bring him to Binji's for dinner this week?"

Aly forgot about holding herself back and threw her arms around Cullie.

"You have to promise not to be weird. We're just friends. It's not a relationship or anything. He's just, he just misses his home, I think. It's not like—"

All Aly could do was squeeze her daughter and laugh until her heart felt like it would burst.

CHAPTER TWENTY-TWO

BINDU

I've encountered few greater tragedies than keeping art from an audience because we're afraid to tip the balance of society with our norms of shame.
I wish I'd had the honor of sharing Bhanu's talent with the world. But even more, I wish it hadn't been stolen from her.
From the journal of Oscar Seth

As a young girl, Bindu had loved to sneak off to the forbidden Foreigner Beaches attached to Foreigner Hotels and spy on the bikinied bodies. It was what her mother believed had corrupted her.

Aie had been right, because that's where she'd met Oscar. Bindu had been snooping around the pool in the red bikini she *hadn't* stolen but had found abandoned on the spikes of an aloe bush when the manager of the hotel caught her. He'd asked for her room number, leering the entire time. Bindu refused to wrap her arms around herself to hide from his ugly gaze. The filth in the way he looked at her was his problem, not hers.

She'd thrown out a number as calmly as she could, trying to figure out how she could make a run for it without her clothes.

There's no room by that number, he'd said, moving too close with his eggy breath, and then grabbed her arm.

Is there a problem? Oscar's voice had been the snap of a whip. *Did you forget our room number again, darling?* he said to her, tone deathly calm, eyes on the manager's hand crushing her arm.

The manager let her go and practically fell to his knees apologizing.

We're here for the next three months, Oscar said, making it obvious why not many people dared to speak in his presence. *I want you to work in a different part of the hotel. Don't let me, or her*—he threw Bindu a look of such fond familiarity, she felt like she really was his darling—*see you again.*

For Bindu, all of seventeen, it had been love at first sight. The way he'd looked at her. Not as though she were a body but as though he *saw* how she wore her body, and it told him what she carried inside it and it changed the way he saw the world. Instead of thanking him, she raised her chin, so he'd know she wasn't about to do anything funny to show her gratitude. Then she attempted to slip past him.

He didn't stop her. *It's seven five two*, he'd said as she tried to make her escape. *My room number. In case anyone else catches you sneaking around.*

Bindu sat up in bed, heart hammering, and wrapped her arms around herself. *Don't check your phone.*

But there it was, another email from Oscar's grandson. Expecting him to leave her alone forever had been naive.

She opened it.

Please, just meet me once. Just one conversation.

Over her cold dead body.

The pain of the good memories was crushing, a vise around her chest that she had to breathe around. Touching the ugly parts was out of the question. She had to find a way to get him to leave her alone before her family found out. Before Ashish found out.

The idea of any of this touching her son made her want to scream. God, she hated men.

Great, now she sounded like the new generation. Casual in their use of powerful words.

I hate broccoli, Cullie used to say.

No, Cullie, you don't like the taste of broccoli. That's not hate.

I hate my computer science teacher.

No, Cullie, your computer science teacher is jealous of you and wants to prove his superiority, and his behavior hurts you. That's not hate.

Hatred was when you felt no pain when madness and death came for your mother.

Hatred was telling your daughter that she deserved to be sold at a brothel down in Baina Beach.

Hatred was what you felt for yourself for not knowing who your son's father was. And for hiding that from him his entire life.

Stop it. She rubbed her arms and tried to find her armor again. This was not the time to lay it down.

There were two other emails, one from Ashish and one from Jane with Connie cc'd. **Pickleball tonight?**

Bindu had been avoiding her Sunny Widows. She didn't want to talk about Richard. Didn't want to be on the courts with judgment being lobbed at her along with the damn ball. But they hadn't been judgmental. They'd given her space, reached out without being intrusive.

She sent off a reply saying she'd see them tonight and then opened Ashish's email.

Richard Langley's children just put out a statement. He'd attached a link to the *Miami Herald*.

"Leave me alone," Bindu said to the phone and got out of bed without clicking the link.

It was still dark outside. Bindu found her way to the living room by the light of her phone so she wouldn't wake Ashish. He was fast asleep on the couch, long hair obscuring most of his beloved face. The quilt had slid off him, and she tucked it back around him. He'd been working late into the night, headphones pulled over his ears, fingers flying on his laptop.

Something fundamental in him seemed to have changed. He was thoughtful about what he said. He helped around the house. He'd even stopped looking like she was embarrassing him when she put on her dresses.

Bindu had a nagging suspicion he was regretting his recklessness with the divorce. As though marriage were playing house and divorce a tantrum.

Making chai would be too noisy, so she grabbed a glass of water and studied the fridge full of fish and meat that she'd bought yesterday. A smile nudged at her. Could there be anything more heartwarming than the fact that Cullie was bringing a friend home, and he loved Goan food?

Today Bindu was going to forget about everything else and cook for her granddaughter. She had it all planned out. Mutton xacuti, prawns kissmoor, and fried fish. And of course made-from-scratch bebinca.

Helping raise Cullie had been the happiest part of Bindu's life, so uncomplicated and pure it had reset her. Cullie's birth swallowed up the insidious emptiness that had crept in after Rajendra didn't wake up one morning. There was something about being a grandparent that freed you from the mistakes of being a parent.

For some reason one got to be much more intentional about it, much less driven by emotion. Much more gentle and driven by love, which constituted wisdom, she supposed. Taking long naps with baby Cullie snuggled next to her when Alisha and Ashish went to work, delighting in her brilliant mind when she started to pick up the world around her, even soothing her when she struggled. All of it had come with not a flicker of doubt or stress.

Raising Ashish had been fraught with second-guessing herself. Until this moment, she hadn't realized how much energy it had taken to navigate Rajendra's silent scrutiny of her parenting. But it had been proof of his love for his son, and she'd held that tight.

When she'd moved to America, she left all that behind. For twenty-three years, their family had rambled through the hike that was life, but the rise and fall had been gentle. Mostly because of Alisha's limitless ability for love. Until Ashish put his decision to "return home" above his family, Bindu had never had the courage to poke at the complicated thing her own marriage had been. There were things about how her son had behaved in his marriage that threw a spotlight on the dark corners of her own marriage that she'd tried so hard to block out.

"Ma?" Ashish said from the couch. "What time is it?"

It was barely five a.m. She should go back to bed and let Ashish get some sleep. But she wanted to get her day started.

"Why don't you go into my bedroom and sleep. The noise won't disturb you there."

He rose, blanket trailing, hair in his eyes, face creased on his sleeping side. Instead of going to the room, he wrapped his arms around her and dropped a kiss on her head. "I love you, Ma."

She had no idea where that had come from, but she soaked him up, finding her own smell, Cullie's smell, Rajendra's lost smell, all of it wrapped up in him. "I love you too, beta."

He blinked the sleep from his eyes. "I have to drive to Miami today to see Radha and Pran. They're looking at some contracts for me. I might as well get an early start and beat traffic." With that he started to make chai.

The urge to stop him was strong, to do it herself, to take care of him. But she stopped herself and sat down at the breakfast bar, watching him with the strangest feeling in her heart. The ritual of making chai was so ingrained in him, it was like watching herself.

The chai too was exactly the way she made it. They chatted about Cullie's mystery man as they dunked Marie biscuits into their tea. He'd always dipped the crisp arrowroot cookies into her chai because he didn't like his own picking up the flavor. He did it now, and she didn't stop him. Not all ways of taking someone for granted were hurtful.

Everyone deserved someone whose chai they could dip their biscuits into without thought.

"Did you look at the article I sent?" he asked as a soggy blob dropped into her tea. He fished it out with a spoon and a sheepish apology.

She hadn't, but they did together. Richard's children had not named Bindu, because Lee hadn't divulged that information. But they had called the woman who had "entrapped" their father several things, including a thief. Her face heated, the feeling of shame she'd wrestled to keep at bay for forty-seven years almost knocking her down.

Her son touched her hand. "Ma, it's okay. They're assholes. The world is full of those."

She swallowed. "I didn't even know he had money." She hated that her voice was a whisper. "I barely knew him."

He threw a glance around her condo, with its ocean view and designer color palette. She waited for him to ask how she was able to afford it. For a moment she forgot that she'd told her family that Oscar's money had come from a wealthy, reclusive aunt. Her shame nudged into panic.

Ashish wrapped an arm around her. "Richard Langley made his own money. Not a cent of it was inherited. It was his talent. Something he suffered for. He can give it to anyone he wants." Her Ashish, on her side. "I'm going to talk to Radha about it today. Maybe we can sue the assholes for slander if they find out it's you and name you."

"No!" Her voice came out firm, and he blinked. "We are not suing anyone. And I'm not taking his money."

"But why?"

Why did everyone keep asking her that? Why was it so hard to understand?

"Because I don't even know why he did it!"

Unlike Oscar. She knew exactly why *he* had.

Whore.

Leave me alone, Aie.

That shame she'd just felt, it had nothing to do with Richard. With Richard she felt nothing but the sadness of an acquaintance. The names his children called her, that was just their greed talking. What did she care?

Ashish squeezed her shoulder. "That's totally fine, Ma. It's your call."

"It is. And I want you to respect that." If the sharpness in her tone surprised him, he took it well.

"Of course I do. How can I not respect anything about you, Ma?" With that he gave her another hug and left to go about his day.

~

A half hour after Ashish left, Bindu's front door buzzed. *Lee.*

He'd taken to coming over for chai every morning, after confirming that she was alone. Turns out he lived in the building next to hers.

"Morning," he said in his gravelly voice. He was freshly showered, hair still damp. Even this early in the morning, his golf shirt and shorts were ironed to perfection. And his eyes shone with that something that made him *him.*

Heart skipping in the most intoxicating manner, Bindu handed him a cup, and they stepped out to the lanai and settled into the rattan couch next to each other. He leaned over and dropped a kiss on her lips. His lips were smooth, moisturized. He cared for himself, his own mechanic. The crisp, clean taste of him was like the first drizzle of the monsoon. Every time.

She smiled against his lips.

The comfort of friendship, with some but not all benefits.

She'd never had this before. No pressure. No need to serve. No desperation to hold on to anything. They'd decided to be friends. Then they'd decided to be the kind of friends who slipped into each other's condos in the light of day and kissed.

It had never been this way for her.

219

Being able to talk. Being able to be silent. She wanted nothing from him but how he made her feel.

She told him about her cooking plans, and he leaned over and kissed her again. It had been a while since she'd been so excited about anything.

"He's coming over tomorrow. Why are we cooking today?"

"Two days of cooking time is the minimum for a respectable meal." She lowered her voice to a whisper. "Not counting the two days I've been prepping."

"Will the poor boy be able to walk after how much you're planning to feed him?"

"He'd better. He's going to have to prove himself. It's the way to an Indian grandma's heart. And the way to Cullie's heart is through me."

"If the reverse is also true, I'm in trouble, because I'm still traumatized by the scolding Cullie gave me."

Bindu wasn't ready to label their relationship or discuss it with anyone, not yet. "You are Weaselly Leslie after all." She laughed. He could handle Cullie. She had no doubt.

"I've been called worse."

"As a lawyer?"

"As the secretary of the HOA."

They laughed together and took their cups into the kitchen.

"You need to sign the papers soon, Bindu," he said quietly, and she thought about him interrogating clients. Soft, lulling you into trust.

"I don't understand why it's a problem that I don't want Richard's money," Bindu said, putting the shredded coconut into the food processor. "Weren't you the one who accused me of having an ulterior motive in dating him?"

He wrapped his arms around her and laid his chin on her head. "I never said that. I said his children suspect that. I'm only interested in doing what Rich wanted me to do with his money. He trusted me with it for a reason."

The racket the food processor made as it ground the coconut gave them pause.

"What about what I want? Does that not count for anything?" she asked when silence returned.

"Once you have the money, you can do what you want with it. The money was his to give."

"But I don't want to be stuck in a legal battle with someone who has more right to the money than me."

Taking the spatula from her, he started to spoon the ground coconut into the bowl she handed him. "Do you know how Rich and I became friends?"

She waited for him to tell her, amazed that the conversation—not the first time they'd had it—was so equanimous. She didn't feel attacked. It didn't feel like she had to prove anything. He was listening to her, but not as though she made him feel silenced or angry.

They moved around the kitchen, he looking to her for directions and she giving them, even though she'd had to force herself to do it at first.

"I met him when Mary—the receptionist at the HOA office—invited me over for Thanksgiving dinner, because Sally and Jake were traveling that year and I didn't go to Michigan. Richard spent the last five Thanksgivings with Mary. Do you know when the last time he saw his children was?"

She waited; the bitterness in Richard's eyes had been so sad. Now she saw clearly that it was loneliness.

"It had been more than twenty years."

"So you want to use me to get retribution on his behalf?"

He thought about that. Taken aback. He barely saw his daughter and son-in-law twice a year. He seemed okay with it. They talked on the phone every week.

She started grinding the next batch of masalas, and the whirring of the food processor forced them into silence again.

What Bindu had was rare and precious. It was her wealth, what she'd worked her whole life for. To love her family wholeheartedly, that had been her choice. Hers. She'd been lucky to have her love returned. But she had also created that luck with her choices.

Other people's choices had guided most of her life, but this she had done herself.

Her parents had chosen honor over her.

Oscar had chosen his family. Oscar had chosen his name.

Rajendra had chosen to save her so he could have her. He'd almost bankrupted himself to pay Oscar off. To keep him from releasing *Poornima*. To hide her obsceneness away from the public eye.

The heat of the lights on her naked body as she threw herself open for the camera burned her skin in another flash of memory.

She had let their choices tear her in half. But her choice to do what she'd done as Poornima had never felt like a choice at all.

All that mattered now was that she was here. In a place neither Rajendra nor Oscar could ever have imagined. In a home that belonged to no one but her, wrapped in ocean and sunshine, in the most free country in the world. With her heels and her dresses. Bindu in all her glory. Not *trouble*, just because she loved herself.

It had taken her long enough to get here. Where the "society" whose opinion her mother and Rajendra, and even Oscar, had lived for—had forced Bindu to live for—meant nothing. Society's opinions were not rules or sentencing, because there was no jury but herself. The realization wasn't a lightning bolt. No, it had been a leak. A slow trickle that had taken years to drain her belief system and reverse it.

Lee was waiting to answer the question she'd asked. Lee, who deliberated everything and took nothing for granted.

"Maybe some retribution is called for? But I'll support whatever you choose to do."

The words fell on her like rain. How she'd hungered for them.

I'm here, she repeated to herself. Where if a man who deserved her showed up with love, she could take it. Without shame. And not Oscar and not Rajendra and not her aie could take that away from her.

"I know you're here, Bindu," he said. Apparently she had spoken her heart. "Let me know when you have a decision."

"I have a decision," she said, wrapping her arms around him. She knew exactly what she wanted to do with Richard's money. But first, she was ready to take her friends with benefits situation with this lovely man to the next level.

CHAPTER TWENTY-THREE

CULLIE

On the day that I ended it, we both told the worst lies of our lives. She never told me that her mother had thrown her out, because she wanted my love, not my pity. I never told her that Hema had swallowed half a bottle of sleeping pills. I didn't want her pity either and I thought giving her something to loathe would make it easier for her to forget me.

From the journal of Oscar Seth

Cullie's feet sank into the sand. She had never given much thought to quite how wildly she loved the ocean. The powdery grains wiggled their way between her toes, and she closed her eyes with a sigh.

Rohan was grinning into her face when she opened them. If looking at a woman were an art, the man's talent deserved to be hanging in the Louvre.

"Let me guess. You love the ocean," he said, the smile spilling like light from his voice.

"You don't?"

"I grew up in Mumbai," he said. "It's my entire childhood. My grandfather used to wake me and my sisters up at four in the morning and take us to Juhu Beach to jump the waves. I'd be up at three and wait for everyone else to wake up, because I had no patience."

"That's funny because Binji took me to the beach almost every day over the summer. She had a giant beach umbrella. She'd set it up, and we'd lie under it for hours. I just had to stay under the umbrella so I didn't get too dark, because my granny Karen—that's my mom's mom—would have a meltdown if Binji let me lose my 'fairness.' She used to wash me from head to toe with milk to get rid of the tan Binji let me pick up. All Binji said to that was, 'It's a small price to pay to get to lie there listening to the ocean, isn't it?' Not that she ever said that to Granny Karen."

"Your Binji wasn't wrong. It's the best sound in the world."

Cullie took his hand and dragged him closer to the ocean. The afternoon sun was high and hot enough to kill those less in love with the sun. *Amhi Govache go*, Binji loved to say. *The sun feeds our souls. It's the sun, the ocean, and the fish. That's what makes us better than everyone else at the arts.*

They found a flat spot across from where the waves were high and frothy from the meeting of two currents and flopped down on the beach blanket. For a long while they just lay on their backs, listening to the ocean, letting the vibrations of their breathing fill them.

"How is the app coming along?" he asked as the silence kneaded every bit of tension out of her.

Something about how she felt about the app had changed. The desperate need to prove Steve wrong, the rage at losing Shloka: she could no longer conjure up the burning sensation they had caused in her belly.

She felt a paralyzing happiness.

Rolling onto her side, she propped herself on her elbow and stared down at him. A whorl dug into his cheek as a smile tugged at his lips. A matching tug pulled deep inside her, across her breasts and between her legs. Something more than just his smile lit his eyes.

"I'm pretty certain I can't write an algorithm for meeting your soul mate. If there even is a way to write code for finding happiness, it's an endless loop of trying."

His eyes blazed at that.

They'd come this close to kissing often but never done it.

She'd tried many times to initiate it, but he always pulled away. Cullie had not a doubt in her mind that he was attracted to her. This thing burning inside her was not hers alone. Maybe he was shy. But he was shy about nothing else.

"But you believe in soul mates now?"

She shrugged and laid a tentative hand on his bare chest. He had the most beautiful body, lean with muscle, not bulky, chiseled into cords and cuts. Detailed in its beauty, like a meticulously efficient piece of code. What man this hot, this *heated*, in his reaction to her would not be interested?

She trailed a hand down the line that separated his perfectly sculpted pecs. Arousal dilated his eyes, and the sun filtered all the way into his golden irises and set them on fire. The flame of his gaze did a quick slide down her body.

She was wearing her black bikini. Her body was thick and lush. It would never make the cover of *Sports Illustrated*, but it made her happy. Obviously, he felt that way too, because his maroon board shorts stirred with his response.

A smile stretched her lips. Knowing burned inside her. She was about to lean over and kiss him when he plucked her hand off his chest and pulled it away.

Rejection stung like a million rattlesnakes, finally shredding through her self-respect. Tears sprang to her eyes, and it was so damned mortifying, she jumped up and broke into a run.

"Cullie, wait." Why was he following her if he didn't want her?

She ran into the water, and he grabbed her from behind.

"Don't touch me if you don't want me." Pulling his arms off her, she flung them away.

"I do want you."

She had to laugh at that. "You could have fooled me."

"Is that all this is about to you?"

How could he say that? She had spent every moment she could with him these past weeks. They'd talked more than she had ever talked to another human being. Everything he was, she saw it. Everything she was, she'd let him see. And she'd never felt so enough in her life. So right.

Until now. Now she felt small, needy. "What? Wanting you is slutty?" she asked as a wave shoved her sideways. But she dug in her heels and stood her ground.

"No." He repeated it again with some force. "No! But why do we have to be in such a hurry?"

"In a hurry?" They'd been eye-fucking for weeks. Could he be one of those puritanical abstinence-before-marriage people?

"Why does physical intimacy have to be such a big deal?" A wave splashed his glistening, golden body.

She was a sexual person, and she didn't give a shit if that was some sort of red flag for him.

"I enjoy sex, and I'm not apologizing for that."

He ran a hand through his hair, so much frustration in the gesture she wanted to shake him. "But you want me to apologize for wanting to take it slow?" His eyes crinkled with such sincerity that a ball of wanting squeezed in her belly.

"If that's how you really feel, then I respect your choice. It's just the way you've been with me. Something feels disingenuous." Disingenuous. That's exactly how this felt.

"It's not. Nothing about what I feel for you is disingenuous. I swear."

Why did she want to trust him so badly? "Is it a religious thing?"

He laughed. Of all things. Then got distraught and squeezed his temples as though this were a choice between sides in a mortal war. "Why do we have to label it?"

So she could understand what the hell was going on. "Labels aren't always bad. Sometimes naming things helps you understand." If she hadn't been able to name her anxiety, she wouldn't have been able to seek treatment for it. Without that she wouldn't be standing here fighting for this.

He was close to her now. He knew what her anxiety could be like. He understood what Shloka meant to her because of it. His film preservation work was in his blood too. *My heart is made of celluloid*, he'd told her over and over again.

"I thought we got each other," she whispered.

"Cullie."

"If you don't want me, you should stop saying my name like that."

"Stop saying I don't want you. I've never wanted anyone this much."

"You have a funny way of showing it."

The saddest smile dug another killer dimple into his cheek. His fingers ran through his beach-swept hair.

"Why is this not making sense to me, Rohan?"

He flinched when she said his name. "We're having dinner with your family today. I don't want to be late."

He was nervous about meeting her family? "Is that what this is about? You don't have to meet them. I thought you wanted to." Although Binji would murder Cullie with her bare hands if they canceled. She'd been cooking for days.

"I do want to," he said with some desperation. "I really want to meet them." His cheeks colored. She couldn't let this torture him so much.

Maybe seeing her with her family would help with whatever he was struggling with. The sense that something about this was eternal, that she had time, swept through her. A confidence that paralleled how she felt about her family and her work.

A huge wave knocked them sideways, breaking the tension, and they came up laughing. "Then let's build up an appetite." With that she dove into the water and took off into the ocean with him close on her heels.

~

By the time they arrived at Binji's building, with an armful of french baguettes to eat with the xacuti, the air between Cullie and Rohan had thickened with a mix of yearning and heat. Cullie felt like she was walking on air, completely off balance.

Eager as he'd seemed to come here with her, his feet visibly dragged as they approached the lobby.

"It's okay," Cullie assured him once again when he stopped outside the glass doors as though he just couldn't get himself to step inside. "My family is really nice. I'm literally the meanest of the lot."

He forced a smile. More like a grimace, but he didn't respond. She wondered again if it was shyness. She could never have pegged him as shy. Then again, people rarely identified her as someone dealing with anxiety. Who knew better than she that people found ways to hide the things they didn't want anyone to see.

"I wasn't kidding when I said we don't have to go. I'll let Binji know that you couldn't make it. There's no pressure."

"No!" he said with too much force and then made his way into the lobby and punched the elevator button. "I have to." He gave her a searching look. "You've already told her we're coming." He squeezed his temples again, hand shaking. "Shit."

"What's wrong?" she asked, a feeling of impending doom brushing her nerves.

He sank his face into his hands and backed away from the elevator. "I can't." He looked at her like she'd done something terrible, but also like she was unutterably precious.

"You're scaring me. What's going on?"

His jaw worked as he tried to get ahold of himself. "Will you tell me something?"

"Rohan? You can say—"

"Why did you come out that day and help me?"

"What do you mean?"

"You know what I mean. We were strangers, and you've helped me for weeks and been my friend. And that day when I lost my work and

I was in a panic over it, you were dealing with a crisis at work, but you were there in fifteen minutes."

She smiled, but her heart stuttered with a new nervousness. "I don't like to see grown men cry."

He looked like she'd punched him, but he made the effort to smile back. "Please tell me you mean confident, handsome, and not pathetic and messy and in need of help all the time."

"I mean nice. A good guy." She swallowed because, what the hell, she'd been honest with him from the moment they'd first met: no point in stopping now. "Someone who makes me feel light with wonder, young and free. I never felt like that. Not even when I was a child." Suddenly she understood; this had become too much too fast. His life was in Mumbai, hers here. That's what this was about. He saw them as doomed.

His smile disappeared. He looked away. Stealing away from eye contact was not something she'd ever seen him do, and it hit a defenseless spot inside her that popped up out of nowhere. He tended to look straight at you. Right in your eyes. As though he were peering into old film to find out if it was worth rescuing.

"Can we go outside for a minute? I need air."

She followed him outside. He sucked in a gulp, chest expanding with the effort.

"Rohan?"

He groaned, the sound tearing from him. "That's not my name."

The eyes he turned on her were so filled with torment, she took a step back.

"My name is not Rohan. It's Rishi, Rishi Seth." He waited as though that should mean something to her.

"You look like you want me to google that."

"You should."

The feeling of doom crashed into her. She *had* googled him and found very little. She'd decided to trust her instincts about him. "Or

230

you could just tell me why it's such a big deal what your name is and why you made one up?"

"I'm a filmmaker." He paused, not pride, exactly, but something like gravitas dripping from his words. "I've directed two of the biggest hits in Mumbai in the past decade. My debut film was nominated for a foreign-film Oscar."

"Congratulations? Why did you hide that?" Did he think she was a gold digger?

He ran his hands through his hair. Both of them, as though he needed to hold his skull together. Another of his huge Bollywood gestures that she'd grown to love.

"My grandfather was one of India's most legendary filmmakers and actors. He's an icon of world cinema."

"That's wonderful, Roh . . . whatever your name is. Why are you telling me all this now?" After lying to her for weeks. "Why did you lie?"

"I'm here to . . . well . . ." Another squeeze of his head. Then he reached out and took her arm as though he needed to hold her in place for what was coming. "I'm in America because I've been looking for your grandmother."

Cullie yanked her arm away. "My grandmother?" A thin beep started in her ears, a needle of rage piercing her brain.

"Yes. My grandfather's journals . . . you remember the woman I've been trying to meet? The one who won't agree to see me."

"My Binji? You know her?" It felt like someone had shoved Cullie off a cliff. With nothing but ice to break her fall.

"Yes. Well, no. I talked to her, but she refused to meet me. And I really need to—"

"You sought me out to get to her." The urge to push her hand to her mouth was strong, to turn her emotions into physical reactions the way she'd picked up from him. In too short a time. "The past weeks . . . running into me in the parking lot, it was all just part of a plan." To trap her. To trap Binji.

"No! Well, yes." He reached for her arm again, but she pulled it away. He was never touching her again. How badly she'd wanted to touch him made her sick. "I . . . I had tracked her down to this community, but they wouldn't tell me where I could find her, and that's when I met you. I didn't seek you out for her. I swear. I didn't know who you were until you told me your name."

How could she believe anything he said? How would she believe anyone ever again? "And then you thought you could get to her through me."

Silence.

Then, "This is incredibly important. Your grandmother is part of something huge. I just need one chance to explain it to her. I just need to meet her once."

His words were a dagger. A cannonball. Her chest felt crushed. Thoughts spun like eddies in her brain.

"But she told you that she didn't want to meet you. So you pretended to be my friend to get what you wanted." All of it had been a lie.

His eyes flooded with pain again, and the stupid hope that he hadn't been pretending tugged at her.

"You have to understand how important this is."

Oh God, that was all he cared about. Whatever this project was. She remembered the way he had clutched the journals to his chest. "Tell me then. Tell me why it's important."

"I can't. I have to tell her first."

Right. He didn't care that he had used her, that he'd made a fool of her. And she'd let him.

"I told you how Steve used me to take the most important thing away from me. And all the while you were doing the same thing. You know what? Shloka means nothing compared to Binji. I would destroy Shloka ten times over myself to protect her."

"I'm not going to hurt her."

"But hurting me was no problem."

Shame dimmed his fiery eyes. "If that were true, I would have gone into that elevator with you. I would have let you take me to her. I didn't. Because I couldn't risk this." He traced the space between them.

"You couldn't risk *this*." She was laughing now. And it hurt far more than tears ever had. How the hell had she been so stupid? Again.

"Cullie, please. These three weeks, they've been . . . it's the first time I've been happy, really happy, since I lost my mother. Since I lost my grandfather. For the first time, I understand what . . . please, you know this doesn't happen. You know how we feel around each other isn't easy to find. This . . . this is what you've been trying to pin down with your app. But how we feel is not something an algorithm can replicate. You said yourself it's an endless loop of trying."

"Stop it. Stop using my life against me. Feel like what? Like a step stool to reach what you want?"

"I wasn't using you." He squeezed his eyes shut again, unable to keep believing his own lies. "Well, I was at first. But that's not all this was."

Maybe. But that was the part that ruined everything. Something cold was spreading through her, gripping her from the inside out. "It doesn't matter. I can never trust you again." She started walking away from him, then spun around again. "Stay away from me. And stay away from Binji."

"I can't do that," he said. For a moment she thought he meant he couldn't stay away from her. But she was wrong. "I just want to give her something. Something I've worked on for years, something my grandfather died without ever being able to give her. She'll want this. Trust me. Please."

It was the words *trust me* that made Cullie laugh as she let the lobby door slam behind her before hot tears started streaming down her face.

CHAPTER TWENTY-FOUR

ALY

"I hate that everyone wants to save me from myself." That was one of the last things Bhanu ever said to me. I wish I'd had a chance to tell her that I'd give anything to make sure she never let anyone change her even a little.

From the journal of Oscar Seth

A blush warmed Aly's cheeks. She still couldn't believe she'd kissed her ex-husband. Fine, it was more than kissed. They'd made out like college kids high on hormones, ravenous for relief. He'd cooked for her and cleaned as promised and played his old keyboard that she hadn't been able to throw away. And hummed their favorite song in his beautiful voice.

He'd asked to come over to talk. Instead they'd put their mouths to other uses.

It was the white linen shirt.

It was the fact that he could cook a pasta bolognese better than anyone.

It was too many pieces of a shared life.

It was celebrating their daughter's being in love for the first time. Or *in like* enough to bring a boy home.

It was the fact that Aly just couldn't replicate the way her body felt with Ashish.

This doesn't mean anything, she'd told him after.

He'd suppressed a world of feelings behind his grin. The bastard knew.

But simply because their bodies had forgotten the hurt didn't mean the way they'd wounded each other's hearts could be healed.

Finally, all these years later, Aly had what she'd fought so hard for.

She had watched the promo video for *Weekend Plans with Aly* on repeat. Joyce had not been able to make contact with Meryl's people, and somehow everyone seemed to have come around to accepting that Aly would be doing the interview. The promo was going live today. The anticipation felt sharply joyous inside her, the pleasure almost painful. She was going to watch it with the team before leaving for dinner at Bindu's.

Bindu had been in one of her cooking trances for days. It had been years since she'd done this. Painstakingly brought together a full Goan meal. Grinding coconut for the xacuti, scaling fish for a crisp fry, fermenting rice for sanna, caramelizing layer upon layer of bebinca, slowly thickening the milk for serradura, and on and on. Hunger had been gnawing at Aly's insides for what seemed like an age. Years and years of denial, and she was starved for fullness.

Suddenly, she had the unbearable urge for Mummy to know it was happening. She had ten minutes before the promo aired. Without thinking about it, she called her mother.

"You sound happy," her mother said as soon as Aly said hello. At least she'd gotten something about her daughter right.

"I am," Aly said, letting it show in earnest.

"So Ash and you are back together!"

Wow, Karen was on a roll today.

"I'm getting the segment."

If the pause was disappointed, Aly didn't care. "Are you sure?" her mother said finally.

"Would I call you if I wasn't?"

"There's no reason to be rude. I just want to make sure you're not going to be disappointed again. You do foolish things when that work of yours frustrates you. And you have a lot on the line right now."

"You're right. I do. But it's not Ashish. Ashish and I are never going to be husband and wife again. I'm finally going to have my own segment, though, and you should be happy for me about that."

This time the pause was definitely disappointed and shocked. "Alisha," her mother said, sounding almost scared. "I am happy. But what does it matter that you have the segment if you don't have a family?"

A groan escaped Aly.

"Child, I mean it. I am happy."

There, was that so hard? "Thank you."

"You're welcome. But can you also please give Ashish a chance?"

Could all your sobs and groans mix into a laugh? "I have to go. I just wanted to let you know." Aly was about to disconnect, but then she added, "I love you, Mummy," because, Why not?

Her mother made a sound that was suspiciously close to "Same." And with that unprecedented concession she was gone.

When Aly entered the screening room, there was no one there. The team always watched the new promos together when they first went live. The usual cascade of doubts kicked in, disappointment crashing like dominos into disaster. She kicked it back. This time she was choosing to believe.

The light in Joyce's office was on, and Aly knocked on the half-open door and went in.

"There's no one in the screening room," she said into the eerily silent room.

Joyce looked up from her laptop, the strangest anger sharpening her eyes. "We're not screening the promo."

Excuse her? "Are we rescheduling?" Aly said as calmly as she could, breath held.

"Do you know who Bindu Desai is?" Joyce asked.

Before Aly could answer, Joyce stood and walked around her desk. "Why didn't you tell me your mother was the one who tricked Richard Langley out of his money?"

"She's not my mother. She's my former mother-in-law." It was the first thing that popped out of Aly's mouth. Even as she said it, she knew it wasn't the right response, but her brain was scrambling to wrap itself around what was happening.

That seemed to give Joyce pause. But only for a second.

She pulled up something on her phone and handed it to Aly.

There was an article about Richard's having died under mysterious circumstances in the home of his latest girlfriend, this time an immigrant woman from India. It said something about his having changed his will a mere month before his death, soon after meeting this woman, who the National Book Award–winning author had been inexplicably smitten by. Friends who preferred to remain anonymous said that the woman had attached herself to him with a speed and force that caused them concern.

The coven had worked fast and struck hard.

"This article has no mention of Bindu."

"My son and his stepsiblings just found out who it is. Since she signed the papers yesterday to take their money. I thought the name rang a bell."

Aly couldn't believe Bindu had done it. Bindu's horror at the fact that Richard had involved her in his vendetta against his kids bordered on rage. She had been adamant about having nothing to do with the money. Had Lee convinced her? Bindu never let other people's opinions influence her. So she had to have found something she wanted to do with the money.

It wasn't their money, Aly wanted to say, but Joyce was in a full mama-bear snit.

"This scandal is really going to blow up. And you know I can't have it associated with one of my anchors. I'm putting the segment on hold, and Jess will do the Meryl interview. I've let Ms. Streep's people know, and they've confirmed the change."

Aly stood there, the floor starting to slant beneath her. She slanted her body with it, slid her reeling mind upright.

Aly had shared the contact once she'd been assured of having the interview. "You're taking my segment away? You're punishing me for what you thought my mother did? When it has absolutely nothing to do with me. When your son would directly benefit from the inheritance?"

"How can it have nothing to do with you? You knew that hussy was trying to trap an old, disoriented man and cheat his children out of what's theirs."

"You mean trap the old, disoriented *narcissistic asshole*?"

Joyce opened her mouth to respond, but Aly cut her off, her mind still reeling from the fact that Joyce had replaced her on the Meryl piece. Without bothering to tell her. Aly's segment was gone. Again.

"And don't call her that." Aly's voice was thin.

"What?" Joyce said, brows fighting Botox valiantly to rise.

"Bindu is not a hussy," she said, voice stronger.

Joyce made a strangled sound.

But Aly was not done with her. "And you can't give the Meryl interview to Jess. Not after how hard I've worked on it."

Joyce let out an incredulous laugh. "Watch yourself, Aly. Because I can, and I did."

"That interview's mine, and I'm not giving it up. That segment is mine, and I'm not giving it up." She pulled herself up to her full height. Joyce loomed over her. But Aly felt taller, filled. Stretched so tight, rips started at her seams.

"Last I checked, I run this place. That's my decision, not yours."

"Sure. But there are antidiscrimination and conflict of interest laws that forbid you from making decisions based on personal interest. You can't use projects to leverage your son's inheritance."

"That's an absurd accusation. I strongly advise you to calm down. Threatening me is not a good idea. It's impossible to prove any of that.

238

With the ratings from your previous pieces, I have no reason to give you the segment."

"Bob and Jess have had worse ratings, and they've been given assignment after assignment."

Color rose up Joyce's long neck. "If you don't like the way things work here, you're free to find another workplace."

"Really, you're threatening to fire me? I strongly advise you to think about that, because I have enough evidence from ten years of you shutting me out of every opportunity to advance myself under the guise of relatability. Which, by the way, is the oldest discrimination trick in the book."

Joyce's temper cooled as fast as it had risen. A glimmer of calculation edged into her eyes. One part disbelief at the fact that Aly actually possessed a spine and one part belief that Aly had absolutely no power in this situation. "Let's both calm down, table this discussion. Take the rest of this week off, and we'll talk on Monday."

Finally, after ten years of fooling herself, Aly knew what that meant. She was never getting her segment. Her dream was over.

~

Where are you? Bindu's text came through as Aly was pulling into the Shady Palms parking lot. The gold lettering on the sign loomed huge in front of her. SHADY PALMS—LUXURY LIVING FOR YOUR VIBRANT YEARS. Aly sat there staring at it. Mesmerized by how she'd ended up here. How she'd had everything and then lost it.

Reaching across to the passenger side, she picked up the wine bag. She'd found a bottle of Goan port in a liquor store in Miami months ago and saved it for something special. Fine, she'd saved it for the celebration when she got her segment.

To hell with that. She was celebrating this day just the way it was. Even though it was a day when she had to give up on a dream. To hell with her dream; she had her backbone.

And yet her hand stilled on the door. She couldn't get out of the car, couldn't move. The huge gold letters of the sign hypnotized her. She twisted open the cap and took a swig straight from the bottle.

The sweet, sharp liquid burned down her throat and tightened her chest. Memories of cousins' weddings in Goa danced around her like the aunties and uncles jiving on the dance floor, henna-reddened hair coifed into bobs, lace dresses swirling.

Aly had hated dancing. Until Ashish had shown her how to love it. How smitten she'd been at how well he led, arms strong and in control, moving her at his will even as he gave himself over to the music.

I'm a Bandra boy, of course I can jive, he'd said with the sense of belonging she'd never felt in her home. *I have you. Let go.*

There was no dance if she resisted. If she let go, she became the music, the swinging, the spinning, the sliding.

Putting the bottle to her mouth, she started chugging in earnest. Sugar and alcohol burned through her body.

She didn't know how long she'd sat there nursing the bottle when a knocking sounded on her car window.

"Aly?"

Ashish?

He gestured at her to unlock the door. She lowered the window and watched as his face appeared from behind the reflected lights. Her lips felt warm and tart from the wine.

"How long have you been sitting here?" His eyes slid to the bottle.

She took another swig before getting out of the car and making her (only slightly swaying) way toward Bindu's lobby.

It took him a while to catch up with her. He took the bottle swinging from her hand, capped it, and put it in the bag, which he'd gathered from the car. He was holding her purse. He'd cleaned up the car after her.

She laughed. Because the role swap was hilarious.

"I'm not getting back with you, Ashish," she said as he followed her into the elevator. It needed to be said. So many things needed to be said.

He didn't deny that's why he was here. Evidently the tongue he had so skillfully shoved into her mouth couldn't make up that lie.

She shoved a finger into his chest. The bastard was wearing a pale-yellow linen shirt with the tiniest cracked hearts. Yup, so many truths in that clothing choice. Her mouth watered at the feel of his chest under the textured weave. The headiness from the wine didn't help. "Don't you want to know why?"

He didn't move. Not even a twitch of an eyebrow.

Well, she was telling him anyway. "I don't think I have it in me to dig up all the patriarchy buried inside you and then fight it for you." She used her hands to dig up the air between them.

His eyes were steady on hers. "What if I fight it myself?"

The laugh that erupted from her almost choked her. "Then why didn't you before? Why didn't you when you had me and I was asking for your help? When I was asking you to examine why you were acting the way you were acting?" Her voice rose and echoed around the mirrored elevator. The force of her feelings, her rage, might have pushed the elevator doors apart because they slid open.

"What if I've done that now?" he said, following her out of the elevator, the corridor lights too bright above them.

She spun on him, and he steadied her because the travertine floor leading to Bindu's new home spun with her. "Don't you see. You're still thinking the word *I. Me.* You think I'll come around just like that. Now that you're ready. Now that you've realized what you want and realized that the way to get it is to do this . . ." She danced her hand around his face. *"This."*

"Is there no place for forgiveness in all this, Aly?"

The bastard had divorced her when she didn't jump at his whim to move across the world. He wanted to talk forgiveness?

A wild craving for the sweet, thick wine that hit fast and furiously stomped through her. She reached for the bag in his hand, and he pulled it away. But she snatched it from him.

"I've forgiven you, Ash. I spent every day during our marriage for-giving you because you were human, because you loved me, because there was so much goodness in you, because I loved you, because you saw me." She counted off on her fingers and followed it up with a long gulp of the wine. "You saw me, and you did the thing that you knew would hurt me the most *because* you saw me!"

How he'd laugh if he knew what had just happened. That the segment was gone from her hands. Up in flames. All the things he'd believed about her were true.

"And I forgave that too. What about me? If I keep forgiving you, keep making excuses for you, then what about me? When do I forgive myself for not having the self-worth to stop forgiving you over and over again, for blaming myself for not being enough. For taking that on for you?"

"I made mistakes. I didn't have the courage to chase what I wanted, and when you did, I had a hard time with that. And it became worse because I didn't accept that I did. But all those other things, was I really all that? My entire life feels like I'm paying for something I never did. Baba's actions, other men's sins. You're not the only person who feels unseen. All I am to you, to my mother, to my daughter, is a sum total of the things generations of men did before me. You throw the word *patriarchy* around to explain your anger. I didn't create any of that, but I feel blamed for it all the time."

"No!" How convenient to separate himself from the privilege he'd milked. "You are a sum total of the things *you* do. You know better. You have information they didn't. You're able to understand the unfairness and the pain it caused. You have no excuse."

"You're right. I have no excuse. I want to do better. But won't you consider for a moment that it's not all privilege, being a man. I was raised to think I had to be a breadwinner. My entire existence was tied to it. Engineering and sales and putting on a suit—that's what gave us the life I was told I had to provide. From where I was standing, I had to put away my dream, and you got to just drop your responsibilities toward our family and chase after your dream."

She was about to scream her frustration, but he held up his hand.

"But I was wrong. You were never irresponsible about it. And if not for you, I would never have gotten to do what I loved. I would have died without knowing what creating sound at that scale felt like. What making a hundred thousand people lose their minds over music feels like." His eyes were on fire. Eyes that had been restless with boredom, with what she'd seen as entitlement, burned with passion.

Great timing, as always, because she couldn't find the passion that had burned inside her. It was gone, lost with the last shot she'd blown.

"Then why are you back?"

"Because none of it means anything without you, and Cullie, and Ma." He was standing too close, and she hated how much comfort her body drew from his nearness. All she wanted was to step even closer. To grab his closeness with her entire body. To use this thing coded into their blood: a comfort in each other.

It had taken leaving for him to see that.

"So you found all this passion, and now you want to give it up and come back because you miss us?"

"I'm not giving it up, but I would. There's a company here who sets up concerts with Indian artists. DesiBeats. They need a sound engineer to run their concerts. I've been interviewing with them. I just got the job. I'll have to travel to where the concerts are, all across the US and maybe Europe. But I can be here and do what I want to do. I'm serious. I want to do better by you, by us."

Laughter spurted up from the very center of her. She couldn't stop laughing. Could it really be this easy? Bitter, jealous rage burned through her. "You want to do better *now*? You walked away. You ended us. And you were right. About everything. About me just not having it in me."

He grabbed her shoulders. "Aly, sweetheart, what happened? Is it the Meryl interview? Did something happen with the segment?"

All the rage and the sadness inside her bloated and rolled. The shaking started deep inside her. "It's gone. You were right. I was never going to get my own segment. It was never about whether or not I'm capable of it. It was about timing, about wanting it before the world was ready to let me have it."

"Oh, Aly." He stroked her back. "You'll find a way."

Now his voice was filled with faith? This was what he'd predicted all along. And now that he had his dream, he wanted to be benevolent?

Before she could push him away with all the force of her frustration, the elevator doors opened on a ding, and they jumped apart because Cullie stumbled out.

Alone.

She doubled over and started sobbing.

CHAPTER TWENTY-FIVE

BINDU

In the end it turned out that I was the trouble, and like the promise of our first meeting, she'd met me without flinching.
From the journal of Oscar Seth

There's a sensor built into every parent. A barometer that can gauge the disasters in their children's lives for intensity. When Bindu opened the door and saw Cullie's face, she knew that something had seismically shifted in her granddaughter. Alisha and Ashish followed close on Cullie's heels, their barometers already pinging with her distress.

For a moment Bindu thought Cullie would fall into her arms and break down, but she headed straight for the food Bindu had laid out on the table and picked up a plate. Without a single word, she proceeded to pile a mountain of food on it and dug right in as tears streamed down her face, liberally salting her meal.

Alisha gave Ashish a death glare and mirrored Cullie's actions exactly, right down to the tears rolling into the food.

"Shouldn't we wait for our guest?" Bindu said.

Cullie huffed out a laugh. The completely uncharacteristic chortles went on and on, until finally the words "He's gone" flew from her.

"Can you give us a little more than that?" Bindu asked. If Cullie's tears had sent the barometer into overdrive, the laughter made it crash past its limit. Bindu sat down next to Cullie.

"This is delicious," Alisha said. "You should eat too before it gets cold." Then she turned to Cullie. "Did you guys break up?" Sneaky sneaky Alisha.

Cullie let out another heartbreaking laugh. "We aren't ceramic vases that had been baked together, Mom." She yanked the central bone of the pomfret from its perfectly fried flesh. "You have to be together to break up."

"Tell us what happened," Ashish said gently and then pushed Cullie's hair off her forehead.

There was so much pain on her face that Bindu had the urge to hunt this Rohan boy down.

"It was never about me," Cullie said, sliding a horrified glance at Bindu. "I'm so sorry, Binji. I swear I had no idea." Now she threw her arms around Bindu and started to sob in earnest.

The ugliest sensation stirred in Bindu's chest. She pulled away from Cullie. "What are you trying to say?"

"He was here looking for you."

Cold dread stabbed across Bindu's skin. With every shred of acting skill she had ever gathered, she dropped a mask of calm over her face. "I thought you said his name was Rohan." Even as she said it, her mind unraveled what couldn't possibly be true.

Rohan could not possibly be Oscar's grandson. A shaking started deep in her belly. Her gaze flew to Ashish. He was staring intently from one woman to the next. *The ABCs of my life*, he'd loved to say. Bindu suspected they'd found Cullie a *C* name just so he'd get to make that declaration.

The glazed intoxicated look was gone from Alisha's eyes, replaced by rage. Everyone seemed to have grasped that this was worse than anything they'd expected. But they didn't know the half of it.

This could not be happening.

Bindu couldn't faint. She couldn't throw up. She couldn't move.

"Binji. I'm so very sorry."

"Stop saying that. This is not your fault." Bindu's voice was wild. The terror in her heart was wild. "You can't go near him. You understand. Not anywhere near him."

"I know. I would never let him hurt you." Cullie was studying her with some alarm. They all were.

"Why would he want to hurt Ma?" Ashish said, and everything started to move in slow motion.

Cullie sniffed and squeezed her temples. "He thinks his grandfather was in love with Binji. Apparently the man left some journals documenting their relationship. He was some big shot filmmaker back in the day."

"Oscar Seth." It felt strange to say his name out loud in front of her family. "He's Oscar Seth's grandson," Bindu said.

"The old Bollywood star?" Ashish asked.

Silence fell between them like a curtain, plastic pushing up against her nose. Bindu struggled to breathe.

Ashish turned the strangest look on her. "How did you know?"

"Binji?" Cullie exchanged a matching look with her father. "How'd you know it was Oscar Seth? I never said his grandfather's name."

The three of them were staring at Bindu now. It struck her that they were her entire world. Outside of them, not a single thing mattered. And she was about to lose them. But how could she not tell Cullie? Not with what all of this might mean for her.

Alisha poured her a glass of water, and Bindu drank.

"I acted in his film when I was seventeen. And we . . ." She cleared her throat. "We had a relationship." She looked at Ashish. "It was just before I married your father."

Ashish dropped into the chair next to Bindu. He opened his mouth, but no words came out. Her son was never at a loss for words. He had never looked at her this way.

He pushed off the chair again and started pacing.

Alisha patted Bindu's hand. "You acted in a film with Oscar Seth?" She sounded impressed.

Cullie stroked Bindu's shoulder. "You were seventeen?"

They both looked at her like they had no idea who she was. And she didn't have the words to bridge that gap.

"Why didn't you tell us?" Alisha, of the hard questions, asked.

If Bindu could find her voice, she might have tried to answer. But before she could, the answer dawned on Alisha's face. Her gaze slid to Ashish, and he stopped pacing.

"Oh God," Ashish said, understanding draining his face of color.

There was no escape left. They knew.

"Beta . . . I swear . . . I never meant . . ." Bindu pushed her face into her hands. *I was seventeen*, she wanted to say, *I was alone*, but the excuses wouldn't come out.

"I need a moment." Ashish's voice was unreadable. When she looked up, his face was unreadable. Turning his back on her, he made his way onto the lanai.

Bindu wanted to follow him, but she couldn't move. Alisha and Cullie were frozen too.

All her life Bindu had been grateful for how much like her Ashish looked. Now she wished she had a sign. Rajendra's nose, Oscar's eyes. Anything. But there was nothing.

Finally, she followed him into the lanai. Silence wasn't going to help them get through this.

"I never meant to hide something like this from you," she said when he didn't turn around, didn't acknowledge her. "But I didn't know what else to do. How do you tell your child you don't know who his father is?"

He stiffened, arms resting on the railing, the ocean breeze swirling a storm in his hair. "Did you know I used to dream that he wasn't my father?" he said, eyes trained on the waves. "I used to wish that I would wake up one day and he'd be someone else."

She wanted to pull him close, but she was afraid to touch him. Her beautiful, sensitive boy, whom Rajendra had tried so hard to "make a man of."

Cullie and Alisha stepped out into the lanai. Alisha looked guarded. Cullie looked like she might be sick.

"I don't know how to make this okay," Bindu said. "I wish he'd been different with you too. I wish I'd known how to make that happen."

He let out a bitter laugh. "I always wondered why you never said anything to him." Finally, he turned around. "But you were protecting me."

She didn't know what she'd expected to see in his face. Anger? Hatred? Sadness? But he was shaking his head, that bitter laugh spilling incredulously from him.

"Dad, are you laughing?" Cullie said, sounding as worried as Bindu felt.

"Ashish, you're scaring me," Bindu said.

He came to her then and took her hands. "Ma, he knew. Baba knew."

"No, he didn't. All he knew was that I acted in Oscar's film."

"No, I mean he knew you had the affair. He suspected that I might not be his son."

Cullie pressed both hands into her face, then pulled them away angrily. Hearing so plainly what this might mean about Rishi's relationship to their family, to her, had to be devastating.

Alisha looked in horror from one face to another.

Ashish's gaze stayed steady on Bindu. He seemed to be reliving something, brows drawn together in focus, eyes filled with memories. "If I hadn't wished so hard for a different father, I might not even have remembered this. But I'm his son, Ma," he whispered. "I'm Baba's son. And he knew that too."

"I don't understand what you're saying," Bindu said.

Ashish's eyes softened, filled with sympathy. "I can't believe he never told you. Never put your mind at ease. He was such a piece of work."

"Dad, please," Cullie said wildly, reflecting Bindu's desperation. "What are you trying to say?"

Ashish pushed Bindu gently into the rattan couch, as though she'd suddenly turned fragile. Then he sat down next to her. "When I was in fifth grade, he had a paternity test done."

That couldn't be true.

Could it?

"It was summer vacation. My friends and I had broken the neighbor's window while playing cricket. So I was terrified when Baba came into my room before he left for work. But he didn't even mention the window." Ashish's eyes were bright with the effort to access the memories. "He told me to pick up the mail that day while he was at work and put it where you wouldn't find it. He told me not to tell you. Which only made me curious. I saw the UK stamp on the envelope and steamed it open and then glued it back before giving it to him."

Shock choked Bindu, constricted her throat.

No one else seemed able to speak either.

Finally Ashish spoke again. "It was a long report with lots of tables that didn't make any sense to me. But there was a letter addressed to him. It actually said the words *Paternity Test* and *Probability of Paternity 99 percent*. Both our names were on it. That evening I remember him squeezing my shoulders. The closest he ever came to giving me a hug. It was all very confusing. Then that night I saw him shred the letter. I didn't think much of it because I didn't understand it. Everything about him was always secretive and withheld, so I forgot about it."

Except, of course, who could forget the only hug he'd ever gotten from his father?

"I still can't believe he never told you."

But how could Rajendra have told her? That would have meant acknowledging he didn't trust her. It would have meant admitting he never believed that she didn't sleep with Oscar: the only lie she'd ever told him.

"But why did he wait until you were in fifth grade?" Bindu asked the most meaningless question, because she'd never have answers for the ones that mattered.

Alisha tapped her phone. "Paternity tests became available in 1985." When Ashish was in fifth grade.

"He'd been waiting for proof that I was his son," Ashish said with an odd calm. "Not that it changed anything. It's not like he got all warm and fuzzy overnight or anything."

Rajendra hadn't had a warm or fuzzy cell in his body. She'd never understood if it was a matter of ability or choice. Unlike Ashish, whose warmth was irresistible to everyone who met him. Bindu cupped her son's face. "All I wanted was for none of this to hurt you. Can you forgive me?"

His eyes were wet, but something fierce shone in them. "Do you know why it didn't matter that Baba was the way he was? Because you never let me feel unloved even for a moment. You were seventeen, Ma. You were an incredible mother. We'll find our way around this."

A giant sniff came from Alisha. The way she was looking at Ashish was probably the only good thing that had happened here today.

Cullie's sniff was far more heartbreaking. "Well then," she said. "At least I'm not related to that asshole." Her eyes were sadder than Bindu had ever seen them. There were so many assholes in play right now, but Bindu was pretty sure she knew which one Cullie meant. Rishi Seth may not be related to Cullie, but he'd obviously found his way past her defenses.

"I'm so sorry to bring this ugliness back for you, Binji." She swiped a determined sleeve against her cheeks. "But I have an app to write." With that she disappeared into the bedroom.

Cullie wasn't the one who'd brought the ugliness back.

The truth just had a way of never going away. A cosmic impossibility, indeed.

"I think I need some air," Bindu said, and Alisha and Ashish pushed her out the door.

"Go, Ma," Alisha said, already cleaning up, furiously trying to set things straight. "We'll clean up and leave."

~

The only time Oscar had ever meant to touch Bindu was when the camera was rolling. He'd been honest with her from the start. So, she'd known it would be the only opportunity they'd have to unleash their feelings, the fevered arousal, the uncontainable yearning. The hungry lens was meant to be the curtain protecting the relief of their coupling, containing their release.

Oscar being Oscar, he'd done every scene in one take, never making a mistake, never botching his lines just so he could touch her again.

When her disappointment had colored her cheeks and wet her eyes, he'd explained himself: *Film is too expensive. It's someone else's money.*

He'd always explained himself. He'd always treated her like she was worthy of that, worthy of his thoughts. He'd understood the demands she'd felt worthy enough to make.

How could I make mistakes when the scene involved laying myself bare to you? The mistakes I make are when I have to hide how you make me feel. His hands had trembled as he shoved them into his pockets as she threw herself at him.

How can you make me live without you? Why is that your decision? Why? She'd been insensate with the injustice of it. Back when she'd still believed that life might be fair, that desire and love might be enough.

Because I have children not that much younger than you.

Your daughter is six. I'm seventeen. You're leaping a bit, aren't you? You're barely thirty. My baba is older than my aie by thirteen years.

What you want is impossible, Bhanu.

Why?

Because I'm married. Because I'm Oscar Seth, and the world will never let us live this down without scandal and ugliness. But it's not just them. I've lived and breathed my work for a decade. All these years I've looked on with disdain as bastards slept with actresses so they could have the roles that would change their lives. Now I see myself in their faces. I see my own face in that ugly currency.

I don't want a role that will change my life. I only want you. How reckless she'd been. How out of control of her treacherous heart. How fearless in asking, begging, for what she wanted.

That, of all things, had broken his heart. *You should want more. Claim this, Bhanu. What you can do in front of a camera, I've never seen anything like it.*

His love of cinema had felt like competition, stealing the love she wanted for herself.

I don't care. She'd said it over and over, believing she would always have the camera, hating the impossibility of having him.

You are the only woman with whom I let my foot slip. I'm married to a woman who struggles with depression. I'm a father. I can't expose them to the kind of public humiliation that will come with this. I just can't. I can be nothing more than your director, your costar.

Their bodies they'd controlled, kept them from burning away in passion. But their hearts, those were unbiddable. The flames fed what bloomed there. Over that winter, they'd become so much more than a slipped foot. They'd been a tumble down the Sahyadri peak. A landslide. A mountain collapsed into an ocean. She'd known this in the deepest part of her heart.

So she told him it was enough, he being her director, her on-screen hero. And she gave him the only thing he felt he could take from her. Her all in front of the camera. Her heart and her body. She became the story he wanted to tell, the colors on his film, the light and shadow in his lens. She let herself dissolve into his celluloid and disappeared into his voice as he sang the love song that had been raging in his soul his whole life.

It was watching on a screen what he'd done to her, with her, in those Eastmancolor tones that had broken him, brought him to his knees.

The rush from the climax scene had been so heady, so intense, it had vibrated through their beings, tied them together in a way no force on earth could untangle.

He'd pushed into her changing room in a trance. She'd fallen into his arms in one of her own. Their joining had been fast and hard, months of foreplay released in one blinding explosion.

Everything after that had been pure pain.

Nothing had hurt more than his apology. *All the beauty I've ever wanted to create. You gave me that. And I have nothing to offer you in return.*

But she'd had him. In those moments, on that hard cotton mattress, on that timeless celluloid, she had him in a way no one else would ever have him. And she had the camera. It had shown her what being alive meant. Two loves too big to fit in her young heart that she lost in one ruthless swoop.

Deep in the throes of his betrayal, she would take years to grasp what he'd sacrificed too. He had offered her everything in return.

He'd shelved the film. Erased his moment of genius. Destroyed the work that he was never again able to create, even though he spent the rest of his life chasing it. This too she knew, because even as he gave her up along with all of that, she followed him. Through the pages of film magazines. Through the movie-theater screen. From the distance of a fan. Her obsession hidden behind the veil of a generalized obsession with cinema. Her one rebellion against Rajendra.

Everything else that the camera had given her she locked away with the pain of losing Oscar: freedom, a voice, heady power over her body. She spent her marriage being what her mother had raised her to be: whatever her husband wanted. Rajendra had wanted the oldest adage in the Book of Marriage. A goddess in the drawing room and a concubine in the bedroom.

It had worked out perfectly. An outlet for her rage and heartbreak after Oscar's betrayal.

Oscar Seth, Bollywood's conscience, the embodiment of integrity, might have called her his greatest moment, but he'd also called her a slip of the foot, a mistake as trivial as tripping on wet earth.

Oscar's abandonment, her parents' shame, Rajendra's greedy charity: they had all piled one on top of the other to break her. Pulled the skin off her body with ruthless tug after ruthless tug. Exposed her powerlessness so completely she'd had to grow scabs so she could have armor. She'd rewritten herself. Become someone who would never feel that kind of pain again. Buried every desire, every dream. She'd believed herself saved. Been grateful for it. Made up and made up and made up for her youthful recklessness. Atoned and atoned until she was gone from inside herself.

Then again, maybe she *had* been saved. The world was different then. She might have ended up on the streets, chewed up and spat out just like her mother had predicted. Bindu had believed Aie, because chewed up and spat out was exactly how she'd felt.

Or maybe she could have changed the world. Walked away from the safety of her family even after Oscar left her to fend for herself. She could have chased the light that blazed inside her when the camera turned on.

If only she'd known then that the cycle of belief, which caused the world to work the way it did, could be broken only by disproving one lie at a time. Women were here today, where they had power, where they had a voice, because molecule by molecule, moment by moment, choice by choice, someone had called out the lies peddled as truth. It had been a boulder the size of the earth, and changing the direction of its spin couldn't happen at one go.

Not when mothers had been enlisted on both sides of the fight.

To have her own mother's hands wrapped around her throat, trying to strangle the life out of her, was a memory no one could live with. So Bindu had cut it out like the bitter innards of a kingfish and tossed it back into the ocean.

She'd never expected it to find its way back to her on a returning tide, forty-seven years later.

Aie had meant to kill her. That was the realization that came back first. Or maybe it had never gone away, like bloodstains on cotton bales and burn marks on raw wood. You had to destroy the thing to remove the stain, and if you couldn't, then the stain became part of its identity. Woven into the fibers, altered beyond repair.

Why didn't you die instead of shaming us like this? Aie screamed into her face.

There can be no shame in this much beauty, Oscar breathed into her ear.

There is only shame if people know, Rajendra whispered into her skin. Then he'd taught her how to hide and to live around what you wanted. A different you in the bedroom—panting over your pleasure, free. A different you in the living room—covered up and protected by domestic modesty.

Far away from the photographs her cousin had stolen from the set and taken to her mother. Proof that her daughter had lost her way. That simple, accidental discovery of the photographs had turned Oscar's search for beauty into ugliness. Pictures of Bindu's shame. Of the nakedness she'd slipped into with such ease, because Poornima's ruin was in her soul and not in her body.

Get out of my house, Aie sobbed as her hands cut off the oxygen to Bindu's lungs.

Her father had simply collapsed, palsied shaking jerking his body as his eyes took in his wife trying to kill his daughter for destroying their family's honor.

Unless Aie's trying to kill her was what had done it. Aie, who had known so little and had wanted to know even less. Because knowledge was dangerous.

When Baba collapsed, pulling with him the dinner laid out on the white tablecloth clutched in his hands, the crash had swallowed the sound of her name on his lips.

Bindu.

She'd been the one to call the ambulance as her mother stood there useless. In the hospital, Bindu had met Dr. Rajendra Desai.

That same day, Oscar's wife had emptied half a bottle of sleeping pills down her throat. So much destruction over one choice. One she'd made in the heady haze of power and freedom.

For days, Rajendra cared for Baba while Bindu refused to leave Baba's side, no matter Aie's silent disdain.

Then one day Rajendra overheard Aie spilling her venom on Bindu and followed Bindu into the stairwell, where she went to spill her tears of shame.

Why she'd told him about Poornima she'd never know. *I did a nude scene in a movie.*

It had changed everything.

He'd told her he didn't care. He wanted to marry her. He'd known it from the moment he laid eyes on her. A line she'd heard too many times in her life. But never after she'd told a man the truth about who she was.

He paid Oscar off. Oscar promised to can the film. To destroy all her scenes. To never contact her again.

No one will ever see the film. No one will ever speak of it.

A handshake between men. Both men kept their promise.

Neither asked Bindu what she wanted.

257

CHAPTER TWENTY-SIX

CULLIE

Bhanu had given me a fake name. I never suspected this. But I can imagine her trying on a new name as she might try on a pilfered bikini.
From the journal of Oscar Seth

What kind of idiot regrets never having kissed a man who betrayed her, who tried to destroy her family?

Cullie shoved a few layers of bebinca into her mouth. She refused to be one of those people who lost her appetite over heartbreak.

Heartbreak.

Yuck. What an ugly, pathetic word.

Heartache. Heartsick. Heartless.

What a bad rep the poor unsuspecting organ got. All day it pumped away, *contract release contract release contract release.* Sped up when the brain and other organs needed more oxygen. Slowed down when the body needed rest. So much work. So much being on top of all the other organs' needs.

Sucker.

Sucker!

The accusation started repeating in her head in an endless loop.

Her Neuroband worked tirelessly on her wrist. *The only way out is through*, she repeated to herself every time a spiral started in her head. The feeling that she was going to be swallowed whole loomed close. But she went through it. Feeling and feeling and feeling.

She'd grown roots into Binji's bed, where she'd been coding nonstop for two days. Stopping her fingers, leaving her computer: it felt inconceivable. It hurt too much to stop. Even making a trip to the restroom meant letting her brain think about something other than the code her fingers were spitting out like rage-y vomits.

How had she not figured this out sooner?

She was coding an app that measured the body's reaction to heartbreak on the Neuroband and matched it with an activity that would raise adrenaline and dopamine levels. Yes, she was writing an app that would help people become a heroine from a rom-com. But instead of forcing you to take solace in tubs of ice cream, this would customize your healing binge.

The way Shloka matched you with chants, Appiness matched you with an activity. Go for a walk, eat a piece of candy, meditate, watch TV, dance, talk to a friend. Even your most-loved ones didn't know what you needed when you felt like shit. Maybe your own body did. Just the way your own body was what told you that your mind needed to calm down, which is what Shloka used.

They had been barking up the wrong tree all along. An app telling you how to find someone who made you feel seen and precious and *right* might be impossible, but it was also less useful than an app that held your hand through the battering this love business put you through.

Thinking the word *love* made Cullie's heart do the most ghastly twist, and she wanted to kick herself.

Appiness kept telling her that she needed to keep coding and eat more of Binji's food. She had worked her way through all the deliciousness Binji had cooked. Every ugly thought stopped when Binji's familiar flavors hit her tongue.

You don't get this, loser. And it's delicious.

One did not hold mental conversations with a man who'd cheated you into thinking you mattered to him.

That was the definition of being pathetic. But Rohan, or Rishi, or whatever the hell his name was, kept making shattered eyes inside her head, and she couldn't care less about being pathetic. She was dehydrated from weeping, so, well, the pathos train had chugged away from the dignity platform long ago.

Cullie stared at her laptop. Endless thumbnail images of his face tiled the screen. She'd googled him. Without meaning to.

She started clicking through. One after another after another. Long hair, short hair, shaved head. Bearded, stubbled, clean jawed. Lean and young, buff and bulky. Head thrown back in laughter, eyes hollow with grief. It was like his entire life was documented right there, and he'd been forever changing. Unlike her, Cullie, who couldn't even bring herself to change her haircut or the color of the clothes she wore.

Rishi Seth.

Director. Producer. Actor. Writer.

Feminist. Activist. Film preservationist.

He was wrapped up in more labels than she'd ever known anyone to have.

She clicked and read. Clicked and read.

All of it. Every word. A bigger hunger than she'd ever known gripped her.

Her fingers stopped on a piece about his grandfather's funeral. Clad in a white mourning kurta, eyes swollen. His Bollywood face broken with Bollywood tears reached into her rib cage and squeezed her heart.

Heir apparent to Seth Films. The only Indian to have studied film preservation under the Swiss grand master Bijou. Responsible for restoring some twenty destroyed films, slices of history that might have been lost to the human race if not for him. Apparently a Herculean accomplishment.

He seemed obsessed with it. This obsession with getting back lost things. "He's an old soul, and I'm a young soul," his grandfather had said in a clip they'd done together to promote the film preservation institute they'd been working on for ten years. "We're the perfect partners in crime."

Binji's face, her smell, the million memories that went with her. It was woven into the fabric of who Cullie was. The pain of his losing his grandfather slashed through her.

I just want to give her something. Something I've worked on for years, something my grandfather died without ever being able to give her. She'll want this. Trust me.

She'd barely seen Binji for the past two days. Her parents had left her alone. Binji obviously needed space too. Those were some potent bombs Cullie had brought home that day. Then been too selfish to think about.

How had Binji lived all those years with such heavy secrets? Love for her father rose sharp and strong inside Cullie. She'd always had his lap to crawl into as a child; she'd always had his brain to pick when a problem challenged her. And he'd had neither of those things from his own father.

Just as Cullie was about to drag herself out of bed to go looking for her grandmother because questions were suddenly exploding inside her, Binji stormed into the room. "Okay," she said. "You've been crying for two days."

"I have not."

"Cullie, when water leaks out of our eyes, that's what we tend to call crying."

Cullie pulled up the neckline of her black tank top and wiped her eyes.

Binji sat down on the bed next to her. "You also haven't stopped moving your fingers on that keyboard."

Cullie held up her fingers and wiggled them. She wasn't writing code right now.

Binji took Cullie's hand and started massaging her fingers one at a time, as though she were counting them. "You didn't shed one drop when Hot Steve went back to his wife." Her grip tightened on Cullie's hand because she'd clearly anticipated that Cullie would try to pull away.

The look in her eyes kept Cullie from putting any force into it. "Tell me what's so special about this Rishi that he's turned my Cullie into this?"

Cullie turned her hand and wrapped it around Binji's.

"I think you're the one with more to tell."

Binji tried to pull her hand away. This time Cullie held on. "Tell me why it took you two days to come to me with that question. This thing with Oscar Seth, it was more than just an affair, wasn't it?"

All the color drained from Binji's face. "I'm sorry you got caught up in all this."

The thought that Cullie wasn't sorry struck slowly. She was livid, but she wasn't sorry she had met him. "What is *all this*, though?"

"Did he not tell you? What happened between you two?"

She'd never known Binji to be cagey. Binji was being cagey.

Maybe if one of them broke the cycle and was honest, they'd get somewhere. Cullie was gripped with the urge to get somewhere, to not feel quite like this. As though she'd lost all control.

"Ever since I met him, he'd been talking about his grandfather's journal detailing a relationship he had with a woman. He was here in Florida to meet her. Turns out the woman was you. Turns out he only became friends with me because he thought I'd get him to you."

Suddenly Binji looked old in a way Cullie could never have imagined, the gentle give of her skin drooping just a fraction more, the familiar pattern of lines on her face just a fraction starker. "Did he say why he was looking for me?" She looked like all her ghosts had come home to roost inside her.

"He wouldn't tell me. He said he had to tell only you. He's oddly . . . what's the word for it . . . principled? Filled with right and wrong.

Filled with . . ." She couldn't say the word *integrity*. If Binji had looked concerned before, she looked stricken now. "All he told me was that he wanted to . . . had to meet you."

"Then why didn't he?"

"Because I wouldn't let him!"

Binji rubbed Cullie's arm, some of the spirit that had been sucked from her returning to her gaze. "But how did you find out what he was up to? How did you know he'd sought you out to get to me?"

Cullie felt that now-familiar electric zap in her chest, the one she felt every single time she thought about him. A heartzap. "He told me." It came out a whisper.

Binji sat there motionless. She didn't press her hand to her mouth, but she might as well have.

Cullie's own heart was hammering in her chest.

I couldn't risk this.

"Why? Why did he tell you before he could get what he wanted?"

It was the question Cullie had been avoiding ever since she'd walked away from him.

"And he didn't tell you why he wants to meet me?"

"All I know is that he has something he needs to give you. Something his grandfather wanted to give you." Something he'd worked on for years. But he hadn't told Cullie any details that might hurt Binji. And he hadn't stepped into that elevator.

Binji pushed herself off Cullie's bed and yanked her up by her arm. "Come on. Time to stop moping."

~

Cullie raised her hand to knock on Rishi Seth's door. Rishi Seth. It helped to think of him that way. Like a stranger, a celebrity. A man whose grandfather had some sort of connection with her grandmother. A connection that was twisting her always-composed Binji into tense knots next to her.

There was no way to know if he was still around. It had been two days. But he'd promised her he wouldn't leave without saying goodbye.

She was about to pull her arm away from the door when it flew open, and there he stood.

He was wearing red basketball shorts and a white tank top. His hair stuck to his forehead in spikes, and his color was high. He'd obviously just worked out. Good to know that his life was going on as though nothing had happened.

Then his caramel-brown eyes met hers, and she knew that wasn't true. There was a deep exhaustion in them. Sharp shadows radiated from the inside edges of his eyes and slashed downward, and his jaw was covered in stubble.

"Cullie," he said. And it made her furious that he got to say her name, one she hadn't lied about.

Binji cleared her throat, and they both jumped.

"You wanted to meet me. I'm here," Binji said.

Purpose had appeared to course through Binji when she'd marched up here. Now she seemed to be reevaluating the very meaning of life.

Rishi Seth dragged his gaze from Cullie and pulled the door wide open. "Please," he said, "won't you come inside?"

Cullie didn't want to. Inside that room she'd felt too light, too fun and flirty. She didn't want to go back in there feeling this heavy with betrayal and mistrust.

"Or we can go down to the coffee shop," he said, eyes on Cullie.

But what he wanted to talk to Binji about was in here. She should have insisted on looking at those stacks of folders and notebooks. She shouldn't have trusted him. "Let's go inside."

They followed him in. The tiny dining table they'd used as a desk was strewn with journals and binders.

An old photo album with a faded brocade cover sat on one of the couches and caught Binji's eye. She picked it up and dropped into the couch. Then, hands shaking, she opened it.

Even for a person as dramatically expressive as Binji, the storm that raged on her face as she looked at the pictures was a lot. And it got worse and worse. Finally, she closed her eyes and shut the album.

When she opened her eyes, she looked at Rishi Seth so steadily it was like she hadn't just practically vomited with emotion over the album. "These look like the stills from a period film. Is this your new project?"

This was obviously the last reaction he'd been expecting.

Cullie shrugged when he looked at her. *Don't look at me; I have no idea what's going on.* Then she realized what she was doing and glared at him.

"It's a film my grandfather made back in 1974," he said in the gentlest voice. "It was destroyed in a fire. A fire he himself set and then put out with his bare hands, because he couldn't finish the job."

When no one spoke, he sat down next to Binji, who had gone ashen again. "He was obsessed with retrieving lost and damaged films. My earliest memories are of him talking about it, and I became obsessed with it too. For years we found celluloid reels and married prints with no dupes and stored them in a climate-controlled facility. We restored stock with minor nicks and damage. I went to Switzerland for five years when I was eighteen to study cinema and preservation. Then I met Bijou, a grand master who was an expert in fire rescue, and trained under him. I didn't know then that this was the film Dada had been doing everything for."

Cullie had never seen Binji hold herself this still. Nothing moved in or around her, and yet it was like watching an implosion. Cullie had been fascinated with demolition videos in high school. Rishi's word's fell on Binji like the precision explosions that made the giant concrete-and-steel towers collapse inward.

When Binji didn't ask the question, Cullie did, speaking to him for the first time. "How do you know this was the film he'd done all that for?"

He turned to her, eyes grateful and somber, filled with memories and grief. "He had a stroke ten years ago. Soon after that I met

Bijou. It seemed to give Dada a second wind. He fought hard on his rehab, pushed himself to recover with renewed force. Within a year, you couldn't even tell that half his body had been paralyzed. He had another stroke two years ago. We'd been able to restore the first of the destroyed scenes by then. This stroke was a bad one. The doctors said it was impossible for him to survive this one. But he hung in there until all four of the destroyed scenes were restored. The morning after he watched the full cut in his home theater, I found him in his bed. He'd passed in his sleep."

Binji's hands trembled in her lap. Her lips trembled, but her eyes were tinder dry. The very air around her felt tinder dry.

Cullie sat down next to her and took her hand.

For the longest time no one spoke. Then Rishi disappeared into a room and came back with what looked like a hat box from an old movie, except it was square.

"I was the last one he spoke to." His voice was gruff with pain. "He told me where to find his journal and all the stills and notebooks from the making of *Poornima*. The last thing I remember him saying was, 'Promise me that no one will see this before Bhanu sees it. Whatever you do with it. Make sure she gets to decide what happens.'"

"I'm sorry, but what does this have to do with Binji?" Cullie asked, not because she didn't know the answer.

Binji stood, and swayed lightly on her feet. "Everything."

Rishi held out the box. "That's why I had to meet you in person. So I could give you the journals and the film."

Binji stared at the silk-covered box but didn't touch it. "I can't."

"Please. It was Dada's last wish. One he dedicated the last decades of his life to. It was worship to him."

"Don't pressure her." Cullie put her arm around Binji.

"Sorry."

The look Binji gave Rishi was filled with so many feelings, a painful lump formed in Cullie's throat.

"What do you want from me?" Binji asked.

He opened the box and extracted a leather-bound diary. "This is his journal. I think you'll want to read it." He held it out. "There's an envelope in there with your name on it. It's unopened."

Binji took the journal and clutched it with both hands, her breathing labored. Then suddenly she gave him a hard look. "Okay. And?"

He looked confused. "I just want you to read the journals."

"No, you don't," Binji said. "What else do you want?"

He smiled and caught Cullie's smile in her eyes.

They watched him, waited.

"And I want you to watch the film."

Binji's grip tightened on the journal, but her gaze was clear and strong again. "Why?"

"Why?"

"You want me to watch the film and then put it away in my cupboard?"

He looked guiltier than a puppy who'd pooped in the house. "Just watch it first. Please."

"Don't manage me. Don't treat me like I'm some little old lady." It was a phrase Binji hated more than anything.

"I would never do that." He looked at once terrified and delighted, and Cullie's heart did another slow melt.

"What do you plan to do with it?"

He tried to look innocent, but Binji's eyes stayed sharp on him.

"Just tell her the truth," Cullie said.

"I want to make a documentary about the making of *Poornima*. With you."

"Absolutely not." For the first time she sounded like herself. Her Badass Binji.

"There's a Blu-ray DVD of the film in there. Just watch—"

"I said no. Thank you for finding me and telling me about Oscar." Her voice caught. "But this is far behind me. I have no interest in digging it up."

"But—"

"Oscar said I get to decide."

He looked at Cullie for help. Cullie had no idea what the film was about or why a man had dedicated his life to rescuing it after trying to destroy it himself. But evidently it was not something Binji wanted to revisit. She wasn't going to budge.

"Will you at least think about it?"

"No." Binji fixed him with a look.

Silence hung in the air.

Binji didn't make a move to leave. Cullie realized she didn't want to leave.

"You shouldn't have lied to my granddaughter," Binji said, finally breaking the silence. "Oscar would have been ashamed of you for that."

"I know."

"Then again, he would have been proud that you didn't go through with it."

Rishi's eyes met Cullie's. "That had nothing to do with Dada." Every bit of charming commiseration was gone from his voice. The sincerity that had felled Cullie was all that was left, his heart naked in his eyes. The heartzap in Cullie's chest felt like live wires shoved into her flesh. "I didn't do that for him. I did it because I couldn't bear to lose Cullie. She's the best thing that's ever happened to me."

"But I don't even know who you are," Cullie said, the words sticking like lies on her tongue.

"You do, Cullie. You're the only person on earth who knows exactly who I am. Everybody else sees a figment of the media's imagination, a story. Even my family, they see themselves, our memories. You see only me."

Binji pressed the journal to her chest. "I'm going to go home now."

"I'll take you," Cullie said, because her heart wasn't being the neutral organ it needed to be. It was being irrational again and hurting in the most unnatural way. And her eyes were wet again.

"No, you won't." The finger Binji pointed from Cullie to Rishi and back was filled with purpose. The look she threw the box was filled with sadness as she put the journal into it and picked it up. But it was neither sadness nor purpose that was in the look she fixed Cullie with. That one blazed with something entirely different, something tinged with hope but also regret, even envy. "You'll stay and figure this out. Because you're lucky enough to still have that option."

"Thanks for staying," he said the moment Binji pulled the door shut behind her.

She turned to him. "Did you mean that?"

"Outside of lying about Dada and your Binji, I've meant every single word I've ever said to you." His remorse shone in his filterless eyes, as bright and huge as all his emotions. "Except for one thing." He took a step closer, and her body leaned automatically into his.

Her own feelings at seeing him again felt outsized inside her. "And what thing was that?"

"That I wanted to take it slow."

Before the words were fully out of his mouth, she grabbed his jaw and pushed her lips into his. And his hands were in her hair, pressing her close, so close it was like he'd never let her go.

CHAPTER TWENTY-SEVEN

ALY

Watching the film stock take up the flames after I set fire to it was like losing her all over again. I had to stop it, and this time I could. That strip of celluloid is the eternity we have together. I knew as the melting film fused with my skin that I would do everything to build it back. I would push back death for it.

From the journal of Oscar Seth

Joyce isn't wrong. Proving discrimination or conflict of interest as grounds for you not getting the segment is going to be hard," Radha said on the phone, unable to hide her glee at finally getting to sue Joyce and SFLN under the lawyerly seriousness she was attempting. As Aly's best friend, she thought it was her duty to get Aly to manage her expectations.

Aly didn't care. "My expectations from this job are already dashed. Maybe this will help the next person who dares to have these expectations."

"Oh, honey, I am so incredibly proud of you. Also, this is not the last job on earth."

"It probably is." Age was not on Aly's side, but she'd never know if that was true until she looked. For some reason she was filled with a belief that she would find something, that everything would be okay. "I've done everything I could. And it's amazing how much knowing that helps."

"You know what else you can take to the bank? That I'm going to make this as hard for them as possible, because the problem is how easy it is to keep doing what they do."

"I know you will. Thank you." That's all she could ask for.

When she let Radha go, she felt good, powerful to be hitting back. She felt rash. RASH. In all caps, it blazed inside her.

"You okay?" Ash asked.

"Not even a little bit," Aly said into the giant—and perfect—cup of coffee he had brought her in bed. "But obviously, I no longer care."

Ash had stayed over again last night. It made Aly feel bohemian and wild. Yes, sleeping with her ex-husband was the wildest thing Aly had ever done. And she didn't care that it was. "It's about time I took a page out of Cullie and Ma's book."

He grinned his lazy Ash grin and stroked her hair. "Maybe they're the ones who took a page out of yours."

For some reason that hit her right in the heart.

Cullie had found her feet again. Actually, it felt like she had found love. Which, surprisingly, made Aly understand why her own mother loved Ashish so much. An unexpected joy gripped Aly every time she was in Rishi's presence, or rather, in the presence of the way he looked at her daughter.

Bindu was fine too, albeit not as fine as she wanted them to think she was. She and Ash seemed to have found a new ease in their relationship that Aly had never noticed had been lacking.

The only thing not fine was Aly's work.

"Well, Joyce really hates my guts," she said.

He looked at her over his own coffee, salt-and-pepper hair skimming his bare shoulders. "She'll get over it. You'll make it impossible for her not to."

This time his words landed on her like a punch. She had the urge to push him off the bed, but they were forty-seven and he might break something. Putting down her empty cup, she snatched his from his hand.

"Hey!" He tried to take it back, but she moved it out of his way.

Instead of fighting her for it, he angled his body so he was leaning against the headboard of her bed. Her bed. Not theirs, because he'd walked away. Because she'd inspired him to chase his dreams. If that wasn't a damned irony, Aly didn't know what was.

"You're mad at me?" he asked. "Why?"

"Didn't you promise to figure things out by yourself?"

"You think I was being critical."

She raised a brow. "Of course you were. You're doing what you always do. You find the thing that plays on every one of my insecurities, poke at it, and then act like you didn't do it? That's the definition of gaslighting."

"Aly, come on. Do you have to bring that psychobabble into every conversation we have?"

Okay, great. This was great. This was great for the feelings she'd started to have again. The fact that something inside her recognized him as a part of her didn't mean anything. It was just comfort. They weren't married anymore. Twenty years of investment in a family wasn't at stake anymore. She didn't need to look the other way when he did this to her.

"It's not psychobabble. It's how I feel. I struggle with my need to please. Look where it got me with you."

The regret in his eyes was real. Not his usual *I want to get you off my back*. "It wasn't gaslighting. I meant it. I can't imagine how anyone might not like you. You wouldn't hurt anyone, even for a price, and you take a personal interest in the happiness of everyone around you. You are literally the best human being I know."

"Don't do this, Ashish."

He pushed a curl behind her ear. "Do you not believe this is how I feel?"

"The kicker is that I know you do. But that's only one part of it. You also know that I torture myself over how important it is for me to be liked. You knew that when you said what you said. You were making fun of my need to be liked. None of this other stuff. Only after you hurt me do you realize you've been a dick. Then you backtrack. But you have the need to be a dick to me, to be hurtful, and I don't understand it. Don't make that face. So much of our marriage was you poking a reaction out of me and me taking the bait."

"Come on, Aly, we had a lot of wonderful times. It wasn't all bad. And these past weeks? Tell me they haven't been good."

They had been fantastic. "You're right, it wasn't all bad. But I'm not the one who gave up on it." She'd asked for one thing. One thing. That he believe that she was capable of something as big or small as being an anchor on TV, something trailblazing, something she'd dreamed of from the deepest part of her.

And he'd used that against her.

Instead of responding, he looked remorseful, for all the good that did her.

"You know what I hate most? What I cannot stop kicking myself for?"

"Tell me." All his attention was on her. Not bored, distracted Ashish. New Ashish. Who made rotis, picked up after himself, and spent hours lost in the music he was mixing.

Is there no place in all of this for forgiveness? he'd asked her. It had made her furious.

Then she'd watched in awe as he let the fact that Bindu had lied to him go. It wasn't a small lie, but he'd understood why she'd told it.

Suddenly forgiveness felt less impossible. But first Aly had to say the things that hurt the most to say.

"You didn't support me when I dared to dream, when I worked my butt off for it. Supporting each other is the heart of a marriage. You kept that just out of my reach, and you did it with brutal precision. I would have told a friend to leave a man for treating her that way. But I didn't. I told myself that one worked on a marriage."

She had to stop and breathe. "And then you were the one who left me. *That*, that's the part I regret most. I let you humiliate me for years, and you got to take that final step. You. When I was the one who should have." There, she'd said it. The heart of it.

"I know. Every word of that is true. I shouldn't have left. I should have figured out what I was really angry about without leaving. I will apologize as often as you need me to. I will change whatever hurts you. I'm here now. But if everything I say gives you déjà vu to when I was a dick, we don't have a future."

She got out of bed. She'd pulled on a tank top over her bare body, and it was armor she needed. "I never said we had a future. I don't want to be a wife." Even before Cullie's dates, she'd known it. She was done with marriage. "I don't want to be the kind of wife I was conditioned to be. Nor the kind of wife you were conditioned to want."

He got out of bed and came to her. "Then don't. Be the woman you want to be. I'm not that man anymore."

"I'm not sure I can put away our history."

"Fine. But can you . . . can *we* put our happiness before our history?"

She'd have to think about it. So she told him that. Instead of a hard sell, she got relief from him. He was happy with what they had right now. She was too. And that was all that meant anything.

CHAPTER TWENTY-EIGHT

BINDU

"I'd rather have a large life than a long one." It was a line from a film Bhanu loved. No life could be large in its entirety. Even a life that looked large from the outside was mostly mundane, filled with day-to-day struggles. But if you were lucky, you got to have moments—experiences and relationships—that were so big they made the rest of your life feel large. What I had with Bhanu altered the dimension of my lifetime.
From the journal of Oscar Seth

Bindu had tucked the red box Cullie's young man had given her all the way to the back of her walk-in closet. Out of sight, where she wouldn't have to think about it. Oscar's journal. A copy of *Poornima*. And his letter.

So, being inside the closet, stroking the red silk box: admittedly, that was a little counterproductive. Opening the box and taking out the letter with her name on it—well, Bhanu's name on it—was *a lot* counterproductive.

The paper was thick, strong, like old-world things. Meant to last instead of being consumed and discarded and replaced. Maybe there was nothing wrong with this new way. Wasn't creation and destruction the inevitability of life? Renewal.

Sliding a finger under the edge where the glue had loosened, she opened it.

And dropped it. Because the last thing that she'd expected to find peeked out from between the thick sheets.

Parijat.

The parijat flowers she'd strung into a garland for him.

She sank to the floor. The flattened and dried-to-membranes blooms had slipped out of the envelope and lay on the floor, faded brown against the white carpet. She'd threaded them together with the needle and twine her aie left in her flower basket next to her prayer altar. Aie, who had always worn flowers in her jet-black hair, day or night.

Such a beautiful thing. Every morning Aie had sat on the front veranda of their red stone house and pierced her needle into the delicate orange stems with exquisite care. If only Bindu had been the recipient of half that care.

Aie had loved parijat. Cursed in mythology to only bloom in darkness. Lord Krishna had brought the plant from the heavens to earth for his wife Rukmini, but his other wife, Satyabhama, had become jealous. So he'd planted the tree in Satyabhama's courtyard. It had grown at a slant and dropped flowers into Rukmini's adjoining courtyard, sending Satyabhama into a rage. She had cursed the flowers to bloom only at night and to fall off the tree as soon as they bloomed.

Every morning, Bindu woke up to a carpet of flowers around the parijat tree, the orange stems sticking up from the white petals like flames. *Fire blooms*, Oscar had called them. *Like you, Bhanu.*

She let one finger touch the papery petals.

Life returned to them in her memory, the white and orange flesh turning plump again. They sat in the palm of her hand as she held them out to Oscar, and his sensitive eyes glazed with tears.

Why? Why did the only man in the world she would ever want have to be someone she could never have? She'd screamed it to the heavens. To all the gods in the universe. Not one of them had an answer. The pain of their silence had been unbearable.

Now the memories pinched at those pain centers again, raking up the powerlessness, and loss, that had erased the life she could have had in its entirety.

As quickly as she could, she put the flowers back into the envelope, then the letter, unread. She pushed everything back into the box and shoved the box back into the closet.

CHAPTER TWENTY-NINE

CULLIE

Poornima will always be the best thing that ever happened to me. But it was also the best work anyone involved in the film ever did. That rare magic that happens when real life intersects art, and the two become married into one indivisible thing.
From the journal of Oscar Seth

In for four, out for six. In for four, out for six. Cullie counted her breaths as she made her way up in the elevator of the building she'd worked at for five years.

Adrenaline was buzzing through her, but she had a sense of rightness about Appiness. She no longer had the urge to consume copious amounts of her grandmother's desserts to fill the hole in her heart. Her heart felt quite filled up, thank you very much. But activities customized to boost your mood were a game changer, and her initial pitch to CJ had reinforced her confidence tenfold.

Rishi had spent the past two weeks with her in San Francisco as she put together her presentation for the board. Their time together had proved three things. One, the man was not, in fact, puritanical about sex. Two, he tended to get recognized in San Francisco a lot and was absurdly charming and gracious when fans took selfies with him. Three, when he'd promised her he wouldn't pressure Binji, he'd meant it, which had made it impossible to not fall even more in love with him.

Bharat and Sam had come to see them last weekend, and Bharat, brat that he was, hadn't been able to stop laughing at how unabashedly smitten Cullie was.

When Cullie got out of the elevator, she was feeling a little bursty with happiness.

She was smiling at the super-cheesy selfie Rishi had texted her of him wearing a shirt that said KNOCK 'EM DEAD, BADASS when she ran into Steve.

Like, actually ran headlong into him. He grabbed her elbows and smoldered at her with what he had to think was sincere concern.

It was hilarious.

She took his hands off her elbows.

"You okay, Cullie?" he said as though he saw something about her that she couldn't. Oh, and he said her name exactly right.

"I will be as soon as you stop following me." She started walking away from him.

"I'm so excited about your new project." He fell in step beside her.

A laugh spurted from her and didn't stop.

"I get that you're angry. I should have supported your decision to keep Shloka subscription-free. I messed up. Let me make it up to you. You know we made magic with Shloka." Had he just made his voice breathy on the word *magic*? "Let's do that again. You know I can help you take a project to market better than anyone else."

Had he always sounded this simpering? "I would love to drag out your miserable groveling. But I'm feeling generous, so I'll save you the trouble. I just told CJ that I'm not making a deal with NewReal if you're still working here. So I'd start packing my bags."

Then, before he could respond, she put a hand up in his face. "This is business, Steve. It's not personal." On that note, she went into the conference room and let the door slam on his face.

Sonali Dev

~

Cullie and Rishi had flown down to Florida to spend time with family before Rishi went back to Mumbai for a few weeks. They had decided to figure out how to be together one step at a time.

They were having dinner with Binji and Lee and Cullie's parents. The six of them, comfortable around a table laden with food. Not the extravagant Goan feast Binji had produced before, but just some xacuti and rice. Mom had brought serradura. Ashish, Lee, and Rishi had marinated fish and chicken and were throwing it on a grill Lee had put in the lanai (possibly to get Binji to stop hanging her bras there to annoy the coven). Cullie had found Goan port.

They chatted easily as they ate and drank, and then moved the party to the couch.

Mom filled everyone in on the lawsuit. She'd had a great conversation with a YouTube arts and entertainment program that was catching fire. They were courting her pretty hard, and it was a beautiful thing to see her negotiate from a place of power.

"I'm proud of you, Mom," Cullie said, tucked into Rishi's side on the couch. She raised her glass. "I'm sorry you lost an opportunity to interview Meryl Streep, but I'm sure there will be another chance."

Rishi sat up. "Did you say Meryl Streep? What does she have to do with all of this?"

Cullie explained how Mom had almost had and then lost the segment she'd always wanted.

"You're kidding," he said, pulling out his phone and starting to tap at the screen. "You do know that Auntie Meryl is my honorary godmother."

A laugh burst out of Cullie. "Auntie Meryl? Really? Why didn't you tell me?"

"It didn't come up. And if you read the tabloids at all, you'd know these things. I just texted her. She would never do the interview with someone else if she knew what had gone down."

Mom looked like she was going to explode. "You don't have to do that."

"I think she has the right to know," Rishi said.

"What other celebrities are you hiding in your closet?" Cullie asked.

"I mean, you could google it," Rishi said and then grinned at her with that incredibly hot knowing look he always got when they shared a reference. "But if you must know, Auntie Judi considers me her adoptive grandson."

"You're not talking about Dame Judi Dench?" Mom squealed.

Rishi blushed. "They always stay with us when they visit Mumbai. They've both done films with Dada and were dear friends of his."

"Holy shit," Dad said. "Mom, you've done a film with the man who's made films with Judi Dench and Meryl Streep, on top of every Indian actor of any repute. How are you not out there screaming from rooftops about this?" Especially now that Dad's parentage wasn't in question.

Binji hadn't been herself since the thing with Rishi's dada had come to light, but she visibly wilted at Dad's words.

She was still refusing to watch the film she'd done at seventeen. A film Oscar Seth had considered his greatest work. Rishi had described Binji's film as one of the most beautiful pieces of cinema he'd ever experienced. To be fair, he generally talked about movies in hyperbole, all his Bollywood effusiveness peaking on this thing he lived and breathed for. Even so, Binji's film was obviously special to him. He'd spent years restoring it and bringing it back to life, and any mention of it tended to move him to tears.

Poornima was the story of a queen being forced to sleep with a stranger for an heir because her king was impotent.

Exactly the kind of thing Cullie would have expected Binji to be proud of. But no, she wouldn't even talk about it. Evidently, this thing with Rishi's grandfather had been something intense. It wasn't every day that an artist destroyed his own work for you and then spent decades trying to restore it. It was the most romantic darned thing Cullie had ever heard. Being embarrassed by it—because obviously she was—was the most un-Binji move ever.

Lee stroked Binji's back, but it seemed to do nothing to soothe her. "I'm not screaming from rooftops because instead of an acting career, I chose to have a family," she said, a tremble escaping into her voice.

The mood in the room shifted. Silence stretched.

"You all carry on. I need some fresh air." Binji went to the door, and everyone stood. "I just need a moment. Please don't let this spoil the wonderful evening we've had."

"I'll go with you," Lee said.

"No. Please." With that she left.

Cullie tried to follow her, but Mom stopped her. "I'll go." And her expression said that she wasn't in the mood to argue the point.

CHAPTER THIRTY

ALY

If I could have a dying wish: I want people to see Poornima. *To know the helplessness and the power that love presents to each of us. In equal parts. And the part we let win is who we really are.*
From the journal of Oscar Seth

Aly found Bindu pacing in the garden behind her building. When she saw Aly, she stiffened. "I guess I would have followed you too if it had been you who left," she said grudgingly.

"It's true." Aly smiled. "And I'm glad it's true."

For a while they just walked around the huge artificial pond edged with perfectly trimmed grass. Landscape beds with clusters of birds of paradise and other exotic native and nonnative flowers broke up the rolling lawn. If plants could scream wealth, these did. They were the greener other side, and they knew it. Even the lights lining the walking path were elegantly concealed to create atmosphere as they went over gentle bridges with curvy railings.

Vibrant years, indeed. A gift for having lived well, or at least for having lived successfully.

"Beautiful, isn't it?" Bindu was the first to speak.

Aly made a sound of agreement. "I can see why you like it so much here."

Bindu threw her a sideways glance without stopping. "I loved living with you, you know that, right?"

"I do."

"My moving here . . . it had nothing to do with that fight we had."

The fight where Aly had said something about Bindu's leaving teacups around as a statement, and Bindu had said, *Why do you have to overcomplicate everything. My son is right about that.*

Aly had been completely thrown. Hitting below the belt was not Bindu's style.

Thanks, Ma! Good to know you agree with your son's criticisms. Not surprising that you do. Aly had no idea where that had come from.

What is that supposed to mean?

It's not that complicated. Actually, it's only complicated if you don't want to see the truth. Another thing Ashish learned from you.

Bindu had gasped, and Aly had quickly apologized. They'd both backed away from the fight, a shared panic making them fearful of losing a relationship that had been a strength to them both. But then Bindu had gone to the open house.

They'd never brought the fight up again.

Until now.

Maybe it was time.

"I know," Aly said. "Cullie's right, your moving here had to do with FOMO."

They grinned with their joint love for their girl, who always saw things so clearly. The way she'd broken out of her comfort zone without changing herself made Aly so damn proud.

"More like FOHMO," Bindu said. "Fear of Having Missed Out." She looked sad, defeated in a very un-Bindu way. "The past tense is so very final, isn't it?"

Aly squeezed her hand. How did one respond to that?

Bindu didn't seem to need a response. "I lied about the money I inherited. There was no rich aunt. It was Oscar."

That explained so much.

"The money brought everything back. Until I came here, I had never allowed myself to acknowledge my sense of not having lived my life. It wasn't like I wasn't happy with our life together. Everything about that was, *is*, beautiful. This"—she threw a glance at the manicured landscape—"this is just experiencing something new. Having some fun. But the real life I love is with you lot."

"We know that."

"But it's not that simple. What I said earlier: that I chose to give up acting to have a family. It wasn't technically a choice. Oscar. The film. It's too many ugly memories." She hesitated, an unusual anger in her eyes. "Painful."

"But also some beautiful ones, right?" If the pictures from that film were anything to go by. Bindu was mesmerizing in them. Different and yet the same. All her spirit concentrated into those moments. A million things trapped in what she told the camera.

"You know how I keep talking about living on my own terms? As a young person, it came easily to me. Then it became something I said all the time, but I knew deep down that I'd lost the chance to actually do it. After the open house, I felt like I had to do something. While I still had the time." The fact that Bindu hadn't responded to Aly's comment about the beauty of the film was telling.

They were having parallel conversations. Bindu seemed determined to keep it that way.

"Is that what you're doing now, by not watching the film? Living on your own terms?" Aly tried to nudge the distance between the conversations closed.

Bindu sped up. "Choosing to let the past go. That *is* living on my own terms."

"Okay."

"Can we skip the passive-aggressive *okays* today, Alisha. I don't think I have the stomach for them." There she was, her ma, back again.

"Fine. Then here is the nonpassive-aggressive version. I know that argument wasn't why you moved here. But we hit a truth that day. About where Ashish learned that ignoring the truth can make it go away."

She waited to see if Bindu would stop her, but Bindu watched her, listening. When people displayed wonder and envy over the relationship Aly and Bindu shared, this had always been the answer. They listened to each other. From the very start, they had listened for each other's feelings and needs, two women hungry for that. It was the key she wished she could hand all her friends who were stuck in tussles with family members.

Then she thought about her own mother. It wasn't that simple. It took two hands to clap, as Karen Menezes loved to say. And in that, Aly and Bindu had been more fortunate than most.

Light from lampposts danced off the water. Silence danced between them. "You blame me for your divorce," Bindu said finally. A statement. A deflection.

"Not even a little bit." Aly blamed herself and Ashish. But Bindu had a role, just like Aly's parents did. Because our parents' marriage is our foundational map for relationships. We either follow it or we don't, but it's there. Always. "Ash didn't think he had the choice to follow his dream either. And it made him angry. And his anger is what finally tore our marriage apart."

"Good thing I don't have a marriage anymore then."

"But you have a life. Maybe it's time to stop being angry at those who took away your chance to live it the way you wanted to. Maybe it's not too late to stop showing them up and really live on your terms, now that you can."

Bindu pressed a hand to her mouth. Then she pulled it away and kept walking. Finally, this silence too seemed to bloat and pop. "What if I can't?"

"There's only one way to find out. I fought for the segment and didn't get it. But I don't regret a moment of it." Then there was Cullie. "Cullie got Shloka back."

"And she never doubted that she would. That she deserved it. She doesn't make herself smaller." Realization dawned in Bindu's eyes. "You did that. You modeled that for her. And I didn't. I thought Karen was the one who didn't, but I didn't either. All I wanted was to treat the two of you the way I wished my mother had treated me."

Aly took Bindu's hand. "You did so much more than that. *We* modeled strength for Cullie. Together. She saw you support me in my goals, in my ambition. Even when my own marriage made that an ugly word. She saw you being comfortable in your skin. Even when it was hard."

A single tear slipped down Bindu's cheek, and Aly laughed through her own tears. Her mother-in-law even cried gracefully.

"You don't understand. The film, it's . . . there's . . ." Bindu swallowed as she met Aly's eyes. "There's a sex scene. A nude one."

Aly's hands went to her face. "Ma!" she said and then burst into laughter. Of course Bindu had done a nude scene in a movie in nineteen-frickin'-seventy-four. Of course she'd had a hot affair with the director that changed his life.

"It's not funny," Bindu said, but she smiled. "It was integral to the story, not gratuitous. It's the most beautiful story." Fierce pride was back in her voice.

"I'm sure it's beautiful, Ma. How can it not be?" Aly squeezed Bindu's arm. "You have another chance. To think about your terms and reclaim them. To reclaim who you were when you were seventeen. A girl who believed in what she wanted, a girl who was glorious in how much she loved herself. It's there in those pictures. I'm sure it's in that scene and in all the others. Let's do it, Ma. Let's actually live on our own terms."

The silence that gripped them as they walked back to Bindu's condo was a potent thing. However easy it might have seemed that Rishi was waiting, with all his resources and passion, to open a portal into the past for Bindu, walking through that portal would take courage.

Aly had told Bindu that her anger was standing in her way. But Aly was angry too. She'd been angry with Ashish for having his dream right there waiting for him when he decided to reach for it. But he'd had to break conditioning too. Coming home to her might have seemed convenient, but that too had taken courage. It had taken the love he felt for her.

Aly was angry because her mountain had proved to be the harder one to climb. But it was the mountain of her choosing, and each mountain came with its own incline. She'd chosen a tough one, maybe an impossible one. But it was the one that called to her. She just had to keep climbing and get as far up as she could.

CHAPTER THIRTY-ONE

BINDU

It had been years since my wife had fallen into mutism, since she had talked to or looked at me or our children. She never left the house she'd cloistered herself in. I did all I could to take care of her, to be there for her. But I'd never been lonely until I met Bhanu. After Bhanu, the loneliness was brutal.
From the journal of Oscar Seth

Watching the film was like having her skin ripped off. But it was also like coming home, falling into her body, into feelings that were at once too stark and too distant. Bindu sat there watching as Poornima stripped down to her soul and Oscar resisted and failed to keep it from destroying him. She felt rage the likes of which she'd never known. And grief. For Oscar and herself and all the many things that might have been. But for Poornima most of all, and what she'd borne.

And hatred for a world that had crushed her like the parijat flowers in Oscar's letter.

Oscar was right. This was the best work of his life.

This time when Bindu opened the envelope, she slid the thick paper out, letting memories slide out with it. They were a flood, a dam burst, a torrential downpour, now that she'd let her eyes soak herself up across a screen, across time. There was no stopping the memories, so she let herself drown.

The shock of Oscar's handwriting was another length of fabric that slid over and around her and wrapped her in coils. He'd been in the habit of making a million notes on her script in that deliberate penmanship. Her copy with all his annotations was impeccably preserved in the box Rishi had handed her.

You can do it, she told herself. She'd watched the film, and she was still standing. She was more than standing. She was filled with fire.

Letter in hand, she went to her lanai and faced the ocean. The tide was coming in, the waves rolling gleefully as they swelled over the shore, utterly certain that no force on earth could stop them.

She started reading.

Dear Bhanu, or should I say Bindu (that suits you so much better),

I write this letter now when I know definitively that there remains no hope of ever seeing you again. Yes, I'd hoped. For the past forty-five years I'd hoped for a glance. For catching up like old friends. Talking about our children and grandchildren. Sharing all the things that happened after us. I'd imagined listening to you talk, the way only you do, with every part of your body.

I missed it. I missed you.

There, I said it. The confessions of a dying man. You already know by now that I tried to keep my promise. I tried to burn Poornima. But as it took up the flames, I couldn't let it go. This was the child we made, the love of our lives. I know that it was yours too. The moment in which we were both more alive than most people ever get to be, and I couldn't let it go. I'm sorry.

Over the years, I've had a million conversations with you in my head, and I wish I could put them all down here, but you'd probably grow bored and bounce on your feet. Or maybe I'm afraid you'd read every word and spend too much precious time on things gone by. There is one thing, however, that I must get off my chest. In leaving you the money, I wasn't claiming you, as I know you think I was.

Before I found out that your baba had a stroke, I had already decided I wouldn't release the film. I knew it even as we shot that scene, that it would be too much. No audience would ever see past the eroticism to the truth beneath it. No censor board would ever allow it, and I wouldn't release the film without that scene.

Isn't it wonderful how far the world has come?

But I digress. I knew all this when Rajendra Desai came to me with his life's savings to buy your freedom, to erase what he saw as your youthful mistake and my predatory exploitation, because he was so smitten with you. I recognized his feelings only too well. But I wasn't sure I liked what I thought the man would do with them. Not that I had done any better.

It was always your money. I added your actor's fee to it and put it away in your name and let it grow. If you needed it during your marriage and if it would have given you freedom, then I'm sorry I didn't tell you it was there. I didn't know how to. Not without breaking my promise to you that I'd stay out of your life.

It makes me happy that it's yours now. I hope you were able to do something wonderful for yourself with it. I suspect you've lived a life that was every bit as beautiful and honest as you. I imagine the kind of mother you are, the kind of grandmother, and I ache with envy for those who got to be around you.

But I would not change what happened between us. You are and always were my Poornima. I would not exchange a second of the time I spent with you for all the wealth in the world.

I would not part with the fullness of one of those moments when you let me into your limitless heart. I don't know if what we had was love, but if it wasn't, then I've never felt love in my life.

Thank you for showing me.

Eternally yours,

Ashishchandra

He'd signed it as Ashishchandra, the love of Poornima's life. The man he'd played when he was hers.

Could your whole body hurt from regret? Could your tears parch you but also wash away a lifetime of grief? She put away the letter and stroked the paper-thin fossils of her past in those parijat petals. Fire blooms. Then she went to the bathroom and splashed her face until the sore throbbing had washed from her swollen eyes.

She'd asked everyone to leave her alone in the condo when she watched the film. She'd promised she would call after. Ashish had gone home with Alisha, Cullie with Rishi. Her family, complete in this moment of happiness. So what if it was fleeting? All we have is now anyway.

Her finger hovered over Lee's number on her phone. The need to talk to him burned softly in her heart, to tell him, to bounce her feelings off him to give them form and weight, to have him listen and color them in with his insight. He'd told her he loved her a few nights ago. She hadn't been able to say it back, but she suspected that she did love him.

The three men who had claimed to love her before this, their love had been about them. She'd brought Oscar's art to fruition. She'd given Rajendra an outlet for his sexual fantasies. She'd given Richard his muse back—for the umpteenth time in his life, if his five ex-wives were to be believed.

It was strange to count Richard with Oscar and Rajendra, but the fool had left her all his money. Even if it was only to use her as a giant raised middle finger for his family. A smile spread across her face. Well, he had come to the right place. She had gotten him retribution, all right.

Family was the most important thing in your life, and that family didn't have to be blood. Only one person had been Richard's family for the past five years. Mary, the receptionist at the HOA office. She was the one who deserved his rage money, and Bindu had given it to her.

If Richard had left Mary the money himself, she would have been the one to deal with his family's anger and the ugly names in the media. Maybe that's why he'd left it to Bindu. Because he thought she'd know what to do. Or maybe she was giving him too much credit.

Lee's love felt easy. Light on her skin, fresh on her tongue, the first drizzle of the monsoon, and just as dependable. It felt fueled by itself, not a mold he wanted to pour her into like molten silver.

Oscar had been able to love her without reservation because he knew he could never have her. Who was it that said, "The only kind of love that lasts forever is the unrequited kind"?

Rajendra had been able to love her, so long as she put parts of herself away except when they served him. He'd had to re-create her so she wouldn't be shameful for him to claim publicly.

Her love for both men had come from a place of self-loathing. From a belief that she wasn't like everyone else, like she didn't fit. She'd believed their loving her despite her differentness was the gift they gave her.

But was that even love? What she'd felt for herself for so many years had barely scratched the surface of the love she was capable of.

She turned on the film again, and love gripped her, so intense that she had to breathe through it. It was the kind of love she felt for Cullie, and Alisha, and Ashish. A love she'd portioned carefully for parts of herself. Today, now, she let it all out. She let herself love the young body that the camera had captured in all its lush, unabashed glory. She loved the spirit that had reveled in the camera, let it in, trusted it enough to show the depth of her pain and pleasure without a single boundary.

She wanted that camera on her again.

She called Lee. "Want to come over?" she asked as she watched herself on the screen, risking everything to get what she wanted, and waited.

In a few minutes she heard the front door open.

"You're beautiful," he said over her shoulder.

She didn't need to ask if he meant her or the girl on the screen. They were one and the same. So she said, simply, "Thank you."

For a long while they watched in silence. A parijat-laden queen in ecstasy.

"That's not all it is, you know," he said finally as Poornima dropped her robe. "Your beauty. That's not the only reason I love you."

She turned the movie off and faced him.

"I mean, you're not that beautiful." He smiled, his lopsided Lee smile. "Fine, I'm lying. You're the most beautiful woman I've ever met. But my point is, that's just one part of it."

"Tell me what the other part is."

"I've never met anyone so complete in her own skin, someone who sees everyone else as complete too. I feel free around you, a deep, true freedom to be me. I'm sixty years old, Bindu, and I've never felt this way around anyone else in my life."

She wrapped her arms around him, and he pulled her close. It was a perfect fit.

"Is that not enough?" he asked.

"It's more than enough," she said. Then she pulled back and met his absurdly green eyes. "I love you too."

And then she told him everything. How losing Oscar had crushed the life out of her. How losing her father had stubbed out what was left. How she hadn't known how to work around the grief and guilt. Maybe she'd punished herself for letting it happen. She'd told herself that she'd already had it all, lived, and now whatever life gave her was payment for that.

She told him about her marriage. Even the parts that she still didn't understand. Why that level of submission had felt both wonderful and terrible.

Her marriage, like every other marriage on earth, had been several parts: one part good, one part difficult, but in more parts than both those put together, mundane. Like life itself. A habit that became more security than a burden. His marriage had been much the same. Solid, but abundant in both disappointment and comfort. Blessedly uneventful for the most part.

Bindu had only ever been able to share all the things she was thinking with two people. Her grandmother when she was a child, before something inside her started to rebel and become like no one else around her. And Oscar.

Her grandmother had always been gleefully proud and maybe a little afraid for her. Oscar had been dazzled by the power of their feelings. Lee listened to her words for what they were.

"Now what?" he asked finally as they sat down with cups of chai.

"Do you ever have a sense that everything you've ever wanted is within reach, but you're afraid to reach for it?"

He looked at her in that way he had. Her skin prickled with the awareness of it. She felt at once young and timeless. "From the very first time I saw you, I've had that sense. As though it's all right here. If I reached out, I could touch it."

"Is that why you called me trouble?"

"I called you trouble because I thought my boring life was about to be upended. I was terrified."

"That I did do, didn't I? You look battered."

"I was a fool. I'm the opposite of battered. I'm filled up, replenished."

"I am too."

He took her hands and stroked her fingers. "If you don't reach for what you want, you'll never have it. I know sometimes that feels safer than reaching for it and finding you were wrong. Or even worse, finding you were right and then losing it. Whatever it is about doing the documentary that you're so afraid of, the only way to not let it win is to walk through it. You can't walk around things without missing what's most important about them."

She picked up her phone and video-called Cullie. "Is your young man with you?"

"Binji, did you watch it? What did you think?" Cullie moved her body so Rishi appeared on the screen too. They were lying on the beach, her head on his chest, the ocean loud around them.

"It's every bit as beautiful as Rishi said it was."

He grinned, Oscar's eyes flashing joy like floodlights in his face.

"Thank you for restoring it."

"Thank you for watching it." He teared up, and Cullie kissed him.

They were beautiful, those tears. Filled with his love for the celluloid he'd built back cell by cell, for Oscar, for his own art. Then he'd risked it for her granddaughter, whose preciousness was a gift.

"Rishi Seth," Bindu said, hope racing like a drug through her system. "Let's make that documentary. But you better make sure it wins us an Oscar." Because Bindu Desai was ready to be a star.

Life.

You blink and it's gone.

The passion. The boredom. The moment lived. The moment lost.

In the end, they're just crumbs stuck in the creases of memory. Remnants of tastes left on your tongue.

Poornima knew this. She knew that she'd have one chance.

As the queen to an impotent king, she'd have this one chance before he took another queen.

One chance.

To bear an heir.

To choose a stranger for seven nights. One week to live.

If she chose someone she knew and the king found out, she'd be punished with death.

But she had one week.

One week to reclaim her love. To gather him up for a lifetime.

She'd walked away from him once when they'd given her to her king. Without a whimper.

Because voice was not among the many privileges princesses were awarded.

He'd moved on too. He claimed to love the wife he'd taken so he too could go on living.

But she was his queen, and she got to choose.

And for that one week she would settle for nothing but him. Nothing but all of him. His golden body. The soul that was the other half of her. All his love. Everything he was. He would never again take another without thinking of her.

And if they found out and beheaded her for it, so be it.

Yes, she'd give her people an heir. But she'd take a fully lived life in return.

ACKNOWLEDGMENTS

I grew up watching Bollywood films. Not just the campy eighties and nineties potboilers but the ones in black and white and early Technicolor from when cinema was a new art and the artists gods who often bought into their own myths. In those old films, I remember being struck by one thing in particular: how the heroines and the vamps / bar girls were unmistakably separate—the modestly clad good girls with the innocent eyes and the sexily dressed cabaret girls with the knowing eyes—and never could the twain meet.

It was probably the first time I noticed how society labeled women in shades of purity and mixed it up with goodness. This realization from way back in my childhood was probably the earliest seed for this story. So, thanks, first and foremost, to those pioneering women of Indian cinema and to my mother for dragging me to the theater and then analyzing stories to within an inch of their lives.

Another seed for this story came from the priceless work Shivendra Singh Dungarpur, Teesha Cherian, and my sister-in-law Irawati Harshe Mayadev and the Film Heritage Foundation do to restore and conserve Indian cinema.

The journey from those seeds to the story on these pages would never have happened without the help of my deadline sisters: Jamie Beck, Barbara O'Neal, Liz Talley, Priscilla Oliveras, Tracy Brogan, Sally Kilpatrick, Falguni Kothari, and Virginia Kantra. From plotting and pep talks to brainstorming and critical reads, you held my hand every step of the way, and I could never have done it without you. Thanks also to Clara Kensie, Robin Kuss, and Heather Marshall for your spot-on critical reads. And to my bestie, Gaelyn Almeida, for letting me vomit ideas in your direction all hours of the day.

Thanks also to Manoj, Mihir, Annika, Aie, Mamma, and Papa for sitting patiently by when I shushed you for an entire year so I could write. Fine, it's been many, many years, every moment of which I've been grateful that you are mine.

This story would be barely coherent without the thoughtful and brilliant edits from my editor, Alicia Clancy. I am incredibly grateful that we found our way to each other. And to my badass agent, Alexandra Machinist, for making things happen even when they weren't easy. Thanks also to Carmen Johnson and Danielle Marshall, Jen Bentham, Brittany Russell, Gabe Dumpit, Adrienne Krogh, Kimberly Glyder, Rachael Clark, and the rest of the team at Amazon Publishing for working tirelessly to get my book in front of readers with such love and generosity. And, of course, my most heartfelt gratitude to the brilliant Mindy Kaling for blazing a trail and changing the landscape for South Asian Americans in media and entertainment. Your love for my book is a shot of adrenaline to my fangirl heart.

And last and most important, thanks to you, dear readers, for coming with me on yet another journey. I hope you laughed and cried and felt my deepest gratitude.

BOOK CLUB QUESTIONS

1. Dating apps are a part of our world today. Have you ever used them? Bindu, Aly, and Cullie find love outside the app, but so many find it within. Do you think there's a way to make that happen, or is it purely accidental when it happens?

2. Aly believes our parents' marriage is our first roadmap for relationships. What role, if any, do you think Aly's and Ashish's parents played in their marital issues?

3. Rishi lied to Cullie about who he was. How justified do you think he was? Did the fact that he told her the truth before he got what he wanted matter? How do you feel about Cullie's decision to forgive him?

4. Everyone around Aly believes she's a diversity hire. How do you feel about her losing her job after the ten years of discrimination she faced under the guise of "opportunity"?

5. Do you think the way society feels about women enjoying sex has changed over the years? How do you think women are perceived by society today if they are up front about their sexual pleasure?

6. How do you feel about Bindu's role in *Poornima* versus her lived reality?

7. "The only kind of love that lasts forever is the unrequited kind." Discuss.

ABOUT THE AUTHOR

Photo © 2018 Ishita Singh Photography

USA Today bestselling author Sonali Dev writes Bollywood-style stories that explore universal issues. Her novels have been named best books of the year by *Library Journal*, NPR, the *Washington Post*, and *Kirkus Reviews*. She has won numerous accolades, including the American Library Association's award for best romance, the *Romantic Times* Reviewers' Choice Award, and multiple *Romantic Times* Seals of Excellence. She has also been a Romance Writers of America finalist and has been listed for the Dublin Literary Award. *Shelf Awareness* calls her "not only one of the best but one of the bravest romance novelists working today." She lives in Chicagoland with her husband, two visiting adult children, and the world's most perfect dog. Find out more at https://sonalidev.com.